TAKE

PAM GODWIN

DISCLAIMER

If you have not read the previous books, STOP!

The books in the DELIVER series are stand-alones,
but they should be read in order.

For Blitz
My little deer
In my heart,
You will never stop spinning.

ONE

Kate had been watching the storm gather strength for two days. Turbulent clouds collided beyond the barred window, howling and banging against the concrete walls of her prison.

The wind wanted in as violently as she wanted out.

She'd been here before. Not in this dingy stone building or in these exact restraints. This place was utterly foreign, the scratchy rope on her wrists too primitive to be real.

But dammit, it *was* real. And intimately familiar. So much so it hadn't taken her long to shake off the shock of being kidnapped. *Again.*

The last time she found herself in shackles was four years ago. Back then, she was just a clueless eighteen-year-old girl. She hadn't understood who had taken her, what they wanted, or how she—a nobody from nowhere Texas—could be of interest to anyone.

But this time was different.

When two men captured her at gunpoint behind

the diner where she worked, she'd guessed why, how, and *who* was behind it.

That was a month ago.

She'd been locked in this room for a goddamn month and still hadn't glimpsed her captor. Not once had she heard his name whispered on the guards' lips.

That didn't stop her from shouting her assumptions from the rafters.

"Tiago Badell!" Her hoarse roar echoed down the dark corridor, aimed at the door that remained closed at the end. "I know you can hear me!"

She'd grown bold in her isolation. Impatient. Desperate. And reckless.

"Show yourself, you fucking coward!" She yanked at the rope on her arms and glared at the end where it secured to the steel beam overhead and out of reach.

With her hands bound together in front of her, she couldn't loosen the knot between her wrists. God knows, she'd tried. Weeks of gnawing on the rope shredded her lips, her fingernails broken and jagged from useless clawing.

She was being held in a second-floor antechamber to another room. Beyond the reach of her leash were two doors. One at the end of the hall. The other led down to the main level and the armed guards who patrolled the property.

The rope allowed her access to a mattress and a doorless bathroom with no mirrors. There was no furniture. No objects that could be fashioned into a weapon.

Hygiene, clothes, and food — the basics were granted and nothing more.

She ached for fresh air, exercise, her friends,

human contact… The list was inconsolably long. But what consumed her thoughts more than all else was the dark, elusive door to the other room.

Someone lived in there, and she was certain that someone was Tiago Badell.

Three times a day, an elderly man delivered two servings of food. With skin the color of midnight, he floated through her chamber like a shadow, never speaking, never meeting her eyes. He always set one serving before her, just within reach. The other he carried to the room down the hall.

He wasn't mute. Sometimes, voices drifted from beneath the door in a language she couldn't decipher — the old man's raspy accent and a deeper, richer timbre.

When she first arrived, the old man would linger in that room for hours. Lately, his visits had grown shorter. He would slip behind the mysterious door and emerge shortly after with empty platters.

He was in there now, having just dropped off her dinner.

Steam rose from the tin plate on the floor. Rice, chickpeas, and grilled meat — the spicy aroma made her mouth water, but she was too focused on the corridor to eat.

Lightning flashed, illuminating the window and strobing the stone walls of her prison. She strained to hear voices from the other room but couldn't detect a word amid the thunder.

"Tiago!" she screamed at the top of her lungs. "Come out, goddammit! Tell me why I'm here!"

Didn't matter how often or how loud she yelled. He never came out.

Was he sick? Hiding? Protecting his identity? She

still didn't know what he looked like.

A few weeks before she was taken, her close friend, Tate Vades, left for Venezuela's Kidnap Alley to penetrate Tiago's compound. It was an insane undertaking, but not unexpected. All her roommates — Tate, Ricky, Martin, Luke, and Tomas — had a habit of running headlong into danger. After escaping Van Quiso's shackles, they banded together to take down as many human sex traffickers as possible.

Camila Dias had been the first to escape. Although she no longer lived with them, she continued to lead their vigilante group of Freedom Fighters.

Tate's latest mission focused on rescuing Camila's missing sister, Lucia, who allegedly worked for Tiago Badell. As if Tate's endeavor wasn't risky enough, he took Van Quiso along as his backup.

How the hell could Tate trust the man who had enslaved and raped him? Sure, Van expressed regret for the hell he rained down on her and her friends, but it was too little, too late. Kate would never forgive him, and she sure as fuck didn't trust him with Tate's life.

The fear she had for Tate before he left was nothing compared to what she felt now.

Now, she was petrified.

Tiago wouldn't have taken her unless Tate's mission was compromised. How else would Tiago know she existed?

That left some devastating questions.

What happened to Tate? Was he still alive? Was he imprisoned within these very walls, gagged and forced to listen to her screams?

Despair crushed her heart in a suffocating vise.

She never mentioned Tate, just in case she was

wrong about his connection to her kidnapping. Instead, she spent the past month telling herself he successfully rescued Lucia and escaped unscathed. If he'd bested Tiago, it made sense that Tiago would go after Tate's loved ones in retaliation.

Of all the people in Tate's life, she was the most vulnerable. The loner. The weakest fighter. The only woman without a companion. Of course, she would be the one to get snatched.

That must've been it, but she needed to know for sure.

"Tiago!" She faced the corridor and raised her voice. "I want answers, and I won't shut up until I have them!"

The door held still.

Restlessness twitched her muscles, reaching into her bones and rattling her sanity.

She paced toward the window and halted a foot short from the glass. It was as close as the rope would allow, but the angle supplied a view of the dusty, barren landscape.

Two stories up, she couldn't see the exterior of the building or any other structure in the vicinity. Two cars sat off to the side, where a burly man loitered, smoking a cigarette with a rifle strapped to his back. Farther out, a dirt road meandered around woody shrubs and cacti before fading into the sandy horizon of nothingness.

She didn't know if the guards lived downstairs or somewhere else. They seemed to come and go in shifts. Five men and one woman, by her count. All heavily armed.

Her journey here had been foggy, muddied by sedatives and shrouded by a blindfold. Multiple transfers between cars, a long flight on a private plane, and more blindfolded car rides had obliterated the odds she was still in the U.S.

Venezuela was the logical assumption.

But this wasn't Kidnap Alley.

While Tate had prepared for his mission, she saw videos, photos, and maps of the slum where he was headed. This wasn't it. Not this arid, desolate wasteland.

She knew her friends would never stop looking for her, but how would they know to come here? *She* didn't even know where she was.

Her throat closed around a hard lump of reality.

There was a good chance she would never be found.

The day she arrived, two guards brought her to this room, stripped her down, and took everything. The cheap necklace from around her neck. The fitness watch from her wrist. The ponytail holder from her hair. They stole her damn dignity.

Then they bound her arms and left her with nothing but a handmade, strapless dress thing to wear.

How long would she sit in this room before she endured the real reason she was here? Her captor wouldn't have gone through the trouble of transporting her unless there was something in it for him.

His specialty was kidnapping. For ransom.

She learned through Tate's intel that Tiago's goons tortured and raped their captives, sent video footage of the brutality to family members, and demanded payment in exchange for the victim's release.

God, how she hoped this was a ransom deal. She and her roommates had plenty of money — *millions* — thanks to the peace offering Van Quiso had given them. If there was a price for her freedom, her friends would pay it.

But in the month since her capture, there had been no mention of payment. No torture. No video recordings. Other than the rough handling during her transport, the guards didn't touch her, talk to her, or visit her room.

If this wasn't a kidnapping for ransom, it was something worse.

She didn't have to imagine the *worse*. She'd lived it. In a windowless, soundproof attic, Van Quiso had whipped her into an obedient slave. An object to be sold for sex. Not to take pleasure but to give it. With her hands, her mouth, and her pain.

Her virginity had been a valuable commodity then. Maybe that was still the case?

Would Tiago sell her virtue to the highest bidder?

Or would he take it for himself?

It was her biggest fear. Her heaviest burden.

At age twenty-two, she should've explored her sexuality like a normal, healthy woman. But she wasn't normal. When she escaped Van, her virginity was all she had left. A precious mercy, and she didn't want to squander it. She longed to give it to someone she trusted. A man who would appreciate the significance.

The naive notion resonated a hollow thud in her head, silencing all other sound.

She managed to escape Van without getting raped. So what? She wasn't stupid enough to believe that would happen again.

Outside, the wind picked up, and with it came the first plops of rain. It would be dark soon, and she'd be forced to endure another night without answers.

She stepped away from the window and shouted,

"Tiago—"

The door creaked open, shooing away the shadows in the corridor.

Footsteps sounded. The clink of dishes. Then the elderly man emerged, balancing empty plates as he closed the door behind him.

"Why won't he come out?" She rushed forward and jerked when the rope caught. "I just want to talk."

He ambled past her, keeping to the farthest wall, beyond the perimeter of her tether.

Vertical scars marred his face, two old cuts on each cheek, perfectly aligned, almost decorative. It was as if he'd them put them there intentionally.

With a blank expression and eyes fixed on the door to the stairs, he moved in that direction, giving her no acknowledgment, not a twitch, like she wasn't even there.

"Just tell me what he wants." Blood pounded in her skull.

He reached the exit and uttered a foreign word. A command not intended for her.

Locks clanked on the other side. The door opened, and a scruffy-bearded guard stepped to the side.

Instead of leaving, the old man turned, lifted his wrinkled face, and rested glassy eyes on her.

"Please." She pulled on the rope. "Untie me. Just let me go."

For the first time since she arrived, he opened his mouth and addressed her in a heavily accented voice. "He's ready to see you."

No shit?

Oh, shit.

Shit, shit, shit.

Her body went taut against an ice-cold shiver, and

the hairs on her nape stood on end.

Don't freak out. Don't fucking lose it.

Sweeping her gaze to the dark corridor, she drew in a slow breath.

This was what she wanted. A conversation with the dickhead in charge. Answers. Reassurances. Negotiations.

But none of that was a guarantee. After watching those videos with Tate, she had only one certainty to go on.

Tiago Badell tortured his prisoners.

A tremor unfurled inside her, crashing its way along her arms and legs.

How badly would he hurt her? How long would it last? Hours? Days? Would he let her live? Would she want to?

The elderly man mumbled something that sounded like Spanish, prompting the guard to step into the room. The massive man strode toward her, removed a pocket knife, and before she could blink, he sliced through the rope between her wrists and the ceiling.

Her arms dropped, and the sudden freedom made her gasp.

As the guard returned to the stairwell, she tensed at the opportunity to attack him from behind. Should she do it? *Could* she overpower him and get away?

He was twice her size, armed with a knife, and her wrists were still tied together. The old man hovered in the doorway, physically frail, but those cloudy eyes watched her with unsettling strength, as if reading her thoughts.

The odds stacked against her, but whatever happened, she wouldn't go down without a fight.

On the heels of that thought, she flung herself toward the guard, her bound arms raised to loop around the guard's neck.

He turned before she made contact, his hand already flying. Meaty knuckles met her jaw and sent her head whirling sideways.

She staggered, momentarily stunned by the jolt of pain. After a soundless choke, she recovered, found her bearings, but not quickly enough.

The door shut with a resounding click.

"Fuck." She raced toward it and yanked on the handle.

Locked.

"Fuck you!" she screamed. Then groaned. *Not helpful, Kate.*

That left the other door.

She trembled to summon movement in her legs, her ears pricked for footsteps in the corridor.

He's ready to see you.

Thunder boomed. Rain pelted the window, and her heart drummed an unruly dirge in her ears.

Apparently, Tiago was too high and mighty to come to her. Whatever. She would go to him, because her curiosity demanded it. But she refused to trudge in there with shaking limbs and hunched shoulders. If he was anything like Van Quiso, her fear would give him a hard-on.

A shudder rippled through her, and she snapped her spine straight.

The only power she possessed here was that over her own emotions. She allowed Van to use her terror to control her and wouldn't make that mistake again.

Rolling back her shoulders, she stood taller, closed

her eyes, and breathed deeply.

She survived Van's cruelty. The experience didn't break her. It made her sharper, tougher, and really goddamn *angry.*

Fuck Van for molesting her, beating her until she bled, and ordering her to suck his dick day in and day out. And fuck Tiago Badell for ripping away her freedom, shoving her into isolation for a month, and summoning her like an object.

Rage scorched through her veins and spurred her into motion.

Her bare feet slapped across the gritty stone floor, her body clad in one of the sleeveless, unfitted rags they provided. The thin gray linen covered her from chest to knees, but if she stood in the right light, the fabric would be transparent.

Nothing she could do about the clothes. If Tiago wanted to strip her bare, she wouldn't be able to do anything about that, either. Except fight. *That* she would do.

Hands clenched around the severed rope, she stormed down the corridor and turned the door knob.

She expected luxurious furniture, plush fabrics, and perhaps the fatal end of a rifle waiting on the other side. But as she stepped in, none of that greeted her. The room was as empty as her prison.

The only source of light glowed from a shadeless lamp on the floor beside a small mattress. Rumpled blankets and a dented pillow suggested recent use. A large duffel bag of clothes sat open near a bathroom door, as if the room's occupant didn't intend to stay.

As for the occupant...

Her breathing stalled as she tracked the reach of

light to the farthest, darkest corner.

A man sat on a two-foot-tall steel safe, his lower body illuminated enough to reveal heavy boots, dark slacks, and a posture that could only be described as an arrogant sprawl. He lounged with his back against the wall and legs spread, his body language insinuating he didn't care whether she entered or not.

The rest of him melted into chilling blackness. His chest, shoulders, face — none of his upper half was visible. He probably positioned the lamp at just the right angle to give the illusion of a predator lurking in the dark, just to ramp up the fear factor.

No illusions needed. She knew what he was, and her knees wobbled with the impulse to cower and beg for her life. But a meek and submissive demeanor would only earn her extended torture. She'd learned that the hard way.

She would rather die quickly than draw out the torment.

Her heart rate accelerated, and she swayed beneath the spinning weight of vertigo. She didn't want to die. But if her life was taken from her, if this was her last stance in the world, she would face it with ferocity and bitter rage.

Shoving back her shoulders, tight as they were, she strode into the room.

"Welcome, Kate." His low, deep baritone curled a shiver around her spine. "Come closer. I know you've been anxious to meet me. Everyone on this side of the continent has heard you begging."

"Cut the shit, Tiago." She paused outside the lamp's glow and swallowed her nerves. "I haven't seen your face. I can't identify you. Let me go, and I'll forget the whole thing."

"Step into the light." Rich and rumbly, his accent swirled with hints of South America and something indefinably exotic.

"You first."

"This will go faster if you follow orders."

"Am I keeping you from something?" She cast a pointed look around the spartan room. "What have you been doing in here for a month?"

The silence that followed closed a fist around her windpipe. It lasted a minute, then several more, until she could no longer bear it.

"Are we in Venezuela? What is this place?"

More silence.

"If you're not going to talk, I might as well head back to the isolation in the other room." She meant to sound bored, but the shakiness in her voice ruined the attempt.

His hand stirred on his thigh. Fingers tapped, *tap-tap-tap*, and fell still. When the shadow finally spoke, it chilled her to the bone.

"Do you want to live, Kate?"

She choked on a whimper. "Yes."

"Are you worthy of mercy?"

"Yes."

"Convince me."

Her nostrils flared, and her neck ached with tension. "I make an honest living and help people in need. I've certainly never kidnapped anyone and locked them in a room for a month." She couldn't disguise the contempt in her tone. "I haven't done anything to you!"

"Feel that high sense of value and superiority? That's pride, little girl. One of my favorite sins."

She drew in a sharp breath. "You asked —"

"I know what I asked. And since you know my name, you know it's not synonymous with mercy."

TWO

No surprise that Kate had been right about *who* had abducted her, but it didn't calm the tremors in her belly. Because let's face it. There was nothing remotely comforting about being held captive by Tiago Badell.

As one of the wealthiest crime lords in Venezuela, he smuggled guns and drugs, kidnapped tourists for ransom, controlled the police force, and made a living off other people's misery. Tate's intel had given her a harrowing overview of the operation, but how would that insight help her? Tiago probably wanted to kill her just because of her association with Tate.

Even if that were true, she wouldn't mention Tate. Not until she better understood the landscape and the man who reigned over it.

Why was he just sitting there in the shadows? Was he aiming a gun? Coiled to strike? Trying to keep his face anonymous? Or maybe he was just a dickhead and wanted to get a rise out of her?

The steel safe he used as a chair was the

freestanding variety, with a combination lock and heavy-looking door. It was probably bolted to the floor and stuffed to the brim with artillery, cash, and enough criminal evidence to earn him a top spot on the *Most Dangerous Men in the World* list.

A quick scan of the room confirmed there was nothing she could wield as a weapon. Except the lamp. Unplugging it would plunge her into darkness. She could use the cord for strangulation or the wooden base as a bludgeon. But not effectively with her wrists tied together.

If she stepped closer, she might be able to see his features. It would also put her directly in the light, with the outline of her body backlit by the lamp. A minor vulnerability, but not one she was willing to concede without negotiation.

"Tell you what." She lifted her bound hands. "I'll come to you, if you remove the rope."

A grunt scuffed from his throat. "With your hands free, you assume I'll wait here while you grab the lamp and swing it at me?"

When he put it like that, it made her sound foolish and predictable.

She clenched her teeth, and another idea struck. It wouldn't help her escape, but she went with it.

Circling backward, she paced away from him, toward the lamp, and approached it from behind. The rope squeezed her wrists as she clutched the base and raised it above her head.

With it tilted in his direction, the light stretched to his chest, revealing a white collared shirt, unbuttoned at the throat and tucked into black slacks. Sleeves covered his arms, the crisp fabric clinging to broad shoulders and defined pecs. Every thread on his body looked perfectly fitted for his tall, lean frame.

Narrow hips, muscular thighs, seemingly hard all over—his athletic physique was unfortunate. She might've been able to outrun an out-of-shape man.

What was with the fancy clothes? Did he dress up for her or was he expecting another visitor? Other than the old man who delivered the meals, no one had entered this room in the month she'd been here. Not even the guards.

"I feel underdressed." She glanced down at the thin dress. At least, she wasn't illuminated from behind.

He didn't move or make a sound, not even as she hoisted the lamp as high as the cord allowed. Because he knew. No matter how she positioned it, the glow wouldn't reach his face.

"Are you finished wasting my time?" He stretched out a leg, reclining farther into the shadows.

"Why am I here?"

"Someone took something from me, so I took something in return." A smile surfaced in his voice. "I took you."

The implication settled through her, loosening her chest. Tate must've succeeded. He must've taken Lucia from Tiago and fled.

They were safe.

Sweet mercy, what a relief. After an eleven-year separation, she couldn't imagine how overjoyed Camila must've been to reunite with her long-lost sister. This was great news. Fucking fantastic.

Except for Kate's part in it. For that, she had no one to blame but herself.

Tate had demanded she not take the job at the

diner. All her overprotective roommates were against the idea because they couldn't keep an eye on her. But she wanted her independence. Her freedom.

Now, she had neither.

She readjusted the light, moving it side to side, desperate to see her captor's eyes. "Are you holding me for ransom?"

"No." The gruff syllable punched from the darkness and hit her in the chest.

No ransom. No negotiations in the works to release her. She was fucked.

Her arms lowered as fear rose to the surface, tightening her face and hunching her spine. She set the lamp on the floor and inched away from it, seeking the cover of darkness.

"I have money." She pressed her back against the stone wall, struggling to quiet her quickening breaths. "A lot of money. I'll pay—"

"*You* are the payment."

Her stomach collapsed. "You're going to rape me."

"If you're offering, it wouldn't be rape."

"I would *never*—"

"You presume I'm interested."

She assumed a lot of things. Sodomy, mutilation, slow excruciating death... Any manner of evil was on the table, in any order and degree of agony.

"I'm not," he said.

"Not...?" Her brows pinched.

"Not interested in fucking you."

Her breath caught and held. She should've felt relief, but she'd seen the videos and knew what he wasn't saying. "You'll let your guards rape me."

He didn't answer, and God help her, the wretched

silence made her blood shiver.

"I have powerful friends." She licked dry lips. "Dangerous allies who are looking for me right now. When they find me, you'll beg for death. You'll beg each time they cut off a piece of you. They'll use fire and chop and cook until there's nothing left but burnt ends and shit stains." She stood taller, her voice stronger. "Let me go, and I'll let you live."

He chuckled, mocking her. "Your friends are cannibals?"

"No, they're…" She clamped her molars together, cursing her bungling attempt to threaten him. "They're coming for me."

"You're a remarkably stupid woman. You know what I am, yet you walk in here, spewing nonsense, as if you actually believe you can control your demise."

Needles pulsated behind her eyes. "So that's it? I'm going to die?"

"Everyone dies. Some more painfully than others."

His cold, callous tone validated her assumption. This wouldn't be a quick execution. He intended to make her suffer.

Terror trickled down her spine, freezing her in place.

Don't just stand there. Move. Run. Fight, for fuck's sake.

She unlocked her legs and bolted toward the door.

Two steps was all she managed before the lamp turned off and pitch-black darkness swallowed the room.

Her heart rate exploded as she strained her eyes. How the fuck did he kill the light?

She couldn't see her hands in front of her face. The exit hovered somewhere to the right, so she crept in that direction, listening for his footsteps amid the eruption of her gasps.

She tried to move slowly and soundlessly, so he couldn't track her. Then her scalp tingled. The air shifted against her, around her. Panic kicked in, and she burst into a blind sprint.

Heart racing, she made it a few more feet before something thumped up ahead. The sound of the door closing, of air being pushed out as it sealed. Then the lock slid into place.

She froze, her lungs shriveling with ice. Energy bounced against her, a disturbance of atmosphere. He was close, but where?

"Turn on the light." She swerved backward, spinning, her bound arms throwing her off balance as she swung at nothing.

He made no sound, yet his presence squeezed in on all sides, taunting her with her fear of the dark.

Her hair ruffled, and she pivoted. Was he circling her?

She whirled back, disoriented. Where was the door? Straight ahead? Behind her? She darted forward, and her throat slammed into an iron bar of muscle. His arm. He fucking clotheslined her.

Pain exploded in her larynx, and she staggered backward, expecting a hand to fly out of the blackness. But it was his boot that hit next. Directly in her stomach.

The excruciating impact sucked the wind from her lungs and knocked her flat on her back.

She landed on the mattress, gulping for air, and in the next heartbeat, he was on her. Powerful legs straddled her hips. His hand collared her throat, and the other pinned her arms above her head.

He was too heavy, too strong. Too fucking close.

"It doesn't matter what you want, who your friends are, or what you think you know about me." His calm breath feathered her face. "You have no opinions here. No privilege or power. Apparently, you didn't learn that the last time."

Her heart crashed against her ribcage as she bucked and twisted beneath his weight. "The last time?"

"Four years ago."

Oh God, he knew her past. He'd done his research.

"That's right." He flexed his thighs against her writhing hips, holding her to the mattress as his hands moved along the rope on her arms. "I know all about Van Quiso and his training."

"Don't do this." She didn't need her vision to know he was tying her to something on the wall. All-consuming fear jangled her insides, violently shaking her. "Let me go!"

"Try not to shit yourself. If you make a mess in my bed, I'll make you sleep in it. Not because I'm into that kind of thing. It's fucking disgusting."

Her jaw fell open, and a stunned whisper tumbled out. "What the hell is wrong with you?"

"We're not going to get into that. Right now, we're focusing on what's wrong with you." He put his mouth at her ear. "It's safe to assume Van Quiso did a number on your head. But instead of learning from the experience, you went and got yourself captured again. Let's be honest, Kate. That was really careless on your part."

"Careless?" she shrieked. "*You* kidnapped—"

He clamped a huge hand over her face, covering her lips and part of her nose. "Another outburst, and my next strike will break something important."

THREE

Kate wrestled for air beneath the press of Tiago's fingers on her face. He already kicked her hard enough to turn her stomach black and blue by morning. If he adjusted his grip by a millimeter, her airway would be completely closed. She had no choice but to heed his threat.

Commanding the rigidness to leave her body, she sank into the mattress and blinked in the darkness.

He released her mouth, then her hands, but his weight remained on her hips.

With her arms stretched toward the wall above her head, she yanked hard. No give. Just as she assumed, the rope was tied to something immovable.

"Now, where were we?" His deep rumble penetrated her chest.

"You were pointing out my faults." She bared her teeth, not that he could see her with the lights off.

"So I was. Among those faults is this withering scorn you carry around." He gripped her jaw, gave it a painful squeeze, and let go. "You're sick of being the underdog, the victim. So you charged in here wearing a cloud of righteous anger, because fuck the man, right? And by man, I mean every prick who's treated you unfairly. The father who abandoned you. The brothers who bullied you. The roommates who didn't protect you. The scar-faced bastard who tried to sell you to some fat fuck with fetishes more unspeakable than his own. Then there's me. You don't even know what I have planned for you."

Horror consumed her, constricting and pulling. He just dissected her with all the boredom of a man playing a child's game. She had no defenses against him, physically or emotionally.

Nothing would stop him from grabbing her throat and ripping out the meat of it. Or breaking her legs so she couldn't flee. Or he could go for her unprotected core. Her abdomen trembled right there between his thighs. He could pummel her until she bled internally.

Any or all of it was possible, and the thought shoved her into a fresh hell of panic.

What about her friends? Would he go after them next? How did he know so much about her life? Her father was dead. But her brothers... No one knew about them.

Except Van.

Tiago coasted his fingers over her hair, slithering a chill across her scalp. "I appreciate your bravado, but it's a portal to make-believe land. It'll get you nowhere." His hand retreated. "It won't save you."

Her head hammered, her eyes wide and unseeing. She might not know anything useful about him, but she knew his type.

Living with five alpha males, she was accustomed

to the overbearing display of dominance. The vibration of confidence close to the skin, the puffed-up chests and unwavering eye contact—every action demanded respect and submission. Which begged the question...

"Why did you turn off the light?" She waited through a span of silence, strangling beneath the press of his proximity. "If I'm going to die, it doesn't matter if I see your face. If you're the one in control, why are you hiding in the dark? You've been holed up in this room for a month. Who are you running from?"

"Now *that*," he breathed at her ear, "is the smartest thing you've said."

The light flicked on, and the sudden brightness blotted her vision. As her eyes adjusted, she glimpsed a remote in his hand. He set it aside, and her gaze tripped along a muscled arm to the column of a masculine neck.

Stubble shadowed his chiseled jaw and outlined sculpted lips. A prominent nose, bladed cheekbones, and eyes so dark they could've been black—the squared cut of Hispanic features formed a ruthless, shockingly attractive face.

As she took in his unexpected beauty, the corners of his mouth levitated in a macabre smile.

He was madness with straight, white teeth. Corruption with glowing skin. A nightmare in a designer suit.

Dipping his head, he brought his eyes into the angle of light. Holographic hues of brown glittered in his irises, but it was the intelligence in that stare that jolted electricity through her heart.

His gaze was deafening. As jarring as a crack of lightning in the night. But instead of chaos writhing in his eyes, she found the steady pulse of self-control and calculation.

He watched her closely, deliberately, as if he knew it unsettled her, and that knowledge gave him pleasure.

His smile widened.

An increase in pressure and temperature swept the room. Her chest rose and fell, fighting for each shallow gasp.

He was so fearsomely, horrifyingly beautiful she had to look away, her focus landing on the only weakness she could find.

A bandage. Multiple bandages, taped in a row from his temple to the back of his head. Thick layers of gauze concealed what lay beneath, but from the size of the wrap, the injury had been severe.

Severe enough to debilitate him for weeks.

"That's why you haven't left this room." Her mind swam as she glanced around at the sparse space, homing in on the duffel bag of clothes. "You fled Kidnap Alley to recover here, to remain hidden until you regained strength. Have you been unconscious all this time?"

"In and out. An inconvenient side-effect of pain killers."

She was surprised he answered so candidly. Did someone shoot him? Knife him? Was it Tate? She returned her attention to his head, scrutinizing the wide swath of shaved scalp. How serious was the damage?

"You want to see under the bandages." His voice purred with provocation, licking a hum across her skin. "You're dying with curiosity."

"Dying is a poor choice of words, considering." She pulled harder on her arms and craned her neck to find her hands tethered to a cast iron pipe on the wall. She returned to his eyes, and a deep inhale helped her maintain that contact. "What happened?"

"Lucia Dias." A twitch feathered along his jaw. "She went vigilante on me with a forty-pound dumbbell."

Camila's sister attacked him? He still hadn't mentioned Tate. Was the attack part of Tate's rescue mission? Did he and Lucia make it out? Were they alive?

Tiago watched her steadily, devouring the trepidation she couldn't hide on her face. If he didn't already know Lucia's name meant something to her, he knew now.

"What happened to her?" A swallow solidified in her throat.

"You tell me."

Was he fucking with her? She didn't know how to play mind games with a psychopath, but she needed to try. Since she couldn't overpower him, she would have to outsmart him.

How had Lucia survived eleven years in his ranks? She worked for him, but no one understood why. There were so many pieces Tate hadn't puzzled out. So many unanswered questions. Hell, he'd traveled to Venezuela uncertain if Lucia would welcome him or shoot him on the spot.

"I don't know her." She held Tiago's intimidating gaze. "I assume you provoked her? The fact that she succeeded in injuring you means you didn't see it coming."

He nodded, eyes narrowing, losing focus. "She was a special circumstance. As fierce as they come. She survived in my outfit longer than any of the men, and that kind of resilience was rare. It made her useful. Worth having around."

Every past tense word struck her like shrapnel, shredding her hope that Lucia was still alive. "How did she catch you off guard?"

"I never trusted her, but we had an agreement." He absently stroked the medical tape on his temple. "I allowed her to live, as long as she followed my rules."

Bashing his head would've been the opposite of following his rules.

"Where is she?" She struggled beneath him, attempting to unbalance his straddled position. "What did you do to her?"

"I let her go."

"You…" Wait. *What?* "You said someone took her from you."

"That's not what I said." He scowled hatefully. "Pay attention, Kate."

"You're speaking in riddles." Her arms pulled at the shoulders, and her hips twinged beneath his weight, compelling her to twist about, seeking distance. "Please, get off me. You're fucking heavy."

He pondered her request for a moment before adjusting his legs and lifting some of that bulk off her lower body.

She released a slow breath, contemplating his cryptic words. "You said someone took *something* from you."

"Yes. I never had her loyalty, but I possessed something more effective. Her *fear*." He tipped his head, his gaze invasive. "You, of all people, understand how every aspect of a person's life can be controlled through terror."

No use denying it. Four years ago, her crippling fear gave Van Quiso power over her entire being. Lucia must've experienced the same with Tiago. Until she attacked him.

"Someone took her fear from you," she said.

"That's right." He flashed an unnerving grin and traced a finger along the gauze near his eye. "I haven't seen her handiwork. Boones says it's healing, but he won't remove the bandages."

"Boones?" She shook her head. No one entered this room, except... "The elderly cook?"

"He's a doctor. A damn good one, despite his motherly approach to my care." He fingered the medical tape, picked at the corner. "Fuck it."

He gripped the edge of the bandage and ripped it off. She winced as he forcefully tore at the pieces, pulling out strips of hair in the process without a twitch of pain on his face.

"Be honest." He gave her his profile and smoothed a hand along a jagged, puffy laceration. "How bad is it?"

She stopped breathing as her gaze locked on the damage.

Jesus. Lucia hadn't just hit him with a dumbbell. Somehow, she'd managed to hit him *twice.*

The first gash sat so close to his eye it was a wonder he survived the blow. The orbital bones around his eye socket should've shattered under the impact. Maybe they did. A yellowish hue discolored his cheekbone where bruises must've lingered for weeks.

The second wound carved a huge crescent-shaped groove along the side of his skull. This one appeared deeper and would've required more stitches, the skin around it still raw and scabbed over, taking longer to heal.

That side of his head was shaved to the peak above

his temple where hair tended to retreat. But there was no threat of a receding hairline. Thick black strands fell over the non-injured side in finger-raked textures, accentuating his rugged features and whiskered jawline.

He was in desperate need of a haircut, one that evened out the sides. The messy-all-over, renegade style no longer worked for him, because hair would never grow in over the deep gouges that ran diagonally from his temple to the back of his head.

Together, the marks would leave a permanent map of scars the length of her hand and almost as wide. A hit like that was meant to be fatal. No doubt he sustained multiple skull fractures.

Too bad it didn't mash his brain to pulp.

She returned her gaze to his and found him watching her, waiting for an answer.

How bad is it?

It didn't diminish his disgusting masculine beauty. If anything, the scars made him even more arresting. But she didn't give a fuck what he looked like. She wanted him to suffer.

"I can't really see from this angle." She bent her neck and squinted. "Can you lean in a little closer?"

As he shifted, she reared her head back and slammed it forward. Aiming for his wounds, she hoped to reopen them with the ram of her skull.

In a blur, he dodged left, fisted the hair at the back of her head, and ruthlessly yanked her flat against the mattress.

"Not exactly the spice of originality." He forced her neck at a painful angle. "I'm disappointed."

She should've known. After Lucia got the drop on him, he'd be hyper-vigilant about strikes to the head.

"You said I don't have an opinion." She squirmed, unable to relieve his eye-watering grip on her hair. "Then you asked me to be honest about your wounds. Excuse me if I'm having trouble with your contradictory rules."

She needed to figure out a different way to fight him. If she could reach him with words, say something he found intriguing, maybe he'd keep her alive.

A heart-pounding smile wrenched his lips. So disturbing, that mouth. As it fell into a slack line, his sudden lack of expression produced a sick, buckling sensation in her stomach.

He released her hair, straightened his seated position on her pelvis, and removed something from his pants pocket. "You might think all human skin cuts the same beneath a blade."

Her pulse quickened as he slipped a small metal instrument onto his index finger and unfolded the tip. It opened like a switch blade and curved into a lethal claw.

All the air vacated her lungs. She couldn't unfreeze her gaze from the glinting steel, couldn't feel her heart beat or move her hands and feet. Her fear was brutal, her mind a torture chamber of the grisly things to come as she fast forwarded the swipe of his finger, the sharp edge slicing her from neck to gut, and the slick gush of blood that would bathe her final moments.

He tilted the razor inches from her face, causing light to dance across the surface. "Cutting a woman, it's different than cutting a man. The blade must be held with a passionate hand, and when feminine skin separates, it doesn't just bleed. It weeps."

Throbbing pressure built in the back of her throat and swelled behind her eyes. His words, the clinical apathy in his voice, the unfeeling look on his face... He was deeply deranged, inhumanly evil, and it scared the living hell out of her.

Tremors crashed through her body. She wanted to believe she was a strong person, that she could endure the worst of his depravity without breaking. But she wasn't and couldn't. She couldn't even rein in her emotions at the sight of his blade.

As she shoved down the panic, it bubbled back up. As she blanked her face, the muscles in her cheeks contracted and quivered. She swallowed ugly, miserable sounds, but they broke through, fracturing the silence and exposing her fragility.

It was such a helpless feeling—the choking breaths, the godawful constriction in her chest, the inconsolable horror. Her chin trembled, chattering her teeth. She blinked rapidly, tried to stop the worst of it before it spilled from her eyes, tried to hold herself together with invisible arms. There was no comfort to be found.

She couldn't remember the last time she was this terrified. Everything inside her twisted and swelled to the point of unraveling. She ached to surrender to it and mentally played out what it would feel like to give in to the tears, to the uncontrollable sobbing, to abandon the fight and let defeat pull her under. She longed for that, to give up and accept her fate. God, the relief in letting go would be extraordinary.

But when her meltdown was over, there would be nothing left. He would still be here, getting off on her pathetic show. He wouldn't even have to cut her. Her misery alone would feed his sadism. It would make him stronger.

He didn't see her as a person. She was an object, a thing to play with and torment. Eventually, he would grow bored and toss away her pieces like a broken toy. Then he would find another.

Fuck that.

A heavy stillness fell over her. A purpose. She wasn't dead yet. That meant she could change her fate, rewrite the ending. But how?

He ghosted the razor's edge along her brow, just a whispered touch of steel that put every nerve in her body into cardiac arrest.

With great effort, she dragged her attention away from the blade and focused on the shadows in his eyes.

What made him become so vicious? Was he born into a life of crime? Did he have any loved ones? Anyone important to him?

He seemed to respect Lucia, said she was fierce and resilient. But Kate wasn't fearless, and he already scolded her for trying to be brave.

There was something broken inside him. That much was obvious. She had no clue how to decode his fucked-up mind, but after her experience with Van, she'd been drawn to documentaries and psychiatric studies about violent criminals.

There was evidential research that linked personal trauma to the making of a murderer. Not all serial killers were victims of abuse, but many experienced brutal childhoods. She couldn't diagnose him or pretend he was anything other than a criminal, but maybe she could reach him in a way no else had tried?

With the glide of his finger, he curved the razor along the side of her face. His gaze followed the movement, and his breathing picked up.

She held still, paralyzed beneath his deadly touch. "You don't want to do this."

His eyes flicked to hers and tapered with warning.

It was a powerful, overwhelmingly desperate moment when the mind recognized that death was only seconds away.

"I can give you something." She swallowed. "Something no one else has offered."

"Don't be naive. You're smart enough to imagine the range of pleasures women offer me." He scanned her body with zero interest on his face.

"Not that." She organized her thoughts and carefully chose her words. "I get the feeling you've suffered things. Unspeakable, horrible things that left a deep impact on your life."

His expression emptied, giving nothing away.

Was she digging her own grave? Her hands slicked with sweat, her lungs shriveling on the cusp of hyperventilation. "Maybe I'm just projecting. When Van Quiso took me, I experienced my own trauma. Whatever happened to you, I can empathize. I don't forgive you for kidnapping me, but I'm capable of compassion." She softened her voice. "Surely, that means something to you?"

"Compassion?" He laughed. "I've heard of it, but not in this world. Not where joy is nonexistent, and integrity is a luxury." He hooked the blade under her throat, skyrocketing her pulse. "In this world, the weak are crushed."

Her chest heaved, and her entire body convulsed with overwhelming horror. Oh God, she didn't want to die. Not like this. She wasn't ready.

But what hope did she have? There was no ransom, no way to locate her, and no white knight riding in on a horse.

What if death was her only escape?

"Okay, Tiago." She wheezed, eyes wide and burning. "I'm scared. Is that what you want? I'm fucking terrified. But I won't give you the pleasure of watching me fall apart. You want to kill me? Go ahead." She raised her chin and pushed against the blade, shaking violently. "You have my fear. You've taken my freedom. I have nothing left to lose."

"That's not true. There is something."

The blade retreated, and he folded it shut. Her heartbeat reeled as he pocketed it and pulled out a phone.

"I have something you and Lucia want." He unlocked the screen, tapped it a few times, and met her eyes.

"I don't understand." Or maybe she did, but denial was easier to swallow.

He turned the phone and showed her the screen.

A live video of a nude man streamed across the display. He stood in a shack with his back to the camera and a sponge in his hand. He was bathing, using water from a bucket at his feet. Even more crude was the shackle connecting his ankle to a chain that snaked along the dirt floor.

What was on his back? She leaned closer to the screen.

Holy fuck.

Blood pounded in her ears, and ice skewered her veins.

Who would have the stomach to carve up that man's back so gruesomely? Her gaze shot to Tiago, her thoughts spiraling to the razor in his pocket.

Dread hardened her gut as she returned to the

screen.

The mutilation spanned from the man's shoulders to his waist, the cuts welted and red, but not fresh. Not only that, there were pink scars on opposite sides of his arm, as if something had been recently stabbed straight through it.

God, the pain he must've endured… She couldn't imagine it. Couldn't take her eyes off the video. She pored over his brown hair, his muscled mid-twenties physique, and the unfinished tattoo on his bicep.

Her breath hitched. *Oh, please, no.* She knew that tattoo.

"As it turns out…" Tiago's deep voice broke through her. "Lucia fell in love."

"No, no, no." She shook her head, denying the truth even as it forced itself upon her. "That's not Tate. It can't be."

"It's him, and the man holding the camera has been instructed to kill him, if I don't call in…" He tilted the phone to check the time. "Five minutes."

Her heart catapulted to her throat. "Call him!"

He regarded her, head canted and expression composed, as if he had all the time in the world.

Everything inside her snapped. She thrashed and spat and went fucking feral as he watched her with a sick kind of curiosity.

"Please!" She kicked her legs, bucking beneath the straddle of his knees. "What do you want? I'll do anything."

"Anything?"

She looked at the phone, at the brutality marring Tate's back, and her stomach sank. "Lucia loves him? And he loves her back?"

36

"Yes." The corner of his mouth bounced. "They risked their lives to be together, and if they're lucky, they'll die together."

"What are you saying?"

"I have a weakness for tragic love stories. It's the only reason I didn't kill them immediately." He shut off the phone, a scowl darkening his inextricable eyes. "Lucia will find him, unless you fuck it up."

"Don't put this on me," she seethed. "I'll do whatever you say. Just make the call."

FOUR

Fucking Christ, Tiago's head hurt. He wasn't in the habit of physically restraining people, especially not while recovering from a fractured skull.

He preferred other means of control, as Kate would soon find out.

"I'm going to remove the rope." He pulled the finger blade from his pocket. "Be a good girl."

Her watery gaze stayed with the phone where it sat out of reach. Her fear for Tate was palpable, paling her pretty face to a ghostly shade of white. She would really lose her mind if she knew her friend was being held within walking distance from here.

Tiago didn't relish the thought of ending Tate's life. It would ruin everything he'd put into place.

But he would follow through on his threat if Kate didn't behave.

"Hold still." He cut through the thick rope on her arms until the fibers unraveled enough to fall away.

She rubbed her wrists, the skin red and raw. A

little rope burn was nothing compared to the hurt she would endure before she died. She might as well get used to it.

He rolled off her slender body, and she instantly tried to scramble away.

"Stay." He pointed the blade at the spot beside him on the mattress.

She froze with a foot on the floor and glared back at him. "You're going to call your guy? Stop him from killing Tate?"

He tapped the mattress where he wanted her.

Her shoulders slumped, and she crawled to the far end, putting her back to the wall and her eyes on his phone.

Another wave of queasiness hit him sideways, and he braced a hand on the bed, catching himself.

Christ, he needed something for the double vision. Being bedridden for a month left him dizzy and weak. Wrestling a pint-sized woman made it worse.

It was time to start working out again. The sooner he rebuilt his strength, the sooner he could return to Caracas and reestablish his reign there.

First, he needed to deal with his prisoners.

"If you make a single sound, Tate will die." He unlocked the phone. "Tell me you understand."

Her blue eyes flashed, and her teeth sawed through the words. "I understand."

He dialed Arturo, the guard who sent the video, and didn't wait for a greeting. "Put Tate on the phone."

Sounds of movement rustled down the line, followed by an angry rush of breaths.

"Hello, Tate." Tiago set the phone on speaker, so Kate could hear the conversation.

Tate made a stricken noise. "Where's — ?"

"If you ask about her, the call ends, and you'll never hear from me again."

It had been a month since Tate and Lucia saw each other. Tate asked about her relentlessly, but his questions went unanswered.

Tiago needed him to assume the worst. "You'll spend the rest of your lonely existence locked away in that shack, wondering why I called and what I was going to say."

Kate sucked in a breath, her expression murderous.

"I'm listening," Tate said.

"I would be there in person, but I haven't been feeling well. I'm sure you know why." As he spoke into the phone, he held her gaze, wordlessly reminding her to keep quiet. "I wanted to offer you something. Let's call it a last request. Anything you want. This doesn't include information, and it must fit inside the shack."

"What is this?" Tate asked. "Like a last-meal request? Am I on death row?"

She tensed, her fingers biting into the mattress.

He shook his head, admonishing her. "I'm offering more than a meal, Tate. You can choose anything — a bed to sleep on, a girl to fuck, a drug to numb your mind. I'm sure you can come up with something creative."

"Why?" Suspicion laced Tate's voice. "What do you want?"

"I've already taken my payment." Given the rancor in her eyes, he might have to kill her before the call ended. "Consider this a thank you."

"What did you *take*?" Tate whispered harshly.

"Not Lucia. I left her to die in prison. What's your last request, Tate?"

Kate pressed a hand against her lips, smothering a whimper.

Tiago had spoken the truth about Lucia, but not the *whole* truth. If Kate sat there and kept her mouth shut, maybe he would enlighten her.

Returning his attention to the phone, he digested the silence on the other end.

Right about now, Tate was likely hitting a very cold, inconsolable rock bottom. Tiago knew too well what that felt like. The suffocating, dire weight of helplessness pulling through the body. The endless chill hardening organs and arteries. The grip of desolation overshadowing self-preservation. An emptiness so profound and consuming there wasn't enough air to return from the dead.

To have and to hold the entire world, then to watch it be violently ripped away... There was no greater suffering.

Kate was right. Some experiences cut so deeply it gutted a man. *Or twisted a good man into a criminal.*

Tate's rasp vibrated the speaker. "Do you have a photo of Lucia?"

"Yes."

"My request..." He coughed, his voice hoarse. "I want to finish the tattoo on my arm, feel her face on my skin, with me always."

Tears welled in Kate's eyes, her nostrils pulsing above the hand she held against her mouth.

Tate had more than proved his love for Lucia in the basement of the Caracas compound. Having her inked into his skin would add a layer of commitment that made his devastation that much more meaningful.

The idea moved Tiago, sinking deep into a

graveyard of memories and resurrecting ghosts. He harbored an ugly past, one that made him fixate on rare and beautiful things, like the mutual devotion between two people.

Wrenching Tate away from Lucia had been as cruel as carving a portrait into his back, but that was the point.

The strongest love rose out of the greatest hurt.

With regard to the logistics of Tate's request, it just so happened one of the local guards was a tattoo artist.

"Very well." Tiago switched the call off speaker. "Return the phone to the guard."

After making the necessary arrangements with Arturo, he disconnected and glanced at Kate.

"Can I see another video?" She wiped her damp cheeks. "Proof that your guard isn't killing him?"

"No." He locked the phone and tossed it aside.

Her lashes lowered, and another tear slipped out. "Please, let him go."

If she thought he kept a watchdog on Tate, she was wrong. The few guards Tiago had with him were needed here, watching the perimeter of the house.

When he was carried out of Caracas a month ago, he was comatose and bleeding from two fractures in his skull. Only Arturo and Boones came with him — the two men who saved his life.

Boones had taken care of everything, treating his injuries and transporting him to this isolated area in the Venezuela desert. Tiago owned this land and had decided days before Lucia's attack that Tate would be captured and brought here. Boones followed through on that plan perfectly.

Only five other guards joined them here, all of which were pulled from Tiago's other domiciles around the country.

His outfit in Caracas didn't know about this place, and he intended to keep it that way. He had countless enemies and trusted no one. Except Boones.

Every day, the old doctor delivered Tate's meals and nursed his wounds. Only then did a guard go near the shack, and that was for Boones' protection.

If Tate managed to free himself from the ankle cuff, no one would stop him from escaping.

Tiago reclined against the wall and captured her gaze. "When Lucia finds him, he's free to go."

"You said Lucia's in prison." Her brows gathered. "You also said you let her go."

"You may not believe this, but I haven't lied to you. I did let her go."

"I don't know what to believe."

"Good, because you have no—"

"Opinions. I heard you the first time." She looked away, giving him the profile of her willful chin.

Why hadn't he sent her back to her room? He wouldn't need her until later, if at all.

He'd captured her to send Tate and his friends a message. *Fuck with the most powerful gang leader in Venezuela and pay the consequences.*

As for Kate's fate, it wasn't pretty. He would offer her to his enemies as a bribe. Or give her to his guards as a reward for their loyalty.

Or he would just kill her.

He tilted his head and let his gaze wander over her, really taking her in for the first time.

Blond hair hung in wild waves to her elbows. Bony shoulders, smallish tits, she was skinnier and shorter than the average twenty-two-year-old.

44

For all the profanity and thunderous noise her face produced over the past month, he'd formed a completely different picture in his head. Between bouts of unconsciousness and listening to her bellow in the other room, he'd imagined a tough Amazonian beast of woman. Someone tall and strong with meat on her bones.

Not that he had complaints about the image before him. That was the problem. Kate was a goddamn knockout.

Her fair complexion, ethereal figure, graceful legs, and fuck, her eyes... As vivid as the ocean and too deep to measure, those bottomless blues could enchant a man, make him change course and lose his way.

He should just kill her now and be done with it.

With a slow breath, she sat taller, pushed back her shoulders, and faced him. "Will you tell me what happened? With Tate and Lucia?" Her eyebrows knitted together as she faltered over her next question. "Is Van Quiso alive?"

Interesting how she asked about everyone else while her own life hung in the balance. And Van Quiso no less. The sex-trafficking rapist enslaved her for weeks, no doubt violating her six ways to Sunday. He didn't deserve her concern.

One might argue that Van couldn't hold a testicle to the crimes Tiago had committed. Nevertheless, Tiago felt a strange itch to answer her and found himself wondering how she would weigh in on his decision concerning her fate.

His train of thought baffled him. She was nothing more than a prisoner. A soon-to-be-dead prisoner.

Her death would be a waste of a gorgeous body. Most men would sell their souls for a night between her legs. But the lure of a beautiful woman had no power over him.

Lucia spent eleven years at his side, naked in his room, and dependent on his mercy. He'd allowed himself to touch her, to indulge in the feel of her every dip and curve. But he never fucked her. That was his rule. His self-imposed penance.

Kate was no different.

He ran a hand along the cuff of his shirt, unbuttoned it, and did the same with the other sleeve. "After a month of bed rest, this is the first time I've put on clothes. Unfortunately, when my bag was packed for me, my casual attire was forgotten in the rush."

Her mouth parted, her eyes bright and watchful. He knew she'd wondered why he'd dressed up. The fact that he answered her unspoken question surprised him as much as it did her.

"I've been straight with you." He rolled up his sleeves, taking his time with each one. "Your life is forfeit. A penalty paid for Tate's stupidity. It's in my best interest to kill you quickly."

She fell unnaturally still, her gaze focusing on nothing. He wasn't sure she was breathing.

Then she blinked and locked onto his eyes. "Do you have anything to drink?"

Her calm response gave him pause, and in that unexpected moment, he found her…spellbinding.

"There's a bottle of tequila in my bag." He nodded at the luggage. "Cups are in the bathroom."

"I'll pour us some shots."

As she stood, her arm wrapped around her stomach where he'd kicked her, her face etched in pain.

He should've killed her the moment she entered

his room.

Why didn't he just do it now? As long as she was alive, her friends wouldn't stop looking for her.

She shuffled through the small space, grabbing the tequila and pulling his concentration along with her. The white-gold of her hair, the unintentional sway of her ass, the irresistible flex of muscle there — the sight of her made him burn, hardening him until there was nowhere to go in his fitted trousers.

He deserved the discomfort, had earned the torment of looking at her without touching. Twelve years ago, he made the gravest mistake of his life and lost everything that made him human. But he still had a working dick, and the damn thing wanted out.

She returned to the mattress, watching him watch her. "Why is killing me in your best interest?"

There were many reasons, but he gave her the one that would hurt her most.

"You said it yourself." He lifted the tequila from her hand, filled the cups, and handed one to her. "Your army of *dangerous* friends is looking for you." He took a hearty draw from the mug, hoping the alcohol would numb his perpetual headache. "I'll leave your body where they can find it."

She tossed back the tequila, gulping it down between hacking coughs.

"Sit." He motioned at the mattress.

She wiped her mouth with the back of her hand, sat at the farthest end, and held out the empty mug. "If you kill me, they'll come for *you*."

"Not with the same urgency or persistence." He refilled her cup. "What will they sacrifice to avenge your death? How long will it take before they refocus their efforts on those they can save? That's what they do, right? They free human slaves."

She averted her eyes, jaw clenched, and looked back at him. "You don't know them."

"When Van Quiso and Liv Reed ran a sex trafficking ring, you were their seventh slave. But they put all that behind them, and now they co-parent the child who came out of their twisted relationship. Van married Amber. Liv married Josh, and they're all one big fucked-up family. You are not their priority."

"Where did you get that information?"

"Then there's Lucia's sister, Camila Dias. She's not only the leader of your little army. She also happens to be married to the capo of the Restrepo cartel. She made quite a leap from Van's attic. Or a fall, depending on how you look at it." He finished off his tequila and poured another. "While Matias Restrepo has the resources to take me out, his focus is and always will be on Camila. If she died by my hand, he'd tear the universe apart in his fury to make me suffer. But I took *you*, and you are not his. You're not his priority. Not his concern."

"Whatever you think." She lifted a shoulder, and the trembly motion ruined her attempt at indifference.

"As for the men you lived with, they're currently seeking refuge in Colombia, under Matias' protection."

"They're afraid you'll come after them. If you kill me, they *will* retaliate."

"Which roommate were you fucking? Martin? Luke? Tomas? All of them?"

He'd investigated the entire crew the moment he discovered Tate Vades sniffing around his domain. While he didn't know who was fucking who in Tate's household, he'd learned enough to determine that Kate was the ideal target.

She wasn't married. Didn't have a romantic partner or monogamous lover. There was no one in her life who would travel to the end of hell and back to avenge her death. And that was where he was headed after he killed her. Back to Caracas. Hell on Earth.

"All your assumptions can fuck right off." She guzzled her drink and shoved the cup aside.

"Your friends might be outraged by your death, but they don't love you. Not the way a man loves his soulmate. You are no one's other half. No one's number one."

She closed her eyes, tucking away her reaction. But he felt the moment his words penetrated. The mattress shook beneath her perch on the edge, her body quaking so loudly and intensely he marveled at the strength of her despair.

Her gaze moved to the exit. Would she make a run for it? If she did, she wouldn't make it past the antechamber. The door to the stairway required a key from the inside, which he kept in his locked safe.

He poured another drink, stalling the inevitable task. She wouldn't be the first life he took. Nor was this the first time he hesitated.

As if she sensed the direction of this thoughts, she turned and gave him her full attention.

Perspiration formed along her hairline, her breaths choppy and rough. "I don't want to die."

FIVE

Smooth tequila, a gorgeous woman, and the thrum of rain on an old roof… Tiago hadn't felt this relaxed in a long damn time.

He didn't want to kill her. Not tonight.

Maybe the month he spent in this room softened more than his muscles. With a grumpy old man as his only visitor, he ventured to guess he was lonely.

He hadn't seen his guards since he arrived. Even though they'd been carefully vetted and handpicked for this job, he didn't trust them in his personal space, let alone his headspace.

He longed for conversation, and Kate wanted answers. He could give her that much.

Wetting his lips with a sip from the mug, he let his mind drift to the past. "Eleven years ago, my men pulled a smuggled slave out of a deadly crash in Peru."

"Lucia," she breathed.

"They found her chained in a truck with a twisted piece of metal protruding from her abdomen."

By some miracle, she'd survived. But barely.

The same could've been said about him at the time.

"When they brought her to me, I knew I'd have to kill her. It was the easiest solution."

"But you didn't."

"I hesitated." He reached for his boot and untied the laces. "It wasn't a matter of morals. I've been taking lives since my early twenties."

Killing was a job requirement, then and now.

Her face paled. "How old are you?"

"Thirty-seven."

Fifteen years her senior.

She touched her throat, eyes round with shock. "You're older than I thought."

He felt old. Too fucking old and jaded to have a meaningful conversation with a girl from the suburbs. But he wanted to tell her about Lucia, needed to get it off his chest.

Removing his boots, he leaned back against the wall, with his legs stretched off the mattress. "Lucia came to me at a time when I needed a distraction."

It had been the worst year of his life. He'd lost everything, moved halfway across the world, changed jobs, and stripped his identity down to the black remains of his soul. All he had left were nightmares and chaos, and he needed to balance that with something constant, something he could control.

And there she was. A woman he could save.

"Boones and his medical team operated on her," he said. "She went through several surgeries and a long recovery."

"He has a medical team?"

"Three other doctors. They followed me to

Venezuela twelve years ago to work for my organization. But they're old, older than Boones, and it was time for them to go home. They left the night Boones transported me here."

"Where is *home?*"

Tiago didn't originate from Eritrea like Boones and the others, but their quiet African village on the Red Sea was the only place he ever called home.

His chest constricted. What bound him to Eritrea was a collection of pervasive, melancholic memories. His life there ran the gamut from extreme joy to unendurable tragedy. None of which he was inclined to talk about.

When her gaze dipped, he realized he was scratching the scars on his forearm.

Lowering his hand to his lap, he skipped over her question. "I didn't keep Lucia alive out of the goodness of my heart. She's attractive and ferocious, and I wanted to mold those attributes into a weapon I could use." He chuckled in remembrance. "She became an invaluable spy, but it took *years* to tame her."

Kate stared at him as if he just told her he ate the hearts of human babies.

She wasn't far off the mark.

He was a self-made felon, feared and abhorred by all walks of life. "I could've killed her. Maybe I should have. Had she fallen into the hands of another drug lord, that's exactly what they would've done. Let's not forget, she was found in a truck full of slaves, destined for a life much worse than the one I gave her."

"She was taken from her home by those slave traders. How did you keep her from running back to her family?" She absently rubbed the red marks on her wrists. "Did you tie her up for eleven years?"

"I poisoned her."

He unraveled the details of his deception — how he'd secretly tainted Lucia's food and made her chronically ill, how he counteracted it with daily injections of the antidote, and how it led her to believe she had a disease that only he could cure.

"My medical team monitored the poison, ensuring the doses weren't fatal," he said.

"That's sick." Kate shook her head, her face scrunched in revulsion. "And unacceptable."

"It was more humane than keeping her in shackles."

"You could've let her go."

He didn't expect this naive girl to understand. Her ordeal with Van Quiso was nothing compared to what existed in the bowels of the criminal underworld.

"I assume she figured out you were poisoning her," she said. "Is that why she attacked you?"

"No. Matias Restrepo was the catalyst for the recent chain of events."

"Matias? How?"

"A week before I took you, Tate initiated contact with Lucia. He approached her in a sex club and fucked her. Or maybe it was the other way around." He smirked. "I knew about their hookup but didn't consider him a threat until her routine changed. She started acting cagey. That's when I dug deeper and discovered his connection with the Restrepo cartel."

"You didn't know Matias was Lucia's brother-in-law?"

"No, and neither did she. It changed the stakes. I was no longer dealing with some clueless American sneaking around my turf. Tate's presence was attached to a cartel, a notoriously ambitious one. I didn't know if they meant to wage war against me, try to seize control of my smuggling routes, or something else. So I took you."

"As payment."

"And to send them a warning."

Kidnapping and murder, business as usual.

"Matias isn't interested in taking your business." Her breathing accelerated. "Lucia is his family. He just wanted her back."

"To that end, he would've gone to war." He cocked his head. "He sent men to the states to gather everyone close to Tate and bring them to Colombia. But when they arrived at your diner to collect you, they were an hour too late. You were already in my possession."

A whimper left her before she cut it off.

"The night you disappeared," he said, "was the same night I captured Tate and Van."

While she was being transported from Texas to Venezuela, he was putting Tate through eight brutal hours of trials and torture.

He gave her a graphic account of the evening—the icepick through Tate's arm, the carving on his back, and the forced sodomy between him and his former captor.

"What?" She gasped, her cheeks damp and bloodless. "You made Tate *fuck* Van? Why?"

"Justice is rarely pleasant, and Van had it coming."

"How is that justice? Tate wouldn't have wanted that. He'd already forgiven Van."

"Are you sure? Have you made peace with Van?"

She glanced away. "Why do you care?"

"I don't like him."

Van was a reflection of himself. Scarred. Splintered. Heartless. There was a reason he never looked in a mirror.

"Is Van still alive?" she asked quietly.

"Yes."

He detailed the events of Lucia's incursion with the dumbbell, her escape with Tate and Van, the gunfight, and car chase. "After they fled, Arturo found me on the floor in my room. By the time I woke, your friends were already recaptured."

"How could you orchestrate that with your head smashed in?"

"Boones arranged things on my behalf, leveraging the police on my payroll. Lucia and Van went to prison, and Tate was taken to the shack as part of the original plan."

"You didn't let her go." She ground her teeth.

"She's free, right now, because I allowed it. While she sat in prison for a week, I could've had her executed or returned to me at any time." He tapped a finger on his thigh, questioning this compulsion to explain himself. "She escaped prison, and I allowed that to happen. I let her go. Her and Van both."

"Why? I mean, I'm happy they're safe, but I don't understand the change of heart."

"I want her to find Tate."

"Then release him! It makes no sense." She tucked her limbs close to her torso, keeping her legs covered by the thin dress. "You poisoned her, tortured him, and separated them when all they want is to be together. Do you hurt people just for the hell of it?" A swallow bobbed her throat. "Because you get off on their pain?"

"You want to know if I'm a sadist." It was a query he didn't mind examining. "I suppose the label fits. Delivering pain is an expression of art. It's inspiring, inherently satisfying, but only when the hurt has meaning, when it serves a purpose beyond cruelty."

She slowly drew her head back, shrinking away from him. It was a sane reaction. Sitting within arm's reach of the man who would end her life, she was probably crawling out of her skin to run far, far away.

He'd told her she had no opinions here, but that was bullshit. He couldn't control the thoughts in her head, and after talking with her, he wasn't sure he wanted to. She was a good listener and spoke her mind, even if he didn't like what she had to say.

It was refreshing.

Her stare lasered onto his, narrowing, analyzing, before traveling down his arm to linger on his scars. "Your cuts are self-inflicted."

"Hm." He didn't move his eyes from her face.

"The lines on your left arm are straighter, cleaner. Because you're right-handed."

Impressive.

She glanced at his head wounds and returned to his arms. "When you asked how bad your injury looked, I thought you were concerned about infection or something. But that's not it at all. You regard scars the way a painter beholds a painting."

He leaned forward, hanging on her words.

"*Delivering pain is an expression of art.* That's what you said." Her nose twitched. "I assume that means you prefer to be the giver of scars, not the receiver. But you gave *and* received those." She nodded at his arms. "I don't know what to make of that. Do you?"

He could explain it, but he chose not to.

At his silence, she drifted closer, inspecting his welted skin with those huge blue eyes. "The designs are incredibly detailed. I can make out a few of the abstract shapes, like the sunset and mountain range. Some of the symbols are animals, but the other marks... They're esoteric." She looked up and met his gaze. "Every cut means something to you."

"Yes." He felt himself warming to her, wanting to give her more than a night to live.

"The image you put on Tate's back..." Her neck stiffened. "I couldn't see it clearly. What is it?"

He described the illustration of the double gate hanging between pillars and the woman floating through the opening. "Lucia was there when I carved it into his back. When she realizes it's a picture of the location where he's being held, she'll find him."

Kate's jaw fell open, her glare livid. "Why won't you just let him go? That's a whole lot easier than cutting a map into his body." She speared a hand through her hair and pulled at the strands. "What you're doing to them... It's insanity."

"Love is insanity."

She blinked. Blinked again. "Okay?"

"Tate and Lucia were an experiment. I wanted to learn the limits of how far they would go for each other. As it turns out, the thing between them is unstoppable. He's alone in a shack under the assumption she's dead, and his only request is a tattoo of her on his arm. She hasn't seen her sister in eleven years, but instead of going home, she's scouring the country day and night. I'm certain she won't give up until she finds him. It's fascinating to watch."

"You're playing God."

"I'm helping them."

"Helping? *Jesus Christ*," she muttered under her

breath. "You're interfering in destiny. Manipulating it."

"Destiny is a power far bigger than my mortal reach. I'm simply providing obstacles for them to overcome, to make them stronger."

"Sounds like a veiled excuse to deliver pain." Emotion leaked into her voice, raising it a few octaves. "Does their agony inspire you? Do you get hard thinking about it?"

"Stop being so goddamn narrow-minded." His pulse quickened, firing through his veins. "Adversity builds character."

"And feeds the sadist."

"Careful, Kate." He hardened his eyes, gripped by an irrational need to make her understand. "If you love someone and they don't reciprocate, what happens? You love them harder, deeper, more obsessively. Roadblocks don't diminish desire. They intensify it. Obstacles heighten the obsession."

"Fine." She blew out a breath, sagging in defeat. "I get what you're saying. Love is insanity. No one can control it."

"Not even me." He felt the glimmer in her eyes, the lingering heat and thrill from arguing.

"Just because I gave the devil his due on one point doesn't mean I agree with your demented methods."

"I don't give a fuck whether you agree or not."

With a harrumph, she tipped her pretty head, studying him. "You're not...quite what you seem."

"Explain."

"Well, you seem to be a romantic, for one. I didn't see that coming. *Wait.*" She straightened, staring at him with a startled expression. "Is that what happened to you? You had your own love story and —?"

"Do you actually believe a woman could love a man like me?"

Her lips parted as she exhaled a slow puff of air. "Am I supposed to answer that?"

He grabbed the tequila and empty mugs and rose from the bed. "We're finished here."

She touched a nerve, and he didn't bother hiding it. He wanted her out of his room.

Heading to the bathroom, he set the bottle on the counter and rinsed out the cups.

The sound of her footsteps approached from behind, pausing outside the door. "Why are there no mirrors in the bathrooms?"

They were removed for reasons that were none of her business.

She sighed into the silence. "Can we talk about the elephant in the room?"

The ever-growing burden of what to do with her unsettled his stomach. With his back to her, he mindlessly dried the cups while making a decision.

If he sent her back to her room and waited until tomorrow, she would spend the evening agonizing over her fate. Unnecessary cruelty wasn't his thing.

He needed to kill her now. No more delaying.

SIX

Some murderers claimed that killing was the same as having sex. Others argued it wasn't about lust. It was about feeling that last breath of life leave a woman, looking into her eyes, and being God.

Tiago didn't have a god complex. Nor did he derive sexual pleasure from killing. He especially hated taking a woman's life, but occasionally things happened.

If he had any human qualities left, he would get to know the stunning woman glaring at his back. He would date her, seduce her, and fuck her until neither of them could walk.

Instead, he was contemplating where to dump her body and how badly it would rot before her friends found it.

"You have four options." Kate's voice strummed with nervous agitation.

That raised his brow. He turned and rested his backside against the counter.

"One. You can let me go." She wilted beneath his

glare and hugged her waist. "But that would make you appear merciful and weak. Can't have that."

He let his silence affirm her words.

Drawing a breath, she released it slowly. "Two. You can keep me locked up. But my friends won't stop looking for me as long as I'm alive."

He slid a hand in his pants pocket and fingered the casing of his blade, the only solution.

Her eyes followed the movement, and a tremor rippled through her. "Three. You can kill me, and maybe my friends won't put a lifetime of effort into hunting you down. Like you said, there are other priorities, stronger passions than avenging my death. But killing me will make them your enemies. It's a small world, and when you cross paths with the Restrepo cartel, they'll remember."

It was a weak argument. His treatment of Lucia ensured that Matias Restrepo would forever be an enemy. "You said there were four options."

"I can make a phone call."

"No."

She cleared her throat and closed her eyes. When she looked at him again, a strange transformation rolled over her, loosening her posture. Her shoulders eased, and she stood taller, lengthening her height with grace and confidence.

"Liv Reed is my closest friend." She smiled, and it glowed so beautifully across her face it was disarming. "I can convince her I'm safe, that I haven't been hurt or touched against my will. Since I've been here for a month, that's plenty of time to get to know you." Her eyes beamed, lashes fluttering flirtatiously. "I enjoy your company. You're ridiculously handsome and protective, and you make me feel things I've never felt. I know it's crazy, but I want to stay. I need this. It's a chance to get away for a while and figure out my life. So there's no need for anyone to look for me. I don't want to be found." She released a shaky breath. "How was that?"

Fucking hell, she was good. Not a hitch or tremble in her voice. She sounded and looked so goddamn sincere he almost believed the lies.

"Did Van teach you how to do that?" He prowled toward her, captivated.

As a trained slave, she would've received lessons in obedience and decorum so that she wouldn't embarrass her Master in public.

"Did Van whip you until you learned how to maintain that pleasing disposition?" he asked. "To hold that smile through the godawful pain?"

"Yes," she spat, all traces of sweetness gone. "I bet that puts joy in your hateful heart."

"Not at all." He circled her, stepping so close he felt a shudder vibrate her tiny frame.

"Shall I grab your phone?" she asked warily.

He kept untraceable burners in the safe. If he went with the *phone a friend* option, what was the risk?

She couldn't tip them off on anything useful. She didn't even know her location. If she meant to deceive him and started begging for help while on the phone, he would just end the call and kill her.

Liv Reed would be skeptical no matter what Kate said to her. But a believable performance would leave her friends wondering, hoping. Just hearing her happy, healthy voice would take some of the urgency out of their need to find her.

"Do it again." He moved in closer, crowding her

back and breathing in the gentle scent of her hair. "Talk through the conversation you would have with her."

With a deep breath, she re-acted the call. Every word and inflection in her voice was just as convincing as the first time. She made references to him throughout, praising his good looks and weaving a tantalizing tale of budding romance and exciting adventure.

Her enthusiasm was so persuasive it drew his body tight, heating his skin and tempting him to touch. The strapless dress exposed her shoulder blades, the top half of her back, and all her delicate arches of feminine bone and muscle. He couldn't resist.

Sweeping her hair to the side, he rested his fingertips on the soft, warm curve of her nape.

Goosebumps rose beneath his hand, but she didn't flinch or stutter. It was a testament to how badly she wanted this phone call. She was determined to prove she could do it, with or without distractions.

As he feathered his touch down the sinuous line of her spine, he interjected questions that Liv would ask. Kate answered with quick-witted untruths and seamlessly redirected the conversation.

She could absolutely pull this off.

He drew his hand away and stepped back. Anticipation hummed through his body as he stalked to the safe and removed one of the phones.

Keeping her alive introduced new problems and temptations, but the challenge excited him. *She* excited him.

He locked the safe and returned to her. "If you're playing me, there will be repercussions."

"I'm not." She picked at her fingernail, avoiding his eyes. "Before I make this call, I need you to promise me two things."

He could guess her demands. "Choose one."

"But—"

"Only one, Kate."

Pressing her lips together, she stared at her bare feet. Crossed her arms. Lowered them. Then she lifted her gaze, decision made. "I need your word that Tate will go free."

"When Lucia finds him—"

"I want a deadline." She raised her chin. "Promise me you'll release him if she hasn't found him in one week."

"One year."

"What?" She gasped. "He's chained in a shack, sleeping on a dirt floor, without a bucket to shit in."

"There is a bucket."

"Please, don't say—"

"To shit in."

Her neck went taut, and she gritted her teeth. "One month, tops."

"Six months."

"Three months."

"Six months. I'll keep him fed and cared for. No harm will come to him."

Her mouth quivered. "Six months is too long."

"That, or we forget about the phone call and go with option three. What will it be?"

"Damn you." She pinched the bridge of her nose, inhaled deeply, and dropped her hand. "If Lucia doesn't locate him in six months, you'll release him, alive, and never hurt him or touch him again. That includes you or anyone under your command. Promise me."

"You have my word."

She gave a stiff nod, set her gaze on the phone, and rattled off a phone number.

He dialed and put it on speaker.

A dulcet, feminine voice answered on the first ring. "Who is this?"

"Liv? It's Kate."

"Kate? Oh, thank God." Movement sounded through the speaker. "Are you okay? We've been worried sick. Where are you?"

"I'm fine. Everything's fine."

She ran through her spiel, her voice as strong and mesmerizing as her eye contact. She smiled and motioned energetically with her hands, one-hundred-percent committed to misleading her closest friend. "So you can stop looking for me, okay? I don't want to be found."

"Wow, I…" Liv released a heavy breath. "I'm relieved to hear your voice, but we really need to see you. Just tell me where you are and —"

"You'll what? Check things out to make sure I'm not screwing up? Don't assume you know what's good for me."

Tiago clenched his hand around the phone, his nerves on high alert.

"You're calling from an untraceable number," Liv said cautiously. "I know I'm on speaker phone. Is he there? Listening to our conversation?"

"You have every reason to hate him." Kate gave him a firm look and held up her palm, staying him. "He poisoned Lucia, mutilated Tate's back, and the thing he forced Tate and Van do together… It's unforgivable."

"He told you about that?"

"Of course. He tells me everything. I know he has

issues. God, they're never-ending."

He narrowed his eyes.

She narrowed hers right back. "But we're working through them. *Together.*"

"He kidnapped you, Kate, and it's not uncommon to become attached and feel affection toward your captor. It's a psychological response, the mind's way of surviving."

"Is that what happened with Josh? You kidnapped and tortured him, so his feelings toward you are just survival tools? Marrying you was his coping mechanism for the hell you put him through?"

"Don't you dare," Liv snapped. "You were there, and you know damn well what he and I mean to each other." Her fuming breaths rattled the phone. "Where's Tate?"

Tiago hovered a finger over the end button and shook his head.

"I don't know." Kate pressed a hand against her breastbone. Her eyes brimmed with tears, but she kept the emotion out of her voice. "I love you, Liv, but I'm going to hang up now. Don't look for me. Don't worry about me. I'm exactly where I want to be."

"Kate, wait—"

He disconnected the call and pocketed the phone, monitoring her expression.

The facade she'd maintained for Liv gave way to a heartbroken stare and hunched shoulders.

"She'll worry. They all will." She inched backward in the direction of the exit. "But they won't look for me."

He let her continue her tentative retreat through the doorway, holding her teary gaze until she turned away in the corridor. When his ears perked to the soft, distressed sounds she tried to swallow down, he stalked after her.

"Kate." He leaned a shoulder against the doorframe and folded his arms across his chest.

She paused in the hallway with her back to him, her posture curling in on itself. The call to her friend marked the point of no return. A decision that would haunt her until she died.

She made a deal with the devil, and in the end, the devil always won.

"You wanted two promises from me." He rested a hand in his pocket and touched the finger blade. "The one you chose guarantees Tate's freedom while sentencing you to a lifetime in captivity. Or worse. Nothing is stopping me from killing you and hiding your body. Your friends will be none the wiser."

"I know." Her rigid back contracted with the heave of her breaths.

"That was your second request, the promise you didn't choose. You wanted my word to keep you alive after the phone call."

"Yes."

She didn't beg or cower. Didn't turn around to see if death was coming. Instead, she placed one foot before the other, eyes forward, and slowly walked to her room.

From his stance in the doorway, he watched her crawl onto the mattress and curl up on her side. With a strange pinch in his chest, he closed the door to his room and locked it.

Tomorrow, he would release her from the confinement of the second floor.

But she would never be free.

If she tried to run, he would kill her.

SEVEN

The next day, Tiago woke before dawn with a sense of levity pulling at his lips. The pounding in his head had abated. His vision was clear. No signs of dizziness. For the first time in a month, he didn't feel like an invalid.

More than that, he had something to entice him out of bed. Something beyond the obligations of running a criminal organization.

His gaze clung to the door as he rose to his feet and stretched. Was she still asleep?

He envisioned all that golden hair fanned out around her serene face. As he showered and groomed, he imagined what her fair skin and angelic blue eyes would look like in the daylight.

By the time he slipped on his boots and stepped into the hall, he was starving for a glimpse of her.

The sun had just risen, spilling faint light into the antechamber, where he found Kate on the bed. Not asleep.

The mattress sat on the floor, and she knelt at the

end of it. With her back to him, her hair fell in wet tangles from a recent shower.

"Come on, dammit." She bent over her knees, scrubbing the bed with a towel. "Fucking shit."

He prowled closer, craning his neck to see around her. "What are you doing?"

Her hands froze, and her head shot up. She didn't glance back or meet his eyes as he moved to stand beside her.

She returned her attention to the bare mattress and the red spot at the center, working the towel over the blotch. All her huffing and rubbing only made the stain worse.

"What happened?"

"What's it look like?" She threw the ruined towel aside. "I started my period."

"Is this the first time?"

She shot him a bland look.

His groin tightened. Her bitchiness did nothing to negate how goddamn striking her eyes looked in the sunlight. Iridescent shades of blue glimmered beneath long, thick lashes. As he continued to stare, her delicate nose twitched, and her full, pouty lips curved downward.

"Answer the question." He strode to the doorless bathroom and checked the supplies. Shampoo, soap, toothpaste, toilet paper…

She climbed to her feet, watching him rummage through the shit under the sink. "This is my first period since I've been here."

It had been a lifetime since he'd given any thought to a woman's cycle. "You've been here for…"

"Thirty-six days." She blew out a breath. "Stress

70

fucks with the body, in case you didn't know."

Boones would've prepared for this, though he'd done a piss poor job of dressing her. She wore another one of those strapless rags, the linen thin enough to reveal the dusky color of her nipples. The style had been practical when her arms were bound, but *Christ.*

He forced his gaze away, irritated by the distraction.

"We'll eat downstairs." He headed to the door and removed the key from his pocket. "You're free to explore the house and grounds."

Her eyes bulged, her whisper a halting, disbelieving exhale. "Really?"

"If you try to run or attack anyone here, you'll pray for death long before I'm through with you. Get me?"

"I get you." She swallowed. "Does Tate know I'm with you?"

"No." He unlocked the door and found Arturo waiting on the other side, as expected.

The six guards on-site spoke both English and Spanish. Tiago was fluent in many languages but primarily used English.

"When she's outside of this room, she doesn't leave your sight." He strode past Arturo and took the stairs to the ground floor.

The wooden steps groaned beneath his boots, and dry heat seeped from the cracks in the stone walls. More stone greeted him on the main level. Old and musty, the building was erected to withstand the arid climate, without comfort in mind. It was barely habitable, let alone anesthetically pleasing.

When he purchased it years ago, he updated the utilities and brought in enough mattresses to house an army. The isolation of the desert made it ideal for a temporary hideaway, and its solid stone exterior should hold up against gunfire. Hopefully, the latter wouldn't be tested during his stay.

A peek through the gap in one of the covered, barred windows confirmed everyone on patrol was positioned appropriately. Spread out around the perimeter, three men vigilantly watched the horizon.

He crossed the main room, passing a row of mattresses. The night shift occupied two of the beds, both guards sleeping soundly.

The large space opened to the kitchen, where Boones sat at the table with his gaze on a laptop.

"You're still on bed rest," the old man said in perfect English. His eyes didn't lift from the screen as he switched to Tigrayit, the Afroasiatic language of his people. "Go back to your room before I—"

"Before you what?" he asked in the same tongue. "Are you going to hit me with those brittle, antique sticks you call arms?"

"Idiot. Suit yourself. When you die—"

"Yeah, I know. You're taking all my money and moving to Florida."

Boones laughed softly, a deep comforting sound. "Where's the girl?"

"Bleeding all over the bed."

The laptop slammed shut, and Boones shoved to his feet. "You've been out of your room all of five minutes, and you're already butchering—"

"She's alive, asshole." He smirked, enjoying the opportunity to rile Boones. "She bleeds every month."

Boones studied him with dark, incisive eyes. Had things gone differently with Kate last night, they would be having a different conversation. Nevertheless, Boones knew her life still hung on a fragile leash. He didn't like it, but it was the way of this world. He accepted that the day he fled Eritrea.

"I'll take care of it." Boones approached, his expression morphing into that of a doctor as he looked over Tiago's head. "You need to sit."

"I need clothes, for her *and* me." He remained standing. "Jeans, t-shirts…"

Boones made a humming noise and prodded a finger around the skull wounds. "Any dizziness this morning? Double vision?"

"No. Add gym shorts and running shoes to the list."

"I didn't approve exercise. Your body needs time to heal and—"

"I need my strength back." He pulled away from Boones' examination. "Stop coddling."

The stairs creaked, and he turned toward the sound.

Kate descended with tentative steps, her eyes taking in her surroundings as Arturo followed closely behind. When she reached the kitchen, Tiago gestured at the massive man at her back.

"Arturo will be your constant shadow when you're out of your room." He clamped a hand on the old man's bony shoulder. "You met Boones."

She offered a tight smile that faded quickly.

"I have a closet stocked with supplies," Boones said in English and motioned for her to follow him to the back wall.

She trailed after him, her movements lissome and unintentionally seductive. She was surrounded by violent criminals, her future dark and nebulous, yet she held her shoulders back and spine straight.

As Boones filled a plastic bag with feminine products, she stood beside him, discreetly scanning the kitchen from beneath the veil of her hair. It wouldn't be hard to find knives, scissors, or any number of things scattered around that could be used to stab or strangle.

Arturo would be on her before she managed to slip even the smallest needle beneath her dress. But Tiago appreciated the fight blazing inside her. He savored it, riveted by the way her hand twitched at her side and how her small toes gripped the stone floor. She had grit.

"I put some weights in the backroom," Arturo said, breaking his trance. "When you're ready to work out again."

Boones glanced back at that, the wrinkles around his eyes deepening with disapproval. But he bit his tongue. He never berated or argued with Tiago in front of others, because he understood the importance of setting an example. Respect was paramount in running a gang.

When Boones shooed her away, she carried her supplies back to her room with Arturo on her heels.

Tiago waited for the door to shut upstairs and switched back to Boones' native language. "Do you have an update on Lucia?"

"She's still working her way along the coast."

"With Cole Hartman?"

"Yes." Boones ambled through the kitchen, setting out a skillet and gathering eggs.

"I need to speed up her search." He explained the promise he made to Kate and the phone call to Liv Reed. "If Lucia doesn't find Tate in six months, I have to release him, which defeats everything I set into motion."

"Let go of this fixation, son. It's not healthy."

He crossed his arms, refusing to engage in another argument about this.

"All right." Boones cut his eyes at him. "What are you suggesting?"

"Leave some bread crumbs. She's looking for the picture on Tate's back. Pay some of the locals in the surrounding towns to tell the story about the *Medio del Corazón* monastery to anyone asking about gates. Once she hears the folklore, she'll know to look for him there."

"Very well. Anything else?"

He ran a hand over his partially-shaved head and eyed the gray fuzz that Boones kept religiously trimmed on his scalp. "Where are your clippers?"

"Bathroom." Boones thrust a thumb over his shoulder.

He strode down the hall, found a zippered black pouch of barber supplies, and exited the bathroom without a glance at the mirror. When he returned to the kitchen, Kate was on her way down the stairs.

She ate her eggs and toast in silence while he conferred with Boones and Arturo about business in Caracas. As they conversed in languages she couldn't interpret, Boones seemed more interested in her presence than Tiago's month-long absence from the city. His questions about her were relentless.

What do you plan to do with her? Will she return with us to Caracas? Is she a replacement for Lucia?

Since Tiago didn't have answers, he didn't give any and instead shifted the conversation back to border issues and smuggling routes.

As they wrapped up the meal, one of the night shift guards climbed out of bed and shuffled into the kitchen, scratching his bald head.

"I thought I smelled breakfast." The man did a double-take at the table, his tattooed eyes fixed on Kate before darting to Tiago. "*Jefe.*" He straightened and held his arms at his sides. "It's good to see you up and around, sir. You look well."

With a nod, Tiago turned to Kate, who sat stiffly beside him with her jaw hanging open. "Kate, this is Blueballs."

"Blueballs," she echoed, staring at the man's blue eyeballs.

Blueballs grinned and widened his eyes to give her a better look.

"How did you...?" She pointed at the freakish coloring of ink that turned the whites of his eyes bright blue.

"The dumbass tattooed his sclera." Boones stood and carried his dishes to the sink. "He's lucky he's not blind."

"Hey! I'm a professional." Blueballs shifted back to Tiago. "Speaking of... I'll get started on Tate's tattoo today."

"What?" Kate gasped. "Is he here?"

Tiago clenched a fist under the table, seconds from cutting the tongue out of Blueballs' blabbing mouth.

"No, he's..." Blueballs paled, gripped the back of his neck, and recovered quickly. "It's a long drive, so I need to head out soon."

When he dared a glance at Tiago, his stupid blue eyes didn't blink. He'd fucked up, said too much, and knew the consequences. He wouldn't be walking out of here alive.

Kate slumped against the back of the chair,

watching Blueballs with a downcast expression. "When you see Tate…" She sniffed and rubbed her nose. "Please, be kind to him. He's suffered enough."

If she hadn't bought the lie about Tate's location, she would've shown signs of edginess and glanced at the door, itching to escape and save her friend. She wouldn't need to run far to stumble upon the gates of the monastery and the shack behind it.

But she believed Blueballs, and her gullibility just saved his life.

"You heard her." Tiago turned back to his breakfast. "Better get going."

"Yes, sir. Thank you." Blueballs made a beeline out of the house.

Without another word, Kate moved to the sink and started on the dishes. During her preoccupation with the task, she didn't notice the container of food Boones slipped into his medical bag.

A moment later, he left without announcing his departure. She had no idea he was on his way to deliver breakfast to Tate.

Keeping her in the dark about Tate's location wouldn't be easy. If she knew he was less than a mile away, there was no telling what she would risk in her attempt to see him.

The solution was to return to Caracas as soon as possible, take her with them, and leave someone here to care for Tate. But Tiago couldn't return until he built some of his strength back. He needed to be able to run when necessary, hold a weapon without tiring, and trust that his vision wouldn't crap out on him.

He needed another week of recovery. Maybe two.

She finished the dishes and turned away from the

sink, staring at him expectantly. "I'd like to step outside for some fresh air."

"You'll cut my hair first." Tiago nodded at the trimmer kit on the table.

"Me?" She shrunk back in revulsion and glanced at Arturo. "Why can't he do it?"

Arturo leaned against the wall, supervising her every move with a deceptively bored expression.

"I said you're doing it." He cast her a hard glare.

"You want to put scissors in my hands?"

"Yes, unless you know another way to cut hair." He unzipped the black pouch full of barber accessories.

She stepped forward, eyes zeroing in on the shearing tools. When she reached his chair, her fingers floated over a pair of sharp blades, lifting them.

"Use this on the sides." He removed the cordless clippers and set it on the table beside her.

She edged closer, but not close enough. He gripped her waist and tugged, wordlessly ordering her to stand in the V of his spread knees.

Her rigid, narrow-shouldered body felt surprisingly curvy beneath his hands. He pulled her another step into his space, and the tantalizing scent of her skin met his nose.

Goddamn, she smelled fantastic. His position in the chair put his face inches from her chest, and at this proximity, the white linen dress was see-through. If she knew he was ogling the supple rings of pink around her nipples, she would be mortified.

She had a modest way of holding herself, as if unaware of her beauty and the power it held over the opposite sex. Her innocence only made him harder.

As she lifted her hands near his head, the round

shape of her tits filled his view, drying his mouth. A glance lower revealed the apex of her thighs and the shadowed patch of hair there. No panties. *Fucking torture.*

The dress fell to mid-thigh, and her bare cunt was right there for the taking. The idea locked things up inside him and scrambled his brain.

He jerked his attention back to her face. Her gaze narrowed on his hair, calm and astute. Her fingers flexed around the scissors, her hands hovering out to the sides.

"Do you know what you're doing?" he asked.

"Sometimes, I shave my asshole. This isn't any different."

Arturo choked on a laugh and coughed into his fist.

The mention of her asshole painted a glorious picture in Tiago's mind — her body spread out before him, her little pucker taking his cock, clenching and dripping with his come.

She called to his testosterone, summoning the most primal part of him to mount, fuck, bite, cut, carve, and make her bleed.

He bit down on a groan, his skin hot and itchy. Christ, he was starting to sweat and needed to get a handle on this. *On her.*

Reaching up, he yanked down the top of her strapless dress and held the fabric tight around her waist.

"What are you doing?" She shrieked and flailed her arms.

He caught the hand that held the scissors, plucking them from her fingers.

"Stop!" She flattened her palms over her exposed chest and twisted, trying to escape his grip on her clothes. "Let go."

He wrangled her arms down and restrained them behind her, holding her wrists in one fist. All that soft, feminine flesh was so damn tempting. He wanted to sink his teeth into her heaving tits, mark her, claim her. But that wasn't how he did things.

Maybe he'd allow himself to touch her, but if anyone fucked her, it would be his guards.

"Do you think she's pretty?" he asked Arturo.

"Very much, *Jefe.*"

She shook her head rapidly, her breaths coming hard and fast, bouncing her gorgeous rack.

He traced the scissors across the slope of one breast, taunting her as he asked his guard, "Do you want to fuck her?"

"More than anything." Arturo stood straighter, interest smoldering in his eyes.

"No, please. Don't do this." She fought harder in his hold.

He yanked her against him and pressed the closed blades of the scissors against her pussy, with only the thin layer of linen between her delicate skin and the steel edge.

"If you cut me, draw blood, or disobey me in any way, Arturo will fuck your ass." He adjusted his grip, angling the sharp tip against her tight, little opening. "When he's finished, I'll yank out that tampon and fuck your cunt with the scissors."

EIGHT

Oh God, oh fuck, oh fuck.

Kate's breath escaped in a shuddering wave, and
her heart banged painfully in her chest. Tiago's ruthless
grip on her wrists made her bones ache, but it was the
scissors he held against her vulnerable flesh that had her
shaking to the point of nausea.

"I won't disobey you. I swear. I'll do whatever you
say." She lifted on tiptoes, unable to escape the bite of
steel between her legs. "Please. You're scaring me."

"Good." He set the scissors on the table, released
her hands, and combed his fingers through his hair.
"Even up the sides and trim the top."

Black spots blotched her vision, and she swayed on
wobbly legs. Wrapping her arms around her waist, she
fought the compulsion to cover her exposed breasts.

The malicious glint in his eyes promised every
horror he'd mentioned if she dared to hide her body.

She'd spent weeks in Van's attic, crawling naked
on the floor in front of Van, Liv, and Josh. It'd been four

years since then, since *anyone* had seen her nude, but she hadn't forgotten how to cope with the humiliation.

Lowering her arms, she focused on facts rather than feelings. She wouldn't die from embarrassment. Tiago pulled down her top to degrade her, but it wouldn't kill her.

She needed to be more resilient and think twice before striking back. For every awful setback and torment he put her through, she would just have to stand stronger, aim higher, and remain true to who she was and what she believed in. He could cut her open and mangle her body, but he could never destroy *her*.

Slowly, her breathing returned to normal, and the tremors faded from her limbs. When her heart settled into a calmer rhythm, she picked up the scissors.

The first brush of her hand through his hair made her sick. She didn't want to touch him, didn't want to give him a damn thing, especially not a haircut with her tits hanging out.

But she powered through it, ran numb fingers through the thick, inky strands, and started clipping.

Growing up in poverty with three older brothers, she used to cut their hair all the time. Basic styles. Practical. Nothing sophisticated or attractive, like what a man with Tiago's wealth and power would expect.

He dressed like a billionaire playboy in his crisp collared shirt, open at the neck, and dark fitted slacks. The cuffs of his sleeves buttoned neatly around strong wrists, his long fingers resting on his thighs.

He didn't have a bulky build, not compared to Arturo or Van Quiso, but he was solid and *tall*. She had to stretch to see the crown of his head, even in his seated position.

As she carefully measured and snipped each section of hair, he didn't leer at her bare chest or grab her ass. He was too controlled for that, too debonair and confident.

But put a weapon in his hand and all bets were off.

The more hair clippings that fell to his shoulders, the more she feared him. If he hated the style, he would kill her. If she accidentally nicked him or bumped his injuries, he would kill her. If she took too long and overextended his patience, he would kill her.

She was a human being with an expiration date, just like everyone else. But her expiration jumped closer with every movement she made. By the time she finished trimming the top of his head, her nerves were frayed and brittle.

His hair spiked in tousled, voluminous layers, each shiny black strand perfectly cut and finger-raked. She still needed to clean up the sides, but damn, it looked professional. The shorter, textured style made the angles of his shadowed jaw seem squarer, his eyes deeper and darker.

Those eyes beckoned like mysterious doors. As she gravitated toward them, they dipped, focusing on her mouth with too much attention.

She looked away and set down the scissors. "What happens if you don't like it?"

"It's just hair." His fingers captured her nipple in an agonizing vise, wrenching her gaze back to his. "If it looks like shit, shave it all off."

She pretended to ignore the stinging burn he'd inflicted on her breast and considered his words.

He wouldn't kill her over a haircut? That was a relief, *if* he was telling the truth.

Last night, he said he wasn't interested in fucking her. But his fingers told a different story as they meandered along the material gathered around her waist. His other hand joined in, and he inched the top of the dress lower, lower, baring her abdomen and the tips of her hipbones.

She held her breath as he lightly placed a palm over the reddish area on her stomach where he'd kicked her. His gaze lifted, narrowing on hers as he pressed his fingers against the soreness.

Her breath rushed out, but she didn't whimper or show signs of distress. Maybe he wouldn't rape her, but that didn't make it easier to share the same air as him.

He was an aficionado of pain, and she was here to absorb the hurt, to wear the bruises of his *art,* until she escaped or died.

The thought was crippling.

She grabbed the cordless clippers and threw herself into completing the task. He sat quietly as she trimmed, shaped, and scattered tiny hairs to the floor. To avoid grazing his wounds, she had to lean in, which felt like she was putting her face next to the jaws of a lion.

He even smelled intimidating. With her nose so close to his neck, she detected notes of cypress, vetiver, and leather, all bound up in the heady scent of an alpha male.

She stepped back, unable to endure another whiff of Tiago-infused air. But there was no escaping his presence. He was everywhere, all around her, overwhelming and watchful. Always watching with those dark, dangerous eyes.

"I'm finished." She glanced around for a mirror, her throat tight. "Do you want to see it?"

TAKE

With a grunt, he skimmed a palm over his scalp.

"Feels fine." He stood and unbuttoned his shirt as he addressed Arturo. "If she goes outside, keep her within eyeshot of the house. I'll be in the backroom."

She'd overheard Arturo mention something about weights. What were the chances she could slip in there while Tiago worked out, steal a dumbbell, and finish the job Lucia had started?

He loosened the cuffs of his sleeves and stripped the shirt. The tank top underneath followed, revealing a heart-stopping landscape of muscle and scars.

The welted designs on his forearms stretched around his biceps and faded at his shoulders. His slacks hung low on narrow hips, his torso a scar-free, concrete wall of virility.

This man had spent the past month in bed? Impossible. He didn't have an ounce of fat on his body. No flab or loose skin. Nothing that resembled weakness or poor health. The last thing he needed was a damn work out.

God help her, she was in trouble.

When she'd stormed into his room last night, she'd been blinded by rage, empowered by the possibility that he was old and out of shape, and floating on the hope that her friends would come. She had none of that now.

Her future rested on the whims of a criminal. A crafty, cold-hearted, beautifully-sculpted criminal, who would end her life without a second thought.

His gaze grabbed hers as he shook out his shirt, draped it over the chair back, and lowered his hands to his belt.

She gave him an incredulous look. If he needed to remove his pants to lift weights, why couldn't he wait until he was in the backroom?

Watching her unnervingly, he slipped the strap from the buckle and emptied his pockets. Keyring, phone, wallet—everything went on the table. Then he toed off his boots and lowered the zipper of his fly.

She didn't want to do this with him. She didn't want him to remove his pants while gazing into her eyes. It felt personal. Intimate. She couldn't breathe.

But looking away would be a sign of submission. Van had taught her that.

So she held fast to that eye contact. She stared as he slowly closed the distance between them. She stared until he ducked his head and dragged his nose across her cheek, her jaw, her mouth, *smelling* her.

She pinned her lips together and remained motionless as he lifted the top of her dress and straightened it into place.

Once her chest was covered, he stepped back and dropped his pants. An arrogant smirk kicked up the corner of his mouth.

She winged up a brow, refusing to glance down or give him a dramatic reaction.

His smirk transformed, curving into a handsome, breathtaking grin. It softened his eyes and altered the very air around him, making him unrecognizable. One smile, and he could be mistaken as human. A hot-as-fuck human with the capacity to shift and melt things inside her.

Holy bejeezus. When he wasn't scaring the piss out of her, he was sucking her in with his glowing charisma.

Lucifer had charisma. It was easy to be both repulsed by evil and drawn to its power. She would do well to remember that.

He tossed his pants on the chair beside the shirt and glanced at Arturo. "Inform Boones that my clothes are covered in hair."

"*Si, Jefe.*"

She waited for him to give her a parting command or threat, but he didn't. He turned away without acknowledging her and strode down the hall, taking every molecule of energy with him.

His command, his influence, his damn magnetism — it created an intoxicating aura around him, freezing her in place as he ambled toward the backroom.

She couldn't look away if she tried. Couldn't stop her gaze from following the ridges of his chiseled back to his trim waist and the fit of the tight briefs across his flexing ass. An unwanted fever heated her skin, and frantic little flutters erupted in her belly.

Why was she checking him out? He was deplorable, mean as hell, and mentally unstable. Pure poison beneath that superficial beauty.

He turned the corner and glanced back, his gaze spearing hers.

Letting her head tip to the side, she plastered on a stoic expression. He already inspired fear in her, and he knew it. She wouldn't give him the impression he was enticing, too.

When he slipped into the backroom and out of view, she glanced around for something she could swipe without Arturo noticing. The scissors on the table? The bread knife near the stove? The keys on Tiago's keyring? His locked phone?

Arturo didn't take his eyes off her as she strolled through the kitchen. She loitered for a few moments, waiting for a distraction, but that only prompted him to shift closer and watch harder.

Giving up on that, she padded through the front room and spied a sleeping woman on one of the mattresses. The sight of the feminine form gave her a sense of comfort. Not that she could trust anyone working for Tiago, but if she had any chance of making a friend here, maybe that woman was an option.

At the front door, Arturo breezed past and led her onto a concrete porch. The shade from the overhang offered little relief from the dry heat.

She stepped off the stoop and lifted her face to the cloudless, sun-bleached sky. Without shoes, the rocky ground burned the soles of her feet, but she didn't care. It'd been a month since she felt direct sunlight on her skin.

There were no sounds, no traffic, no roaring of ocean waves, no signs of civilization in any direction. Unmarked nothingness embraced her with empty arms.

She paced a circuit around the house, examining the barred windows and probing for weak exit points. If she decided to run, the front door would be the only way out. Not that she would make it two feet with the silent, intimidating barricade hovering at her elbow.

Arturo's presence made her skin crawl, especially after hearing him admit he wanted to fuck her *more than anything*.

A shudder gripped her as she returned to the porch and sat on the steps.

"Are we in Venezuela?" She squinted at him.

He leaned against the awning support and said nothing. At six-foot-and-too-many-inches tall, his thirties-something gladiator build backed up the combative vibes that emanated from him.

"How long have you worked for Tiago?" she asked.

No response.

"I'm not comfortable with what you said about me inside." She rubbed her neck. "Please, tell me you weren't serious."

He grunted a huff, and his pockmarked cheeks bounced with sick amusement.

"So it's true." Her face turned to ice, despite the suffocating heat. "He lets his guards rape his prisoners."

"He likes to watch."

NINE

Kate's stomach plunged to her feet.

Tiago liked to watch his men rape women. Of course, he did. He was a criminally insane psychopath.

And she'd been sleeping next to his room for the past month.

Her heart sprinted as she honed in on the car parked thirty feet away. What were the odds she could outrun Arturo, hop into the front seat, and find a key in the ignition?

Not a chance in hell.

She slumped. "Where did Boones go?"

One of the cars was missing, and she hadn't seen the doctor since breakfast.

Arturo stared at the hazy horizon, as if she weren't speaking.

"What animal best represents your personality?" she asked, trying to startle a reaction from him.

His eyes narrowed, but he didn't glance at her.

"I'm thinking a bear." She tapped her chin. "But

could you survive in the wilderness?" She sighed at his muteness. "A teddy bear, then."

A raping, murderous, gangster teddy bear.

He crossed a booted ankle over the other and rested his fingertips in the front pockets of his baggy jeans.

"What do your clothes say about you?" She pursed her lips, frustrated by his refusal to talk. "Say something. I dare you. No, really. I totally dare you to utter one word."

He was a statue. A voiceless, expressionless sentinel.

Over the next two hours, she continued to toss out questions, hoping he would bite. She wanted him to slip up and tell her something useful. But the comment about Tiago watching his guards rape prisoners was the only information she managed to coax from him.

The sun beat down on the cracked earth, brutally hot and smothering. Nevertheless, she remained on the shaded porch, preferring the limited freedom of outside to the stale confinement of the stone walls indoors.

Eventually, Boones returned.

As he parked the sedan and climbed out, Arturo straightened, assuming a more attentive stance. She didn't know how many weapons the massive man concealed beneath his clothes, but she wouldn't try to steal car keys from Boones and risk a bullet from Arturo.

Her escape would require more stealth than a grab-and-run.

"Help me with these." Boones handed her several shopping bags and carried the rest into the house and up the stairs.

There were stores nearby? Close enough for

Boones to buy all this stuff and return within a few hours? She still didn't know what country she was in. Maybe there was a receipt with an address in one of the bags?

Arturo relayed Tiago's message about the hair-covered clothes in the kitchen. Then he hung back in the stairwell as she followed the old doctor through the antechamber and down the hall to Tiago's room.

Boones heaved the bags onto the mattress and removed the contents. Running shoes, active wear, jeans, t-shirts, underwear… As he separated the clothes into two piles, she realized one of the stacks was meant for her.

She emptied the other bags and helped him sort, unable to locate a receipt or anything that identified her location. "Are we staying here? In Venezuela?"

"This place is temporary." His cloudy eyes glanced at her sidelong. "But we won't be leaving Venezuela."

Finally, an answer!

"Why is this temporary? Where is he going next?"

"You'll have to ask him," he said in a foreign syllabic rhythm she couldn't place.

"Is your accent Hindi?"

He snorted. "No."

"British? South African?"

"No."

"Caribbean?"

"You're getting colder." He shifted back to the clothes. "No one ever guesses correctly."

"You're not going to tell me."

"No."

With a frown, she lowered to the mattress on the floor and helped him remove the tags. "Why doesn't

Tiago sleep on a real bed?"

"He prefers to live modestly."

"But he's wealthy?"

A low chuckle creaked in his throat. "He has more money than God."

How much of that money came from blood, drugs, and ransom payments? She gritted her teeth. "Is that why you work for him? He pays you well?"

"Loyalty keeps me here." All humor vanished from his wrinkly face. "Tiago means a great deal to me, and I'll remain at his side for as long as he needs me."

There was a story there, thickening his accent with deep emotion.

"Your markings..." She motioned to the vertical welts on his cheeks. "Tiago has them on his arms. Did he give you those?"

"No." Boones pushed up the sleeves of his linen shirt, exposing a faded tapestry of scars on his dark forearms. "Where I'm from, we believe scarring connects us with our ancestors. It's an ancient tradition, one that's rarely practiced anymore."

"Where are you from?"

"That, I will not say."

Somewhere in Africa, if she had to guess. "Did Tiago adopt the practice from you?"

"I taught him, but his scarification has nothing to do with tradition." He lowered his sleeves and turned back to sorting the clothes. "For him, the scars convey a message."

"What message?" She leaned closer. "What do his scars mean?"

"Beware, there is pain in the world, and you cannot run from it. But if you endure it, if you accept the suffering, it will stop."

"Oh." She let that soak in. "You're talking about emotional pain."

"*All* pain. He carries more than most." He gave her a sad smile and handed her the stack of women's clothing. "Take these to your room and change out of that dress."

She did as he instructed, anxious to wear something other than a transparent rag.

It was interesting how easily Boones talked with her when she couldn't pull a word from Arturo's pinched mouth. Was Boones trying to make her sympathize with Tiago's actions?

Clearly, Tiago had a different relationship with Boones than he did with his guards. He and the old man shared a bond, a history, that piqued her curiosity.

After slipping on cotton panties, jeans, and a soft gray shirt that fit her perfectly, she returned to Tiago's room and helped Boones fold the remaining clothes.

She favored Boones' company over Tiago's, but it didn't stop the monster from occupying her thoughts.

Was he still working out? In his underwear? If she asked him to show her another video of Tate, would the request infuriate him?

She lifted a pair of gym shorts and eyed the new running shoes on the floor. She could take the clothes to him as a gesture of kindness and weigh his mood.

The thought of seeing him made her insides float and drop in a roller-coaster of sensations. He provoked every emotion at its extreme. Terror, excitement, hatred, curiosity, attraction... She really hated herself for that last one.

The reality was she couldn't avoid him. She was

stuck here, stuck with him, until she found an opportunity to escape.

"I'm going to run these down to him." She didn't look at Boones as she gathered the exercise gear and headed out of the room.

Arturo waited at the top of the stairs. He let her pass before trailing on her heels.

In the living room, the mattresses sat empty. Where did the woman go? Where was everyone else? She strained her ears, listening. Then she heard it. The deep, gravelly rumble of Tiago's voice in the backroom.

He was speaking to someone in Spanish, the words flowing so melodically it sounded like a sensual song. She followed his timbre, marking the pauses between sentences. He must've been on the phone.

She hit the hallway with Arturo in tow, passing a bathroom. Then a bedroom, where a mattress sat in the corner on an actual frame. Was that where Boones slept?

Moving on, she stepped through the last doorway and slammed to a stop.

Tiago stood near a rack of free weights, one hand braced on the wall in front of him, and the other holding a phone to his ear. With his head tilted back and eyes closed, he intoned a string of Spanish between heavy breaths.

He wore only a pair of tight black boxer briefs, his muscles pumped, veins bulging in his arms, and sweat clinging to miles of shredded, bronze skin.

It was a carnal, painfully arousing sight, potent enough to send her into cardiac arrest. But that wasn't what stopped the blood from pumping to her brain.

A woman with short black hair knelt before him. Her mouth pressed against his abs, teeth scraping skin and tongue tracing the V-shaped indention near his hipbone. Her hands wandered everywhere, gliding down his back, kneading his ass, and trailing his waistband back around to the swollen bulge between his legs.

Every muscle in Kate's body tensed to turn heel and run. Her vision clouded, and adrenaline flooded her system. If he wanted to fuck his security guard, fine. Good. Better that woman than Kate. But why leave the door open? What the fucking fuck?

She burned to smash his face in. With one of those heavy barbells. At the same time, she trembled to scurry away like a simpering, prissy, little virgin.

Fuck.

She hovered in the doorway, holding his sneakers and gym shorts, while Arturo breathed down her neck. Her chest hurt. Her throat filled with cement, and nausea seared her stomach.

There was no rational explanation for her raging disgust. But as his breathing grew deeper and roughened his voice enough to affect his phone conversation, she saw red. The whole fucking thing was making her stabby as hell.

The woman lowered her hand to stroke along his rigid length, and thoughts of murder were eclipsed by the need to vomit.

Tiago's eyes snapped open, and he stepped out of the woman's reach before she made another pass over his cock. Then his gaze flicked to the doorway, locking on Kate.

Fuck him.

She rolled her shoulders back, lifted her chin, and stepped into the room.

He barked a few Spanish words into the phone and

tossed it aside.

"Sorry to interrupt." She set the clothes on the rack beside him and met his hungry stare head-on. "Boones got you some clothes, and… You should really wear foot protection while working out."

What the fuck was she saying? She needed to get the hell out of there.

She turned toward the door.

"Kate." His stern voice pierced through her. "Come here."

Her ribs squeezed, and her fingernails pierced into her palms. After a few slow, deep breaths, she relaxed her hands and forced herself to face him.

"This is Iliana." He glanced down at the kneeling woman. "Stand up."

Iliana didn't just rise to her feet. She slithered up his body in a sexual undulation of hips and tits. With a nip at his chest, she pivoted and held out a hand to Kate. The same hand that had rubbed his dick.

No, thanks.

"Do you shake hands with all the prisoners?" Kate asked.

"No, I…" Iliana dropped her arm. "I guess not."

She smiled sweetly at Kate. It seemed genuine. As did the lust in her eyes when she sidled up to Tiago and tiptoed her fingers across his flat stomach.

The woman embodied all the allure of a gorgeous Latino fantasy. Fit body, great skin, beautiful hair, exotic accent, and sexual confidence. She and Tiago looked outrageously perfect together.

"You didn't come in here to bring me clothes." He grabbed the shorts, lifted them for inspection, and slid them on. "Tell me what you want."

She wasn't inclined to ask for anything in front of his lover, but Iliana didn't appear to be leaving.

"I was hoping…" She smoothed a hand over the coarse tangles of her hair. "I want to see a live video of Tate."

"No." He shifted away, punctuating the finality of his answer.

Making the rejection even more unbearable was the woman pressing up against his back and pawing at his body.

Hatred sizzled in her gut like a hot ember.

She hated him.

Hated Iliana.

Hated her illogical jealousy.

She held tight to that hatred, let it carry her out of the room and into the hell that followed.

TEN

Every day was the same. Same prison. Same guards. Same hell.

The ruler of hell spent most of his time working out. When he wasn't grunting and clanking weights in the backroom, he was holding meetings with Boones and his minions in languages Kate didn't speak. Every foreign word was meant to exclude her, to keep her isolated and uninformed.

Her hatred for him endured, strengthened, and all that animosity sharpened her focus.

The problem was, while she never took her mind off escape, her captors never took their eyes off *her.*

Arturo trailed her relentlessly. The other guards formed a vigilant wall around the property. Then there was Tiago. He ate his meals with her, shared the second-floor with her, and watched her with an awareness that raised the hairs on her neck.

Even if she managed to sneak past his sentinels, he would hunt her down before she made it to safety. Then he would kill her. Slowly and horrifically.

She thought a lot about her phone conversation with Liv. Had she been *too* convincing? Had her friends completely given up on her? They probably had all their resources tied up in looking for Tate, as they should. Thinking about him sitting in that shack made her heart hurt.

"A penny for your thoughts?" Iliana sat across the kitchen table from her, smiling over the lip of a coffee mug.

"Nope." She pushed the syllable past the thousand vindictive things she wanted to say.

A week had passed since she walked in on Tiago and Iliana. Every time she saw them together, Iliana had her hands on him, touching him in a suggestive way. He tolerated the attention to a point.

When she tried to kiss him, he jerked away. If her fingers dipped below his belt, same response. But none of that was required for fucking. Which they were doing. Why else would they be in the backroom together every day?

Iliana didn't hide her intentions. She was obnoxiously flirtatious, not just with Tiago but with everyone, including Kate. Sex dripped from every glance and gesture, but Kate sensed something reserved and steely behind the bawdiness.

"You have great tits." Iliana cocked her head. "Every time those little nipples harden, I get wet."

The wardrobe Boones had bought didn't include bras. It wasn't her fault she nipped out, and whenever Iliana brought attention to it in front of Arturo, Kate wanted to rip out the woman's tongue.

Pushing away from the table, she grabbed her

dishes and rinsed them in the sink.

"Hey." Iliana caught up with her, leaning close to tuck a lock of hair behind Kate's ear. "I'm sorry."

"Don't touch me." She ground her molars.

"Shit, Kate. It's just…" Soft brown eyes blinked beneath long lashes. "You're so beautiful. I totally get why he's crazy about you."

"What?" Her pulse quickened. "Who?"

"*El jefe*." Iliana scraped a hand over her black pixie cut and sighed. "Your naivety makes you even more desirable." She glanced at her watch. "Damn. Gotta run, babe. I'll see you at dinner." She turned and winked at Arturo. "You, too, handsome."

Kate gripped the edge of the sink and waited until the front door shut before releasing a heavy breath.

"She has no off switch." She peeked over her shoulder and met Arturo's eyes. "Are you fucking her?"

He shrugged, expressionless.

"Well, your boss is fucking her, too, so enjoy those leftovers." She twisted to face him. "Why did she say he's crazy about me?"

The only thing that moved was his eyes. One slow blink.

"I'm not naive, Arturo." She crossed her arms. "Tiago doesn't get crazy about people. He's just crazy. Period."

No response.

"Great talk." She swiveled back to the sink and tackled the rest of the breakfast dishes.

A few minutes later, something thumped in the hallway. Footsteps sounded, staggering from that direction and closing in. She turned just as Tiago stumbled into the kitchen.

"*Mierda.*" He gripped his head, his face creased with pain. "I need…"

He pitched forward with a lurch. She tried to jump out of his way, but he landed against her, trapping her back against the counter.

Did someone attack him?

She scanned his sweaty, half-naked frame for blood and found none. "What do you need?"

"Goddamn head. Fucking kills." He let his weight slump against her, holding his skull in one hand while swinging the other across the counter behind her and knocking dishes to the floor. "*Agua…*"

He looked like he needed more than water. He'd pushed himself too hard. Even the healthiest man would eventually collapse beneath the rigorous exercise he'd been putting himself through. But what did she care?

"You're crushing me." She shoved at his steel chest.

"Jusss a *minuto*," he slurred, dropping his brow to her shoulder and breathing heavily.

His proximity saturated her senses, the length of his body smothering her from head to toe. His thighs against hers, the cage of his arms holding her in place, she couldn't evade the heat of his flesh, the stroke of his breath on her neck, and his scent…

Sweet hell, he radiated the scent of a man when the exertion of work warmed his early washed skin. She tasted the potency of it on her lips, breathed him into her lungs, and somewhere low in her core, she *throbbed.*

"Drink." Boones appeared out of nowhere, holding a glass of water to Tiago's mouth.

Tiago pushed off her and gulped down the fluid as Boones rattled off a string of short, unfamiliar words.

Despite the calmness in his voice, the old man's eyes flashed with ire.

A conversation ensued between them. It sounded casual to the ear, but she sensed the undertones of a heated argument. It ended with Tiago staggering toward the stairs alone.

Boones watched him go and gripped her arm. "I'll make lunch, and you'll deliver it to him."

"I'd rather not."

"That's an order. *His* order." He pointed at the far cabinet. "Grab the medium pot."

Fifteen minutes later, she trudged into Tiago's room, carrying a tray of heated soup for two, crusty bread, bottled water, hot tea, and various pills.

Her stomach tumbled as she searched the empty space and paused on the bathroom. Steam drifted from the doorway, bringing with it the aroma of masculine soap.

"Tiago?" She willed him to be dressed, even as her mind entertained erotic images of his sculpted, nude physique.

He emerged from the bathroom and leaned a shoulder against the doorframe, his hair wet and body clad in sweatpants.

"Where do you want this?" She held up the tray, staring too long at the mist beading on the hard ridges of his chest.

He gestured at the mattress and gripped his forehead. A hiss pushed past his clenched teeth.

"There's some medicine for the headache." She set the tray on the floor near the lamp and backed toward the door. "I'm sure Boones will come—"

"Sit. You're eating in here." He made the short

walk to the bed, dropped to his knees, and collapsed with his face in the pillow. "Fuck."

"Maybe you just need to sleep." She lingered by the exit, rubbing clammy palms on her jeans.

"I won't repeat myself." He angled his neck to glare at her.

"Fine." She strode toward him, grabbed the food, and sat beside him on the mattress. "I don't understand why Iliana isn't in here with you instead?"

"I don't trust the guards in my personal space."

She jerked her head back. "But you trust me?"

"Not at all. Pass me the water."

He drank, refused the pills, and after some grumbling in Spanish, he accepted the soup.

They ate in silence, and with each bite, the pain lifted from his face.

Over the past week, he seemed to be on the mend. She'd caught him holding his head a few times, but he hadn't slowed down his workouts or shown any signs of weakness. Until now.

"Why are you exercising so much?" She collected the empty dishes and set the tray aside.

"I need strength to return to Caracas." He rolled to his back and closed his eyes. "Too many people want me dead."

Her friends included. Except they weren't looking for her anymore.

"You don't have to go to Caracas." She considered his wealth and all the places he could live. "You can go anywhere, do anything, right? Why not retire?"

"I chose this life. End of." He rested an arm across his brow, his expression relaxed, almost sleepy.

She'd never seen him asleep. He kept his door

locked at night and was downstairs before she woke most mornings.

A peculiar blanket of warmth settled over her, and her fingertips tingled. Why did she suddenly feel so weird?

What were they just talking about?

She blinked, trying to remember as a strange pull urged her to stretch out beside him on the mattress. Something was wrong.

"I think Boones drugged the soup." Holding her hand in front of her face, she marveled at its weightlessness. "I feel stoned."

"Probably. He knew I wouldn't take those pills." He patted the mattress beside him. "Lie down."

"That doesn't make you mad?" She gave in to the heavy weight in her limbs and lay on her side, facing her captor without a twinge of worry or panic. *How weird.*

"Can't be mad at Boones." He shifted to his hip, bending an arm beneath his head and mirroring her position. "He cares."

Fringes of thick lashes swept downward, hooding his brown eyes as he reached across the space between them. The pad of his finger rested on hers, barely a touch, yet it shivered every nerve ending in her body.

She held still, studying his slack expression. He seemed different, less threatening. Normal. Like a person capable of having a conversation without kicking her in the stomach.

"How do you know about my brothers?" she asked.

"Public records mostly." His gaze lifted to hers. "Are you aware all three of them are in prison?"

"No." She waited for a simmer of emotion behind

her breastbone and felt only a brief pinch of anger. "For drugs?"

"They were smuggling *cocaína* for a Mexican cartel. Someone ratted them out."

They deserved it. After her mom died, they were supposed to be her protectors. Instead, they turned her childhood home into a crack-house, exposed her to a world of drug dealers and addicts, while chasing away every boy who showed interest in her in high school.

In the end, they were the reason she fell onto Van's radar. He'd overheard them talking about their little virgin sister in a bar, *bragging* about how they'd protected her virtue. Van followed them home, abducted her, and she hadn't seen or talked to them since.

Her hand curled into a fist. "Fuck them."

He pried her fingers open and rested his huge palm over hers. "Tell me about your time with Van Quiso."

"I don't want to talk about that." She slid her hand away.

"I'm not asking." He caught her wrist and used it to yank her chest against his.

She shrunk back, straining to hold a sliver of space between them. "What do you want to know?"

"Everything."

Why not just tell him? He probably already knew the details anyway.

With a deep breath, she talked through the ridiculous requirements Van had beaten into her. Kneeling, eyes down, constant nudity, perfect dick-sucking techniques… She was vague about the sexual training, and Tiago didn't press for details. Just mentioning *blow job* seemed to put him on edge.

His fingers tightened around her wrist with bruising pressure. "I despise that ceremonious BDSM bullshit."

"There was nothing sane or consensual about it." She twisted her arm in the shackle of his fist. "You're hurting me."

He released her, and she rolled away from him. But his arm hooked around her midsection and hauled her back against his chest.

"What are you doing?" She shoved at the bar of muscle across her stomach, unable to move it an inch.

"Go to sleep." His breath caressed her hair.

"Release me." She squirmed in his grip. "I'll go get your girlfriend, and she'll make it real good for you."

God, she sounded snarky, but she couldn't stop picturing him fucking Iliana, pile-driving her against a wall or whatever they did together. Her jaw stiffened, and her insides boiled. She needed that venom to remind her she didn't want to be here, cuddling with a gang leader.

"You're jealous." He dragged his nose along her neck.

She flinched at the sensation, confused by his gentleness. "Captives don't get jealous. They get Stockholm syndrome."

Soft laughter vibrated his chest. "Tell me about Texas."

A safe topic. She calmed down, as much as she could in the iron bands of his arms, and shared some impersonal details about home, highlighting scenery, culture, and local food.

She missed it, her friends, the simplicity of everyday life. The more she talked about it, the heavier her heart grew. He listened without comment, and eventually, the effects of the drugged soup pulled her into a heavy sleep.

When she woke, Boones was standing over the bed with a peculiar look on his scarred face. Tiago stirred behind her, his arm still locked around her waist.

"I brought dinner." Boones pointed a gnarled finger at the tray of tacos on the floor and squinted at Tiago. "Rate your pain on a scale of one to ten."

"What's the rating for *drugged*?"

Boones flattened his lips and blinked. "You're staying in bed."

"Good idea." He pulled her to his chest, fitting her buttocks tightly against his hips and upper thighs. His cock, neither soft nor swollen, rested along the crack of her ass.

And so that was how it went for days. Every hour sanded away the distance she so desperately tried to maintain. She couldn't avoid him, couldn't breathe without his eyes on her.

Because he didn't just confine himself to his room.

He locked her in there with him.

ELEVEN

Kate's demands to leave his room were met with silence.
Tiago Badell and his goddamn smugness incited a level
of anger unlike anything she'd ever felt. But she'd agreed
to obey him. The night she met him, she'd agreed to do
anything in exchange for Tate's freedom.

For days, he abstained from exercise and limited
his activity to eating, showering, and napping. There was
no Iliana. No business meetings or phone calls. And no
fucking freedom.

It wasn't the confinement that made her feel
restless and trapped. It was him.

This lazy version of Tiago was suspiciously
pleasant, talkative, and sometimes, he was clingy. Not
clingy in a dependent, insecure way. But in a growly,
aggressive, bring-your-ass-here way.

The next three days came with some startling
revelations. Behind the face of a crime lord was an
intelligent conversationalist. They talked for hours on
end, analyzing Venezuelan politics, arguing about

American football, and while finishing off the tequila, he shared his thought-provoking views on religion, extraterrestrials, and the future of technology.

She philosophized with him late into the night, floating in a bubble of complacency, where she let her guard down and basked in his company.

When he flashed that infectious smile, her bitterness dissolved. When he held her tight against the heat of his skin, she didn't pull away. At some point, her brain decided he wouldn't hurt her, not here in this quiet one-room world inhabited by two.

Even as she knew he hadn't earned that kind of trust, she struggled to maintain distance. Meanwhile, he seemed to have no trouble keeping his defenses in place.

He napped with her tucked in the curve of his rock-hard body, but he didn't sleep soundly. Whenever she thought he'd fallen into a deep slumber, she would move ever-so-slightly, and those sinful eyes would pop open without fail.

Like now.

"I thought you were asleep." She lay on her side, her legs trapped beneath one of his, and his mouth so close she smelled mint tea on his breath.

He grunted softly and stroked a knuckle along her cheekbone. Heat rolled off that touch, and the air around him vibrated with power and dark suggestions. Her body tightened in response, fearing what he was while aching for what he could offer.

"Christ, you're stunning." He said it spontaneously, vehemently, his expression unguarded.

"Thank you." Captivated, she leaned closer and hovered a hand over the wound near his eye, too scared to touch him. "How's your head?"

"Fine." He curled his fingers around her wrist. "Ask my permission."

The words clogged in her throat, her mouth parched. It was in these suspended moments that he posed the most danger to her, when he made her want things she should never want from him.

Something had happened to him in his past, something deeper and more painful than the wounds on his head. Though he refused to discuss his life prior to Caracas, she ached to show him compassion. She just didn't know how.

"I'm growing impatient." His hand clinched around her arm, fingers biting into bone.

Her eyes felt too wide as the question fell past her lips. "May I touch you?"

He gave an inviting growl and guided her palm to his cheek.

Thick stubble shadowed his face, and beneath the tickle of hair, his jaw felt like solid metal. Not clenched. Just...*hard*.

Were all men so sharply cut and rigid to the touch? She'd only put her hands on Van Quiso and the few boys she fumbled around with in high school. The sensations from those encounters weren't worth remembering.

She let her fingers dip, roving past the squared underside of his chin to explore the column of his neck. Sturdy and so very masculine, he felt as strong as oak and granite, any of nature's most durable materials.

Her gaze darted to his, and the intimacy in that eye contact stole her breath.

"Don't you get sick of looking at me?" She withdrew her hand.

"You have one-hundred-and-ninety-three

eyelashes on the top lid of your right eye."

"You did *not* count them." She rubbed the lashes in question.

"Stop." He gripped her arm and drew her gaze to the single brown eyelash stuck to her fingertip. "Now it's one-hundred-and-ninety-two."

A profound *happening* pulsed between them, a metamorphosis she couldn't explain away. It flapped loudly in her chest and sizzled static across her skin, refusing to be ignored.

Maybe she was having a mental breakdown.

"You can't say things like that." She wiped her hand on her shirt.

"Things like what?"

"I don't understand why I'm here."

"We talked about this. You're a payment—"

"No. Why have I been in this room for the past three days? Am I one of your experiments?"

"What does your gut tell you?"

"I only hear my captor, and not once has he told me I'll survive."

His expression closed off, and he rose from the bed. "I need to take a shower."

He wore jeans today, and off they went on his way to the bathroom. Kicking them free at the doorway, he disappeared around the corner, wearing only boxer briefs. A moment later, the shower turned on.

Panic crept in. She'd pricked the bubble they'd been floating in and sent them plunging back to reality. This wasn't some profound happening. He was her captor, holding her against her will. That was the ugly truth.

She climbed from the bed and paced, eying the

door to the corridor, the door to the bathroom, and pausing on the jeans he left on the floor.

Her pulse sped up. It wasn't uncommon for him to leave his clothes unsupervised within her reach, as if he thought she were too afraid of him to try anything. Well, fuck that.

She raced toward his pants on silent feet and searched the pockets. Phone, finger blade, keyring, wallet — it was all there.

The splash of water around the corner announced his movements in the shower. She focused on the phone, tried to unlock the screen and make an emergency phone call. It required a code, and after too many attempts, the keypad prompt locked her out.

Shit!

She tossed it aside, removed the cash from his wallet, and shoved it into her pocket, along with the finger blade. Arturo would follow her down to the ground floor. If she could lead him outside, catch him off guard with the blade, cut his throat if she had to, she might be able to make a run for it.

Her heartbeat shot into overdrive, nearly exploding. It was a risk, one that would either set her free or end her life.

Palming the keyring, she bolted out his room, down the hall, and paused at the door to the stairs. Pipes groaned in the old walls. He was still in the shower.

Her hand grew slick around the keyring. One key unlocked this door. The others could've been for the cars, the house, a safe? She didn't want to tip off Arturo, so she tried the handle first.

It gave beneath her grip, and she sucked in a breath. Then she opened the door.

Arturo stood on the other side and leveled his eyes at her. Then they lifted, pointing at something behind her.

Sinister energy crept over her back. The hairs on her arms prickled, and her stomach rolled over in violent waves. Reaching through the paralyzing dread, she gathered the courage to peek over her shoulder.

"You disappoint me, Kate." Tiago's gaze, black as coal, burned into her face from a few feet away.

Dressed in the jeans she'd ransacked, he prowled toward her, holding a bundle of rope. His hair was dry. Not a drop of moisture on his shirtless chest. Yet the sound of water still ran through the pipes.

The fake shower, the discarded jeans… It had been a test. One she failed.

"I'm sorry." She whirled to face him and inched back. "I was scared and—"

The cold, sharp edge of steel caught her beneath the chin, driving her head upward. With a gasp, she dropped the keyring, grabbed Arturo's arm, and teetered back against his chest.

"If you speak or move a muscle without permission, Arturo will slice you open from ear to ear." Tiago tossed the rope at her feet. "Drop your arms."

Tears burned the backs of her eyes and scorched down her throat as she obeyed.

He gripped the front of her shirt with both hands, ripped it down the front, off her shoulders, and flung it aside. When his fingers bumped her bare chest, she bit down on her lip and tasted blood.

She trembled to scream, beg, bargain, to do anything to remove that heartless, frightening look on his face. But it was too late for that. She'd fucked up and

wrecked their imaginary peacetime.

Crouching before her, he removed his belongings from her pockets. Then he yanked down her jeans and panties, stripping the last of the clothing from her body.

A feverish chill swept through her, simmering into convulsions that wobbled her knees and dotted her vision.

He didn't grope her or stare at her nudity, didn't so much as look at her.

"Take her downstairs." He picked up the rope and tossed it to Arturo. "Tie her to the table."

TWELVE

Four limbs tied to four table legs, Kate lay face up and stretched open, her nude body arranged like an X-shaped centerpiece for the sick and depraved. She shook so viciously the table rattled beneath her. Because she knew what was coming.

He lets his guards rape his prisoners.
He likes to watch.

When Arturo had dragged her into the kitchen, Boones took one look at her and disappeared into the bedroom down the hall. Tiago hadn't come downstairs yet, but there were two others in the kitchen, staring, *anticipating.*

Iliana perched on the chair to her right with a hand gently massaging Kate's wrist near the rope. If the touch meant to calm her, it was a wasted effort.

Sitting at her left, Arturo braced his elbows on the table and held the tip of his knife against her neck. Dishes cluttered the tabletop around her, emitting aromas of fried meats and stomach-turning spices. She was going to throw up.

Her mouth flooded with saliva, and she swallowed, battling the fear that attacked her so cruelly. She hadn't spoken, hadn't moved without permission, acknowledging the verity of Tiago's threat in the blade at her throat.

Arturo and Iliana didn't speak, either. The entire room held its breath, waiting for *el jefe*.

Too soon, the tread of boots sounded on the stairs, triggering a fresh surge of shivering panic. He strolled into the kitchen, showered, and decked out in black dress pants and a white collared shirt, unbuttoned at the throat.

Trenches rutted his wet black hair from his fingers pushing through it, his jaw cleanly shaved and hard as stone.

Approaching the table, he paused at her feet. A short conversation with Arturo followed in Spanish. Then he looked down and helped himself to an eyeful of her spread thighs and everything intimate and vulnerable in between.

Liquid fire filled her eyes, blurring her vision and spilling from the corners. She glued her gaze to the ceiling, pinned her lips together, and bit back the sounds of her grief.

Since the night she'd been taken from the diner, she knew it would come to this. The past forty-six days had only dragged it out, delayed the inevitable. Crying about it wouldn't change a damn thing.

That was exactly why she'd jumped on the opportunity to steal his weapon and escape. She wouldn't regret the boldness of her actions. She only wished she could dredge up some of that bravery now and face her punishment.

TAKE

The soles of his boots scraped the stone flooring as he stepped closer and leaned in. Bent over her, he braced his hands on either side of her hips. The heat of his gaze ghosted across her pebbled flesh, his presence a smothering, inescapable force.

Now would've been the time to beg, but a mere swallow jogged her throat against Arturo's blade. Her heart thundered, every thrashing beat a plea to survive.

She didn't want to look into the eyes of the crime boss, but she needed to know. If there was any trace of the man who counted eyelashes and snuggled during naps, maybe she could connect with him, make him remember she was a person.

With agonizing effort, she inched her gaze to the buttons on his shirt, up to the bronzed skin of his throat, and higher to his sculpted lips, straight nose, and the coldest, darkest eyes she'd ever seen.

There was no soul in the depths, no humanity or mercy as he silently commanded, *Don't move. Don't make a sound.*

How could something so evil be so enticingly, flawlessly beautiful?

She'd fallen for the devil's trickery, and now she would pay the price.

Letting her muscles go slack in the restraints, she conceded. There was no escaping his intent, and she would need her strength for it.

"Let's eat." He lowered into the chair between her bound feet and filled his plate.

The meal was an eternal hell. The chewing, the leering, the laughter from discussions in a foreign language... They carried on while she slowly died inside. The one time she glanced down the length of her body, she found Tiago with a knife in his hand, cutting his meat and glaring at her pussy.

He was a psycho with the face of a model in a men's fashion mag.

Please, make this end.

When utensils finally clattered to empty plates, Arturo started clearing the table.

Tiago turned to Iliana, his lips lifting in a chilling smirk. "Remove your clothes."

A growl clawed up Kate's throat, and she trapped it behind her lips.

Iliana rose from the chair, eyes smoldering as she slowly peeled away her shirt, jeans, and everything underneath.

No matter how hard Kate tried, she couldn't look away. The woman had a body that wouldn't quit, all hourglass curves, heavy breasts, and toned, tanned flesh.

She sashayed toward Tiago and wriggled her way between his chair and the table, blocking Kate's view of what they were doing.

If he intended to hurt her by fucking Iliana in front of her, then… Yeah, that would do it.

Her hatred for him stabbed punishing heat through her veins, spawned from a jealousy that made no sense. She hated him too much to want him. She hated him for making her think that wanting him was even a possibility. She hated him for fucking with her head so thoroughly she didn't know what to do or feel.

Don't give up. How about that? Pull your sniveling shit together and stay strong.

There was nothing stronger than the human spirit. She needed to stop underestimating herself. She'd survived horrors worse than this. She'd obeyed Van's countless rules and restrictions, watched him fuck Liv for weeks, and came out of that experience smarter and tougher than ever. She would survive this.

"Turn around and bend over the table." His deep, husky voice sent her fingernails into her palms.

Iliana twirled in place and leaned into the triangle of Kate's bound legs, with her nose right there, up close and personal.

Kate screwed her eyes shut, but her imagination choreographed Iliana's ass in his face, his fingers between her legs, and his hard prick straining beneath his zipper.

In a burst of anger, Kate jerked her arms, her legs, and twisted her hips, fighting against the rope. Until a knife skimmed the curve of her throat.

She flinched, and her eyes flashed open, colliding with Arturo's narrowed glare.

Don't move. Don't make a sound.

She swallowed a whimper and held herself as stiff as a board.

"Put your tongue in her cunt," Tiago said to Iliana.

Kate's mouth opened on a horrified breath, unable to silence the wheezing from her lungs.

Arturo inched back the blade just a little as Iliana edged closer, focused on her target.

Detestation curdled in Kate's stomach. Iliana might've been following orders, but the woman was going to enjoy every second of it.

Refusing to watch, Kate closed her eyes again.

There was no build up. No easing in. Iliana stabbed her tongue inside, fast and deep, with a harsh suck of her lips. A scrape of teeth. A hungry moan. All of it rolled into a rude, nauseating open-mouth kiss.

Enduring the invasion wasn't physically painful,

but humiliation and helplessness built a searing pressure in Kate's throat. Tears clamored in, burning their way across her vision and dripping down her face.

She opened her eyes and found Tiago staring at her from behind Iliana's bent position.

Heat inflamed that vicious glare as he watched with an invasiveness that felt more penetrating than the tongue lashing inside her.

He was doing this, commanding this cruel molestation for his own perverted pleasure. His eye contact struck her with the severity of a fist. She couldn't look away, couldn't hear or feel anything but rage as a million rapid-fire heartbeats pounded into the space between them.

If she thought he had a heart, she'd been wrong. There wasn't a hint of humanity or softness in the sharp angles warping the sick perfection of his face.

The slash of that hard mouth parted, speaking to Iliana without looking away from Kate. "Describe the taste."

"Sweet. Lively. Heaven." Iliana leaned up, blocking the view of Tiago as she met Kate's gaze. "The essence of want-to-get-fucked."

Bitch, Kate mouthed.

Iliana laughed, a tinkling sound of joy. She was in her happy place, stark naked between Kate's legs, with her ass arched in his face like a cat in heat.

He stood and moved his chair a few feet away, positioning himself with a sidelong view of the show. "Arturo."

The massive guard pocketed his blade and lumbered around the table to stand behind Iliana. A zipper sounded, and a heartbeat later, Iliana's mouth fell open in a silent scream of rapture.

Good for her.

She writhed and bucked and bounced her breasts in the spread of Kate's legs. Arturo didn't hold back, his gaze locked on Iliana's backside as he slammed his hips and scooted the table across the floor.

Each thrust evoked the groans of impending orgasm. Their bodies heaved and slapped together, but no part of them touched Kate. They didn't have *his* permission.

She didn't look at him. Not as the scent of sex infused the kitchen. Not as five minutes pounded into ten. But eventually, her eyes moved on their own, rolling in his direction.

He wasn't watching them fuck. His stare fixed directly on *her*, his jaw tight and hands fisted on his thighs.

Fire spread through her, chilling her skin and hardening her nipples. She sucked in a jagged breath, detesting the effect he had on her, hating that he hadn't forgotten she was here.

He was just biding time, tormenting her with it, until he could hurt her in deeper ways.

Jerking her gaze to the rafters, she couldn't help the tears that trickled down her temples and collected in her hair.

Eventually, Iliana moaned and trembled through her climax, marking the end of the pre-show.

Kate's pulse detonated. She was up next.

"Move her to the edge of the table," Tiago said, his voice a languid drip of sex and smoke.

Iliana floated around Kate, adjusting the rope for the new position. As the tension on Kate's wrists released, the bindings on her ankles took up the slack.

Calloused hands gripped her thighs and yanked her to the end of the table, drawing her attention to Arturo. He was still clothed, save for the sag of his pants and the angry, wet erection jutting from his open fly.

Bile hit the back of her throat, and her insides clenched against full body tremors.

He couldn't put that thing inside her. He wasn't gentle. Or small. It would rip her apart.

He stepped between her legs, his fingers biting into her thigh as he positioned himself.

The trembling in her chin shook more tears loose.

Why was she so terrified? It was just sex, just sex, just sex. People did it all the time.

She needed to loosen the tension down there, make her inner muscles more pliable. Liv had coached her about that, hammering on the importance of relaxing the rectum during anal. But her body refused to calm down. She felt as though she were careening toward a complete loss of heart function, breathing, and consciousness.

"Shhh." Iliana put her mouth at Kate's ear. "He's gonna feel good, babe. I promise he'll be the best you've ever had."

She'd never had vaginal sex, anal sex, or any kind of sex. Who knew which hole he would tear open? She only knew she didn't want it, not like this. Not tied to a table, against her will, in front of an audience.

"Fuck her, Arturo." Tiago's voice thrummed with impatience. "Make sure she feels it."

She locked her jaw down so hard it throbbed. The pain flared into defiance, and she twisted her neck, giving Tiago the full force of her eyes.

As he met her glare with a meaner one, she poured

all her fear and misery into that shared look. He didn't twitch, didn't react with a trace of emotion. There was no moving him.

In a desperate last-ditch attempt, she let a whisper tumble out. "Please, don't take this from me. It's all I have left."

His spine snapped straight, his expression frozen in malice.

Shit. She'd made a sound, broken his rules. This was about to get a whole lot worse.

Arturo's hips bumped her inner thighs, and her entire body locked up on reflex. She sealed her eyes shut, willing the trembling to ease from her muscles.

His breathing grew heavier, closer, and fingers dug into her leg.

"*Basta,*" Tiago barked. Footsteps sounded his approach, and his next words came from above her. "Open your eyes."

She couldn't look at him.

Keeping her eyes squeezed tight, she angled her head away.

His fingers stabbed into her hair, fisting it near her scalp. Then he yanked, wrenching her face to his and forcing her to meet his terrifying gaze.

He looked at her, really looked for an eternity, as if searching for some answer behind the anguish in her eyes.

Whatever he found there slackened his expression. He released her head and stepped back.

"I changed my mind." Gripping his nape, he swung his glare to Iliana, then Arturo. "No one touches her but me."

THIRTEEN

What the fuck am I doing?

Tiago scraped a hand down his face, reeling from shock.

She's a virgin.

It shouldn't matter. It shouldn't mean anything at all.

But it fucking did.

Actually, the only thing that mattered right this second was getting her away from Arturo, who was standing there with his mouth ajar and his dick in his hand.

"Iliana." He gestured at Arturo. "Finish him."

She crooked a finger, and Arturo followed her into the front room. As she pushed him onto a mattress, Tiago didn't miss the suspicious look she flung in his direction.

Yeah, something was definitely off with him. He never reacted on impulse or emotion. Everything in his life was studied, rehearsed, designed with patience and purpose, and meticulously positioned to prevent undesirable outcomes.

Except this.

Kate lay on the table, motionless, watchful, her face pale and soaked with tears. Long golden hair rippled around her head, and full lips bowed downward, conveying all the ways she wanted him dead. As her steely glare held fast to his, he reminded himself to breathe.

She was the fiercest, most exquisite creature he'd ever laid eyes on, and she was his.

His prisoner.

His property.

His only source of light, glowing through a crack in the coffin of a twelve-year purgatory.

Grunting sounds drifted from the front room, breaking his trance. He fished the finger blade from his pocket and tackled the rope on Kate's arms and legs.

The instant she was cut loose, he tossed her over his shoulder.

There was no reason to carry her. But he was operating on instinct, and for the life of him, he couldn't stop.

He left the kitchen, took the stairs, her warm body draped over his as he navigated each step and turn. Her sweet natural scent was so pervasive his skin heated, and he quickened his pace, speeding toward a delirious unknown.

Every movement was unpracticed, every step uncharted. He had no strategy, no agenda but one.

Claim her.

Blood rushed to his cock, making him thicker, hungrier, more impulsive. He charged straight to his room. Shut the door behind him. Locked it. Carried her to his bed.

The second her feet found purchase on the mattress, she attacked.

In a whirlwind of fangs and claws, she went for the wounds on his head.

Knocking her arms away was easy. Sweeping her legs out from under her and dropping her onto the bed with a knee on her chest took less than a heartbeat.

Her eyes illuminated with blue fire, signaling her next move before she swung a balled fist toward his groin. Even with the warning, that bony-knuckled punch required him to jerk back. She missed but kept coming, flinging herself at his chest with a glorious, bloodthirsty expression on her face.

He caught her, rolled them onto the mattress, and landed with her on her back and his weight pinning her down. But she wasn't finished.

With a battle cry, she reared back an arm, and for reasons unknown, he let her have the hit.

Her fist skidded across his jaw and mouth. He tasted blood, a kiss of pain, and grinned. "That's the only one I'll give you."

"I hate you." She bucked and thrashed underneath him.

"I'd question your sanity if you didn't."

With the rope still tied to her wrists, he secured the ends to the cast iron pipe on the wall. She held her murderous rage behind clenched teeth until he finished restraining both arms above her head.

"You're a heartless kidnapper," she spat.

"Can't argue with the evidence."

"You're a murderer."

"Yes." He put his face in hers and smiled a

humorless smile. "I'm the reason people lock their doors at night."

She took a breath, one that seemed to go all the way through her, and released it. "What are you going to do to me?"

"Everything you're dreading and more." He pushed off the bed and unbuttoned the cuffs of his sleeves.

A tear slipped from her eye, but she didn't sob or beg for mercy. She simply glared, and in that single chilling look, he knew she was his perfect match.

Bending at the waist, he removed his boots while letting his gaze travel along the porcelain skin of her thighs, the dramatic tuck of her waist, and the delicate curves of her small breasts. His hunger for her was sharp and sick.

She looked like an angel, her body too pure and ethereal to touch. But she wasn't innocent. Even though Van Quiso hadn't fucked her, he'd put her through weeks of hands-on training. She probably learned techniques Tiago didn't even know existed.

"Explain something to me." He removed his socks, his shirt, and stared down at her. "How are you still a virgin?"

"I'm not."

"Lie to me again and there will be consequences." He unlatched his belt.

Her eyes flashed, and a huff gusted past her lips. "Van couldn't rape me. The slave buyer paid for a virgin."

"That was *four* years ago. Since then, you've been free to spread your legs for any man you desire." Cocking his head, he absorbed her blinding beauty, savored every detail, utterly gobsmacked. "You lived with five hard dicks, and none of them fucked you."

Her face turned ten shades of livid. "There's more to life than sex."

"Not for a man. Your roommates are pussies."

"And tying unwilling women to your bed makes you a man?" She dug her feet into the mattress and scooted back against the wall, tucking her knees to her chest. "You said you weren't interested. Then you learned I'm a virgin and changed your mind? Is that your thing? You prefer your victims unsoiled, so you can be the one to plunder and defile them before you cut out their throats?"

He was many things. Many repulsive, unforgivable things, but she was wrong about this. So fucking wrong on all counts. He'd never fucked a virgin in his life, not even when he lost his virginity at sixteen. He didn't understand the appeal.

Even now, imagining hurting her in that way, taking something so intimate and precious brought him no satisfaction.

Worse was the thought of Arturo or any other *cabrón* touching her.

This inconvenient possessiveness wasn't new. He'd successfully ignored it since the night he met her. Didn't matter that he wanted her with every vile, undeserving bone in his body. He never intended to fuck her.

Until he heard her whispered plea.

It's all I have left.

He would die before he'd let Arturo take that from her.

Of all the women who tempted him over the last twelve years—the parade of virgins, prostitutes, and every level of experience in between—he couldn't fathom why this mouthy, petulant, argumentative vixen was the one who had pierced through the tough, shriveled crust of his dead insides.

Of all the goddamn women, why was she the one he wanted for himself?

He had but one explanation, which wasn't an explanation at all. "You're mine."

"Oh, for the love of caveman clichés." Her mouth twisted into a snarl. "Just kill me already."

Brave words, but she didn't mean them. Her will to survive blazed in the molten core of her being. Not even he could douse those flames. And he wouldn't.

While the rational part of him analyzed all the reasons why he couldn't wrap his life around this woman, the rest of him didn't fucking care.

This wasn't him. This wasn't how he operated.

He flexed his hands, seconds from putting a fist through the wall. He wanted to hear the bones crunch, feel the hot gush of blood between his fingers, and remember the paralyzing pain. He needed to remember his penance.

Tipping his head back, he stared at the rafters, exhaled roughly, and leveled his gaze back on her.

Those destructive blue eyes fired a barrage of animosity and judgment. He could drown in her hatred and rise out of death in the intensity of her passion. Because she wasn't just malice and vengeance. There were so many facets to her he wanted to carve her open, bleed all her layers, and preserve her strength in a canvas of beautiful scars.

Fuck his penance.

He was doing this.

He was going to break his own rules.

Resolve kicked his pulse into a gallop. He whipped his belt free and dropped it. His pants followed. Then he knelt on the mattress, wearing only his briefs.

"What are you doing?" She squeezed her thighs together.

"I'm going to hell, and I'm taking you with me."

No mistaking her terror. It drained the blood from her face and saturated the air with the short, frantic sounds of her breaths.

That added another punishing scar to his miserable existence. The past six weeks hadn't been easy for her, and every time he breathed in her direction, he hurt her more.

He regretted what he was and the shit he'd done, but the shame wouldn't stop him. It never did.

A criminal with remorse was still a criminal.

"You're a rapist." She flattened her back against the wall.

"I'm not. But that's about to change."

With her legs free to kick, she swung them wildly, desperately, at his head.

Putting an end to that, he closed his hands around her ankles and pulled. She fought uselessly as he hauled her down the mattress on her back toward his kneeling position. When the rope on her wrists snapped her arms above her, he pinned her knees to her armpits and spread her thighs open.

Everything stopped — his heart, breath, all sound and motion. The room faded until all that existed was the view beneath him.

He stared at her, at her slit, at the dark narrow breach within. His face was just a kiss away as he gazed earnestly, devoutly, memorizing and cherishing her gorgeous design.

The flesh around her tiny holes was so pink and taut he couldn't stop himself from running his nose deep inside the cleft, devouring the scent of sweet torture from her pussy to her ass and back again.

His fingers curled around the backs of her thighs, and all the heat in his body descended south. Fucking hell, he'd never been this hard, this reckless. His mouth watered to taste, eat, and consume.

"Untie me, Tiago. Let me go. Right now!" She jerked her head, the only thing she could move. "I don't want this."

"I know you don't. But I promise, before I finish tonight, you'll experience pleasure unlike anything you've ever felt." He was nothing if not thorough.

"The only thing I'll feel is the seething, poisonous, undying desire to castrate you with my bare hands."

"That's your fear talking. You know I'm right, and the thought of enjoying sex with someone like me scares you more than anything."

"I'm not scared." She sawed her teeth together and roared, "I'm fucking pissed!"

He was going to fuck that temper out of her with only his tongue. It would take a while, possibly hours to thaw her enough to climax. Christ, it had been a long damn time since he put his mouth on a woman. But he had all night to relearn.

Settling in on his chest, he wrapped his hands around her thighs, trapping her legs on either side of her torso.

She went crazy trying to break the position, but he was bigger, stronger, and more determined.

"Be still." He nipped her thigh. "You'll wear yourself out before I get started."

"Fuck you, you miserable piece of —"

He buried his face in her pussy and stole the breath from her voice.

Her back arched as drugging sips of honey flooded his mouth. Her taste, her velvety warmth, the frantic rush of her gasps — she became his entire existence.

Carnal need took over, pulsing through his veins and turning him into a mindless starving animal.

His tongue delved into her depths, curling, licking, and moving on its own. He couldn't control his aggression, and she was too tense to enjoy it, fighting and spitting through every second of it.

She would continue to fight until he drove her to exhaustion. Only then would her anger retreat long enough to free the sexual energy that buzzed beneath her skin.

Eventually, he reined himself in and eased into a pace he could maintain for as long as it took.

Teasing a finger around the entrance of her cunt, he marveled at her silky heat. It felt unreal. Impossible.

He hadn't planned for this, hadn't even allowed himself to fantasize about it. Yet here she was, every inch of her beauty exposed beneath him, legs spread wide, with the intoxicating scent of her sex in his lungs. It wasn't just a new feeling. It was monumental and absolutely necessary.

He had to physically restrain himself from plunging in and decimating the depths of her body. "How often do you fuck yourself?"

"Rot in hell."

He caught her clit between his finger and thumb

and squeezed until she screamed. "Answer me, and be specific."

"I...I used to do it all the time. Every night. Before you took me."

"Did you put things inside you? Toys? Your fingers? I don't want to hurt you more than necessary."

"Oh, is that right?" Her tone grated with resentment and hostility. "You want to force yourself on me the non-painful way? Instead of the fun, bind-and-torture-because-it-makes-you-feel-like-God way that rapists luxuriate in?"

He pinched the swollen nub harder.

She jerked beneath him, unable to escape the pain. "Jeeeesus, stop! Fuck! I use a dildo. My fingers. Whatever. Just... Please, stop!"

Good, so there was no hymen to tear.

He released her. "You come that way?"

"Yes."

Thank fuck. He didn't have the know-how or finesse to teach a virgin how to orgasm.

Snugging closer into the juncture of her legs, he lightly stroked her inner lips with his tongue, around and around, following the edge of her opening without penetrating.

She was wet with his spit, not with arousal. Using his mouth, he lubricated a finger. Then he kissed her cunt again, deeply, voraciously, leaving enough slickness to slide a digit into the hot, sucking glove of her body.

As he slowly pushed in to the last knuckle, he groaned at the inconceivable tightness, the heat, while battling the overwhelming instinct to climb on top of her and rut like a raging beast.

Her pussy quivered and shuddered against his

mouth and hand. Her breathing accelerated. The lobes of her ears turned pink, and far quicker than he expected, her cream began to soak his finger.

Her brain didn't want this, but her libido was powering up, humming to come undone.

He teased her with one finger, then two, determined to send her over the edge before he fucked her. The firmness of his purpose pulsated between his legs, hot and swollen, so damn stiff and trapped at a painful angle against the mattress.

The steady stream of her gasps wove through the room, spurring his tongue deeper as he focused on her pleasure. His teeth scraped in his urgency, and he fell into a zone, lost in her addictive beauty, the sublime fragrance of her skin, and the breathy sounds of her cries.

He ate her for so long his mouth became one with her body, sealed to her delicate, delicious heat. He'd never been so blindsided by desire, so overcome by the need to lick every crease, kiss every curve, and plumb every hole. Her pussy, her ass, no inch between her legs was neglected by his tongue. He couldn't get enough.

He kept the thrusts of his fingers slow and consistent, careful not to overstimulate, chafe, or scare her so much she completely shut down. He could finally taste her arousal, the crisp, intoxicating tang of it telling him her body was reacting.

When her hips lifted toward his mouth, that tiny reflex compelled him to move in closer and sink deeper. He was spiraling, falling, and fucking God, he didn't want it to end.

Where did his infatuation with this woman come from? Somehow, she'd reached straight into his chest and dug up something so vital and needy there was no turning back.

His entire body shook with ravenous energy, his hips grinding against the mattress, breaths panting, and hands clenching so tightly his fingers imprinted on her legs. Nothing compared to this. To *her*. Just the feel of her satiny flesh against his lips drove him to madness.

Time ceased to exist as he kissed her cunt the way he burned to kiss her mouth, as he devoured her soaked flesh until his jaw wore out, as he gorged on her again and again. Now that he accepted this indomitable attraction, he was possessed with it. Ensnared. He would never quit.

Eventually, he lowered her spread legs, let her tired muscles relax, and flexed his stiff fingers. She sagged onto the mattress, boneless and breathless, too exhausted to fight.

With her thighs resting on his shoulders, his hands were free to roam. He caressed her slender hips, her high round breasts, every part of her he could reach, and all the while, his tongue continued to worship her cunt.

He fucking loved her body, especially her tits and the perfect way they fit his hands when he palmed them. He curled a thumb over a nipple, tormenting the taut bud as she rocked her head on the pillow and gulped for air.

But she still wasn't with him. Amid her husky moans snapped the cutting words of *no* and *stop* and *hate you*, reminding him she didn't want this.

He needed her to want this. In fact, his need for her to want this became the most important thing in the world.

"Kate." Her name scraped from somewhere deep and echoed outside of him like a prayer in an empty church. "Let go."

Her glistening gaze crept down the length of her body and landed on his. When their eyes met, it was a connection so welcome it trembled through his chest.

Shifting his mouth to her clit, he flicked his tongue. Drew the nub between his lips. Sucked gently. And never looked away.

That was when he sensed it. The shattered sigh she couldn't hold in. The softening in her bones and muscles. The tiny twitches along her inner thighs. The reluctant longing in her expression.

Her crumbling resistance.

He finally had her.

FOURTEEN

Under duress, a woman would do whatever she could to cope with the pain and justify its cause. Kate could endure physical abuse and all its malicious faces, and she had, many times over. But this? She had no defenses against Tiago's gentle manipulations.

The blade of his tongue ravished her relentlessly, weakening her willpower. The suction of his mouth was cruel in its devotion and so damn pleasurable her eyes blotted with wet stars.

She would die if she didn't come soon.

She would hate herself if she did.

But she might not have a choice. Not with her clit caught between those wicked lips as he suckled and tortured and plotted her ruination.

"Stop." Her chin quivered, and she twisted her arms in the rope, too bone-tired to put up a real fight. "Enough."

The wound beside his eye twitched with the flex of his jaw. It was a reminder that even he had weak moments, that he could be hurt, that he could bleed, just like other people.

All thought vanished as his tongue knifed between her legs, slicing from her pussy to her ass and spearing both holes. His mouth was hot enough to melt iron and tenacious enough to liquefy every ring of muscle he kissed, loosening every opening he violated, and consuming her with one. Simple. Lick.

Don't come.

Don't come.

Everything below her waist felt like warm butter — soft, wet, melted, and gooey. He'd reduced her to a throbbing puddle of lust, and at this point, he could fuck her without resistance. There would be no reflexive tensing, no self-preservation. Her body was enervated, wide open, soaked to the needy core, and humiliatingly primed for him.

Frenzied sparks of electricity swept through her nerve endings, replacing her torment with a passion that answered his.

Good God, he had never-ending passion. Every time he touched her, fevered energy rolled off him and caught her up in the surge. With her arms bound above her, she could only lay there and absorb the frantic caresses of his lips, the trembling reverence in his hands, and the intensity in his dark wolfish eyes.

His hunger blanketed the room, smothered her senses, and turned her body against her. His tongue laved. His fingers adored, and his breathing ran away from him. He was climbing, building to a crescendo, and taking her with him.

Her inner muscles found a rhythm, pulsing, squeezing, knotting, needing. Soon, every part of her locked onto that steady throb, matching it, heightening it, until all she felt was one banging heartbeat against his mouth. It propelled her toward the precipice, gathering, contracting, and launching her in the wrong direction.

No, no, no, no, no!

Tears hit her eyes, clogging her voice. "I won't give this to you."

"Then don't." He reached beneath his hips and shoved off his briefs, the last of his clothing gone. "Take it, Kate. Take it from me."

He set his vicious mouth over her clit, clamped back on, and sucked, hellbent on forcing her surrender.

Her body engaged, glued to those lips, everything inside her heating and tightening without her permission.

Seized by resentment, she glared into the face of the beautiful monster as it bored down upon her, tunneling in with fingers, teeth, and tongue. She scrambled away from the edge. Tripped. Lost her grip. Spiraled.

And fell into his dark hell.

He groaned as she plunged, and goddammit, she groaned back, shaking, writhing, unable to stop the orgasm. Then she screamed, and the world exploded as her consent ripped away, and a ballistic eruption of heartbeats blew apart the darkness in shimmery bands of color.

She came until his breath broke. Until his hot mouth left her pussy to the cool air. Until his bare chest appeared over her, his hands tangled in her hair, and the penetration of hard, heavy fullness raided her body.

She was still coming as he thrust, slamming his hips against hers. It happened so quickly. A single swift stroke, and that was that.

He took her virginity.

Buried to the root, he didn't move, didn't shift those arresting brown eyes from hers. His fist hung tightly in her hair, as if forgotten amid the joining of bodies. His mouth parted, but there was no breath, as if he were paralyzed by shock.

It didn't hurt. She wished it did, so she could focus on the pain. The anger. But all she felt was confusion and sadness. And pressure. The pressure of all of him inside all of her.

His girth swelled against her inner walls, stretching her to the point of discomfort. There was so much of him she didn't think she could hold him in any longer. But instead of feeling the need to push him out, she willed him to move, to slide and rub inside her like her dependable dildo.

Her reaction was so fucked up and shameful she could never speak it aloud. But there was one thing she needed to say.

"Put on a condom." She squirmed beneath him. "Please, don't get me pregnant. You don't want that."

She didn't want that. It would be the worst possible outcome, outside of death.

"I can't have children." Pain slipped into the creases of his eyes and vanished just as quickly. "I'm sterile."

"Oh." Startled, she glanced away, blinking, stalling, and looked back. "What about—?"

"I'm clean."

Of course, she was, too. Clean as a virgin.

But her virginity was gone. The one thing she had left was no more. She couldn't stop herself from mourning the loss of it, couldn't stop the ache in her eyes or the silent stream of tears that ran into her hair.

He watched her, his gaze inches away, chillingly still, barely breathing. Was that look on his face one of contrived regret? Or was it genuine sympathy as the reality of abduction, abuse, captivity, and manipulation rode on the waves of pleasure?

How messed up was she that she craved that pleasure? Not the kind she gave herself at home alone. But a pleasure so filthy and twisted it could only be derived from a rapist's tongue, lips, fingers, and cock as he invaded her body, weighing her down with his sickness, ruining her in the best and worst way possible.

Staring down at her, he just held himself there, his thick cock firmly seated inside her, with a strange expression on his face. He didn't speak, but his eyes didn't shut up, the depths crowded by a storm of churning thoughts. She couldn't read him, not for the longest time. Then he blinked.

"This means something." His breath carried the bladed words, slashing them against her lips.

"No. You're wrong." She didn't want to hear this and shook her head, knocking more tears loose.

"It means something to *me*." He gripped her chin and wrenched her face back to his. "You have no idea."

Then he moved. Tiny, shallow, shaky thrusts. Mouth parted, cords straining in his neck, his eye contact was deafening, broadcasting something she didn't understand.

Soft, secret grunts reverberated from a hidden place inside him. The sounds shivered into strangled noises, reminiscent of fragile things breaking apart. Noises she never imagined coming from such a hardened, vicious criminal.

With a hand in her hair and one framing her face, he fucked her slowly, delicately, as if committing every sensation to memory. He fucked her as if this were his first time, too.

What a ridiculous notion. He hadn't gone down on her like a novice, and he certainly didn't fuck like one, either. But there was an innocent attentiveness in every thrust. A thoughtful slide of motion that implied this was more than sex to him, that it was grave and significant.

She knew she was just reading into his deceptive words and strangling herself with misguided trust. No doubt he fucked Iliana with the same dedication.

"I hate you." She yanked on the rope, desperate to break free.

"Ah. We're back to that." A smile twisted the aroused male's gorgeous features.

His skin was on fire, burning against her. His weight, solid and hard as cement, tacked her to the bed from chest to feet. She registered every point of contact, every quiver that ran through his muscles, every hitch in his breath. All of it affected her deeply, the intimacy shredding and destroying her. She wanted this to be different so badly it broke her fucking heart.

"You're raping me." Another shameful tear slipped out.

The hand on her face glided through the wet track, wiping it away, stroking with too much tenderness. "If you need to hate me, then hate me. Use me. Take pleasure from my body."

"You're confusing me."

"I'm a bad man, Kate. Never confuse that."

She should've nodded her head emphatically. But

she could only stare at the stunning paradox of beauty and atrocity that embodied Tiago Badell.

Was he really as terrible as he claimed? Did true evil admit to being evil?

What was she thinking? He was the absolute worst. He'd poisoned Lucia, mutilated Tate's back, kicked Kate in the stomach, locked her in a room for a month, tied her to the dinner table. Raped her.

But he raped her gently.

Gently?

Could that word even be used in this situation?

She was losing her goddamn mind.

"Hate is a feeling." The warm wetness of his mouth brushed against hers. "As long as you feel something, you're with me. I need you with me."

"Fuck what you need." She gnashed her teeth, aiming to bite off his tongue. "Go talk about your *needs* with someone who cares."

His cock jerked inside her, triggering an unwelcome clench in her pussy. He lowered his head, and her pulse jumped through her veins. She tasted his minty breath before his mouth closed over hers.

She tried to fight, lips pinched and neck arching away. But the hands in her hair held her to the pillow, trapping her face exactly where he wanted her.

Then he plundered. Just like when he put his mouth between her legs, this assault wielded the same skill, potency, and seduction. Demanding full lips coaxed and pried until they caught her bottom lip between them, tugged roughly, sucked deeply.

His teeth joined in, nipping in warning, biting when she tried to pull back. The longer she refused to kiss him, the harder his hips plowed against hers. He wouldn't allow her to escape his gaze, his kiss, or the toxicity of his presence.

"Give me your mouth." His voice dropped low, his heavy cock sliding in and out, faster, deeper, scrambling her mind.

She searched for a breath, unable to catch it through her nose. When her lungs burned, she had no choice. She gulped, gasping, and he dove in.

Sweeping past her lips, his tongue hunted hers, lashing, curling, claiming in a vigorous ambush of breathy kisses. He moaned into her mouth, and rumbling vibrations spiked through her, annihilating her pleasure zones.

Her body yielded. Melted. Sighed.

Because the man knew how to kiss. Sweet hell, he knew exactly how to own her.

Every nibble and lick carried just the right tickle, taunt, and floaty, languorous pull. The stubble on his jaw inflicted just the right burn. The firmness of his lips created just the right cushion to caress and bruise. And his taste... Oh God, his mouth burst with flavors that were uniquely him. A fusion of sharp mint, warm caramel, and dark, bold decadence. He tasted like sin.

He didn't just kiss her. He devoured her with his entire body. His hands were everywhere, kneading her ass, coasting up and down her thighs, palming her chest, her neck, her face, and tangling in her hair. All the while, his hips never stopped moving, a constant piston of endless energy and forbidden pleasure.

Frenzied ripples of sensation swallowed her resistance as he stroked his length along her walls, digging in, reaching deep, jerking, and stirring. Tongues locked, hands trailing, cock stabbing, he meant to own her. And in that moment, he did.

It was the kiss. His fucking kiss had the power to crash walls, fuck minds, and bleed souls. It threaded between vulnerable and arrogant, selfless and greedy, polished and primal, silken and brutal, and she sucked it from him helplessly, needfully, knowing it was wrong, which only made her want it more.

He didn't dominate with just one technique. He mastered them all, licking the corner of her mouth, sinking his teeth into her lips, sipping at the seam, sweeping deep into the recesses, quick pecks, long deep perusals, and everything in between.

He kissed her, and kissed her, and kissed her until she couldn't feel her tongue, couldn't unlock her jaw, and couldn't taste anything but him.

When he finally came up for air, she floated in a fog that smelled only of him—his breath, the swollen flesh of his lips, the skin on his masculine face. Even his whiskers had a warm, rough, comforting scent.

Comforting? No, it was…

Familiar.

She'd been naked with him for hours, *with* him in ways she'd never been with anyone else. He was the most familiar thing she'd ever known. The kind of familiarity that cultivated a sense of safety and attachment.

A vein of fear ran through her, sharp enough to shake her from his spell. "This isn't real."

"It feels good and ugly, painful and fucking extraordinary. That's life, Kate. That's *real*." Lines formed between his dark eyes as he searched her face. "It doesn't get more real than this. I know you feel it."

"It's Stockholm syndrome."

"Don't give a shit what you call it." His accent thickened, sliding across her skin. "Doesn't change what it is."

The frantic wallop of her heart rang in her ears. "What do you call it, then?"

"Ours." He drifted closer and stabbed his hands in her hair, holding her lips to his. "You and me. Wide awake. Alive. This is all we have left, and it's the only *real* we'll ever need."

He captured her mouth in a brutal attack, sucking her in, commanding her heart rate, possessing, always taking. His tongue controlled hers, hot and strong, feral and unstoppable. His terrifying power curled around her, summoning her darkest shame. Promising to fulfill every depraved fantasy. Vowing to hurt and cherish her in equal measures.

Diabolical hands found the flesh of her ass and squeezed aggressively, achingly. Palms inched over her hips, fingers splaying as they skimmed up her ribs to her chest and continued along her arms.

The kiss didn't slow as he reached the rope around her wrists, tugging at it.

He was untying her?

The restraints loosened and fell away, and her breath caught.

She stared into his eyes, her hands lowering, free to grip the first thing she encountered—the hard bulges of his shoulders. She meant to push him away, but he was too big, too heavy, too overwhelming.

She held on, sinking fingernails into puckered scars.

Yanking one of her legs around his hip, he pressed his weight into her body and effectively trapped her against the mattress.

His eyes narrowed, and ruthlessness strewed across his handsome face. "I'm going to fuck you now."

"What? You already—"

"Don't let go."

Then he went off the rails.

FIFTEEN

The moment Tiago relinquished his self-control, Kate realized just how much he'd been holding back.

She lost track of time as he fucked, kissed, and tumbled her over every inch of the bed. It was nothing like before. This was a rebellion of chaos and mastery, thunder and liquid smoke.

His thrusts trailed fire. Fingers bruised flesh. Teeth caught lips, and his sounds lost all traces of strangled vulnerability. He growled and grunted from some deep chasm in hell, roaring like a majestic beast in battle, pounding his cock inside her, fighting to get closer, raging, rabid, and petrifying.

Shredded muscles rippled and pumped beneath her hands. Sweat squelched in the creases of their bodies. Her arousal leaked to her legs and spread between their grinding hips. His, hers, they were drenched in wetness, sliding together and burning up.

His broad torso blocked her view of the room, the lamp light, the entire world as he bowed over her, pommeling into her body with the stamina of a fully-charged machine. Ramming. Heaving. Groaning. Kissing.

His kiss owned her soft parts, her compassion and humanity. But this… This brutal, unruly savage of a man owned something darker, something innately carnal and animalistic inside her. He'd woken her from dormancy, ripped her away from shelter and safety, and preyed on the hunger she couldn't hide from him.

A turbulence of conflict tore through her gut. She feared him down to the marrow of her bones. Desired him with every fiber of her sexuality. Cursed him to the ends of her pride and back.

She shouldn't have to remind herself this wasn't consensual, yet as he took her mouth with those fierce, unapologetic lips, she fell in, aching for more, drowning in the overload of his terrible beauty and passion.

"Fucking goddamn." His huge hand cupped the side of her face, stealing her breath and pieces of her soul. "Feels so good, Kate. So fucking honest and real. I need to come. I need…" He pushed deep inside and choked. "I can't hold off much longer."

Hold off? He'd been fucking her all night.

He shoved up just enough to reach between them and rub her clit. His fingers had gravitated there countless times since he began, constantly focused on that overly-sensitive nub. He'd loved it so hard it hurt to the touch.

Then it dawned on her. "You've been waiting for me to come?"

Stormy, hungry eyes hardened and flared, as if he had the right to be offended by her ignorance.

"Well, don't!" She slapped his hand away from her abused clit. "In case you forgot, I was a virgin, and I don't want this. I'm not willing. You've pounded my insides into hamburger. I'm sore, raw, and bruised, and I will *not* come for you."

"You came on my tongue."

Shame. It crashed in from all sides and collided in her gut.

"No more." She pushed at his shoulders, unable to move his bulk. "Please, just stop. Or finish. I don't care. Just do it without me."

"Only with you." His hoarse, gravelly voice brooked no argument.

"I'm with you in all my hatred and venom."

A huff released from his throat, and she heard the relief in it, the smile.

She didn't expect him to relent so easily, but as he folded his arms beneath her back and pulled her deeper into the heat of his body, she felt the twitchy, fiery fatigue in his muscles.

With a hand flattening on her spine and the other cradling the back of her head, he rested his brow against hers and began to drive into her with purpose.

Flexing his hips, he caught a fast, steady rhythm. The warm softness of his tongue traced her lips. His heartbeat thundered against her chest. Breaths heavy, grunts deepening, eyes locked on hers, he chased his release.

She hadn't moved her hands from his shoulders since he'd freed her, but his unguarded expression compelled her to move them now.

Feathering fingertips along curves of biceps and brawny ribs, she suppressed the moan that rose in her throat. Feeling brave, she sought out his hip bones, and around to his lower back, marveling at the sinewy strips of muscle and sculpted grooves she would never find on her own body.

Dipping lower, her fingers bumped the cleft of his ass. Tentatively, she explored the tight divide between rock-hard glutes. Hot and sweaty, his buttocks squeezed with the smack of his hips. Each cheek formed a globe of steel wrapped in silky satin skin.

What a magnificently built man, all bold lines and chiseled strength. And so responsive. He groaned and shivered as she caressed his backside. She knew it was wrong, stroking such a private part of him, especially since she didn't want this.

But she reveled in the feel of his body, feasted on his reactions.

How incredible that her fingertips could alter the tempo of his breathing and spread goosebumps across his flesh. It felt powerful and strangely addictive.

Four years ago, she'd learn how to touch and please a man in every way. Van Quiso had seen to that. But he'd never responded to her hands, and she'd never responded to him.

Why was this so different? The circumstances were the same. Captor and captive. Abuser and victim.

The difference was the man behind the sins. The soul beneath the skin.

The heart of Tiago Badell lay hidden under blood, teeth, and vicious threats, but it was there, calling to her, beating for her. She felt it every time their eyes connected.

Like now.

"Kate." He clutched her neck and tilted up her chin, his thumb stroking the hollow of her throat as he stared, pupils wide, his pelvis slamming her into the bed.

"I'm going to blow my load. Fucking fill you up with my come. Tear up that pussy." His accented English stumbled into Spanish, rolling together syllables that sounded like a vulgar plea to God. "Fucking fuck, fuuuuuuck!"

His hips lost rhythm, jerking wildly, and his jaw turned to stone. He pushed up, his gaze dropping to where they were joined as he pumped, coming without sound or breath, the length of his body shuddering, stiffening, strung like a bow.

Then he groaned, long and deep, his eyes finding hers and his lungs releasing in a guttural whoosh. "Jesus, fuck."

She'd never experienced anything like that and didn't know what to expect or how to react. So she just lay there, motionless, quiet, and invisible.

He pulled out and stared at his flagging erection soaked in their combined fluids. Her first glimpse of his cock didn't leave her gasping at the generous length and thickness, because she already knew it so well. She'd felt every fat inch inside her.

Sitting back on his heels, he dragged his gaze over her flushed body, probing, scrutinizing, heating her skin anew. Hadn't he seen enough?

The only blanket had been tossed out of reach. With nothing to cover herself with, she pressed her arms to her sides and met his hooded eyes.

Without looking away, he cupped a hand between her legs. Placing his other over the juncture between her shoulder and neck, he curled his fingers around her nape. A covetous hold. Possessive and weighty.

Neither of them spoke. There were only the sounds of their breaths, the slam of a door downstairs, the wind whistling across the thin roof. And something else. The stillness between them. It swelled with hurtful words, conflicting thoughts, and promises she didn't want him to make.

With his hands at her throat and pussy, he held her there for a long moment as his gaze made a vow he didn't need to voice.

He would never let her go.

Then his face blanked. He pulled away and shifted to the foot of the mattress. There, he lowered to the floor beside his clothes but didn't pull them on.

He sat with his back to her, unabashedly nude, with his legs bent and his arms dangling over his knees. He seemed to be finished with her. At least, for tonight.

What now?

She wasn't restrained, didn't have anything to wear or cover up with. Every part of her ached and burned from hours of his brutal attention. She just wanted to curl up in bed by herself and escape into sleep.

Staring longingly at the door, she started to climb to her feet.

Until his low, creaky rasp shuddered the air.

"My wife was murdered twelve years ago." His voice lapsed to a monotone, and every word pulled his shoulders down, slumping his powerful body. "I walked in while it was happening. Too late. Too slow. Couldn't put her back together. Didn't save her. I failed her in every way."

Ice trickled down the base of her skull, and her throat tightened around a hot ember.

His wife.

He was married.

She couldn't wrap her mind around it, even as

she'd known there was *something*. Something horrendous that had left a bleeding scar on his life.

Tucking her thighs to her bare chest, she hugged her legs and watched the painfully slow break down in his posture.

An elbow wobbled on one knee, his head sinking toward his chest with a hand over his eyes. She guessed they were closed, his expression lost in memory. Or maybe his face was as tortured as his body language.

She hated that she couldn't see his eyes, but she didn't dare move.

He was quiet for so long she didn't think he'd speak again. When he finally stirred, it was a jerky movement. His arm moved out to the side, sifting through the pile of clothes and disappearing in front of him again. He shifted, shoulders twitching, his hands fidgeting or doing something out of view.

His silence loaded the space between them, a roaring freight of heaviness, too loud in her ears.

She swallowed. "What was her name?"

His back tensed, relaxed, and he raked a hand through his hair. "Semira. She was a doctor, like her father. Grew up in a small village in…" He cleared his throat, his tone strained with pain. "In a faraway place."

"What happened?"

"Someone I trusted turned on me. An assassin came. Gutted her from hip to hip. Let her insides just…spill out. He made sure I saw her bowels hit the floor as I walked in the door."

"Why?" An outcry of emotions tangled in her chest, and she pressed a fist against her mouth to keep it all in.

"Why does anyone rape and butcher innocent

women? Why am I hurting you? Everyone has their reasons. Pain is constant and everywhere. All you can do is endure and fucking accept it."

God, that was heavy. Some of it echoed her own sentiments, slicing like hot knives in her chest. But he didn't just accept the pain in the world. He added to it, made it worse. She couldn't reconcile that.

"Before Semira died…" He hunched forward, further hiding his expression from her line of sight. "I was what society considered a *good man*. I had a lawful job, paid my taxes, and followed all the fucking rules. But there were conversations I should've had with my wife. I should've asked her if she was conflicted about the things I did and the man I was."

So many questions piled up, most of which she knew he wouldn't answer. "Why would you become like the man who had her killed?"

"I didn't. He was my colleague. When he betrayed me, I became the opposite of him. I became his enemy."

"It doesn't make sense. What was your job?"

"This isn't about the job. It's always been about her."

"I don't understand."

His arms twitched with movement, his torso blocking her view. What was he doing with his hands?

"When she looked at me," he said, "she saw what I was. What I am. I didn't even know it was there, this egregious thing inside me. But she saw it."

Had his wife seen the rapist, the murderer, the gruesome artist who carved images into living victims?

She squinted at the back of his head. "You said you were a good man."

"Whatever she saw when she looked at me was

neither good nor evil. It just *was*, and it killed it for her. It killed the love she wanted to feel for me long before that knife killed her." He drew in a breath and let it out. "Some men simply have something inside that makes them impossible to love."

"I don't believe that. All humans are capable of giving and receiving love. Everyone has a *someone* out there."

"Semira believed the same when she married me. I loved her deeply, and no matter what I did to earn her love, her feelings never developed. It was hard for her to bear, knowing that while I cherished her above all else, she couldn't bring herself to reciprocate. She wanted to fill that void with children, and I would've done anything to give her that. But I couldn't. It was another part of me that didn't work. Another thing for her to resent."

Jesus. He had years to dwell on this, to let it eat at him, and now his infatuation with the romance between Tate and Lucia had an explanation. It seemed his own failed relationship had fostered a fascination with happy endings.

Was it possible that he craved love?

She wanted to know about his wife's death. It seemed that was the key to everything. "Why did your colleague betray you?"

"Because the good guys aren't always the good guys. Integrity isn't a guarantee, just because you're fighting on the right side of the law."

"So your colleague was a traitor?"

"I can't talk about the fucking job." His voice vibrated with so much threat it stopped her heart.

"Will you just explain one thing?" Swallowing

hard, she sat taller and glared at his back. "You went from a straight life to that of a crime lord. It changed when your wife was murdered?"

"Yes."

"You said it isn't about the job, yet the job was connected to your wife's death. You must hold resentment for everything that life represented—the legitimacy of it, the paid taxes and moral righteousness. Could it be that if you let go of that grudge, you might—"

"Be a better man?" He barked out a self-depreciating laugh. "When I held Semira in my arms, with her intestines in her lap and her life spilling through my fingers, it was neither love nor hate that shone from her eyes. The last look she gave me was saturated with pity. Pity for a husband she couldn't love, even in death. Pity because she knew that without her, I would forever be alone, because no one would put as much effort into me as she did. I hated her for that. I hated her pity to the depths of my soul, and I made damn fucking sure no one would ever give me that look again."

He became a monster.

In a deranged, fucked-up way, it made so much sense. Monsters were abhorred and feared, but never pitied. In that, he'd succeeded.

Kate had never felt bad for him. Never felt sorrow or disappointment. Not even now. Because it was inconceivable to think of him as weak or helpless. He didn't evoke that oh-you-poor-thing, head-patting kind of emotion from anyone.

What she did feel was compassion. That innate goodness that most people possessed was what compelled her to sway toward him, filling her with the perverse need to comfort him for the pain *he* had inflicted on *her*.

Talk about messed up. But the more she thought about it, the more she understood. For the first time, she felt a real sense of hope.

Hope for him.

He was a self-aware bully, open-minded and regretful, imperfect and *human*. She could work with that, relate to it, and maybe, just maybe, she could convince him to let her go.

"A terrible thing happened to you." She quietly inched to the side of the bed. "But it doesn't have to be this way. You can change the course of your life. Stop kidnapping and terrorizing people."

His neck slowly turned, bringing the intensity of his eyes over his shoulder to grab hold of hers. "I'll stop being heartless when you stop looking at me like it's the only thing I am."

She emptied her expression but couldn't clear the guilt. It stuck in the press of her lips, accusing and judgmental.

"Or don't stop." He jerked back around. "Either way, it doesn't change your circumstances."

Reality crashed in, banging in her chest. What was she doing trying to reason with her captor? He just fucked her ruthlessly, while she screamed *no* until her throat bled. He didn't give a shit about her.

Except something was happening deep in her gut. She felt this coiling, fierce objection to putting him in a category marked *Irredeemable*. He was so much more than a bad man, and she'd only scratched the surface.

Or maybe she really was just suffering from Stockholm syndrome.

Why had he shared his past with her? Was it a call

for help? Was he begging her to see past his imposing, brutal good looks? Or was it a trick? A ploy to engender feelings from her so he could use them against her later?

An unusual sound broke through her introspection.

The plop of wet drops hit the floor near his position.

Plop. Plop-plop.

Was the ceiling leaking? It appeared dry.

Was he crying?

She craned her neck, straining her senses, listening.

The wet sounds sped up. More liquid. A slow trickle.

"What is that?" Chills swept across her scalp as she stood from the bed.

Scanning the room, she scrambled for the closest thing she could grab. His shirt. She spread the crisp material against the front of her body and slowly stepped around him. And lost her breath.

Blood.

Oh God, it was everywhere.

Rivers of crimson snaked along his forearm, forking stained lines down his fingers and dripping to the floor.

Hot red splatters. There were so many dots between his feet they overlapped.

She teetered, lightheaded, and focused on the source of the bleeding.

A razor. He wore that damn finger blade like a claw, dragging it over old scars.

"What are you doing?" she whispered.

He was cutting and not answering her, because it was a stupid question.

She took a shaky step closer. "Why?"

"Punishment." His voice lacked all emotion, and the blade continued to carve.

Balling a fist in the shirt, she clutched it tighter against her chest. "Punishment for what?"

"You."

She flinched, and her gaze flew over the scars on his arms. So many marks. Faded ones. Newer ones. "Do you do this every time you fuck a woman?"

The razor paused. He lifted his head, his expression empty, voice emptier. "The last person I had sex with was my wife."

"What?" Her naïveté plummeted to the floor and shattered. "That was—"

"Twelve years ago." He returned to his cutting.

"You haven't had sex in twelve years?"

"That's what I said."

She recalled how incredibly experienced he was in bed and stared at him in disbelief. "You're lying."

His nostrils flared, and he dug the razor deeper into his arm.

Thick droplets oozed free, flowing off his skin and soaking the flooring.

Dark red against dark wood.

The scent of copper in the air.

She wished it would stop. She needed it to stop.

"Tiago, can you just..." Now within reach, she stretched an arm toward him and held the other against her chest, trapping the shirt. "Please, just stop for a second and talk to me."

He looked up, stared blankly at her face then her outstretched hand. She wanted to yank her arm back, but she refused to look scared, even if everything inside her screamed to run.

His bladed finger twitched as he raised his slashed arm and curled a bloody hand around her wrist. He pulled, forcing her to shuffle into the space between his legs.

The soles of her feet sopped up the gore on the floor. She tried not to think about that, and instead focused on what he'd said.

"You fucked Iliana." She held her arm still in his grip. "In the backroom, every day."

"I've *never* touched that woman."

Cycling through her memories, she couldn't identify a single time he put his hands on Iliana. Not even tonight in the kitchen. It was always the other way around.

"She's all over you," she said.

"Iliana throws herself at everyone." His fingers tightened around her arm. "She will *never* touch you or me again."

"What about Lucia?" She squinted. "She was your captive for eleven years. You can't tell me nothing happened."

"I touched her body and imagined my wife, but I never kissed her. Never fucked her."

He released her wrist and yanked the shirt from her grasp. Blood-soaked fingers curled around her hip, and he lowered his head, touching his brow to her stomach.

Was he staring at her pussy? Or were his eyes closed? She kept her attention on his bladed finger and held her breath.

"When I was with you tonight, I didn't think about Semira. Not once." He pressed his lips to her belly button. "Celibacy was my penance for failing her. It was my choice. Until you."

He broke his twelve-year abstinence. For her.

It means something to me.

As if pulled by an invisible string, her hand floated toward his head, where his soft hair lay against her abdomen. Before she made contact, she snapped out of the enchantment and dropped her arm. "Why me?"

In a swift glide of powerful muscles, he unfolded his body and rose to his full height, towering over her, completely nude. "You're mine."

Mine. That fucking word set her teeth on edge. He could say the same about this house, his security guards, the stupid blade on his finger. He could take his property and all his precious little possessions and shove them up his ass. She refused to be one of his belongings.

Stretching her spine, she tried to add length to her height, to stand taller than eye-level with his chest.

"Why did you cut yourself?" She lifted her face. "What was the punishment for?"

He narrowed his eyes.

She narrowed hers back. "For everything you've done to me?"

"No, Kate." He cocked his head. "For everything I'm *going* to do to you."

SIXTEEN

The heat in Kate's cheeks gave way to numbing chills. She didn't have a chance to stammer a response before Tiago grabbed her hand and hauled her into the bathroom.

"What are you doing?" She dug in her feet, slipping in the blood that trailed him.

"Get in the shower." He pushed her in the general direction. "Back against the wall. Hands at your sides."

He didn't need to flash the blade on his finger. His tone was sharp enough to send her running.

"What did I do?" She pressed her spine against the shower wall and pinched her arms close to her ribs. "If I angered you—"

"You meant to. You'll fight me at every turn." He set the razor on the counter and prowled toward her with a terrifying glint in his eyes. "I look forward to it."

"Don't hurt me." Her breathing quickened, knocking her chest into a heaving jog.

"Too late for that." He stepped into the shower and

wrapped both hands around her neck, forcing her head back with his thumbs beneath her chin. "I fucked you thoroughly and completely, and I've only just begun."

Warm blood dripped from his arm to her chest, and she shivered. "You need to get Boones. Let him look at your cuts."

"Tell me you care if I bleed out."

"No." She set her jaw. "I don't care."

"So fucking honest." He leaned in and licked her lips. "Tell me more."

"You're a possessive, duplicitous, unreasonable nutjob."

"Your insults make me so damn hard." He dropped a hand to her ass and squeezed it painfully. "*Me encanta tu culo.* When I put my mouth here…" He wedged a finger into the crack, making her clench. "When I lick this tight rim, tell me you hate it."

She couldn't. Just thinking about it hardened her nipples. She knew it was happening when he glanced down at her chest and grinned.

"I waited twelve years for you." He touched his mouth to the corner of hers.

"Don't say that."

The wet sound of dripping drew her attention to the tile floor. Red splatters hit the drain. One heavy drop landed on her foot and worked its way between her toes. They both stared at it.

"I've seen a lot of shit in my life. What's normal to me would be shocking by society's standards." He wiped a hand over the cuts on his arm, collecting a palm full of blood. "Don't move."

He set that hand against her stomach and smeared the scarlet wetness across her hips, her thighs, and between her legs.

Horror hit her in a surge of tears, trembling her chin and burning through her sinuses. She closed her eyes, desperate to unsee the blood he was rubbing into her pussy.

"I've been a voyeur for twelve years." His hands cupped her face, warm and sticky. "Always watching from the front row, close enough to smell the tang of a soaked cunt, to hear the hungry slap of balls. I collected a lot of fantasies, and the things I've imagined... The dirty, filthy fucking things I've played out in my head never had an outlet."

Until now.

Until *her*.

She kept her eyes squeezed shut and bit down on a sob. But it found her vocal chords and vibrated in her throat.

He moved in closer, his wet palms sailing downward, lingering on her chest, tweaking her nipples, then continuing south to her waist and hips. No inch of her was left untouched. He was so attentive that way, achingly affectionate, and it fucked with her head.

Reaching her balled hands at her sides, he pried them open and guided one to his groin.

"Let go of your self-imposed restrictions, Kate." He forced her fingers around his heavy testicles.

When she tried to pull away, his free hand flew to her throat and applied pressure.

"Let go of every preconceived notion you have about sex." Holding her neck in a threatening restraint, he slid her hand to his cock and molded her fingers around the girth. "Fuck the stigmas and labels and society's definition of what's proper. Stop thinking about what you *should* do and fight for what you *want*."

"You know, maybe I'd feel more liberated if the roles were reversed." She swallowed against the collar of his fist and opened her eyes. "I have no power here. I'm completely at your mercy, and as you already pointed out, you have none."

His lips split in a feral smile, a menacing spark lighting up his eyes. "Fucking love your mouth."

The hand on her throat crept into her hair, and he clutched a hunk of it to yank her lips to his.

Stubborn as she was, she tried to resist. But she just couldn't. Not with his hot, beautiful cock in her hand, his fingers holding that grip, and his mouth setting her on fire.

The kiss went from playful to starving in seconds. Her body craved him. It recognized his touch, his mouth, the scent of his skin, and the rumbling sound of his voice. Didn't matter how selfish or cruel he was. The brainless, fleshy parts of her loved the way he made her feel.

While his tongue chased and licked hers, he guided their hands along his shaft, angling to rub the head between her legs, touching her, touching himself.

It was erotic and tantalizing and so fucking wrong. She loved it. She hated that she loved it. He was corrupting her, and her mind seemed hellbent on rationalizing and justifying every illogical reaction.

"You're right in that you have no power here," he breathed against her lips. "Not while I'm holding you against your will and you're constantly looking for an escape. But you have the power to take from me. When we're together like this, you can take as much pleasure as you want. Deviate from everything Van taught you. Break free from your hang-ups. Explore whatever you desire without judgment."

She wanted that, but she didn't trust it. Not with him. He was spinning her around so fast she didn't know which way was out.

Her eyes fluttered closed. "I don't know how."

"Look down. Look at us."

She lowered her gaze, taking in her bloodstained body, his hand holding hers around his cock, and the semi-hardness of it gliding between her thighs, seeking entry.

He adjusted his grip to drag a finger along her slit, collecting the ejaculate he'd left there minutes ago. Then he smeared that into the blood on her thighs.

It didn't feel forced or planned. He wasn't pretending to be something he wasn't. This was Tiago, the man no one else saw, in all his crude, natural, horrifying glory.

No one had ever captivated her the way he did.

"You're covered in me." He tipped her head back to stare into her eyes. "You're wearing my spit, sweat, come, and blood. Give me *your* definition for that. The first word that comes to mind."

"Raw." Her brows pulled together.

"Yeah." The corner of his mouth curved up. "Raw isn't a bad thing, Kate, and I'm not finished."

He swooped in and caught her lips, stealing choppy breaths from her lungs.

What did he mean he wasn't finished? Would he cover her in his tears next? Or... *Oh, God.*

A hot, wet stream flowed down her legs. The length of his dick rubbed against her hip, warm and half-hard in their hands. His mouth moved over hers, distracting her with the potency of his assertive tongue and sultry lips.

But she knew what was happening. A steady rush of liquid warmth drenched her lower half, tickled her feet, and stirred an appalling reaction between her legs. He was peeing on her, shamelessly pissing on her body, and her pussy *throbbed*.

It wasn't the shocking dirtiness of it that turned her on. It was the intensity of his arousal from it. The quicker his breaths grew, the faster her heart panted. He kissed her harder, more frantically, and she met him lick for lick, bite for bite.

She clung to the sounds of his groans, the confident way he held his cock in their hands, and the sensation of his body's hot fluid soaking her skin. It was the rawest form of intimacy she could've ever imagined.

Urinating wasn't much different than climaxing. There was a need for privacy while doing either action. The urge to hold it, stall it, then the tightening, building internal pressure, until the burst, the gushing flood, and the overwhelming relief. It made her want to release her bladder and orgasm all at once, just to share in the freedom he was experiencing, to let it all go without the judgment of prudes in the outside world.

Because a prude was one thing Tiago was *not*.

As the warm trickle slowed, he sighed as if he'd just jerked himself off on her legs.

"Look at you." He swayed back enough to let her see down the length of her defiled body. "So goddamn beautiful."

"Yeah." She unraveled her hand from his as modesty and shame crowded in. "I'm a glowing matriarch for women's rights."

Somehow, she'd forgotten to scream and fight him

off while he was peeing on her.

"Hate me all you want." He clutched her chin and put his face in hers. "But never hate your desires. Never be ashamed of what you want."

"You pissed on me. I can't want that."

"Says who? You? Or the world you were raised in?" He released her to turn on the faucet and adjust the water temperature.

"It's dirty," she said lamely.

"I don't have an infection." He positioned her under the shower head. "It's sterile enough to drink."

"Where do you draw the line?"

"No shitting and no sharing." He grabbed a bar of soap. "Those are our limits."

"You can't tell me *my* limits."

"I just did."

He proceeded to wash her body. Then his own. His dick, fully erect now, jutted from the apex of his powerful legs. But he ignored it as he focused on cleaning away the blood and urine.

She was at a loss. Part of her warmed at the thought that he didn't want to share her. When he'd offered her to Arturo in the kitchen, it had been the worst possible scenario. Worse than Tiago finishing the job himself.

Why was that? Wouldn't a quick fuck by a random guard have been better than the hours she endured with Tiago?

The voice in her head screamed no.

"Do you still want to kill me?" she asked quietly.

"No." Grasping her hips, he spun her to face away. "Put your hands on the wall."

Exhaustion sluiced away her resistance. She

flattened her palms on the tiles and let her head drop between her arms. "But you'll kill me if you need to."

"I should've killed you weeks ago." He set the soap aside and ran lathered hands up and down her back and shoulders. Then his fingers curled around her throat. "There are other forms of punishment if you try to escape."

"Torture."

"I have endless energy when it comes to you." He lowered his other hand to her abdomen and sank his fingers between her legs, pushing one inside. "I can torture your pussy for days. If you lose consciousness, I'll dunk you in cold water and start again, sucking, licking, biting, fucking, and never letting you come." He thrust that long digit in and out, racing her pulse. "If that doesn't convince you, you should know I won't hesitate to hunt down your friends."

The implication he would kill them slammed into her gut, but he didn't voice it. He didn't need to.

I hate you leapt to her tongue, and she bit it back. She'd said it so much it'd become trite and predictable.

"What are the rules?" she asked. "How do I guarantee their safety?"

"Don't try to escape and no murder attempts against me or those in my employ."

"But I can defend myself? I can fight and disobey you if I don't like what you're doing to me?"

He leaned his chest against her back and put his mouth at her ear. "Be my guest."

Strength revisited her muscles and joints. Determination wound around her spine. As he kicked her feet apart and sped up the finger inside her, his intent was clear.

She pulled in a breath, knowing he expected her to start struggling. Instead, she held still, anticipating the right moment.

He seized her from behind, banding both arms around her. His teeth went to her neck, and she dropped like a rock to the floor, breaking the hold. He lurched after her, but she was already swinging.

Her fist collided with his erection and the meaty sac of his nuts. She put all her strength into it, certain the hit was hard enough to drop him.

Except he remained on his feet. He didn't even let out a grunt or reach down to cup himself. Pain drew his lips into a flat line, but that was it.

She gave him a point for barely reacting, knowing full well that behind that stoic expression, he was battling the need to double-over and roar.

Water rained down upon her, and she blinked through the deluge, watching him, terrified.

After several heartbeats, he glared down at her and blew out a swift expulsion of air. His body seemed to widen before her eyes, flexing with testosterone and aggression, his nostrils flaring with a surge of heavy breaths. Like a bull preparing to charge. To fight, fuck, and maul.

Instead of attacking, he tilted his head and considered her. "I didn't give you that hit."

"Yeah, well, I took it." Point for her.

Begging for forgiveness was her best option at this point, but she wasn't feeling apologetic. So she swung again.

This time, he caught her fist and wrenched her to her feet. The shower stall spun around her, and her cheek smacked against the tile wall. His body pinned there, his hand at her throat, cutting her air.

He was teaching her a lesson, proving he had the upper hand. He could crush her throat—her trachea, esophagus, and whatever else she needed to stay alive— with nothing but a squeeze of his fingers.

Pain pulsed beneath his grip, and she pawed at it, eyes watering and lungs burning for oxygen. Her fear was deep and cold, stinging without mercy. He said he wouldn't kill her, and she hung onto that promise as dots blackened her vision.

"I'm going to take you right to the edge, Kate. Over and over again." He let go of her.

She gasped, clutching at her throat and savoring the weightlessness of unbridled breath.

Wrapping his arms around her from behind, he pressed his mouth to her jaw. "You hate me for it now, but someday, if I earn your trust, that razored edge will set you free."

He was completely unhinged if he thought she could ever trust him.

Grabbing her hands, he placed them on the wall before her. Then his fingers slid between her legs.

He worked her the way she knew he would— passionately and persuasively. Every touch rubbed salt in the wound of desire. His lips at her neck wobbled her knees. His hard, long cock against her backside coaxed cravings she didn't want.

Engaged in a constant war, with him, with herself, she was tired. So goddamn tired.

As he sensed her body begin to yield, he braced his bleeding arm on the wall beside hers and guided her other hand between her legs. She was wet, not just from the shower but from her treacherous arousal.

Twining their fingers together, he glided them through her folds and around her clit. He stroked himself, stroked her, his foreplay an endless night of mind-fucking torment.

By the time he stuffed his cock into her from behind, she was grinding in his arms and panting raggedly.

He banged her against the wall, with his hand trapping hers where they were joined. Just another of his wicked tortures, forcing her to feel his strokes with her fingers, using their hands to caress each glide of his length as he thrust.

That erotic touch brought an awareness to the connection she couldn't ignore. Sparks of pleasure shimmered across her fevered skin. Pleasure that belonged only to them. She couldn't fight it, didn't want to.

Greedy and mindless, she surrendered to the climax, moaning and rocking and clawing at the shower wall.

He pulled out, spun her around, and took her again, chest to chest, mouth to mouth, hiking her up his body, so he could kiss her as deeply as he pounded into her. He came fast and hard, roaring her name and shaking from head to toe.

"Never letting you go," he whispered long after he finished, still buried inside her, still chanting her name as he caught his breath.

It wasn't the last time he fucked her in the shower. Over the next two weeks, he took her there, on the mattress, the floor, and everywhere.

He moved her into his room, made her sleep in his bed, and spent more time inside her than out of her.

His headaches came and went. Some days, he exercised downstairs. Every day, he worked out in her body.

When she found the energy to fight him, he restrained her with rope. When she felt herself slipping under his seductive spell, she remembered Tate.

Tate, sitting alone in a shack, with a bucket to shit in and a tattoo of the woman he loved.

That reminder helped her cling to her hatred. But she knew she wouldn't be able to hold onto the anger forever.

Tiago was inside her, possessing her like a demon and cherishing her like a man.

She saw the truth in the devoted way he kissed her, in those breathless moments when she returned his passion with a fire of her own, in the homage that scratched his voice as he said her name.

The chemistry between them burned so hot she had to shield her eyes and look away. But she still saw it. It was Tiago who didn't know it went both ways.

She told him she hated him, and he never doubted it. He didn't know about the times when she felt herself swaying, softening, falling.

Someday, Tate would be free, but she would still be here, staring at the crime lord who stood at the edge of hell, with his arms open, waiting to catch her.

SEVENTEEN

Tiago pushed through his work out, tossing up weights and annihilating his cardio routine with a nourishing burn in his lungs.

His strength had returned, his headaches completely gone, his health back to normal.

He might've been fifteen years older than Kate, but he'd spent the past two weeks fucking her like he was in his twenties.

With a grunt, he grabbed a heavier weight and heaved it through a set of bicep curls. He should've been focused on his upcoming return to Caracas, but his thoughts constantly wandered back to her.

What was she doing right now? Was she staring at the front door and plotting her escape? Or was she caressing the lush curves of her greedy body and thinking about his hands?

She despised him with every breath she took, but she loved the way he touched her, kissed her, and moved inside the tight clasp of her cunt.

"Goddamn." His skin tingled and heated.

He dropped the weight and dragged a towel down his face.

They were leaving for Caracas in just a few days. He didn't want her anywhere near the cesspool of his organization, but he would never leave without her. Hell, he couldn't even bear being in a different part of the house than her.

Finished with the work out, he exited the backroom and stepped into the hall.

Iliana had stayed out of his way since he set the record straight. She and the other guards received the same message two weeks ago.

He and Kate were off-limits.

No more touching or flirting.

No sharing.

Kate would be treated with the same respect as Boones. Keeping her and the old doctor safe was his top priority, and he made certain his security team knew it was theirs, too.

As he prowled down the hall toward the kitchen, the sweet sound of her voice reached his ears. He peered around the corner and found her at the table with Boones.

Arturo stood in the front room. When Tiago gave him a nod, he soundlessly headed down the hall in the direction Tiago just came from.

With their backs to the doorway, Kate and Boones didn't notice the change of guard.

"Who is she?" She leaned over a crinkled photograph in Boones' hand, the one he always carried in his pocket.

Boones stroked the black-and-white image of the

gorgeous Eritrean woman. "Her name was Semira."

On a stunned exhale, Kate whispered, "Tiago's wife." Another gasp. "She was your daughter?"

"My only child."

"I'm so sorry for your loss."

In the doorway behind them, Tiago stared at his feet as a mace of memories formed in his stomach, all sharp, pointy spikes, piercing and heavy.

Semira wore a traditional Tigrinya dress and gold head jewelry in that picture. Tiago had been behind the camera, capturing the snapshot of the mischievous smile she'd so often thrown at him. As beautiful as she was strong, she'd ripped his heart out of his chest the first time he'd seen her.

"He told you about her?" Boones clutched her arm, his toothy smile glimmering with hope.

"He shared some of the painful highlights but was rather stingy with the details. I'd love to hear more." She entwined her fingers with his. "How did he meet your daughter?"

Tiago silently shifted back into the hallway and let his head rest against the wall. He trusted Boones to share only the parts that were safe to speak out loud. Her question was one Tiago would've answered himself. But she hated him too much to ask him directly.

"Tiago met my daughter when his family moved to my country," Boones said. "His father originated in Venezuela as a pharmacist, and that's where Tiago was raised. When Tiago finished school and took a job in America, his father moved his mother and younger brother out of Venezuela. His father's expertise in medicinal botany brought him to…" He coughed. "My village."

"Why is the location of your home such a big secret?"

"Tiago has enemies from his old life, as well as this one. Now that my brothers have returned home, he can't keep them as safe as he would like. He doesn't want anyone to know where to look for them."

"Wait. Your brothers? They're the other doctors on your medical team?"

"Yes. Semira, her uncles, and me. All doctors."

"So Tiago was raised in Venezuela? And when he returned, you and your brothers followed him back here?"

"Of course." A sad smile sifted through his voice. "We're his only family."

"That's why he's so protective of you." Realization softened her tone. "His parents...? They're not alive?"

Tiago ran a tense hand through his hair, fighting the impulse to make his presence known and end the conversation.

"They died," Boones said. "His father was my dearest friend. We worked together for years, while Tiago was off traveling the world, immersed in his career. But Tiago visited my village often, mostly to court my daughter. He loved her."

"He said she didn't love him back."

Boones sat quietly for a long moment. Tiago didn't need to see his father-in-law's scarred face to read the troubled thoughts in his head.

"She fell in love with his looks and the safety he could provide," Boones finally said. "He has a big presence, powerful and handsome, but you already know that."

His military background in America was what

drew Semira to him. The political climate in Eritrea wasn't good, hadn't been good for decades. Repression ran rife throughout the country. Citizens lived in constant fear, unable to speak out against the government. News outlets were closely controlled. Everything was locked down.

For Semira, Tiago had represented freedom. A way for her and her family to escape the repression.

He'd been in the process of moving them out of the country when she was attacked. How ironic that instead of keeping her safe, he was the one who got her killed.

"She never loved him the way he loved her." Boones' voice carried years of regret. "We fought about it, she and I."

"Because *you* love him," Kate said.

"Like a son."

Tiago closed his eyes. The best thing that came out of Eritrea was that stubborn old man. Boones had stuck by his side through the worst, brought him back to life multiple times, watched him do things no one should ever have to witness, and not once did Boones give up on him.

"You have to understand," Boones said. "Tiago didn't just lose his wife that day. He lost his father, mother, and little brother. His entire family was slaughtered in front of him."

Her gasp cleaved through Tiago, but it was Boones' next words that twisted the knife of shame.

"He needs a woman's love."

Enough of this.

Tiago charged into the kitchen, circled the table, and stood on the other side to glare down at Boones, then Kate.

He braced himself for the pity she wouldn't be able to hide in her honest eyes, but when he peered closely, he didn't find it.

She tilted her head and raised a brow, her lips pursing as if she were annoyed by his intrusion.

Fucking incredible.

He turned his gaze to Boones and spoke in Tigrayit. "I don't need love, you meddling old fuck."

"Idiot," Boones said in the same language. "You need it more than ever now that you have brain damage."

"You said the injuries didn't damage my brain."

"I changed my mind."

Irritation slithered beneath his skin. He switched to English. "Tell her what happened after I watched my family die."

Boones bit down on his thin lips. He didn't like this part.

"That's okay." Kate patted Boones' arm. "I have a pretty good idea."

"I don't think you do." Tiago paced around the table, his hands clasped behind him. "I killed everyone involved. Those who coordinated the attack on my family and everyone associated with those people. I murdered handlers, operatives, and officials, which put me on wanted lists for multiple countries and all the three-letter agencies."

Her face paled.

"I didn't just walk away from my job." He paused beside her and leaned down, gripping the edge of the table. "I went rogue, killed a bunch of important people, and took Boones and his family down with me."

"Don't you start on that." Boones stood and

pointed a finger at Tiago. "We demanded to go with you."

"I shouldn't have allowed it." He'd ruined their lives, tainted their gentle souls with his filth.

Boones slammed a fist against the tabletop, his body stiff with rage as he turned to Kate. "I was as close to his father as he was. We were all close, his family, my family. The day they died, we *all* changed. My brothers and I needed revenge just as badly as Tiago. That's why we went with him." His accent thickened, vibrating with vehemence. "We followed him from city to city, waited as he took each life, and patched up his broken bones and wounds. Then we followed him here to Venezuela." He cut his eyes to Tiago, the white scars on his cheeks glowing against his black skin. "I made my own choices. You don't get to take credit for my crimes."

He gave Boones a tight nod, willing to give the man anything he wanted. The last twelve years had been painful for both of them.

"Thank you for sharing that with me." Kate glanced from Boones to him and squared her shoulders. "I didn't mean to open old wounds."

"Don't worry about that. Tiago has been opening a lot of wounds lately." Boones pointed his cloudy eyes at the cuts he'd treated on Tiago's arm two weeks ago.

Tiago hadn't touched his razor since then, but he wanted to. He longed to draw blood, fantasized about it constantly, and it wasn't his flesh he imagined cutting.

His gaze shifted to hers, and his groin tightened.

Boones ambled toward him, obstructing his view of blue eyes and flawless skin.

A bony hand gripped Tiago's neck and dug in with surprising strength. "Let her see you," Boones said in

Tigrayit. "All of you. Even if it invites her pity. Then she can decide whether to love you. And you'll know if she's worthy of the man in here." He tapped Tiago on the chest.

His hackles bristled. "Semira was worthy. She was just ambitious, focused on her career. She was a good woman."

"I loved my daughter, but she wasn't good for *you*."

With that, Boones left the kitchen and slipped out the front door.

"I'm willing to bet some of that exchange was about me." Kate rose from the table and gathered the dishes from lunch. "It's rude to talk about people in a language they don't understand."

"Leave that." He snatched the platters from her and held out his hand. "Come with me."

Ignoring his command, she walked past him and headed for the sink. "I figured out why there are no mirrors upstairs."

He caught a fistful of her hair and yanked her around. He wanted to look into her eyes while she called him out on his shit. "Tell me."

"You hate your reflection." She jerked in his hold, swinging and kicking until he released her. "Not your appearance. You know how damn…" She growled and waved a flippant hand in his direction. "You're ridiculously good-looking. It's not that. You don't like what you see in your eyes. The cruelty. The hypocrisy. Your family was murdered, and what did you do? You went to Caracas and became a kidnapper and murderer. Your cold eyes are windows into that hell, and I have to stare into them every time you fuck me. Because you hold my head and make me look and…" She spun away, fists clenched at her sides. "You're pure evil."

Fucking Christ, she was fiery today, itching for a fight.

There were no guards around to witness her disrespect, so he let her continue the rampage, because she wasn't wrong.

She stormed to the sink, clanked a few pots around, and charged back. "And another thing. I'm over the whole *mine* declaration. That's something an insecure guy says to a girl when he doesn't want her fucking other guys. When you say it to the woman you abducted, it's psychological warfare. Not sexy."

He laughed, loud and deep, because fuck him, this woman had balls. Huge fucking lady balls. "I don't give a fuck whether it's sexy. You won't be fucking anyone but me."

Her spine went straight, and her cheeks burned into an angry shade of red.

But this wasn't anger. She was scared. Beneath her surly bravado lurked a deep sense of dread. She feared what it meant to belong to a man like him. She feared for her friends if she tried to break free. And she feared the day she would stop thinking of escape and yield to the force that knotted them together.

Every time he entered her body, he wanted their roles to disappear. But how could he move them away from being captor and prisoner when he was unwilling to let her go?

He didn't just want to keep her. He wanted to bind her, spank her, cut her, and fuck every hole. He wanted to share every depraved fantasy with her and earn her trust at the same time.

He didn't need a woman's love. He'd survived thirty-seven years without it.

But he ached for *her* to love him.

Him, a thing that couldn't be loved.

He wanted the impossible.

All humor gone, he extended his hand again. He'd told her to come with him, and he wouldn't repeat himself.

The atmosphere shifted and tightened. She stared at his mouth, his chest, his hand, and shifted her weight from one foot to the next.

Then she ran.

EIGHTEEN

Kate bolted toward the front of the house, the perfect curves of her ass flexing in denim shorts, and all that blond hair swinging around her tiny waist.

Energy swelled, heating Tiago's muscles. His cock lengthened and hardened for the chase. The thrill of the hunt.

She veered around mattresses and tripped over backpacks, her noisy breaths spurring him into motion. When she reached the front door, she fumbled with the handle, and it cost her.

He caught her from behind, an arm against her stomach and a hand around her throat.

"What did I say about trying to escape?" He sank his teeth into her shoulder.

"I wasn't! I just need..." She twisted in his hold, an attempt to break away, but ended up with her chest against his and her mouth so close he tasted lemon tea on her breath. "I just need some air."

"What's wrong with the air in here?"

On an exhale, a pleading look seeped into her eyes. "You."

Gripping the backs of her thighs, he hitched her up his body. The position forced her to hug his neck and hook her legs around his waist.

"Explain." He tangled a hand in her hair and seized her molten blue gaze.

"How can I explain *you*? This?" She feathered her fingers along his whiskered jaw, cupped the side of his face, and touched her forehead to his. "You make me crazy."

"Goes both ways, Kate."

"Then let me go."

"Never." He turned and climbed the stairs.

Her limbs tightened around him, and her breathing accelerated. She thought she knew what would happen when they arrived in their room, but she didn't have a clue.

"I won't surrender," she whispered fiercely against his mouth.

"You always say that."

"I don't want this."

"Always say that, too."

She lowered her head to his shoulder, resting her cheek there, with her warm lips against his neck. "I'm tired, Tiago."

Tired of fighting him.

She'd been here for two months and spent every second of it resisting, defying, spitting, and fighting. Always fighting.

He didn't intend to break her down or defeat her. He wanted her arguments, her wrestling matches, and her rebellious spirit.

"Don't give up." He pressed a kiss beside her ear. "Never."

There's my girl.

In the bedroom, he locked the door and set her on her feet.

"I need to use the toilet." She backed away and vanished into the bathroom.

While she did her business and washed her hands, he removed the rope and blade from the locked safe. Then he grabbed the bag of medical supplies Boones kept near the door.

When she stepped back into the room, Tiago was sitting on the mattress, holding his phone.

She stood there in little jean shorts and a tank top, with her arms rigid at her sides and her head held high.

Just like the first time she walked in here and raised that chin at him, he was sucker-punched with the fiercest, rawest form of perfection. She was so much more than he could've ever fathomed.

Except now, he knew that devastating beauty ran through the deepest parts of her, and his heart longed for it, hammering and stretching to sink inside of hers.

He could make her come on his mouth and fall apart on his dick. But he couldn't make her love him. He couldn't even hope for such a thing.

Nevertheless, he wouldn't stop fighting for it, knowing he would lose in the end.

Turning his attention to the phone, he opened a screen and held it out to her.

"What is it?" She inched closer, her long lashes hooding the curiosity in her eyes.

"I had a camera installed in the shack."

She erased the distance in three running strides

and snatched the phone from his hand.

Arturo had placed the solar-powered recording device on the roof and angled the lens through a hole to capture the interior. Tate didn't know it was there, and no one would spot it from the outside.

"Oh my God." She clutched her throat, eyes wide and glued on the live streaming video. "That's Boones. How is he with Tate?" Her gaze snapped up and landed on his, the depths clashing with relief and accusation. "Tate must be close by."

"Within walking distance. Come here." He leaned against the wall, stretched out his legs, and opened his arms.

She came right to him, somewhat absentmindedly as the video held all her attention.

Gathering her on his lap, he tucked her back against his chest. With a hand stroking through her hair, he watched her watch the live footage.

"That's where Boones goes every day." She pulled in a serrated breath and released it. "He's been taking care of Tate."

"Yes."

On the screen, Boones knelt behind her friend and applied a balm to the man's back. He would do the same with the arm injury, the new tattoo, and check for any health issues.

"This is so much better than I've been imagining." Her fingers tightened around the phone. "It's still horrible and inhumane, but knowing he has Boones, that he's so close, it means everything."

"I installed the camera so you can check on him. Before we leave for Caracas, I'll take you to see him."

"What?" She spun on his lap to face him, dropping

the phone in her excitement. "Really?"

"I can take it away just as quickly as I've given it." He locked the device and set it aside. "Remember that."

She looked up into his face and adjusted her legs to straddle him, to stare a little closer, a little deeper, with a strange tumult of emotions flitting across her expression.

"You tortured my friend and chained him in a shack for two months. I can't forgive you for that. But..." She swallowed, breathed in slowly through her nose, and placed her soft hands on his jaw. "It's funny how you throw me a few scraps, a video, a chance to visit him, and follow it up with a mean threat, and all I can think is... Here's a glimpse, a tiny peek of goodness. This is the moment when I don't see the fearsome, ruthless gang leader you created twelve years ago. I see *you*, the man who mourns his wife and family. The man I want to know. The man I want to kiss."

Erratic and unstable, his pulse careened through his veins. "I'm not a good man, Kate."

"No, you're definitely not that. But you're not the one-dimensional creation you show the world, either."

"I believe your exact words were *pure evil*."

"I was angry."

"And now?"

"I'm moved."

She leaned in slowly and skimmed her fingers into his hair. A puff of breath. A gentle brush of lips. Everything inside him clenched and locked.

It was the first time she initiated intimacy, and the kiss was so delicate it shivered with fragility. It took every bit of strength he could muster to stop his hands from flying to her head, to stall his tongue from sweeping in and taking over.

She was such a sexual creature she couldn't breathe without radiating the sizzling, ignitable energy that lived beneath her skin. His entire body recognized it, fed on it. But he wrestled down the need to control this and closed his eyes, savoring the tenderness, the exquisite affection.

The peaks of her supple, braless tits dragged against his chest. The heat of her cunt burned against his cock through their clothing. Her tongue found his with licking, curling, divine sweetness, and perspiration formed on his spine. She was killing him.

Then she grew bolder. Her hands wrapped around the base of his skull, bringing him closer, angling his head for a deeper kiss. Her tongue slid over his, tasting, exploring as she panted against his mouth.

It was the most exhilarating, most sensual kiss he'd ever experienced. All his senses telescoped to her lips, her soft, wet tongue, and the maddening way she tunneled her fingers through his hair.

She transported him into a fantastic dream and smothered him in layers of emotion. She didn't just kiss with her body. She fused to his mouth with her whole being, all tongue and breath and deep, swirling feelings.

When she broke for air, her fingers clung to his neck, pupils blown, and lips swollen. For a moment, she seemed disoriented, stunned. Then she blinked, and her expression glowed with wonderment. Maybe even fondness.

"I like you like this." She stroked a thumb along his bottom lip. "Kind and unassuming."

His stomach hardened.

She thought she was looking at him, but she was staring at a stranger. He wasn't a man who let a woman straddle his lap and dole out vanilla kisses. There wasn't a docile breath in his body.

He needed pain to feel alive. Perversion to stay focused. He needed the razor-sharp edge.

Let her see you. Then she can decide whether to love you.

"You're only seeing what you want to see." He touched her cheekbone and traced a path to her perfect mouth.

"I haven't forgotten what you've done or why I'm here."

"You don't know the half of it."

She ghosted a hand along the scars on his forearm. "What haven't you shown me?"

His brutal cravings.

His darkest hunger.

His deepest hurt.

He pointed his eyes at the rope and blade beside the mattress, and she followed his gaze.

"No." She tensed and started to pull away, shaking her head. "You don't need that."

He yanked her back by her hair. "There's a lot of pain in the world. You can't avoid it."

"If you endure it, accept it, it will stop."

His breath caught. That was *his* mantra, something he'd only ever repeated to…

He narrowed his eyes. "You've been spending too much time with Boones."

"I adore him."

"He had his scars deliberately put on him. Does that disgust you?"

"Not at all. They're an important part of his culture." She circled a finger around a raised welt on his wrist. "Did your wife wear scars, too?"

"No. She thought it was outdated and crude. But

many of the women still practice the art. I find it seductive, exotic, and beautiful." He met her eyes. "I've never cut a woman."

In his mind, he'd carved countless elaborate illustrations on Kate's body, but there was one in particular that made his fingers twitch for the blade.

"You haven't?" Her head flinched back. "But you said cutting a woman is different than a man. Something about a passionate hand and weeping and…" She choked on a gasp of realization. "You were referring to your wife. When she was…"

"When I watched that knife slice her open, I *felt* it. I felt myself bleed. I heard myself weep. Then all I knew was rage. I emulated that exact cut on the man who killed her, the men who killed my family, and all the others associated with the attack. The more men I sliced, slashed, and carved, the more I liked it. *Craved* it. So much so I became less discriminatory about my targets."

"You turned the blade on innocent people. Like Tate."

"Yes. But I've never cut a woman." He opened his expression and let her see every nefarious intention in his mind.

"No." She scrambled off his lap so fast she tumbled to the floor. Scooting backward on hands and feet, she screamed miserably, "Stay away from me!"

He sprung after her and seized her ankle, yanking her back to the mattress.

She went crazy, all flailing fists and snapping teeth. He held her to the bed and snatched the rope, making quick work of the knots around her wrists and the cast iron pipe.

Then he sat back on his heels, his legs straddling

her hips, restraining her lower body in place. The position reminded him of the night they met, the first time he tied her up.

"We've been here before." He planted his hands on either side of her face and leaned down, biting her lips.

She tried to bite him back, missing his mouth in her outrage. "Let me go!"

"I need you to listen."

A tremor rippled across her jaw. "Are you going to cut me?"

"With pleasure."

"Fuck that." She thrashed. "Fuck you. I won't let you do this!"

"Stop." He grabbed her chin and held her head still.

"Please, don't kill me." Tears spilled from her liquid blue eyes.

He loosened his grip and glided his fingers along the side of her face. "I can't lose you."

It was the most honest, vulnerable thing he'd ever admitted aloud.

"But you're going to hurt me?" More tears escaped.

"God, yes." He bent down and ran his mouth over her wet cheeks, kissing away the pain he'd caused her.

"Why?" She gulped air and swallowed back her sobs, a noble effort to pull herself together.

"It's a need that drives me. A comfort I can't live without."

Cutting was a purging, an outlet for the nightmares inside him. As much as he cut himself, it wasn't the same. He needed the connection to her pain.

Her arms trembled in the rope. "Does it arouse you?"

"With you? Yes."

"You're a sadist. I get that. It's part of what makes you so intense, unusual, and terrifyingly captivating. But Tiago, there's a difference between hurting a woman who gets off on it and hurting a woman against her will."

It was a moot point. He didn't ask permission when he fucked her, and he wouldn't ask permission for this.

"I won't surrender to that blade. Not ever." Her lashes fluttered, and her eyes flicked back and forth before pausing on his. "But I'll make a deal with you. We're leaving for Caracas in…?"

"Three days."

"What will you do there? Kidnap more people? Torture them and hold them for ransom? Kill them if their families can't pay?"

She knew what he did. He didn't need to fuel her hatred with a response.

"Retire." Her expression morphed from fearful to determined. "You don't need the money."

"No."

"Can't or won't?"

"Both."

"Then change your business model. You want to live a life of crime? Fine. Stick to victimless crimes."

He laughed heartlessly and stopped short when he realized she was serious.

"No more kidnapping. No more hurting innocent people. Make me that promise, and I'll…" Her nostrils widened with a slow, deep inhale. "I'll be whatever you need me to be."

"No deal. I want you exactly as you are."

"If you don't make me that promise, all you're

going to get from this point forward is a plastic, hollow version of me." She leaned up, as much as the rope allowed. "Don't forget. I was trained how to please a sadist. I can make this a memorable experience for you or I can turn it into a robotic musical of fake moans and cheap quivers."

"You said you wouldn't surrender." He rubbed his brow. Christ, this woman. Why was he even entertaining this conversation?

"I can't surrender to this. Pain doesn't turn me on. At all. But I can give you the real me." She pulled on the restraints, trying to lift her face closer to his. "I know you, Tiago Badell. You need this to be mutually honest. No games. No bullshit. Just you and me."

Heat surged to his balls and swelled his cock.

She jutted her chin. "Stop. Kidnapping."

"What you're asking for is ridiculous." He sat up and hardened his eyes. "Caracas is the kidnapping capital of the world. You don't survive Kidnap Alley without playing by the rules."

"If you're the king, you can do whatever the fuck you want."

NINETEEN

No more kidnapping.

Was it as easy as just deciding to stop? Tiago never had a taste for abducting people off the streets, but he had a reputation to uphold and hundreds of powerful men in his pocket, including law enforcement and politicians. If he so much as appeared weak, he wouldn't just lose their protection. They would turn on him and everyone loyal to him.

The deaths of his family had led him to this corrupt life. His last revenge kill was in Caracas, and when he finished, he stayed.

He'd slunk into the deepest, darkest corner of Kidnap Alley and became one of them. One of the irredeemable who lurked in the shadows, smuggling contraband, kidnapping tourists, and killing at will. Within a year, he'd become their leader.

His fate was sealed. He was hunted by government agencies, cartels, crime lords, influential people. They wanted him imprisoned, tortured, dead, dismembered, his head on a stake in town square. Didn't matter. They wanted him gone.

If he left his life in Caracas, he left the protection of his crime syndicate. Walking away was the same as walking toward death row.

But he could make a minor change to the business. If he refocused his efforts on gun smuggling and expanded his routes, he could make the argument to his money-hungry constituents that it was more lucrative than kidnapping for ransom.

He could give her this one thing. He wanted to, and not because he was receiving something in return. He wanted to give her this because it was the right thing to do.

It might be the only good thing he could ever offer her.

"No more kidnapping." He ran featherlight fingers down her neck, eliciting a shudder in her breath. "Consider it done."

"Thank you. And you'll take me to visit Tate before we leave."

"You have my word."

All she had was his word, and he could break it at any time. But he wouldn't. She seemed to know that. She trusted it.

"Untie me." She stared at him, a silent bid to trust *her*.

"No." He climbed off the bed and collected the blade and Boones' medical bag.

The air between them assembled and charged, a palpable battle of her fear against his anticipation. As he readied the supplies, her anxiety pressed against him, the shallow sounds of her breaths accelerating his.

She deserved so much more than the sickness inside him. But she would remind him of that. The hatred in her eyes, the derisive words from her mouth, she would never quit fighting. He counted on it.

Moving back to the bed, he climbed over her and shimmied her tank top over her head, up her bound arms, and left it gathered around her wrists. Then he lowered his hands to the button on her shorts.

"Do you already know the design you're going to cut into me?" A sheen of wetness spread over her eyes.

"Yes." He released the fly and dragged the denim and panties down her legs and off.

"You planned this."

"Weeks ago."

"Of course." Her jaw set, and a quiver raced along her nude body. "How big will it be?"

"The size of my hand." He splayed his fingers over her thigh, magnifying her shivering. "It'll wrap all the way around your leg."

This twenty-two-year-old, petite wisp of a woman, whose hair tangled wildly around her bare chest and bound arms, didn't flinch.

Life hadn't been kind to her. She was abandoned by her parents, betrayed by her brothers, tortured by Van Quiso, and now this. Life should've broken her, but instead of shattering, she became her own hero. She didn't even realize she'd saved herself. And in doing so, she saved him.

He cleaned the blade with Boones' antiseptic and rubbed the homemade compound into the skin on her thigh, something he never bothered to do with anyone, including himself.

And because he couldn't control the impulse, he

leaned down and kissed her pussy, dragging his tongue through her velvety flesh and taking generous sips of her intoxicating essence.

Her hands fisted around the rope, her eyes never leaving his as he worshiped her body.

He needed her in ways he didn't understand. She satisfied every sexual craving, but this wasn't just lust. He needed her strength, her defiance, every nuance of her ferocious spirit.

If there was ever a woman mighty enough to break her restraints and stand as his equal, she was it.

She was the one.

With the preparations finished, he fitted the sharp blade onto his finger. The custom-made scalpel extended like a claw, enabling him to cut detailed swirls and precise lines.

Kneeling in the spread of her legs, he lowered the blade to her thigh.

His nerves fired and exploded with excitement. He wanted this too deeply, too vehemently. He could see the finished image in his mind, imagined her wearing his scars for the rest of her life. He was overcome.

"It's beautiful." Her shaky voice drew his gaze to hers.

"I haven't started yet."

"Doesn't matter. I have a choice. I can spend the rest of my life loathing the scars every time I remove my clothes. Or I can decide right now they're as beautiful as the ones that cover you and Boones." Her eyes flashed. "I already made up my mind about it. Every time I look at the scars, I'll remember that a crime lord gave up kidnapping in exchange for art."

Fuck him, she was remarkable. Rare. Perfect.

Mine.

"Hold still." He steadied his hand and spread her skin taut beneath the scalpel. Then he drew the first cut on her upper thigh.

Her bleak blue gaze creased with pain, but she didn't look away. Didn't twitch or scream. She watched him with the eyes of a tortured goddess. Proud. Fierce. Distressed, but not defeated.

Gathering the gauze he'd set aside, he went to work, focused on the design, and dabbed at the trickles of blood.

He dragged the blade the way a tattoo artist dragged a needle—hunched over, breaths calm, eyes glued to the art, every mark deliberate and meticulous.

Cutting Kate was different than cutting anyone before her. He felt the vibrations of her labored breaths, the wetness of her silent tears, the very fluid of her life slicking over his hands.

Time became irrelevant. Seconds leaked into hours. He was lost in it. Lost in the passion of creating, the release, the bleeding.

The bleeding.

The bleeding.

It was flowing too fast. He held the gauze to the deepest slash, but no matter how much pressure he applied, blood gushed between his fingers, pooling under his hand, drenching his arm, the bright ruby rivers quickly darkening, tangling, growing thicker.

Organs spilled. Ropes of viscera. Heavy, wet things. The pungent scent of bowels. And blood. God, the blood oozed from everywhere and nowhere, staining everything it touched.

How did he get here? Did he kill someone?

Silence crashed in, thumping hollowly in his ears as he watched Semira die again and again, the pity in her eyes vivid and alive, making him pay.

His pulse went berserk, the agony hitting in waves and turning the blood to acid. All he could do was rock in place, the occasional whimper ricocheting off the walls.

"Tiago!" A faraway voice pleaded with him. "Look at me!"

Everything sharpened, narrowed to a pinpoint of purpose.

Kill.

A flash of glinting steel.

Destroy.

Deadly shades of red.

Slaughter.

"Tiago, dammit! Stay with me!" That voice again. That heavenly voice.

He jerked his head up and looked into the eye of his storm. She stared back, gaze glowing, expression soft, his perfect calm and clarity.

"What happened?" She tilted her head.

"Nothing."

"That wasn't nothing. You look like you're seconds from blowing a gasket, and I don't want to be under that blade when it happens."

He glanced down at his hand, at the razor on his finger. Blood didn't flow. Organs didn't tumble.

What he saw was her pale, toned leg across his lap, her skin etched with the birth of a painting, a carved outline, and the budding blooms of something beautiful.

The sight of his design heated his soul to burning.

"Untie me." She kicked him in the hip with her free leg, her voice gentle. "Let me touch you. The contact might help."

Pain would've been deep within her thigh now, stinging and smoldering, as if the bone had caught fire. She couldn't veil the agony on her face, her lips stretched taut, and her forehead beading with perspiration.

But it was the concern in her eyes that moved him up her body. This woman, whom he'd hurt so ruthlessly, had the capacity in her heart to help him.

It made no sense, but he didn't question it. Instead, he untied the knots on her wrists.

She tossed the rope and tank top from her arms and grimaced at her leg.

"I'm not finished." He shifted back into position, resting her thigh across his lap.

"I know." She lay back and gripped the arm he held across her midsection. "I'm not surrendering."

"I know."

She turned her gaze to the ceiling, and he returned to the design, cutting a braided pattern across her thigh.

"You had a flashback, didn't you?" Her body quivered beneath the blade, her teeth sawing the hell out of her bottom lip.

"Yeah." He reached up and tugged on her chin. "Stop that."

"Does it happen often? The flashbacks?"

"Never." He nudged her to her side and continued the lacerated braid to the back of her leg.

"Maybe this is helping?" She whimpered as he carved along a tender spot.

"Helping with what?"

"Your terrible personality."

He glared at her through his lashes without lifting his head.

"Yeah, you're right." She glared back. "Your personality can't be fixed. But maybe reliving your past is better than bottling it up. It should be cathartic."

"This, us, *you* are cathartic."

She fell silent after that but never removed her touch.

An hour passed before another flashback sneaked in.

She sensed it before he did, and her hand sank into his hair, fisting, pulling, until his gaze latched onto hers. "Stay with me."

And so he did. He focused on the warmth of her fingers against his skin, on the way they trembled and flexed with her pain. He marked the rapid pace of her breaths and paused often to let her calm down, kissing her body during each break, his lips on her knee, her chest, and everywhere in between before starting again.

Blotting each drip of blood, he felt that flow of life roll through his veins like lava. Soon, he fell into a rhythm, a sensual slide of his hand, the scalpel seamlessly slicing her gorgeous flesh.

Dark, depraved pleasure circulated through his system. Indecent and drugging, sensations swarmed his nerve endings and heated his skin. Christ, he'd needed this.

He flipped her to her stomach to finish the back of her thigh. Numbing balm went into the incisions as he went along, and he forced water to keep her hydrated.

Dinner had long passed by the time he sat back and wiped off the blade. She'd stopped watching a while ago but not once had she withdrawn her touch.

He marked the heavy sag of her eyelids and the slackness of her mouth. "Where are you, Kate?"

"Floating on hatred."

More like floating on endorphins, high on spikes of pain and stress, exhausted from hours of shivering, and probably lightheaded from the burn out of an adrenaline rush.

She looked ready to pass out, and he was hard as a rock. Cutting her had aroused him to the point of distraction. But this was Kate. Every time he touched her, his cock lengthened.

"Finished?" She inched her gaze to his.

"Yes." He set aside the supplies. "Ready to see it?"

"It's beautiful." She closed her eyes.

"Bullshit." He gripped her under the arms and lifted her to a sitting position. "I know you made up your mind about it, but you're going to give me your honest opinion."

"Fine." She blew out a resigned sigh and looked down.

As her gaze flicked over the design, her sexy bowed lips separated. She leaned forward and twisted to see around the sides and underneath.

Her bright, glossy eyes and appreciative noises shifted things inside his chest.

"My God. It's... I have no words." She hovered a hand over the design, as if itching to touch it. "Why did you choose this? What does it mean?"

"The image will be clearer as it heals. It's a rope, coiling around your thigh."

"With a flower trapped under it?"

"Not trapped. It grows out from beneath it, blooming despite the confinement." He ran a hand along her calf, cupping it to drag her closer. "There are twenty-two petals on the flower, each representing a year of your

213

life."

"Why?" She blinked, and a tear skipped down her cheek.

"You're the miracle that grows in the smallest crack of sunlight. The bloom that never gives up."

"Tiago." A teary hiccup teetered to her lips, and she smothered it with the back of her hand.

"There's something that thrives within all living things, a force that drives us to want to live more than anything else. You're the essence of that. The purest example of resilience. No matter what direction you need to grow — out of the darkness of an attic or from beneath the constriction of braided rope — you do it fiercely, tenaciously, and without fail." He clutched the back of her neck and brought her face to his. "There's nothing more vibrant, more beautiful, or more treasured than the flower that blooms in hell."

"That's… I don't…" Her voice creaked, and she feathered fingertips around the perimeter of cuts on her thigh. "How long will it take to heal?"

"Two months. It'll fade to pink. With time, it'll be completely white and blend in with your pale complexion. But unlike a tattoo, it has a tactile element."

"It'll be raised like yours." She tickled a hand over the welts on his arm, but didn't look down at his scars. Those huge, glistening eyes fixed on his. "I like the way they feel."

Compelled by a force he'd only ever felt with her, he ducked his head and kissed her, running his tongue along the seam of her lips the way he'd imagined for hours.

Soft and wet, her mouth opened for him, salty with her tears, warm with the gust of her breaths.

He plundered her with urgency, devoured her with hunger. Hauling her onto his lap, he took her mouth with feverish strokes, his body moving of its own volition, grinding against her, mindless with desire.

The need between them swelled, and he didn't hold back. They were an explosion of motion—hands gripping, tongues battling, breaths heaving, hearts pounding. All of it burst into a consuming, soulful integration of her and him.

Her mouth dove to meet his in a kiss that was so unexpected he groaned and shook to his core.

She was unexpected, yet it felt as if his entire life had been building to this. Every tragedy, every crime had brought him here, to this woman, who kissed him with all the hatred and goodness inside her.

Her fingers lifted to his hair as his hands lowered to her chest, cupping and caressing her nude flesh. She rocked on his lap, and he gripped her firm ass, jerking her body harder, faster, until he felt wetness bleed through his gym shorts.

"Kate." He grunted against her greedy lips. "Kate, wait."

She pulled back, dazed.

"Your leg. Hang on." He swept her onto her back and fumbled for the package of gauze. "Don't move."

He re-cleaned the incisions and dressed her thigh in soft bandages. She watched his movements with labored breaths, her cheeks flushed, and eyelids at half-mast.

Then her brows pulled together, the depths of her gaze flickering with an inner war.

At any moment, the words *I don't want this* or *I hate you* would fire out, but instead, she reached for his face and traced the line of his jaw.

He lowered his body into the cradle of hers, falling. "You're wrecking me."

"You deserve it." She hooked her legs around his hips.

Shoving down the elastic band of his shorts, he slid the head of his dick along her slit. "You're mine."

A pretty growl vibrated her throat. "Shut up."

"You want my cock."

"Not even a little."

"You want to come all over it."

"Lies."

Her body didn't lie. A sweep of his finger through her cunt released a gush of arousal. She made a strangled sound and pressed her hands against his bare chest.

When he pushed back, her fingers caught his nipples and locked on, pinching with an alarmingly strong bite.

He choked, seated his cock against her pussy, and shoved home.

With a yelp that rivaled his throaty groan, she wound her arms around his neck.

"So fucking wet." He rotated his hips, grinding into her soaked heat, teasing her. "Hear how sloppy you are? You're creaming all over me."

"You're a good kisser, okay?" Her hand speared through his hair and clenched. "I still hate you."

"You want to hate me, but I don't think you do."

Her eyes shuddered, and she looked away. "I want my freedom back."

"Can't release you." He shifted to his side, taking her with him so that her bandaged leg rested over his hip.

"Then, for now, I'll take a different release." She rolled her hips, catching a slow ride on his cock. "We both need this escape. You can take from me. I'll take from you, and just for a little while, let's get lost in it."

Her words gripped him deeply, every part of him bowing toward her. An honest touch from her fingers could sustain him forever.

"No more resistance," he ordered.

"No more restraints," she ordered back.

He palmed her ass and drove harder inside her. "No more holding back."

"I'm sick of fighting this." She gasped on his next thrust. "But I won't stop fighting everything else. Especially when you're being a total dick, which is pretty much all the time."

"Except now."

She raised her face to his, her expression drunk on desire. "This is a good moment."

Lying on their sides, he wrapped his arms around her. Then he fucked her gently, taking, giving, fusing them together. She cried out, her mouth agape as he drove into the hot, tight fist of her body.

Hands down the best thing he'd ever felt. Soft lips on his mouth. Thick blond hair against his arms. Lush, toned curves beneath his fingers. Wet, warm pussy sucking in his cock. Heaven. Salvation. She made him feel again.

She made him want to be a man she could love.

Wrapping up the length of her hair in his fist, he forced her gaze to his. Slowed his pace. Stroked in and out in a steady, desperate grind.

Eyes locked, mouths connecting and separating, the connection was raw, unhurried, and heavy. Every kiss thrummed with what-ifs, every touch a climbing step to something huge and unstoppable.

A fever of lust.

A bolt of energy.

A blissful fall.

He came with her, syncing their orgasms by eye contact alone.

Her body clamped down on him, spasming, squeezing, as unholy pleasure hit him from all directions. Her hungry mouth crashed down over his, stealing her name as it rode on his groaning breaths.

After, he lay on his back with her body splayed across his chest and her eyes losing the fight against sleep.

When her lashes stopped fluttering, the fringes spread over her cheeks, he started counting each one.

His heart knocked an unusual beat.

Relaxed.

Peaceful.

Happy.

But it wouldn't last.

In three days, he would come out of hiding and take Kate with him.

There was no way around it. He'd been holed up in the desert for two months. Eventually, his enemies would find him, and here, he only had the protection of a handful of guards.

He needed to get his ass back to Caracas, where he would be surrounded by the fortification of his neighborhood and the hundreds of loyal criminals who worked for him.

But once he arrived in the city, his enemies would know.

Twelve years ago, he killed some important people and painted a target on his back. That had never mattered to him. Until now.

Until Kate.

There were so many ways he could lose her. So many fucking enemies. DEA, FBI, local crime lords, the Mexican government, neighboring cartels who fought for his smuggling routes, and of course, Lucia's brother-in-law and capo of the Colombian cartel, Matias Restrepo.

The biggest threat, however, was Cole Hartman.

Hartman had steered Tate directly to Lucia, and now he was helping Lucia locate Tate. Once that job was finished, he would come after Kate.

If anyone could separate her from Tiago, it was that fucking guy.

A tremor attacked his muscles, the barbs of dread sinking in and shredding his insides.

Tightening his arms around her, he pulled her closer against his chest and buried his nose in her hair. In her sleep, she burrowed into the shelter of his body and sighed.

When he lost Semira, he surrendered his humanity.

If he lost Kate, he would surrender everything.

TWENTY

Tiago woke with a start, his pulse pelting against his throat as the hum of a distant car engine lingered in his mind.

Had he dreamed it? Or had he heard it in his sleep?

The sky hung beyond the barred window like a black velvet blanket, hours before dawn.

No one should've been coming or going. Not the guards. Absolutely no visitors.

He held himself motionless, his hand possessively gripping Kate's perfect ass beneath her panties.

He didn't wear a stitch of clothing. No weapons within reach. He could only stare across the dark room in the direction of the locked door and listen.

The pitchlike silence heightened his paranoia, making him twitchy.

Seconds pounded by. Minutes. His hearing strained against the hush. No sounds. No movement.

Probably just remnants of the dread he'd carried into sleep.

But he couldn't shake the feeling something was wrong.

Reluctantly, he untwined his arms and legs from Kate's slender limbs, despising the separation from her soft, warm skin.

Moving quietly in the dark, he was careful not to wake her. But as he unfolded from the mattress, her groggy whisper floated up.

"Where are you going?"

He lowered back to the bed and kissed her parted lips.

"Getting some water." He traced the scalloped hem of her panties and fingered the bandage on her thigh, checking that it hadn't unraveled. "Need anything?"

"More sleep." She rolled away, her breathing instantly falling into an even rhythm.

He ran a hand down her spine, smoothing the oversized shirt. *His shirt.*

He'd fucked her so many times last night she hadn't been able to keep her eyes open. Eventually, he'd put her in the panties and his shirt, because sleeping beside her nude body...

His dicked jerked. Started to harden.

Yeah.

Rising to his feet, he navigated through the dark room, located his bag of clothes, and pulled on the first thing he found. A pair of sweatpants.

Then he grabbed his phone and checked his messages on his way to the stairwell.

Just after three in the morning. No notifications. No missed calls. A quick peek at the live video of the shack confirmed Tate was safe and asleep.

At the bottom of the stairs, he scanned the main

room. Muted light from the kitchen illuminated one occupied mattress. Arturo.

No reason to wake him. Not yet. The other guards would've been outside, patrolling the perimeter.

Except there should've been more of them asleep at this hour. Three on the day shift. Three on the night shift.

But only Arturo was required to sleep inside as a last layer of defense for Boones.

Pacing to the covered windows, he peered through the slit of one and probed the shadows.

The cars sat where expected. Stillness stretched to the horizon. Too dark. He couldn't see shit from this position. He would have to go out there to investigate.

He slipped into the kitchen on silent feet and grabbed the largest knife from the butcher block. Then he headed to the hall and made a beeline to Boones' room.

The door stood ajar. He stepped in.

The faint sound of snoring drifted from the bed, but it wasn't enough to calm his nerves. He needed to *see* Boones alive and free from harm.

He approached the bed and crouched beside it, straining his eyes in the dark until he could make out sheared gray hair, black skin over sharp bones, and the rise and fall of a scarred chest.

He exhaled a sigh of relief.

The snoring stopped.

"What's wrong?" Boones asked in his native tongue.

He lowered the butcher knife out of view. His scalp tingled, his senses telling him a tendril of unrest was creeping toward the house.

Or, most likely, it was just his overactive paranoia taking shape in imaginary noises.

"Just checking on you." He rested a hand over the welts on Boones' sternum, finding sanctuary in the thumps of a strong heartbeat. "If you die in your sleep, I'll have to find someone else to make breakfast in the morning."

"I spit in your eggs." Boones smacked him away, a smile in his voice. "Shut the door on your way out."

He did more than that. As he slipped into the hall, he turned the handle and engaged the lock from the inside without sounding the click and worrying Boones.

A hard kick would break the door, but it would take an extra second or two to bust in.

In the front room, he returned to the gap in the window. Outside, the landscape was a black tarp of empty silence.

Nothing moved. No guards in sight, which meant they were stationed where they were supposed to be, spread out around the property, watching the perimeter from every angle.

Still, he couldn't shake the tingling along his nape. His senses hummed on high-alert, the hilt of the knife hot in his hand.

He prowled through the front room, listening, waiting, second-guessing the foreboding feeling in his gut.

"Jefe?"

He turned toward the sound of Arturo's gruff voice and squinted at the silhouette sitting on the mattress. "Who's on watch right now?"

"Blueballs, Iliana, and Samuel." Arturo rose to his feet and said in Spanish, "Or maybe it's Alonso, not Iliana. I don't know. They switched up the schedule last night." A pause. "Juan was in here when I dozed off."

Alarm spiked his heart rate, hardening his body into battle mode.

"The guys rarely sleep in here." Arturo scratched his whiskers, wearing only a pair of boxers. "The desert is making them restless."

Tiago strode into the kitchen and removed all the bottom drawers in the cabinets. Behind each one waited a stash of weaponry and ammo. He grabbed a .40 cal pistol, two loaded magazines, and glanced down at his pants.

No pockets. No shoes. No shirt. He wasn't dressed for combat.

Tension stifled the muggy room as he loaded the magazine in the gun and set the extra one aside. Then he grabbed the knife, both hands armed.

Silence buzzed in his ears, a haze of muted light shining down from the ceiling. His skin itched, sticky with sweat, his pulse thick in his throat.

"What is it?" Arturo approached, zipping up the fly of his jeans. Eyes wide and alert, he loaded his own weapon. "You hear something?"

"Not sure. I'm going to take a walk outside. I need you to stay here with—"

The boom of gunfire sounded in the distance.

He froze, blinked, and in a blur of sharpness, he sped in the direction of the stairs.

Except Boones was down the hall.

His footsteps faltered, skidded.

Kate or Boones.

Kate or Boones.

Indecision cost him half a second.

He swung toward Arturo, pointing the knife. "Go to Boones. No matter what happens to me, you'll protect him with your life. Don't let him out, and do *not* leave his door. Swear to God, Arturo, if any harm comes to him, I will haunt you long after I'm dead."

The hard edge of his voice sent Arturo running toward the hall, carrying an armful of artillery.

He swiveled back toward the stairs.

Kate.

Flying into a sprint, he made it halfway through the front room before the windows exploded in a shower of glass and lead.

He shielded his face with an arm and ran into the shrapnel, hunching low to avoid a wayward bullet.

The front door crashed open, followed by a stampede of boots. Then the rapid firing of popped rounds and ear-splitting, disorientating chaos.

His military training kicked in, revving his pulse, sharpening his awareness, and focusing his mind on one objective.

Kill.

The Glock in his hand held fifteen rounds, and he used every bullet to clear a path to the stairs. When the pistol clicked empty, he whipped it across the face of the nearest intruder and threw it at the head of the next one.

Down to the knife, he slashed it along a heavily muscled arm. The man's firearm dropped out of reach. Tiago slashed low and opened the man's gut.

Five intruders left. Two swept up the stairs.

Kate.

Fury flogged him, but he couldn't chase them. Three men were already on him, punching, kicking, and swinging knives.

He tackled the only one with a gun, gripping the man's arm and guiding the automatic weapon as the fucker squeezed the trigger.

TAKE

The spray of bullets went wild, punching a zigzagged line along the floor, up the front wall, and taking out one of his own guys.

He swept the man's legs out and wrestled him to the ground.

Gunfire sounded from the direction of Boones' room, ramping his pulse to a dangerous level, distracting him.

An elbow slammed into the back of his head. He coughed a pained grunt and lost his balance.

Adrenaline flooded his veins as he rolled, swept the blade wide, and cut a deep gash across the man's chest. Hardened eyes rounded in shock then tapered with the drive to kill.

With a grunt, Tiago flipped to his feet and spun as another guy jumped on his back. A backward stab with the blade relieved him of the threat behind him.

He rammed his forearm against the throat of one in front, pinning him against the wall.

Footsteps erupted on the stairs, descending at a run.

He swiveled his neck and marked two men making an escape from the second floor.

One of them carried Kate, her unconscious body dangling over a bulky shoulder, blood dripping from her face.

Heat smothered his brain and blinded his vision.

She'd put up a fight and received a knockout punch for the effort, which meant this wasn't a rescue attempt. It was a kidnapping, and he knew exactly how it would play out.

Her chance of survival was nil.

Rage detonated in his chest and hit the air in a

blistering roar. He seethed, breaths shaking, teeth cutting the insides of his cheeks.

With a surge of strength, he pushed harder against the throat beneath his arm. Holding the knife in his other hand, he buried it in the man's skull, pushed it in to the hilt, and yanked it free.

The body dropped, and he launched for the stairs. Until someone slammed into him from behind.

The wind evacuated his lungs as he collided with the floor, his shirtless chest skidding through shards of glass beneath the weight of the man on his back.

He trained his eyes on the front door, where those dead motherfuckers had just carried out his whole fucking world.

They knew it, too. They knew exactly what she meant to him, because one of his own goddamn guards had tipped them off.

Someone had told them to head straight for the stairs.

An arm hooked around his neck from behind, the heavy drive of a knee against his spine. He shoved his upper body into a push-up, dug in his toes, and dove into a somersault. The man lost his grip and came up swinging.

Fists flew. Elbows. Shins. Bone-crunching smacks. Tiago wouldn't feel the pain from those hits until later. Right now, all he felt was pure, raw aggression, scorching his blood and driving him forward, toward her.

If he didn't get her back, he would burn the whole fucking country to the ground.

Venom seared through him, powering his punches, propelling each strike harder, faster, spraying blood, breaking teeth, bone, and cartilage, until the man

228

slumped to the floor.

Legs quaking, heart thrashing, he grabbed a pistol off a dead body and bolted out the door and into the night.

At the end of the drive, taillights glowed red in the blackness. They already had her in the van. Already driving away.

Bullet holes littered his cars. Tires deflated. Hoods ablaze with fire.

He was too late.

Grief tried to suck him into the earth, but he pushed forward, throwing himself into a burning sprint.

Serrated air sawed in and out of his lungs. He pumped his legs and leveled the gun on the van's tires. Fired. Missed.

As he emptied the magazine, the van sped away, vanishing into the darkness.

He careened to a stop, braced swollen, bloody hands on his knees, and attempted to stymie the insufferable pain closing around his heart. If he let in the anguish, it would kill him.

This wasn't over.

He couldn't fail her.

Her captors would contact him, before or after they killed her. It depended on who they were and what they wanted. He had an hour at most to organize an attack.

First, he needed to find out where the fuck they were taking her.

Spinning, he raced back to the house as his mind pored over what he knew and everything that had just gone down. He recalled faces, accents, weapons, and fighting styles.

They were Mexican cartel.

When he burst through the front door, he barreled into Boones.

"What are you doing out of your room?" He ran his hands over Boones' shirtless torso, front to back, shoulders, legs, his frenzied search fueled by fear.

"Calm down." Boones gripped Tiago's arms, hindering his hunt for injuries. "I'm fine. Not a scratch."

His hands shook as he stepped back and locked onto Arturo's eyes behind Boones. "Search the property for survivors and bring the old truck around from the back. We're going to need it."

"*Si, Jefe.*" Arturo headed toward the door with a rifle.

"Arturo." He waited for eye contact, trying his damnedest not to fall apart in front of his guard. "Thank you for keeping Boones safe."

With a stiff nod, Arturo lumbered out the door.

"We need information." He combed the room littered with dead bodies and found one breathing.

The man lay on his back, his face and stomach soaked in blood as wet gurgling sounds wheezed from his mouth.

Boones stared down at the injured man and ambled toward the kitchen. "I'll get the sharpest knife."

Twenty minutes later, every inch of skin had been flayed from the squealer's chest. He didn't survive the torture, but Tiago now had a location and an identity.

The orchestrator of the attack was the *comandante* of a Mexican cartel. Hungry for money and power, they operated without borders, trafficking worldwide in drugs, prostitution, stolen cars, and contract murders. But it wasn't enough for them.

The *comandante* wanted Tiago's gun smuggling

routes. Tiago had refused every offer and negotiation over the past couple of years, and thus, infuriated the ruthless, brutal man.

A man who now had Kate in his custody.

Tiago rose to his feet and stared down at the gore he'd strewn across the floor. Boiling rage lined his insides and scalded his throat, the taste of death coating his tongue.

During the skin-flaying session, Arturo had returned carrying Blueballs, the only survivor. The tattoo-eyed guard had been shot in the stomach and lived long enough to explain that he, Samuel, and Alonso were on the night shift.

Iliana and Juan had wandered off to fuck when the attackers arrived on foot. While Tiago's guards were picked off one by one, a van showed up. The occupants captured Iliana as she tried to race back to the house.

The same van that had taken Kate.

Blueballs had managed to wheeze out every detail while Boones worked tirelessly to save his life. When he died, Tiago knew Blueballs hadn't betrayed him.

Another concern was Tate, but a check on the video footage of the shack verified Kate's friend hadn't been touched.

The cartel had known exactly *who* to target. They knew Kate's capture and ultimate death would hit the deepest, most vulnerable part of Tiago.

There would be no negotiations.

The *comandante* would make contact in the form of body parts. Proof of Kate's death.

Normal behavior for a violent, power-hungry criminal group.

"You'll get her back." Boones cleaned away the

blood from Tiago's trembling hands and shoved a clean shirt against his chest.

Tiago looked at him and Arturo, the only two left standing.

They seemed nervous amid the storm whipping off him, as if waiting for him to pull his shit together, anxious for a plan.

"Right. Okay. This is what we'll do." He outlined a strategy, called in fifty of his best men in Caracas, and sent them to a small town a couple of hours away, where Kate would be held.

Then he strapped on as many weapons as he could carry and rose out of hiding.

TWENTY-ONE

Taken.

Again.

Kate might've laughed at her absurd misfortune if she weren't so fucking terrified.

Handcuffs shackled her arms behind her, and the hood over her head confined her within a black, sightless world.

Sweat coated her skin, made worse by the chills that came in feverish waves. She licked her cracked lips, tasting blood. Probably from the fist that had knocked her out in Tiago's room.

Where was she? Who had taken her? What happened to Tiago?

She'd woken in the back of a moving vehicle. It had traveled another hour or so before stopping here.

Here was some kind of city, an urban area. She couldn't see through the hood, but she smelled the asphalt, felt the heat of it beneath her bare feet. The sounds of motor traffic rumbled nearby, as well as in the distance.

Men surrounded her, marching along in heavy boots, their deep voices firing words in Spanish.

Her insides buckled to the point of nausea. Her lungs couldn't gather enough air.

The cold metal of guns prodded at her from both sides. When her toes caught on a curb or a crack, someone pushed her from behind.

After a few minutes, the crumbly concrete underfoot smoothed into polished cement, and the scuffing of boots echoed off walls that closed in around her.

She'd just entered a building.

Ushered forward by barking shouts and urgent hands, she was forced into a jog. She imagined a winding hallway with countless turns and stairs going up and down.

With her hands fettered behind her, it fucked with her balance. The whole thing was a stumbling, falling, slipping all-out run to some unknown destination.

Eventually, calloused fingers yanked her to a halt.

More voices. The same ones, new ones, all yelling in Spanish. The scent of motor oil and gasoline permeated the hood, tickling her nose.

"Who are you guys?" She spun around, blind and winded. "Where am I?"

A hand caught her neck, squeezing her airway, strangling. Hot breath saturated the outside of the hood, seeping through the material and heating her face.

Her mouth gulped for oxygen. She couldn't breathe, couldn't escape the choking grip.

He held her there, waited as the very end of her life crashed toward her in a chest-squeezing, lonely, black wave of nothingness.

Alone.

She would die alone.

The collar of fingers released her with a vicious shove that sent her careening across the floor on her back. Boots shuffled out of her way. One of them kicked her into a corner.

She pressed herself there, curling into a ball, gasping for life, and swallowing silent tears.

Time passed in frantic heartbeats. Her pulse hammered for an hour. Maybe two.

The cement floor grew unbearably hard beneath her butt, grinding against her bones. Her legs bare, her body covered in only a shirt, she was overly exposed and unarmed. But still alive.

Not once did she let herself consider the possibility Tiago was dead. He was too untouchable, too impervious. Too goddamn mean to die.

He would hunt her down. Find her. Hopefully, before it was too late.

Footsteps came and went. Others scuffed around her, lingering, guarding. The men never shut up, their voices charged with energy, fear, excitement.

Then she heard a word she recognized.

Comandante.

A horrible feeling overtook her, running chills down her spine. She was already in the worst situation she could imagine. But hearing the mention of a *comandante*, she knew this was either a rebel group or a cartel.

She wouldn't escape this alive.

That suspicion solidified when another set of boots entered the room and paused before her.

The hood lifted, and florescent lighting blinded her eyes. She blinked through the brightness as the cold press of steel caught her beneath the chin.

Her heart stopped.

Holy fucking goddamn, that was a huge fucking knife.

The man holding it crouched before her. Black hair and a mustache, pockmarked cheeks, and soulless eyes, he smelled of cigarettes and torture.

She scanned the surrounding shelves that lined the wall, taking in stacks of machinery, tools, a random tire, and things made of steel. A supply room full of automotive parts? A mechanic shop, maybe.

Nothing within reach to slam into his face. Not that she could with her arms handcuffed at her back.

Another man stood beside her and gathered a fistful of hair on her crown, pulling, elongating her neck.

And she knew.

They were going to cut off her head.

Her insides turned to ice as her mind spun, quickly forming an idea and weaving a bogus story.

"I've been waiting for you guys." She met the eyes of the man with the knife.

He arched a brow.

"Do you speak English?" she asked.

"Yes."

"Take me to the *comandante*." Her bladder threatened to release beneath the force of her almighty fear.

"I am the *comandante*."

Oh God, oh God, oh God.

With a deep breath, she raised her chin above the knife. "I work for Matias Restrepo. Do you know —?"

"Everyone knows Restrepo." His gaze pulsed with interest.

"He planted me inside Tiago Badell's organization. The assignment was to grow close to Badell, become his lover, and wait for your infiltration. Matias Restrepo knew you would capture me, and that you would feel inclined to…uh…" Her teeth chattered. "To send my head to Badell."

The man grinned with yellow teeth. "Go on."

"Restrepo wants you to contact him."

"Why would I do that?"

"Because I have information. Intel I've been gathering on Badell. And because you just extracted me from the hands of Restrepo's enemy, he's now in your debt." She hardened her jaw. "Call him. Tell him you have Kate, and you'll be generously rewarded."

It was a risk. He could just as easily torture her for the intel she boasted about. Of course, she didn't know shit about Tiago's business dealings, so it would be a slow, bloody, horrifically gruesome way to die. Much worse than getting her head sawed off.

But she was offering the *comandante* an opportunity to join forces with Matias Restrepo, an offer no one ever received. She didn't know who this man was in the underground world, but she hoped her bullshit story carried some weight.

If only for a little while.

She just needed to buy some time until Tiago arrived.

Swallowing against the blade, she held the *comandante's* oily gaze. After an eternity of wordless torment, he lowered the knife.

It took everything she had not to pass out in relief.

He rose to his feet and barked a string of Spanish words. The room erupted in a scurry of squeaky boots. Everyone evacuated except the man fisting her hair.

His hand tightened, yanking her forward. She fell with a yelp, her cheek pressed against the cement as he unlocked the shackle on one of her wrists.

Oh, thank fuck.

She rolled her stiff shoulders, started to rise, and heard the clicking sound of handcuffs latching onto something.

"You just saved your head." The *comandante* lingered in the doorway, staring down at her. "Until I reach Restrepo, you are ours to enjoy."

He slipped into the hall, and her stomach turned inside out. She scrambled away from the other man, but the snap of her arm yanked her back.

The son of a bitch had handcuffed her to his wrist.

"This is a mistake." She scooted on her back and stretched her free arm out to the side, floundering for something to grip, a heavy piece of steel, something sharp, anything she could brandish as a weapon. "Restrepo will kill you if you rape me."

Her fingers gripped the leg of a steel shelving unit. She pulled, and he pulled her back by her leg, dragging her across the floor.

At the center of the room, he dropped her feet near the door, dove on top of her, and ripped off her panties with a violating fist.

"No!" She thrashed beneath him, smacking at his greasy face and kicking her legs. "No! Stop! Get off me! You'll regret this."

He was thinner, smaller than Tiago, but still twice her size. She couldn't get leverage, and even if she did, she was fucking handcuffed to his arm. Where would she go?

Didn't stop her from putting up the biggest fight of her life. She went crazy, bucking, screaming, scratching, and biting. She lost her mind, flailing in a fog of desperation and horror.

Seconds felt like hours, and her body started to give out, draining energy fast.

He forced her thighs apart with his knees and unzipped his pants. She released a blood-curdling roar, and his hand clapped over her mouth as his other fisted his swollen dick.

She sank her teeth into his fingers. He bellowed, face red, and reared back his arm.

Her heart slammed. She saw it coming and instinctively closed her eyes, knowing she couldn't dodge the impact.

He made a choking sound, and a hot wet drizzle dripped across her thigh.

She opened her eyes to a sharp object protruding from his chest.

Her brain couldn't make sense of it, and he seemed to share her confusion as he stared down at the serrated steel edge that stuck out several inches beneath his breastbone.

Then it moved, slicking upward in a vertical line, cutting his torso from bottom to top.

Blood poured in a bright red stream from the wound, from his mouth, bubbling down his chin.

She gulped, gulped, gulped, with no sound. No air. Her pulse throbbed so loudly it created a vacuum in her ears.

The blade pulled free. Life leaked from the man's

eyes as he tipped to the side and hit the floor, unblocking her view of the door.

Tiago stood over her, glaring at the dead body before leveling her with force of his terrifyingly potent presence.

A machete dangled from his hand, magnifying the fury and testosterone pouring off him. Brown eyes darkened into hues of feral. Speckles of red splattered the shadows on his face. God, that strikingly beautiful face, all brutal angles, sculpted lines, and dangerous scars.

The air left her lungs in trembling gasps.

He'd abducted her, fucked her, pissed on her, scarred her.

And saved her.

She squeezed her legs together and shook beneath the press of his power. The most arresting kind of power — lawless, savage, protective.

He wore a black leather jacket and jeans, both stained in blood. No telling how many people he'd slaughtered on his way here.

"I've never been more happy to see you." She pulled her feet under her but couldn't stand. Not with her arm handcuffed to the dead body.

Tiago knelt between her legs and trapped her fingers between his and the floor. Then he swung the machete, cutting off the man's hand.

Bile hit her throat. The sight and aroma of so much gore numbed her brain and chilled her from the base of her skull to the tips of her toes.

Wriggling the handcuff from the severed limb, he circled the rotating arm all the way around, which left it unlocked and hanging from her wrist.

"I'll remove this later." He gripped the cuff still

attached to her.

"With a key, I hope."

A big hand lifted to cradle the side of her face, commanding her gaze to his.

"I almost lost you." He swallowed hard.

The jog in his strong, muscular throat reminded her this brutal, hardcore criminal was human.

She'd been taken from him, nearly beheaded and raped, and the starkness in his eyes told her he knew. He knew exactly the sort of horrors she'd just evaded.

"You weren't too late or too slow." She touched her forehead to his, replaying the words he said about his wife's death. "You don't need to put me back together. You didn't fail."

Tilting her chin back with his finger, he scanned her face with a flicker of vulnerability in his eyes. There and gone in a flash, his handsome Venezuelan features went from gentle to stony.

"I killed the man who hit you." He prodded a thumb around the cut near her eye. "Got him on my way in."

"How do you even know—?"

"Did he have a crucifix tattooed on his neck?"

Yeah, he sure did. Tiago must've identified him while she was transported out of the house.

"Don't we need to go?" she asked.

"Arturo," he called over his shoulder.

The burly guard poked his head into the room, held up a finger, and returned to the hall.

"We're waiting." He slid off the backpack that hung from his shoulder and removed a pair of shorts and running shoes. "Put these on."

"Waiting for what?" She pulled on the shorts, sans

underwear.

As she shoved on the sneakers, his hand wandered to her thigh, smoothing over the bandage where he'd cut her.

"There's a gunfight outside." He withdrew his touch and glanced at the door. "Not taking you out there until the numbers have dwindled."

"Gunfight?" She listened for a moment and was met with silence.

"We're deep within the warehouse." He grabbed her hand and stood, lifting her with him. "One of their chop shops."

"Cartel?"

"Yes."

"The *comandante* – "

"Killed him, too."

Before or after the man called Matias Restrepo? Didn't matter at this point. Matias might've been in route here, but he'd still be hours away.

"Hold onto my waistband." He pulled out two handguns and swung the backpack behind him. "We're going to run into some resistance on our way out. Stick to me like glue until I tell you otherwise. Understand?"

"I want a gun."

"No." He turned toward the door.

"Why not?"

"Because you have me," he growled.

"But—"

"If you shoot me in the back, accidentally or deliberately, your chances of escape drop to zero."

Well, shit. She didn't like it, but she understood. Those were his guys out there, fighting and dying under *his* command. They were loyal to him, not her. If he died, she was fucked, with or without a gun.

"We're not returning to the desert, are we?" she asked.

"No."

"Is Tate—?"

"*Jefe.*" Arturo appeared in the doorway and lowered a phone from his ear. "It's time."

"Tate is safe." Tiago gave her his back and adjusted his grip on the pistols. "Hands on my belt."

She curled her fingers around his belt loops, registering the small gun between his tailbone and waistband. Multiple knives strapped to his hips, legs, and boots. Loaded magazines filled every pocket and holster. He was a walking armory.

"Let's go." He charged into the hall.

She did her best to keep up with his long-legged strides. Arturo stepped in behind her, pacing backward to cover the rear.

Her breathing sped up, tripping in her throat as Tiago navigated a maze of never-ceasing turns and stairs.

The muffled report of gunfire alerted her they were getting close, and she silently thanked him for coming for her.

His body felt like steel beneath her hands, shifting and flexing through a seamless glide of muscle. Her gaze traced the sinewy cords in his thick neck, taking in the strength of it, the harsh cut of his rigid jaw, and the profile of a face chiseled in stone.

He was such a devastatingly sexy man. If he were normal and this was normal, she might've told him he was the most beautiful man she'd ever seen.

The boom of guns came in bursts, slowing between each report but growing louder as he crept to a doorway.

It opened to a massive garage crammed with more luxury cars and motorcycles than she could count.

Armed men patrolled the space. Just outside the wall of garage doors waited more men, who fired off sporadic rounds and shouted at one another.

"This is the only way out," he whispered so low she had to strain her ears. "I need to clear the room."

Before she could draw a breath, he was on the move. Arms stretched out before him, he trained the pistols and sidled along the back wall, using his body as a shield in front of her.

The men in the garage didn't spot him creeping amid the shadows. Arturo veered off in the opposite direction, rifle raised, headed toward the huge garage doors.

Her pulse pommeled, her stomach a block of ice, as her fingers dug into Tiago's hips.

He reached a wall covered with small hooks holding keys. Flicking his gaze over it, he examined each one.

What was the plan? Would he steal a car?

He snatched a key, apparently the one he was looking for, given the glimmer in his eyes. Then he pivoted, gripped her arms, and shoved her into a nook between a workbench and concrete wall.

"Stay," he mouthed.

She locked her legs as he spun and blitzed through the garage toward the enemy, his guns up and firing.

Two men went down. Others shot back. He found cover behind an engine block, but the shooters closed in, surrounding him.

On the far side, Arturo hoisted one of the rolling garage doors, letting in a flood of morning light.

TAKE

The distraction allowed Tiago to fire off another kill shot. But more men flooded in, through the open door and from the other side of the garage.

Her heart pounded so hard it made her lightheaded. She felt helpless, useless, her hand clutching her throat as she watched without breath.

Arturo volleyed bullets from the shadows, taking down the men Tiago missed. But there were too many.

They were outnumbered.

Bullets pinged off steel casings and pelleted beautiful cars. Glass shattered. Dying groans sounded from fallen bodies.

Arturo let out an enraged shout, dropping beneath a flurry of fists and losing his gun. A moment later, he found his feet and launched into a bloody brawl with multiple men, punching and choking and spitting blood.

She searched the space around her and spotted a tire iron. Dropping to hands and knees, she crawled to it, curled her fingers around the cold metal, and waited with her heart in her stomach.

Tiago must've run out of ammo, because he chucked his last gun and reached back to free the machete from his backpack.

In a blur of incredible speed and strength, he ran through the half a dozen attackers, taking down the ones with guns.

The din of bullets fell silent, replaced by the panting grunts of hand-to-hand combat.

She trained her eyes on the open garage door and spotted a clear path.

Gripping the dangling handcuff against the tire iron so it wouldn't rattle, she drew in a deep breath and ran.

The shadows along the back wall concealed her escape. No one noticed her. Those who were still alive were fighting to stay that way.

Twenty feet from the exit, Arturo bent over a man, pummeling his fists, over and over. Farther away, Tiago took on three others, slashing the machete with the skill of a professional assassin.

She reached the exit and peered outside.

Bodies scattered the parking lot. The gunfight had moved down the street, and the number of shooters seemed to have been drastically reduced.

Buildings lined the narrow roads. Plenty of places to hide and provide cover as she fled this nightmare.

This was it.

She could make a run for it and find a way to contact Matias.

Her hand slicked around the tire iron as she stepped into the parking lot and tasted the bright light of freedom.

Another step and the space between her shoulder blades itched.

He had come all this way for her. Protected her. Shielded her with his body. And she was bailing on him?

Her chest squeezed, and her throat closed.

Fuck!

She couldn't leave. Not without looking back. Not without seeing him one more time.

TWENTY-TWO

Twisting her neck, Kate scanned the garage behind her. As she honed in on the powerful body laid out on the floor, a sudden coldness hit her core.

She'd expected Tiago to be the only one standing, not face down in blood with a man pounding fist after fist into his ribs.

Her hand squeezed around the tire iron, clanking the handcuffs.

She needed to leave.

Right now.

Tiago stretched an arm toward the machete, but it lay too far out of reach.

Her shoes turned into blocks of cement.

Fucking goddammit!

Across the garage, Arturo wrestled another man in and out of a choke hold. The rest were dead or too injured to move.

Tiago continued to lie there as that fucker pounded fists into his back and ribs. He just took it, his legs twitching as he absorbed every strike.

Her heart cried out, and her molars slammed together, grinding hard enough to break enamel.

Before her brain caught up, her legs were moving, carrying her toward him as fast as she could run.

She was neither stealthy nor strong. But she was quick, approaching the man's back and smacking the tire iron into his head before he knew what hit him.

He toppled over, and she continued to swing, slamming the metal rod into his skull, again and again. She didn't stop hitting until strong arms banded around her, yanking her back, pulling her away.

The weapon fell from her hands, and she turned, stunned so completely she felt as though she were floating outside of her body.

Lifting her head, she stared into Tiago's impossibly gorgeous eyes and swayed. Or maybe the room was swaying.

No, it was him.

She grabbed his leather-clad arms and steadied him. "Are you okay?"

"I am now." He tiptoed ice-cold fingers along her jaw, leaned in, and stopped before their lips made contact. "Got a lot to say and do to you, but we need to go."

A scream sounded from an office-like room in the front of the garage. A woman's scream.

His face tightened, and he bent down to snatch the machete from the floor.

On the other side of the room, Arturo snapped up his head, where he stepped through piles of carnage, stabbing anyone who still lived.

"Who is that?" Kate shifted toward the office.

A slender figure emerged in the doorway. Short black hair. Seductive mouth. Iliana.

Why was she in that room and not fighting alongside the others? Was she hiding?

Iliana spotted Tiago and ran toward him. "*Jefe,* oh my God! You made it!"

He gave Kate's hand a squeeze and prowled ahead, toward the approaching woman, slowly, stiffly, letting the machete hang from his lolling fingers.

Was he tilting a little to the side?

Blood covered him from head to toe. His clothes were an utter mess and would need to be burned, but there weren't any concentrated stains. Nothing to indicate the blood was coming from him.

As she studied his gait, he seemed steady. Strong. He'd taken a helluva beating and was probably in a world of hurt.

"I was so afraid they got you." Iliana raced toward him and raised her arms, as if to embrace him.

Two steps away, he stopped, flexed his hand. Then he ran the blade of the machete through her stomach and out the back.

Her mouth gaped, eyes wide with shock as she doubled over the hilt.

He twisted it, gave it a hard shove, and yanked it free.

Kate cupped a hand over her mouth to smother a whimper. What the unholy fuck?

When Iliana hit the floor, he wiped the blade on her shirt and jeans until it was clean. That done, he rose and stalked toward Kate.

Her heart pounded as she shuffled back. "Why?"

"She betrayed me." He strode past her, grabbed

her hand, and hauled her with him. "She took you from me."

"How do you know?"

"Why do you think she tried so hard to get in my bed?" He veered toward a row of motorcycles, his gaze sweeping over each one. "She was feeding information to the cartel."

"Why would she do that?"

"Money. Protection. Who knows? Maybe they were holding something over her." He punched something into his phone and pocketed it.

"That's how they found you in the desert."

"And how they knew you were important to me."

Her chest constricted. "You knew she was a traitor all this time?"

"No." He paused beside the biggest, meanest-looking bike and inserted the key from his pocket. "I'm suspicious in nature. Never trusted her. When she vanished after you were taken, I knew."

So he killed her.

There was a time, not too long ago, when he would've run that blade through Kate.

He removed the backpack from his shoulders, stored the machete in it, and strapped it onto her back.

"Arturo!" he shouted across the garage. "You good?"

"Never been better." The guard strode toward the open garage door, his face a mask of blood as he took off in the direction of lingering gunfire.

Tiago mounted the motorcycle and fired up the engine. "Hop on."

"Helmets?"

"Afraid not."

"Shouldn't we take one of the sports cars, instead?"

"If we're chased, this is the best option." His eyes turned flinty. "I'm getting impatient."

Grateful he'd brought her a pair of shorts and shoes, she swung a leg over the huge hunk of steel and scooted in behind him.

The handcuff on her wrist caught against his leather jacket as she wrapped her arms around his chest.

He tensed and adjusted her hold to squeeze him lower around his abs. Then he zoomed out of the garage, polluting the air with a hard rev of the engine.

Turning in the opposite direction of the gunfight, he hit the narrow streets at a speed that stole her breath.

Her hair whipped around her head, her body bending with his as he ducked low, his face protected by the small windshield.

She tucked in tight against his back and squinted her eyes away from the blasts of air. The sun sat just over the horizon, the humidity clinging to her pores despite the constant lashing of wind.

He didn't slow. Not through stop signs or intersections. He raced out of the small, concrete town scattered with sagging buildings and minimal traffic and arrowed into a thick copse of trees.

The winding road snaked through a jungle-like terrain. Twenty minutes in, asphalt turned to dirt, and civilization faded behind her.

Did he know where he was going?

She clenched her arms around his waist, blinking through the windblown tangles of her hair.

Another twenty minutes zipped by, taking them deeper into the tropical wilderness of massive trees and hanging vines.

He'd stopped maintaining a constant speed. The motorcycle slowed, sped up, teetered a little, and thrust forward again.

Why did he feel so rigid in her arms?

Slipping a hand under his zipped jacket, she followed the grooves of his hard stomach to his chest. He felt really cold and sweaty through the shirt. His breaths heaved shallowly, erratically against her palm.

Then her fingers encountered wetness.

She yanked her hand back and held it up.

Blood.

"Tiago!" She grabbed his arm. "Stop the bike."

"Almost there."

"How far?" she shouted into the gust.

"Two hours."

"You'll be dead by then!"

He hit the gas, refusing to stop. The next mile blurred by. And another. Then the bike wobbled.

She held onto his waist, eyes closed, bracing for impact. But he kept them upright and found a turnoff, veering onto a trail and slowing through overgrown foliage.

Woody branches scratched her bare legs as he eased them to a stop without crashing.

She jumped off and spun in a circle, scanning the surroundings.

Trees. More trees. So much green and buzzing insects and endless nature. They were in a fucking jungle, without doctors or medical supplies.

"What the actual fuck, Tiago?" She whirled on him. "Were you shot? Stabbed?"

He killed the engine, slid off the bike, and walked to a nearby clearing. "Just need to sit for a second."

His gait was wrong, lacking his usual power and confidence. He stumbled into a lopsided step, and she raced to his side, hooking his arm over her shoulders and lowering him to the ground.

Kneeling before him, she shrugged off the backpack and inspected his face.

Clammy complexion, pained eyes, sinful lips, he looked so damn beautiful, even in agony.

"Where's your phone?" She patted the front pockets of his jeans. "Need to call Boones."

"Already sent him an alert. My phone has a tracker. He'll find us."

A smidgen of relief loosened her shoulders.

"I have to remove your jacket." She yanked down the zipper.

The instant she wrangled it off his arms, her heart plunged to her sneakers.

Multiple stab wounds gouged his shoulder, and it looked like a bullet went through the side of his chest. And the blood... God, she could taste the gravity of it on her tongue.

No wonder he'd moved her arms to his waist when she mounted the bike.

"Why didn't you tell me?" She ripped his t-shirt down the front, carefully removed it from his body, and shredded strips of it to use as bandages.

"The knife wounds are superficial, and the bullet just grazed my side."

"Why is there so much blood?"

"You were going to run."

The rapid change of subject stammered her breath, and she dragged her gaze to his. "What?"

"At the warehouse. You started out the garage

door. But you came back. You chose *me*." His voice broke on the last word, at odds with the smug look in his eyes.

"Don't misunderstand me. I want my freedom back." She tore open the backpack and dug through weapons, searching for medical supplies. "Do you have anything in here — ?"

The *click-click-click* of metal yanked her attention to her wrist.

The open end of the handcuffs, which had hung from her arm a moment ago, was now shackled around his.

She pulled, and his hand came with it, snug within the cuff. Locked. "You did *not* just do that."

"I'm not letting you go." His eyes hooded, heavy with pain, but his timbre carried all the weight of a possessive, overbearing man.

"Where's the key?"

"Don't have it."

"What if you die?" Outrage screeched into her voice.

"Not gonna die."

"You're bleeding all over the fucking place, and I don't even know if the bullet is still in you."

"Check the jacket." He lowered to his back and dropped his unshackled arm across his forehead.

She snatched the pile of leather, swinging his cuffed hand around with hers as she hunted for a bullet hole.

There it was, a tiny tear in the back of the jacket. How had she missed that?

A knife had cut up his shoulder pretty good, but the leather wasn't torn all to hell. The jacket must've been hanging open, which meant he'd zipped it later to hide the wounds from her.

Grinding her teeth, she ripped up the rest of his shirt and stared at the battlefield on his chest. "I don't know what to do."

"There's a first-aid kit at the bottom of the backpack."

He talked her through how to clean and dress the injuries. There was enough gauze to wrap the wounds, and his instructions were precise and calm. Given the number of scars on his body, he knew his way around an injury.

"How long before Boones arrives?" She wadded up the jacket and propped it under his head.

"Don't know." His voice took on an edge of pain. "An hour-ish. Maybe more."

"What about Arturo?"

"He went to the desert with another guard. Need them there to look after Tate."

Tiago could've just freed Tate and eliminated that complication, but this was neither the time nor place for that argument.

"Can we call someone else?" She used the extra pieces of the shirt to clean his mouth, cheeks, and neck.

"No." He lay on his back and stared up at her, the look on his face *not* like a man who lost a lot of blood.

His tongue peeked out, wetting his lips, his gaze alert and watchful. Always watching, staring as if he were seconds from swallowing her whole.

"You must be hurting." *And delirious.* She rummaged through the first-aid kit. "Do you have anything to dull the pain?"

"You."

"Get real."

"*You* are going to take the edge off."

She let out a tight laugh and glanced down. He wasn't even hard.

His eyes lost focus through a long, slow blink, as if he were fighting to stay awake. "Sit on my cock."

"You've lost your damn mind. How can you think about that right now? You just killed like fifty men, drove an hour on a motorcycle while bleeding and half-dead. Not to mention you don't even have enough blood in your body to get it up. Oh, and we're probably surrounded by snakes, spiders, and random other venomous—"

"Shut the fuck up, Kate." His pale lips failed to form the *T* in her name.

"Shit." She reached for the red-soaked gauze on the side of his chest. "You're still bleeding."

"Apply pressure." His voice was weak, reedy. He was fading fast.

Flattening her hands against the wound, she pressed hard and held it. His lashes lowered, hiding the agony in his eyes.

"Tiago." She didn't know if his injuries were life-threatening, but keeping him awake seemed important. "Stay with me, dammit."

His eyes snapped open, sharpened, drilling into hers. "Need to tell you something."

"What?"

"I love you."

Her heart skipped. "You're insane."

"Love is insanity."

Desperate to keep him alert and talking, she leaned in and asked, "What do you love about me?"

"First off..." He lifted his unshackled hand to her

face. "Everything."

His eyes fluttered shut, and his arm dropped.

Passed out.

TWENTY-THREE

I love you?

Kate blew out a ragged breath.

Maybe those words would've meant something if Tiago weren't caught in the delirium of blood loss, but right now, he didn't know what he loved.

"Tiago." Pressing against his wound with one hand, she pried open his eyes with the other. "Wake up."

Nothing.

Her nerves rioted, quickening her pulse. "Tiago!"

When he didn't stir, her anxiety burned to anger.

She was shackled in the middle of a jungle in Venezuela. At any moment, she could be ambushed by a rebel group, attacked by a man-eating panther, or strangled by an anaconda.

If he died…

She eyed the machete sticking out of his backpack, recalling how he'd freed her from the last dead body.

Fucking hell, she didn't have the stomach for that.

"Wake up!" she shouted in his face.

Was he even breathing? Her heart raced as she scanned him for signs of life.

"Damn you, Tiago. Nothing says *I love you* like handcuffing me to your dead body." She pressed shaky fingers against the pulse point on his throat, panicking. "This is sick and fucking twisted, even for you."

A breath huffed past his lips, and he cracked open an eye.

"I'm not dead." He shifted, groaning in pain. "Would drag my ball sac through ten miles of broken glass for another chance to be inside you."

"Oh my God." She groaned with a mix of relief and annoyance.

"You're so beautiful." His eyes glossed over and faded beneath the descent of thick lashes.

"No, no, no. You need to stay awake."

"Did you fuck me unconscious?" The corner of his mouth crooked, but his eyes remained closed.

"You wish. Where's your phone?"

"Boones will come." A slurring whisper.

"Before or after you die?"

No answer.

She gripped his square jaw. Too slack. Too cold. Too unconscious.

Fuck.

If he survived this, she was going to kill him.

She eased the leather jacket from beneath his lolling head and located his phone in the pocket. It was locked, of course, with a passcode she couldn't hack. She couldn't even tell if there was a signal.

What if they were in a dead zone? Was cell service required for tracking?

She checked the bullet wound, and it appeared to

stop bleeding. Turning her attention to the backpack, she removed all the knives and tried each one on the handcuffs. None of them made a dent in the chain. Not even the machete.

She tried to pick the lock. That only ended in cursing, screaming hysterics.

Her mouth felt like stale toast, despite the mugginess in the air. There was no water, no way to hydrate. She hadn't had anything to drink since last night.

Out of options, she turned her anger to the unconscious man at her side. "I hate you."

The words tasted sour and made her stomach hurt.

She needed to hate him, but she couldn't. She needed him to live, because if he didn't, she would feel that loss in ways she didn't want to examine.

An ache burned the backs of her eyes, and her chest caved beneath the constriction of fear.

"Don't die." She stretched out beside him and snuggled in under his uninjured shoulder, pressing herself so tightly against him she felt the slow thud of his heartbeat.

"Don't you dare give up." She buried her face into his neck and let the tears fall.

With her free hand clinging to the hilt of the machete, she forced herself to stay awake, her awareness heightened with every rustle and buzz in the jungle.

As the residual effects of adrenaline abandoned her, exhaustion barreled in. She fought the overpowering need to close her eyes, perking her ears, watching the trail, waiting.

When the rumble of a distant engine broke the silence, she shot to her feet and heaved the machete out in front of her.

Her pulse exploded as the vehicle approached. It could be anyone. Someone more interested in killing Tiago than saving his life.

A van emerged through the trees, slowing on the road at the entrance of the trail. Twenty feet away.

Only the front of the vehicle had windows, and through the glass, she made out two faces.

Faces she didn't recognize.

Her hands shook as she planted her feet on either side of his body, crouching over him and holding out the machete.

The arm connected to hers limited her range of motion, but she had a weapon. Multiple knives. They would have to go through her to get to him.

The doors opened and shut. Her muscles trembled with enough force to stop her heart.

"Don't come any closer!" She adjusted her grip on the hilt and bit down on her cheek, sawing through tender tissues.

Footsteps approached. Big men, wearing sunglasses, heavy boots, and armed to the gills with holstered guns and knives.

They didn't run at her. Didn't free their weapons and start shooting.

"Who are you?" she shouted. "What do you want?"

A creak sounded near the van. The back door closed, and a tall, gray-headed, black man emerged on the trail.

The warm, familiar face swarmed her with overwhelming emotion. The surge crashed through her so violently she nearly fell beneath the weight of it.

The machete tumbled into the foliage, and she buckled over, giving into the sobs that piled in her throat.

Boones reached her side and gripped the handcuffs on her wrist, staring at the link to Tiago's arm. She didn't know what she expected, but it wasn't the laughter that burst from his chest.

The comforting sound of it combined with the gentle squeeze of his fingers around hers reduced her to a hot mess of sobbing, laughing, maniacal hiccups.

"He's lost so much blood." She sobered and quickly walked him through the gruesome points of Tiago's injuries.

The other two men gathered the backpack and weapons, and two minutes later, they had Tiago in their arms, up the trail, and laid out on his back in the rear of the van.

The handcuffs pulled her along. Boones joined her in the cargo space, which was loaded with multiple medical bags and equipment.

As much as she wanted the damn manacle off her wrist, she didn't mention it as Boones went to work on Tiago's wounds.

The light in the roof illuminated his steady scalpel and meticulous stitches, his face aglow with remarkable concentration.

She found a case of water amid the supplies and guzzled three bottles. She used another to wet Tiago's lips and clean the blood from his body.

As Boones taped on the bandages, she filled him in on the events at the warehouse, explaining how things ended with Iliana.

He caught her up on what happened during the attack at the house. The news that Arturo was the only surviving guard hit her harder than she expected.

When Boones finished the last bandage, he nodded at the driver waiting in the front seat.

The engine rumbled to life, and the van shot into motion, speeding toward Caracas.

She took in Tiago's rapid breathing, slack face, and bruised body, willing him to look at her. But his lashes didn't stir.

It tightened her chest. "Is he going to live, Dr. Frankenstein?"

Boones cut his eyes at her, his expression disgruntled.

"You didn't create the monster." She clutched Tiago's limp hand, linking their fingers. "But you've been patching him up for twelve years."

"He's not a monster."

Flashbacks of the past few hours peppered her mind in blood and bullets. "He is when he needs to be."

His face softened, relaxing the scars on his cheeks. "I've been his accomplice through it all. He will always have my support, even when he makes mistakes."

"He's made a lot of mistakes, Boones. Just in the past couple of months. With *me*."

"Yes, but he'll learn from them. I don't always agree with his actions, but I believe in him." He crooked a finger at her. "Let me look at you."

She scooted around Tiago's body and let Boones clean the injury on her face. Then he removed the bandages on her thigh. His body language gave nothing away as he cleaned the swirling cuts and applied a tingling cream.

"It's beautiful, isn't it?" She searched his eyes.

"Yes." He redressed her leg with clean bandages.

"You're healing him."

"What do you mean?"

"He's been hurting for a long time. I can only heal the body. But you..." He clutched her hand and placed it against Tiago's chest. "You heal the rest."

She didn't know about that, but there was one milestone she could share with him.

"He's giving up the kidnapping business." At the widening of his eyes, she felt a shimmer of pride. "He made that deal with me last night."

Boones studied her with an unreadable expression. Then a smile broke through. "See? You're good for him."

She nodded, accepting the truth in that. "So how about helping me out of these handcuffs?"

"Not a chance." He turned to his medical supplies and started putting things away.

"Why not?"

"He secured you that way for a reason, and they will stay until he decides to remove them."

Dammit.

"You didn't answer my first question." She took in Tiago's pallid complexion and the bandages that covered half of his torso. "He's going to live, right?"

"He's very lucky. If the bullet hit anywhere else on his chest, even just slightly to the left, it would've damaged organs or bones. Surgery in a van is less than ideal."

"He would've died."

"Yes."

"What about the blood loss?"

"No arteries were nicked. He'll be weak for a while, but he'll recover. The priority right now is getting him to safety."

The hairs on her nape lifted. "Are we in danger?"

"He's a wanted man." He stared down at Tiago's face with a troubled look. "There will always be danger."

She considered the long list of enemies he'd acquired over the years. No matter what he did going forward, he would never escape what he'd done.

"He can't leave this life, can he?" She swallowed. "Even if he wanted to?"

"When he avenged my daughter's death, he was labeled as a criminal and forced to live like one. He's safer here, among other criminals, than out there in normal society. Here, in the heart of hell, he's protected."

She shivered at what his words meant. What they meant for *her*. If she didn't escape, his violent world would become her life. If she managed to get away, she would lose him.

"Are we going to his compound?" she asked. "That's where he lives, right?"

"He *did*."

"What does that mean?"

"I'm taking you to his penthouse in Caracas."

"He has a penthouse?" She couldn't imagine it.

"It's a luxury he owns but never indulged in. He kept it for my brothers and me. He didn't want us sleeping in the filth of his slum, and he doesn't want you sleeping there, either."

"No more mattresses on the floor?"

"He has a very nice, very large bed in the penthouse that has never been slept in." He cast her a knowing look. "Or used in any way."

She refused to acknowledge his response and held up her shackled arm. "What happens when we get there and I need to pee?"

TAKE

"Hold it or release it. The handcuffs stay on."

TWENTY-FOUR

Tiago woke to the immaculate face of an angel. She floated over him, her vivid blue eyes backlit by a halo of golden hair. The seam of her cupid lips separated, and he wanted nothing more than to hear her voice, taste her kiss, and lose himself in her ferocity.

"I must be dead." Confusion poked at his muddled brain. "Except angels don't exist in hell."

"Not dead." The angel scowled. "But you should be."

Kate.

Alive.

Relief cut through the dull pain in his chest. "Where are we?"

"The garage of your penthouse." She leaned to the side, revealing the interior of a cargo van.

At the rear, Boones stood in the open doors, flanked by two men. Tiago didn't know them, but he trusted Boones to choose only the best for his personal security.

There would always be traitors, but Iliana's death should serve as a deterrent for the time being.

He flexed his arms and rolled his neck, testing his strength and mobility. Muscles protested, but the pain didn't make him want to hurl his guts. Definitely an improvement from the jungle.

"What's the damage?" He glanced down at his torso but could only see clean bandages.

"You'll live." Boones stepped back and motioned at the men. "They're going to carry you up."

"Fuck that." He pushed to a sitting position and swayed beneath an onslaught of vertigo.

"Tiago." Kate gripped the metal bracelet on his wrist and tugged at the other half still attached to her. "Remove the handcuffs. It'll be easier if you're not dragging me along beside you."

No way would he release her until she was safely locked behind the doors of the penthouse.

Shifting to the rear of the van, he lowered his boots to the ground, rose to his full height, and waited for the dizziness to pass.

The walk to the elevator was a short trip of staggering steps, grabbing hands, and glowering disapproval. Most of the scowls came from Kate, but her fingers gripped his arm with the kind of support no one could give him but her.

By the time he entered the top floor, his body was drenched in sweat and the pain had morphed into a fire-breathing entity inside his chest.

"Idiot," Boones said in his native tongue and walked past him, heading toward the master bedroom.

"If the roles were reversed..." She trudged along beside him, surveying the contemporary interior of the penthouse. "I'd be draped over your shoulder like a caveman's whore."

"Give me a couple of hours, and I'll carry you like that again." He caught himself on the doorframe of the master bedroom.

"A couple of hours?" She gaped at him. "You're going to be in bed for days. Maybe weeks."

He refused to admit she was right.

The rush of water sounded from the master bath as he forced his heavy feet across the bleached wood flooring.

Bold, colorful artwork punctuated the white walls, and the sleek, minimalist furniture satisfied his modern aesthetic. The penthouse didn't drip in gold accents or conform to the lavish styles of a moneyed Venezuelan, but it was exorbitant, nonetheless.

"I ran a hot bath." Boones stepped out of the en suite. "Use it, but keep your chest above the water."

A bath sounded perfect, especially with the woman handcuffed to his arm.

"You can't leave the penthouse." Boones ambled toward the hall. "No one knows you're in Caracas, and it needs to stay that way until you're recovered."

Because of Kate.

Word of Tiago's return would spread, and when that happened, Matias Restrepo and Cole Hartman would learn her location.

Tiago had planned for this complication upon his return, but those plans hadn't included getting shot and stabbed.

He needed to meet with the biggest, most powerful constituents in his network, attend their parties, and prove to them he was still strong and undefeated. Only then could he petition them for their support in keeping her friends out of Caracas. If he didn't, Matias Restrepo would snake his way in and turn the entire city against Tiago.

"I want you in bed after the bath." Boones gripped the doorframe, looking as tired as Tiago felt. "Breakfast will be brought in shortly."

"Thanks, Boones."

The penthouse had a full-service staff, such as an on-site maid, cook, and personal guards who had been here for Boones since the beginning.

Tiago owned the entire building, and the security was the best money could buy. No one could penetrate these walls without getting blown to bits in the process.

He made his way to the desk in the corner of the bedroom, with Kate keeping pace at his side. She angled toward the nearby window that overlooked the violence, poverty, and despair of the slums below.

"It's weird." Her brows pinched as she took in the view of crumbling concrete and rusted metal roofs. "The top floor of this building feels like a palace, and it stares down at *that*. It feels wrong."

He agreed, which was why he'd never stayed a single night here. He deserved to be down there amid the strife and misery, but she didn't.

"When the economy went to shit, many of Venezuela's aristocratic families moved to Miami, including the untouchable *enchufados*." He dug through the desk drawer and grabbed a paper clip. "I bought this abandoned tower for a steal and fortified it to keep Boones and his brothers safe."

"Do you think Boones will ever go home to be with his brothers?"

"No. I've tried to make him leave. He's stubborn."

She nodded, her expression contemplative. "What now?"

"Bath, food, sleep. In that order." Forcing his heavy feet across the room, he pulled her along.

When he reached the massive tub, steam rose from the water, infused with the calming scent of Boones' herbs. She hung back, as far as the handcuffs allowed, and shifted her weight from foot to foot.

"What's the problem?" he asked.

"I need to pee."

He pivoted, somewhat clumsily, and led her to the toilet. "Sit."

"How about you use that paper clip you're hiding in your fist and unlock the handcuffs?"

Christ, she was perceptive. And sexy as fuck.

If he weren't seconds from face-planting on the marble floor, he would plant his face between her gorgeous legs.

Instead, he hardened his expression in silent command.

Her glare sparked with objections as she kicked off her shoes, shoved off the shorts, and plopped down on the toilet with an urgent release of her bladder.

While she peed, he stripped his clothes from the waist down. He was already shirtless, but every movement ignited an inferno in his shoulder. He gripped the edge of the counter and breathed through the pain until it passed.

"If you removed the handcuffs, I could help you into the bath." She hit the flusher and stood.

"You're getting in with me."

A tsunami of resistance came at him, emanating

from her rigid posture.

He nudged her to the side, braced a straight arm on the wall above the toilet, and used his shackled hand to angle his dick while he peed.

She watched for a second before pressing her lips together and looking away.

"I want to piss all over your tight little pussy," he said, just to further ruffle her feathers.

She ground her teeth.

"I'm going to cut you again." His tone was flippant, but there was nothing casual about his intentions. He meant every word.

She tensed. "Can we just…not have this conversation right now? I don't have the emotional bandwidth for it and could really use a couple of days without any blood or violence."

The cynical side of him wanted to push her even more, but there was a stronger impulse to do something completely foreign. She needed rest as much as he did, and he felt an overwhelming need to simply take care of her.

He flushed the toilet and led her to the edge of the bath.

Adjusting the paper clip in his hand, he bit the end of it and made a dent. A quick twist inside the keyhole on her bracelet released the ratchets of teeth.

When the cuff swung open, she yanked her arm free and rubbed her wrist.

"Remove the shirt." He picked the lock on his and set the handcuffs aside.

She obeyed without argument and stood before him wearing only the bandages on her thigh.

Crouching to one knee, he peeled away the medical

tape and unwound the gauze. A fresh sheen of ointment coated the clean incisions. Boones must've treated her on the way here.

Tiago took his time examining her, admiring his work, and memorizing the stunning contrast of deep red lines against her pale skin. Then his gaze drifted to the flawless shape of her body, traveling along the sexy curves of her hips and smooth undersides of her pert tits.

He leaned in and skimmed his nose along her flat stomach. Her fingers feathered through his hair, and the soothing contact made him lightheaded.

Too soon, her touch retreated. She stepped into the water and held out a hand, offering to help him in.

The gesture surprised him, and for a moment, he didn't know what to do with it. She was too nude to conceal a weapon. Maybe she intended to drown him. But even in his weakened state, she would never be able to overpower him.

Perhaps she was just tired and wanted to get this over with.

He rose to his feet, gripped her offered hand, and lowered into the water.

Shifting to face him, she fit her legs on the outside of his and straddled his thighs. Then she went to work, lathering a washcloth with soap and cleaning his arms and the exposed skin around the bandages.

Assuaging fingers washed every inch of him, her mouth a kiss away as she finished her task with concentrated focus.

"Careful, Kate." He sank deeper into the water, his body giving into the tranquilizing comfort. "I might get the impression you care."

"Well, don't. I have Stockholm syndrome."

"You sure about that?"

"When I stepped into that parking lot with no guards, no shackles, and no confinement, freedom was right there." A tumult of emotions scrunched her features before settling into the vertical grooves between her eyes. "All I had to do was run. I wasn't even thinking about your threat against my friends. I want to escape that badly. But I didn't." She stared at her hands. "I looked back."

His pulse thumped in memory. He'd sensed her escape from across the garage and started to go after her. The distraction had earned him a knife in the shoulder and a crippling drop to the floor. If she hadn't come back for him, he would still be lying there. Dead.

She lifted her head and wrecked him with her crystal blue gaze. "This isn't real. It's just my mind's way of coping."

A fist of hurt slammed through his chest, one he'd earned through a lifetime of destructive choices. "What do you feel when you're with me?"

"Fear."

"What else?"

"Physical attraction. Desire. But you already know that."

"You don't think those feelings are real?"

"I don't know. It's not just that. I…" She closed her eyes, drew in a breath, and looked at him. "I feel protective of you, like I would choose your life over all else. I mean, I already did. I chose you over my freedom, and it doesn't make sense. If that's not Stockholm syndrome, I don't know what is."

He hated it, fucking despised her assessment of the intrinsic tether between them. But he knew what he was

276

and what he'd done to her. Expecting her to hand over her heart to a warped bastard was inconceivable.

That didn't, however, change his feelings for her.

"You're probably right." He toyed with a lock of wet blond hair that curled around her nipple. "But *I* don't have Stockholm syndrome. For me, this doesn't get any more real."

Her expression fell. "You only feel that way because I'm the first person you've had sex with in twelve years."

"No, Kate. You're the one I had sex with *because* I love you."

A quivering twitch pulled at her mouth, and her gaze dropped to the carving on her thigh. "You can't love me. If you did, you would let me go."

"Bullshit. You're fucking essential, as necessary as water, air, and blood. I can't give you up." He gripped her chin, pulling her face to his. "If you truly love someone, you don't let them go without a fight."

"Even if not letting me go makes me miserable?"

"Are you? Miserable?"

"I have no freedom, no independence, no rights." Resentment leeched her voice, sucking the calmness from her words. "If you loved me, you would at least let me leave the penthouse to take a walk or—"

"Absolutely not. You would be kidnapped within seconds."

"Kidnapped by people like you? Or taken by my friends?"

"Both. If Matias Restrepo found you, do you know what he would do?" He clamped a hand around her nape, seizing her gaze. "He would confine you to his compound in Colombia, with no way to leave, no access to the outside world, no freedom."

"He would only do that so you couldn't take me again!"

"Think through that, Kate. He doesn't want me to take you from him. I don't want him to take you from me. Same. Fucking. Thing."

"He's never hurt me."

"No, he hasn't. He's safe, because you don't owe each other anything. Is that what you want? To spend the rest of your life surrounded by risk-free bets? If that's the case, stay far the fuck away from love. Growing close to someone, becoming attached to them, that shit doesn't come with a guarantee." His voice roughened, haunted by the reality of his past. "There's no guarantee they'll outlive you or love you back. It's a fucking risk that could end in a lifetime of hurt."

Her breath cut off as she searched his face. He didn't expect her to risk anything for him, but he knew she felt something. He wasn't alone in this unfathomable connection.

"I hate when you say things that make sense." Her heavy exhale cumbered the space between them. "It feels manipulative."

Fatigue fanned in lines from the corners of her eyes and hunched her shoulders. The conversation wasn't helping.

"Come here." He guided her to lie against his uninjured shoulder and used the washcloth to clean away the long night.

When he started to shampoo her hair, she took over, lathering and rinsing and teasing him with all that velvety blonde cascading around her arms and back.

She was such a pleasure to watch. The fluidity in

her movements, the nuances of her expressions, and the sweeping dips and arches of her nude form—all of it sent a rush through his veins, invigorating him.

"If I knew then what I knew now…" He let his head fall back on the edge of the tub, regarding her beneath the weight of his eyelids. "I would do things differently."

"Like what?"

Everything.

No, not everything.

He would never regret taking her.

"I'm sorry you didn't see Tate before we left the desert." He handed her a towel from the rack beside the tub.

"Me too." She rose from the water and dried off. "I know you can't go back now that the house is compromised, but doesn't that mean he's in danger there?"

"He's safely hidden behind a monastery." He grabbed a towel and followed her out of the tub. "No one will find him unless they're looking for him."

Once they had a full sleep, he would show her another video and ease some of her worry.

In the bedroom, a tray of breakfast food steamed from beneath metal domes. They ate quickly. Then he directed her into the massive bed and slid in behind her. She didn't roll toward him but didn't pull away, either.

Lying on his uninjured side, he tucked her backside into the bend of his hips and held her close.

Within minutes, her breathing evened into the steady rhythm of sleep. Every bone and muscle in his body thrummed to join her in slumber, but his mind refused to shut down.

With his entire world in his arms, he lay awake and made plans.

TWENTY-FIVE

Recovering from a gunshot wound was a bitch.

Tiago should've been thankful the through and through injury had missed bones, arteries, and internal organs. It healed fast, and within three weeks, he could move the damaged flesh and muscle without nauseating pain.

But three weeks of recovery meant no exercise and no leaving the penthouse.

Word had gotten out he'd fled the gunfight on a motorcycle. Since that was the last time he was seen, there were all sorts of rumors in the air about his inability to maintain his power in Caracas.

Many assumed he was too weak or too dead to be a threat. His allies dwindled with every meeting, dinner, and party he failed to attend, no matter what excuses he gave.

His rivals launched attacks against his operational locations and smuggling routes, thinking they could overtake his syndicate. His men managed to hold their ground, but the constant fighting was wearing on them.

Still, he wasn't ready to announce his location. Not until he was one-hundred-percent confident the city and its constituents would stand against Matias Restrepo when the capo attempted to retrieve Kate.

Tiago spent his days on the phone, barking orders, making deals, rallying new supporters, and repairing relationships in the criminal underground. Business as usual.

His evenings, however, belonged to a blonde spitfire.

Blindfolded and naked, she lay face up on the bed, with rope crisscrossing her body from neck to feet.

She hadn't gone into the restraints easily. After all her thrashing and cursing, he could still feel the burning scratches from her nails on his face.

"Untie me! Right now!" Her hands flexed under the net of knots as she swung her head, trying to knock off the blindfold. "Where are you, motherfucker?"

Across the bedroom, he reclined against the wall and devoured her sublime anger.

The redder her skin flushed, the faster his heart beat. The louder she screamed, the harder his cock grew. He should go to her, calm her, but he couldn't stop staring at the beauty of her distress.

He might as well have been a psychopath. Most of the time, he could control his urges and find a release valve in his workouts. But without exercise, he didn't have a way to burn off the need for pain.

Did he think about whipping her, spanking her, applying clamps or constriction bands?

Nah. Not his thing.

Did he want to cut her skin, piss on her tits, and

insert needles into her tender female parts?

Fuck, yes.

Blood, come, and urine — any or all of it covering Kate's body made him painfully hard.

"Tiago!" She tried to arch her back but couldn't gain a millimeter in the restraints. "I won't surrender to this, you son of a bitch. Let me go!"

Although she had no idea what he had planned, she still wasn't receptive.

In his estimation, it took some level of mental scarring for a person to be open to the indulgences of a sadist.

He didn't buy into the delusion of a power exchange that was prevalent in the BDSM community. People abused those positions of power, and he was no different.

Kate was smart enough to understand this, and maybe that was why she wanted no part of it.

That didn't mean he would change. Not that he could, even if he wanted to. He was warped beyond hell, with warped problems that had no simple solutions.

But none of that mattered tonight. The sexiest, most desirable woman in the world was trussed up in his bed, and he intended to put a smile on her angelic face. And maybe a few tears.

Pushing off the wall, he prowled toward her on soundless feet. With the blindfold on, she didn't sense his approach, didn't know he leaned over her until he fisted her hair and yanked her lips to his.

She gasped at the sudden contact, and he swept his tongue in with hungry lashes, kissing her hard and deep. His need for her raged, and he didn't hold back.

His hands went everywhere, pulling, bruising, and

grabbing at her beneath the rope. He consumed her lips, licked the graceful column of her neck, and sucked the rise of her perfect breasts before returning to her mouth.

She whimpered beneath the harsh strokes of his tongue, fighting and yielding, giving and taking, drowning and resuscitating, and no doubt hating him to the end of hell and back.

People like him should never fall in love. His wife couldn't reciprocate. Kate was smart enough to guard her heart. But it was too late for him.

He loved her at a deadly, explosive, unstoppable level.

He came up for air, his mouth hovering a fraction away.

"Please, Tiago." She panted. "I need to see."

"The blindfold stays." From the bedside drawer, he removed the jewelry he'd sterilized and the supplies he needed. "I have three gifts for you. The first one will make you angry as hell."

"I'm already angry." Her chest heaved, causing the rope to pinch her tits. "Gifts are supposed to make people happy."

"This might bring you happiness someday."

"Oh God." Her face paled. "You're going to cut—?"

"Shhh." He pressed a finger against her mouth and sat on the bed beside her hip. "No cutting tonight."

She looked so breathtakingly erotic lying there on her back, with her legs and arms tied to the mattress.

He'd stretched the rope across her torso in an X pattern that made her breasts accessible while preventing movement in her core. She couldn't lift or twist or do anything below the neck.

He leaned down, examining the three new cuts that sketched along the side of her ribs. He'd added those swirls a week ago, without her consent. Nothing like the one on her leg, the small carvings had only taken minutes, just a few quick turns of his blade before he'd buried himself inside her.

"What are you doing?" Fear trickled into her voice.

He pinched her nipples and tugged hard, elongating the peaks. "Tonight, I'm going to pierce these."

"Fuck," she said with a gulp. "Can we talk about it?"

"No." Bending close, he spoke at her ear. "This gift means the most to me, Kate."

"Why? Because it's going to hurt the most?"

"That has nothing to do with it."

Maybe someday he would tell her exactly what he was giving her.

"Stay still." He squeezed her left breast, letting her know which one he was starting with.

Boones had instructed him on how to safely clean and pierce the area. With the preparations done, he didn't draw it out.

Hands steady, he stabbed the back end of the barbell into one side of the nipple. The front of the bar pierced the other side.

The pain was probably so intense she felt it in the pit of her stomach. But she didn't scream or fight in the restraints. Her hands balled in the sheets. Her teeth dug into her bottom lip, and the sinews in her neck stretched taut.

Goddamn, she was devastating.

As he repeated the steps on the other nipple, heat

simmered beneath his skin. Just imagining the sharp puncture of her sensitive tissues made his cock swell.

It wasn't a fast pain. He'd never done this before, and each nipple took about a minute to pierce the ruthless rod all the way through.

He thought her stoic composure would snap by the end, but she persevered without crying. Anyone else would've screamed bloody murder beneath his inexperienced hands.

When he finished, he put the antiseptic away and pulled off the blindfold.

Her watery eyes went straight to her chest and widened. "Gemstones? Are they garnets?"

"They're called painites."

The double-prong barbells held a one-carat precious stone on each end. Four stones in total. He had the pieces custom-made so that her nipples would fit snugly between each pair of deep red gems.

"Fucking beautiful." He circled a finger around her breast, eliciting a shiver.

She twisted her neck away and stared across the room at nothing.

"If you don't like the piercings, too damn bad." He roughly cupped her tender breast, making her gasp. "You will *not* remove them. Understand?"

"Yes." Her jaw set.

He turned his attention to the knots and spent the next few minutes untying her. When the rope fell away, so did some of her indignation. She really didn't like to be restrained.

Scooting to the headboard, she sat with her back against it. Her nipples would be sore for a few days, and though the jewelry wasn't heavy, it would feel like a constant bite, an ever-present reminder of him.

"Will there be more?" She pulled the sheet over her lap but didn't try to cover her chest. Instead, she stared down at the piercings with bitter curiosity. "Will you cover my body with jewelry until I look like a pincushion?"

"No more piercings, but there will be needle play in your future."

She closed her eyes and choked. "Sorry I asked."

"The second gift is some news I want to share." He shrugged out of his shirt, grimacing at the tightness in his shoulder.

His shoes and jeans hit the floor next. Then he joined her on the bed.

"I finalized some negotiations today with three of the largest gangs in Caracas." He leaned his head back against the headboard, watching her sidelong. "I traded some of my smuggling routes for their kidnapping operations."

She whirled on him, her blue eyes burning. "You promised you wouldn't kidnap anymore."

"I keep my promises, Kate."

"So you gave them your smuggling routes in exchange for...?" Her gaze flicked over his face, her expression etched in confusion. "For their kidnapping operations? What does that even mean?"

"Their territories are now mine. It's a lot more complicated than that, but the gist is I control the bulk of Kidnap Ally and the surrounding areas. With the exception of a few rogue gangs, I'm the only one who can kidnap in Caracas."

"Except you don't do that..." Realization penetrated her voice, soaking the words with stunned tears. "You found a way to stop *everyone* from kidnapping."

"Not everyone. But I'm working on it."

There was the smile he'd hoped to see. It stretched her honeyed mouth, lifted her cheeks, and glistened in her eyes.

"That's a great fucking surprise, Tiago." She slid onto his lap, enticingly nude as she straddled his thighs. Her fingers braided through his hair. She touched their foreheads together, and her mouth closed over his gently, briefly. "You did good."

"Sometimes I do the right thing, but it's usually by accident."

"How does it feel?" She ghosted her lips along his jaw and softly sucked behind his ear.

"Keep doing that, and I'll skip the third gift and show you exactly how it feels."

"I'm not afraid of you." She leaned back and coasted a hand along the scar on his head. "The cutting and piercing and all the other pain you put me through really pisses me off. But then you do things that surprise me, like abolishing kidnapping in Caracas. Tell me that good deed doesn't feel amazing."

"It feels good to make you happy, Kate." He stroked a thumb along her bottom lip. "That's all that matters."

She made a humming noise and ran her fingers through the messy strands on his head. "You have great hair. Who's your stylist?"

"She's a foxy little thing. Likes to put her tits in my face when she's giving me a trim."

"She also now knows how to stitch up your next knife wound."

"Boones taught you that today?"

"He *showed* me. I haven't actually held a needle."

While Tiago spent the past three weeks running his business from the penthouse office, she passed the time with Boones, learning the basics of emergency medicine. She initiated the instruction, and Boones was more than willing to share his knowledge.

"If you ever decide to become a doctor," Tiago said, "Boones would be an excellent mentor."

"I know." She gave him a small smile.

He clasped her tiny waist and lifted her to fasten his mouth to hers. After a few dizzying sips, he adjusted her legs around his and reached for his phone.

"One more gift tonight." He unlocked the screen.

"I don't think the last one can be topped."

A swarm of energy buzzed in his gut as he handed her the phone. "The video is a couple of hours old."

She glanced at him, directed her eyes on the screen, and stopped breathing.

TWENTY-SIX

Tiago's back rippled with tension as he absorbed Kate's reaction.

She held the phone tightly, her gaze glued to the screen. Face contorted. Lips pinched. Tears breaching the waterline.

The recorded video showed Lucia entering the shack with Cole Hartman. Tate looked at her, and it took a moment for him to come to terms with her presence. But once he did, he pulled her into his arms and held onto her like he would never let her go.

"I've waited three months to see this." A keening sob tore from Kate's chest.

"I know." He hadn't expected to feel so relieved by the reunion. It put a strange warmth in his chest and shifted the shape of his mouth.

"You're smiling." Her own smile trembled beneath streams of drippy tears as she watched the video until the end. "I guess you're happy about your experiment."

"No." He took the phone from her and set it aside,

tasting the thick onus of his words. "I regret it deeply."

She traced gentle fingers along his hairline, her eyes bright and wet as she watched his face, waiting for him to elaborate.

"I shouldn't have separated them." He reclined against the headboard, his stomach a hard knot. "If someone did that to me, if I lost you for three months…" He dragged a hand down his face. "I can't even let my mind go there."

Crushed by guilt and unbalanced with relief, he wanted to end the bleed of vulnerability and kiss her until neither of them could think straight.

"He's free." She touched her brow to his and breathed a blissful sound against his lips. "In the end, you did the right thing. You let him go."

But she wasn't free. She wanted autonomy more than anything else, and he couldn't give that to her. He would never let her go.

"Thank you for the video." She touched her lips to his cheek. "For putting a stop to kidnapping." She kissed the corner of his mouth. "For never breaking your promises."

She trailed a sensual path of sucking nips down the line of his neck, across his shirtless chest, and lower, arrowing straight toward his hardening cock.

"Kate." Lust ran riot through his body, tensing muscles and tightening his balls.

She inched down the length of his reclined frame, nipple piercings glinting in the lamplight and blue eyes peering up through long lashes, drawing him in, pulling him deeper.

She'd never gone down on him, and he never forced it. Her ferocious temper and sharp teeth wasn't a combination he'd wanted near his dick.

Her hands slipped beneath the waistband of his briefs, as if to relieve him of that last bit of clothing. But she hesitated, head down, hiding her face.

Images of his cock sinking between her pillowy lips heated his insides to a smoldering boil. He snared her by the hair and wrenched her head back. "Don't fucking tease—"

"I'm not." Her eyes snapped to his, her expression a composition of longing and moxie, at odds with the tears flitting down her cheeks.

"What are you doing, Kate?" He released her hair.

"I don't know." She sniffed and tugged his briefs down his legs, freeing his erection. "I guess I'm trying to properly thank you, but also..." She clutched the base of his erection and gave him a hard, confident stroke. "I want to do this for myself."

His head rocked back, and he gasped for air as his entire body stiffened and throbbed, strumming beneath her wicked touch.

He tolerated it through a few more strokes before he closed a fist around hers and took over. Kicking his hips, he drove hard and fast into the clasp of their hands.

Her eyes found his. She yanked her grip away, and in the next heartbeat, she replaced it with the hot, wet heaven of her mouth.

"Holy fuck." He clutched her head and worked himself deeper into the back of her throat, shaking and thrusting with urgency. "Jesus, Kate. That feels fucking incredible."

It had been twelve years since he'd let anyone suck him. It was long enough ago that even a half-ass blow job would feel extraordinary right now.

But nothing about this was half-ass. The swirling, sucking motion of her lips and tongue delivered the perfect pressure and rhythm, just the right amount of teasing and manipulation to drive him out of his fucking mind.

He couldn't stop his hands from holding her in place as he fucked hard and deep into her throat. She swallowed through it without gagging, but after a few breathless seconds, she smacked her palms on his abs and pushed away.

Leaning up, she got in his face and growled. "I was trained how to do this by a scary, cold as fuck sadist." She wrapped a hand around his length, torturing him with diabolical strokes. "I want to do it *my* way, for *me*, and I don't need your damn guidance."

"Christ, you're fucking fierce." He was so goddamn hard his dick felt like cement beneath the pressure, like any moment he might crack in the vigorous vise of her hand.

"I've never done this without..." Her brows furrowed. "Without giving my consent." She edged back and lowered her head, her gaze locked on his. "Let me do it."

"Okay." He relaxed into the mattress, his head tipped back against the headboard and his hands at his sides. "Do it. Suck me."

She did. She sucked him until every nerve in his body sparked and sizzled with need. The rolling sweep of her tongue brought him back from the dead. The suction of her lips banished the nightmares, and her tear-stained cheeks filled him with an overpowering sense of responsibility.

His love for her resembled a blade, a source of

pain, but vital. He would always protect her, however she needed him, even when he was the cause of her suffering.

Their relationship was unconventional, dark in nature, almost unworldly. Although she resented it, he knew she cherished it just as deeply.

He felt it in the veneration of licks along his cock, heard it in the emotion-soaked panting of her breaths, and saw it in the sodden depths of her watchful eyes.

She wasn't just giving him a blow job. She was surrendering pieces of herself. Tiny, rare, invaluable pieces of her soul.

Possessiveness growled in his throat, and his muscles clenched with desire. He wanted to erase her past and be her forever. He wanted to disintegrate everything from her life until he was the only thing she needed to breathe.

He wanted her to love him.

As her mouth moved along his shaft and her gaze clung to his, he could almost pretend she was with him willingly, that she wasn't locked in his penthouse with twenty guards preventing her escape.

Sucking in air, he swallowed the urge to flip her over, sink into her heat, and pound home the message that she belonged to him.

Instead, he simply let go. He let her set the torturous pace, let her add a teasing nip here and there, and let her decide when to send him over.

The moment she took him to the back of her throat and kneaded his balls in the cup of her hand, she knew she had him.

He surrendered, gasping for breath, groaning incoherently, and coming for the woman he wanted to fuck for the rest of his undeserving life.

She swallowed him down, every single drop, and by the time her sexy lips slid free, he only vaguely remembered how he got there.

"*Hostia puta.*" His lungs stuck together, gasping for oxygen. "It's never been that perfect."

"Well, you have no recent comparisons. It's been a while since someone gave you head, right?"

"Twelve years." He stared at her mouth, obsessed with every little twitch within those lush arches.

"I like that." She crawled up his chest and rested her head on his shoulder. "I like that there hasn't been anyone since your wife. But it also feels intimidating, like her shadow is constantly hanging over me. No matter what I do, I'll never be *her* in your eyes and—"

"Stop." He crushed her close, forging them together as her fragile truths winged through his soul. "I haven't thought about her nor will I ever think about her when I'm with you. My past is where it belongs. I don't want it or her, not even a little. I want *you.*"

The fact that she was dwelling on this at all was progress. Huge fucking strides in the right direction. If she didn't care about him, she wouldn't have brought up his sexual history, marriage, or any insecurities about it.

She was jealous, and she hated him. He was possessive, and he loved her. Together, they were a combustion of extreme emotion that burned without boundaries or expiration.

Didn't matter how far he took her or how hard she fought, she was with him, kicking and kissing, punching and fucking, with her heart engaged and her mind challenging him as nothing less than his equal.

He ran his fingers down her side, veered around

her hip, and dipped into the valley between the firm globes of her ass.

"Lie on your back and spread your legs." He clenched her buttocks hard enough to make her squeak.

She lifted her head, and it wasn't resistance that glowed in her gaze. It was heat. Desire. Acceptance.

"I want to come." Her lashes lowered, transforming her petite features into pure seduction. "I like that you always give me that."

As she slid off his lap and stretched out on her back, a second heartbeat took up residence between his legs.

The fluidity of her lithe figure made his mouth water. The tight buds of her nipples pinched erotically between the precious stones, and if that weren't enough to make him hard again, she had the brazenness to meet his eyes and open her thighs.

In a blink, he shifted from man to beast. His hands landed on her knees, spreading her wide as he went after her pussy with tongue and teeth.

She moaned beneath the attack, and her body trembled against him, filling his mouth with feminine hunger.

No matter how many times he went down on her, it was always explosive. Her responses, his need — the air crackled and sang with the sounds of fighting, snarling, mating animals.

As she climaxed, she did it with her entire being. She let go of everything — her hatred, her fear, her painful past — and for those few fleeting seconds, he glimpsed a woman who was capable of seeing what he was and loving him despite it.

In that moment, something awoke between them.

Something deep and untouchable. On the surface, they were captor and captive, but at the heart of their connection, they were one.

"Tiago." She opened her arms, panting through the remnants of her release.

He prowled up her body, lowered onto her, and buried himself in her hot, tight pussy.

Pleasure zinged through his veins, and he snapped his hips into a frantic, urgent rhythm. She answered with a cry, and her hands gripped the muscles of his ass.

But it was her eyes that held him. Those vibrant oceans of blue called him into the rippling vastness, pulling him in so close and deep he didn't know where he ended and she began.

With his hands tangled in her hair, he thrust again, and again, harder, faster, with a desperation that echoed in his heart.

All his life, he'd been alone. In marriage, he'd been alone in love. In his career, he'd fought his own battles. In hell, he reigned from a solitary throne.

What would it be like to have Kate's love instead of her hate? To have her fighting beside him instead of against him?

The notion was unattainable but not unimaginable. He imagined it every day, in every possible way.

With a low, deep moan, she came undone. Her orgasm swelled and crashed around him, contracting her inner muscles and tossing him into a delirium of ecstasy.

"Kate." He groaned, holding her tight as she milked him, draining him into exhaustion.

Spent and sated, he rolled to his back and gathered her in his arms.

It was easy to give up everything for her, but there

were some things that required time and planning. He was willing to surrender whatever was needed to earn her love, as long as it didn't compromise her safety.

Letting Tate go had been the right thing to do, but it came with a cost.

Cole Hartman was no longer occupied with the search for Tate.

Now he had a new job, a new target, and by this time tomorrow, he would know where to find Kate.

Tiago had to leave the penthouse tomorrow, and she would be at his side. It was a risk to take her to his compound, but it was even a bigger risk to leave her in the care of someone else.

No one would protect her like he would.

If Hartman meant to take her, he would have to pry her out of Tiago's cold, dead arms.

TWENTY-SEVEN

The grungy, menacing atmosphere set Kate's instincts on high alert as she followed Tiago through his Caracas compound.

The bones of what was once a regal hotel hid behind fumes of cigarette smoke, spray paint, and decay. Sheet metal covered the windows. Bullet holes pocked the ceilings. Brown stains blotted the worn carpet, and sweaty, heavily-armed men stood at attention in the dark hallways.

Hard to imagine Lucia had lived within these claustrophobic walls for eleven years.

The absence of light disorientated Kate, but she stayed close to Tiago's familiar frame. Not that he would let her drift out of arm's reach.

He didn't glance at her, hold her hand, or touch her the way he did when they were alone, but the weight of his attention never left her. Whether he was navigating winding passages or briefing dozens of guards on business deals, he knew where she was and what she was doing at all times.

His awareness of her was an unexplainable sense in her gut, one that had evolved from a collection of shared experiences during their inseparable months together.

Strange as it was, she seemed to be constantly aware of him, too, in the warning tingle across her skin, the rash of heat in her cheeks, and the hum of energy in her chest.

Outside his inner circle, however, no one was privy to the constant storm between them. No one knew she was the object of his dirtiest, darkest, most intimate desires, that she wore his scarred artwork, that she slept in his bed, or that he would kill anyone who tried to take her from him.

Her role at his compound was simply to look the part of Lucia's replacement.

When he'd strapped an unloaded gun on her hip before they left, his expression had been strained so tightly with worry it bordered on anger.

He couldn't stomach the thought of leaving her in the penthouse, where he couldn't watch her. At the same time, it terrified him to take her into this world. He told her none of this, but words weren't necessary. She read it in the intensity of his eyes and felt it vibrating from his anxious posture.

Maybe his protectiveness was a symptom of obsession. Or maybe it came from a place of twisted love.

He'd said the words. Three words no man had ever given her. But she couldn't let his declaration sink its poisonous hooks into her psyche.

As long as he was her captor, love didn't have a damn thing to do with it.

But as she followed him through the dark halls of his lair, she soared on wings of gratefulness. After being locked up for months, she was finally out, even if it meant wearing an unloaded gun and pretending to be one of his guards.

None of his men questioned her presence. In fact, they couldn't seem to take their eyes off Tiago.

It had been three months since he'd shown his face here. Three months since they'd seen their leader alive and breathing, and he was really something to behold.

The dark stubble on his jaw accentuated his masculine bone structure as he spoke to them in Spanish, the soft J's and double R's rolling off his tongue with seductive authority.

Inky black hair raked back from his strong brow in tousled, spiky rebellion. Deliberately rebellious, as if every strand had been commanded into perfect disorder. She felt a disturbing urge to tangle her fingers in all that sexiness.

She'd recently trimmed the sides of his head, making the scars stand out in stark relief. They added a dangerous edge to his appearance, as if he needed more of that with his black jeans, leather jacket, and shit-kickers.

Strength and power radiated from him, and it wasn't just for show. He'd returned to full health, exercised daily, and stood before his adherents with all the potency of a confident, merciless crime lord.

And so he was back to work. For the next week, he spent every waking moment at the compound, catching up with his men. She remained at his side from the second they left the penthouse to the moment they returned, sitting through business meetings held in languages she didn't understand.

The night Tate walked out of the shack, Arturo returned to Caracas and resumed his position as her constant shadow. Between him, Tiago, and the hundreds of guards in his regime, escape was impossible.

By the second week, the bustle of Tiago's return had calmed down. He found some time to give her a quiet tour of the old hotel floors, including the basement cells, where he'd held Tate and Van and countless other victims.

As his monotone voice recounted the things he'd done over the years, his expression lacked smugness and aggression. She hunted for hints of regret in his eyes, hoping to glimpse something human during his narration, but he remained guarded and closed-off.

Until he took her to the room where he used to sleep.

"This is it." He shut the door behind her, leaving Arturo in the hall.

She paced through the sparse space, marking the empty safe, the bare mattress, and the wooden chair at the center.

"It's almost an exact replica of your room in the desert." She paused beside the dumbbell on the scarred floor, and her stomach caved in. "Except this."

He leaned his back against the door and tilted his chin down, wearing a pensive, darker-than-usual expression. "She should've hit me one more time and made it count."

"What?" Her head kicked back. "Why would you say that?"

"You think I deserve to be alive?" His jaw flexed, and his eyes lifted, glowering from beneath thick lashes.

"Look around. This room sums up the last twelve years of my life."

She scanned the impenetrable lock on the door, the empty bed, the scarred surfaces, the suffocating darkness, utter vacancy, and isolation.

Maybe the space defined his experiences, but it didn't personify the man.

He'd committed unforgivable crimes. Heartless acts. But over the past few months, she'd come to realize Tiago Badell was in full possession of both a conscience and a heart.

Complex, sentient, and deeply honest, he had the capacity to hurt and love in equal intensities. He gave and received all ranges of emotion, more so than any person she knew.

And to think, he spent twelve years in this empty, lifeless, dispassionate cell.

She hated it.

Even as she knew it was a means of self-punishment, it hurt to imagine him sleeping here alone for so damn long.

She rubbed her chest, and her gaze landed on the dumbbell, a symbol of his constant drive to be strong and invincible. It also represented his pain.

Lucia had every right to attack him with it, but from his perspective, it probably felt like a terrible betrayal. His closest confidant had turned on him, and from what Kate understood about his wife's death, it wasn't the first time he'd been betrayed.

"When we leave this room," he said in a rough, heavily-accented voice, "I'm going to lock the door and never open it again."

"Good idea." She stepped toward him. "The past

stays in the past, where it belongs."

"I have a lot of regrets, Kate." He rested the tips of his fingers in his front pockets. "Too many to fit inside this room."

Agitated energy, *his* energy, swarmed around her in dizzying waves as he stared at something behind her.

She followed his gaze to the chair. Not just any chair. "That's where you sat with Lucia on your lap every day?"

"Yes."

Right there was where he gave Lucia the injections that counteracted the poison he put in her food.

Her insides constricted.

"You know my sins. I've disclosed them all in detail." He pushed off the door and prowled toward her, quickening her breaths. "What I haven't done is repent for them."

She held still as he circled her, every cell in her body pinging at his nearness.

"I'm sorry for what I did to Lucia." He paused before her and curled a finger under her chin, lifting her gaze. "I'm sorry I kicked you the night we met."

Her lips trembled, and she locked her knees to prevent them from wobbling. It wasn't his words that knocked her off-balance so much as the raw contrition shining in his eyes.

"I'm sorry for letting Iliana touch you." His hand skimmed along her jawline, making her pulse sputter. "I'm sorry for raping you. I'm not proud of it."

She sucked in a slow, shaky breath, bringing the dark scent of leather, cypress, and dangerous man into her lungs.

"I'm not asking for forgiveness." His fingers wove

through her hair and clenched. "I just needed you to hear it."

She didn't just hear it. She felt it stretch and pull inside her.

"Why now?" Swaying toward him, she burrowed into the warm den of his jacket. "What prompted this?"

"You." He leaned back and cuffed a strong hand around her neck. "Your eyes. It's impossible to feel heartless when you look at me like I'm not."

"Tiago." Her heart thumped heavily, catching in her throat.

"Also…" He brushed his nose against hers. "I'm in love with you."

Every word was a razor, reopening the cuts on her body. Lancing pain shot beneath her skin, burning, aching, inflaming the wounds.

His confession of love had never hurt before. So why did it hurt so much now?

An inner voice begged her to ignore it, to hold onto her hatred and feed it with her need for freedom.

But he was in her face, infiltrating her breaths, and staring down at her with a foreboding glint in his eyes.

Dark and tempting, indecently gorgeous and sickeningly filthy in bed, he knew he could set her on fire with only the force of his will. He was always just one impulse away from nailing her against the wall and driving her to the sublime edge of pleasure and pain.

His physique alone was a chiseled altar upon which any woman with a pulse would sacrifice her soul.

But he would never touch another woman.

He belonged to her.

Mine.

Well, maybe not *that.*

But he was her protector. Her lover. There.

If you truly love someone, you don't let them go without a fight.

Maybe she needed to be reminded of what she already had and trust that it was all she really needed.

She just didn't know how to separate the horrible things he'd done from those glimpses of goodness she'd seen in him.

"You're not heartless." She sighed. "Just complicated."

"And selfish." He swooped in and stole a greedy kiss from her lips. "Because Kate..." Another kiss. And another. "I know you can't love me, but I'm not sorry I took you. I won't apologize for it." His mouth sealed over hers, devouring her gasp before he pulled back. "If it came down to it, I would take you again."

With that, he released her, leaving behind the hot imprint of his touch on her skin.

As he turned toward the door, a thought tapped at the back of her mind, something she'd been meaning to ask him.

"Tiago?" When he glanced back, she raised her chin. "While we were holed up in the penthouse for a month, I know you were making plans."

"Go on." He shifted to face her and clasped his hands behind his back.

"My friends know where I'm at now?"

"Yes." A muscle bounced in his jaw.

"I assume some of your planning involved keeping them out of Caracas?" She stepped toward him, searching his unreadable expression. "Have they tried to enter the city or make contact?"

"Not yet."

Because of her phone conversation with Liv? She'd told them not to come. "Can I just call them and see —?"

"No. Stop asking."

Same answer he'd given her the last hundred times she asked to contact them.

"If Matias Restrepo comes for you…" He grasped her hand and pulled her into his space. "It won't end well for him."

"What do you mean?"

"I negotiated a deal with the President."

"What? The President of…?"

"Venezuela. His armed forces will not allow Restrepo to cross the Venezuela-Colombia border."

Her stomach sank. "What did you have to offer in exchange for that deal?"

"Nothing as valuable as you."

"You're evading the question."

"For now." He gripped the door handle and paused. "I accepted an invitation to one of his dinner parties. It's a formal affair this weekend. You're going with me."

"You want me to go to the President of Venezuela's party?" She gulped, seized by panic. "Will I be there as your captive? Your whore? Your fake guard?"

"You'll be there as *mine*."

Her growl came out as a choke. "I need to understand the landscape. Will you have enemies in attendance? Will I be expected to hold conversations? I don't know the language, and I definitely need a gun or something to —"

"If I asked any other woman to accompany me to a Presidential dinner, her first and only question would be what to wear."

"I don't give a fuck about that. I'm more concerned about—"

He captured her mouth in a demanding kiss and smiled against her lips. "I'll take care of the dress."

TWENTY-EIGHT

The dress encased Kate's body like liquid gold, as if each shimmering thread had been cut and woven in veneration of the female form. Fashion never meant one iota to her, but holy shit, this gown was empowering.

She paced to the full-length mirror in the master bathroom, nervously fluffing her long hair. She should've pinned it up or curled it or something, but the girly stuff was beyond her expertise.

Anchoring a hand on her hip, she extended a leg through the slit of the dress and gave herself a final once-over.

Her makeup was modest. A little mascara. A glide of lip gloss. But the gown and the heels and God, the whole look… She'd never felt so glamorous.

The satiny material clung to her slight curves from her chest to the floor. The cut up one side reached high on her thigh, enabling normal strides when she walked.

The slit fell along the leg that bore his artwork. No doubt, intentional. With each step, the fading pink welts of rope and petals peeked through the opening of the floor-length skirt.

Tiny shoulder straps held the top in place, and the deep scoop between her breasts exposed the length of her breastbone.

The gown and gold stilettos had been waiting for her in the bathroom when she exited the shower. No bra or panties. Not that she could've worn anything beneath the unforgiving material.

At first, she thought the gold color had been selected to match her hair. But it was much darker, more bronze-ish. Like the metallic hues in Tiago's brown eyes.

She hadn't seen him yet. Hadn't worked up the courage to step out of the bathroom.

Stop stalling.

Adjusting a shoulder strap, she drew in a calming breath and opened the door.

Across the room, he sat on the edge of the bed, dressed in a jet-black tuxedo. Head down, he wrestled with a cuff link, his face pinched in concentration.

"I can do that for you." She strode toward him, stepping carefully in the skyscraper heels, and slowed at the lift of his head.

He straightened. His mouth parted, and his eyes went from wide and stunned to heated and wolfish as he ate her up from head to toe. He made a few more passes, slower each time, lingering on the outline of the nipple piercings beneath the satin.

The heady caress of his gaze touched her everywhere, stroking, tingling, his breaths growing shallow and hungry.

She swallowed back a whimper. Swear to God, if he stared at her much longer, she could have an orgasm.

Just from the potency in his eyes.

The tuxedo wasn't helping. Sweet hell, the man wore the fuck out of tailored threads.

The black trousers and white collared shirt fit his hard body with mouthwatering precision. The dinner jacket cut a crisp outline across his broad shoulders. A gold square, the color of her gown, peeked out of the front pocket, and a black bow tie sat at the base of his tanned neck.

Every hair on his head fell together in unruly perfection. His cleanly shaved jaw showed off all his square angles and outrageously handsome Latino features.

Looking at him was a treacherous trap. He was too attractive, too addictive to take in all at once.

Desperate to break his spell, she focused on her feet and approached the bed. "Need help with the cuff links?"

"You're blindingly beautiful." A fingertip skimmed along her collarbone, teased the pocket of her throat, and dipped to follow the line of her breastbone. "I can't think straight."

"I could say the same thing." She peeked at his face, and if she thought she felt pretty before, her self-appraisal didn't hold a candle to the awe-stricken approval shimmering in his eyes.

His hand shifted to cup her breast, a possessive hold that turned wickedly mischievous as he flicked a thumb against the piercing.

Heat flashed through her, and she stepped back. "Let me see your sleeves."

He held out the cuff links and offered his wrists. "I need to be inside you."

"Too bad." She attached the gold links through the buttonholes.

Despite her resolve, she couldn't stop herself from glancing at his lap.

The outline of his cock formed an impressively long, rigid bulge that lay trapped against his thigh. Harder than hard, he looked ready to tear through the tuxedo pants.

A molten fever gathered between her legs, and her nipples tightened, the unbidden reaction further stimulated by the barbells.

She needed to stop melting all over the place and focus. He hadn't answered any of her questions about what to expect tonight. She didn't know what she would be walking into or how to conduct herself.

"Aren't we supposed to be there at seven?" She secured the last cuff link and sidled out of his reach.

"We're going to be late."

"If we leave now —"

A rough hand grabbed her arm, wrenching her into the space between his knees. "I'm going to fuck you."

Flames swept around them, from his gaze burning into hers, his fingers trailing heat up her arm, and the fire igniting inside her.

His other hand slipped through the slit of her gown and sank between her thighs, finding her embarrassingly wet.

"Fuck." He gripped her waist, dropped his forehead against her stomach, and twisted two fingers inside her. "Fucking drenched. Dripping for a cock."

"We're not doing this." She teetered in the heels and caught his shoulder for balance. "We're already dressed, and I'm too nervous about the dinner."

"I'll take the edge off." He thrust his hand, fingering her harder, deeper, until the line between *yes* and *no* blurred, and her thighs clenched together. "Sit on my cock, Kate."

"Stop." Throbbing, aching, and growing wetter, her body betrayed her. "I don't want to ruin the dress or take it off. It took me forever to make everything look just right. And you're wearing black. The smallest stain will glow like a spotlight. Do you really want to introduce me to the President with come stains on your pants? God, I'm already sweating, and you're making it—"

"Hey, Kate." His fingers slipped to her inner thigh and clenched, his voice chillingly quiet. Deadly serious. "Reach into my pants, pull out my cock, and fucking sit on it."

Her gaze dropped to the captivating curves of his bossy mouth, lingering there before lifting to his eyes, to the swirls of brown glowing in the lamplight.

A tremor erupted low and hot in her belly.

The way he looked at her, the piercing glare that cut right through those dark lashes, grabbed her deeply and completely.

She shivered with goosebumps in her heartbeat.

What was it about this man? This scary, stubborn, rude, horribly sexy man? He tied her up in knots, sometimes literally, and she wanted it.

She really did.

She fucking ached for him.

"You want me to fuck you?" she asked quietly.

"That's what I said."

The fact that they were discussing it instead of doing it gave her pause. Usually, he skipped the conversation and went right to stripping her clothes and working over her body.

Something had changed.

He'd apologized for raping her. Did that mean it wouldn't happen again?

She yanked her arm out of his grip and backed away, testing his sincerity.

He remained seated, his lips twisted in frustration and anger as he tracked her retreat to the door.

When she reached the hallway, her pulse pounded, and her muscles tensed, braced for him to chase her.

But he didn't. He slowly lowered to his back and rested an arm over his eyes, breathing heavily.

"You're not going to force me?" She clutched the doorframe.

"I'm trying, Kate." He adjusted the rigid length of his cock. "Go on. I'll be out in a second."

She stepped into the hall, squinting at him.

He would be fine. It was just an erection, and it was good for him to be denied.

Except she was denying herself.

Her need for him dripped and pulsed between her legs. What was the point in opposing something she wanted? Just to be stubborn?

Maybe this was a sick game of reverse psychology? But why would he bother with a mind fuck when he could just pin her down and fuck her like all the other times?

This wasn't a game.

He regretted forcing her, and she felt that at gut level.

They were already late, and the truth was she couldn't leave him like this. It went against every instinct inside her.

Fuck it.

She strode into the bedroom and shut the door. "I feel like the flakiest woman in existence."

He raised his head and lifted to his elbows, his gaze following her approach, pupils flaring.

"I changed my mind."

"Thank, fuck," he growled.

"But I want this on my terms." She glided her hands along the back of the gown, trying to locate the invisible zipper.

"What are your terms?"

"I get to be in control." Her skin heated, and her body bloomed into a galloping throb, fortifying her decision. "Can you handle that?"

"I don't know." He watched her hunt for the zipper and gripped his dick through the trousers. "Leave on the dress."

After a few more seconds of searching, she gave up and reached for the floor-length hem.

There was a lot of material to collect, and as she gathered it up her legs, his hands ghosted up the backs of her thighs, caressing, urging her to move faster.

Once the dress was ruched around her waist, he held it in place while she crawled over him and opened his fly.

He lifted his hips as she dragged the pants and briefs to his knees. His cock jutted upward, beautifully shaped and leaking a clear bead of moisture from the slit.

She wanted to taste it, ride it, and come all over it. Maybe that was wrong for someone in her situation. Maybe it was a psychological condition. But it didn't change how she felt.

"Don't just stare at it." He dug his fingers into her

thigh.

She clutched him, enclosing both hands around the thick, turgid, burning hot length.

A groan rumbled in his chest, his thighs flexing as he pushed himself into the squeeze of her fists.

"Fuck, Kate." His hand enclosed hers, tightening her fingers the way he liked it. "Goddamn, I need you. Come here."

"Stop bossing." She inched up his body and straddled his hips, careful not to mess up his tuxedo. "We're going to do this quick. I'm worried about our clothing and—"

"Shut up, and put me inside you." His hand guided her fingers up and down his cock, angling his hardness to fit at her entrance.

She knocked his arm away and took over, stirring his plump crown through her folds, readying her body, making herself wetter, hungrier.

His fingers joined in, stroking her pussy and rubbing her arousal over the head of his cock.

What now? She'd never done this before. What if she bent his dick when she sat on it?

"You're ready." His voice cracked, his bedroom eyes reading the expression on her face. "Just slide down. You won't hurt me."

He laced their fingers together, and his other hand went to her waist, pushing down with impatience.

"I've got this." She braced herself on the twitching bricks of his stomach. "Relax."

His grip loosened on her waist, and she lowered her body, taking him in inch by hard inch. His jaw stiffened, and the cords in his neck strained taut as he groaned deep and long in the back of his throat.

"Holy fuck, Kate. So good." He kicked his hips, thrusting to get deeper. "*Mierda*, you feel sinful."

"Stop moving." She pressed a hand on his thigh beneath her, trying to calm his need to dominate. "Let me do this."

"Then do it. Fuck me."

Holding their entwined fingers against her midsection, she flattened her other hand on his abs and rocked her hips.

Each movement wrenched a groan from him. When she lifted and lowered, sliding him in and out in languid rolls and undulations, he started to pant.

His hungry responses spurred her faster, harder, until their gasps became one. She threw her head back and writhed on him, losing herself in the pleasure, until his fingers closed around her nipple piercing and painfully tugged.

"Eyes on me." His accent rolled over her, as thick as the Venezuelan humidity.

She met his gaze, and in one look, he obliterated everything between them. There was no air, no fear, no words.

It was a monumental moment. She was on top of him, controlling the pace and rhythm, fucking him into the bed. Something he'd never allowed anyone else to do and would probably never allow again. It was all there in his eyes, drowning her in the gravity of it.

"Give me your mouth." He caught her neck and yanked her to him.

She fumbled around his tuxedo coat until her arms found a safe place to land. Then she leaned up, her chest flush with his, and kissed him.

He let her take a few gentle licks before he

annihilated her easy pace with his aggressive, sinful tongue.

That tongue was a weapon, wielded by a wicked, kinky, eternally horny man, who was wrinkling the hell out of his formal wear and thrusting his hips like he didn't have a care in the world.

No, that wasn't true.

In a disturbing, deeply moving way, he cared about *her*. She felt it in the massage of his fingers on her thigh, heard it in the unbridled rush of his breaths, and saw it in the beautiful, extraordinarily thoughtful design he'd carved into her skin.

She'd never been this close to anyone, physically or emotionally, and she felt forever bound to him. Not by handcuffs or threats or the cock inside her. This connection ran deeper, beyond anything she could touch with her hands or see with her eyes.

They were joined on an inexplicable level, and it scared the hell out of her. Because nothing was more terrifying than the beautiful, dangerous threat beneath her and his total and utter possession of her senses.

Pressing closer, she ate his mouth with all the confusion and passion burning inside her. Her hips moved with abandon, chasing the release they both needed.

Tongues moving in tandem, hands kneading and clinging, they groaned together and came up for air.

A pained sound pushed past his lips. The muscles in his face pulled taut, all those gorgeous, masculine angles unable to conceal his discomfort.

"What's wrong?" She froze. "Did I hurt you?"

"Trying not to come." He captured her hand and pressed it between her legs. "Touch yourself."

That she could do.

Sitting up, she circled her fingers around her clit and quickly found the right pace and pressure. Swift, consistent movements, in sync with the snap and twist of her hips.

His gaze smoldered, bouncing between her eyes and her touch, back and forth. He licked his lips, bit down on the bottom one, and his legs began to tremble.

He was fighting it, trying to hold back his orgasm, waiting for her.

Watching his groaning, shaking effort was enough to send her over. The climax tore through her in dizzying, magical ripples of electricity.

"Kate," he moaned, clutching her waist and staring into her eyes. "I'm coming. Ahhh, fuck!"

With a guttural groan, he jerked into her erratically and buried himself deep, holding her against him as he filled her with his come.

"Fucking amazing," he said on a long, languorous sigh. "Thank you."

"That's a first." Twitching with the sparkling remnants of ecstasy, she collapsed on his chest.

"Which part?"

"*You* thanking *me* for anything."

"I'm working on rectifying that." He brushed her hair behind her ear and blew out a breath. "We need to go."

"I'll get a towel to clean us up." She lifted, letting him slip from her body.

"Don't." He straightened his pants and tucked his dirty cock behind the zipper. "You're going to wear my come to dinner."

"How romantic."

He rose to his feet, pulling her with him. His hands smoothed over the dress, straightening and adjusting, and all the while, she could feel his ejaculation leaking down her legs.

She would just have to use the bathroom on the way out and clean up the mess.

As if reading her mind, he sneaked a hand under the gown and smeared the come down her thighs and in her pussy.

She gasped. "What the—?"

He rubbed those same fingers across her mouth. "Let's go meet the President."

TWENTY-NINE

During the two-hour drive to dinner, Kate fretted over whether she reeked of sex or had a wet spot on the back of her gown. As it turned out, the President of Venezuela was in no position to notice.

Not only was he a busy man, life hadn't been kind to him in the hygiene department.

As Tiago clasped his outstretched hand in greeting, she had to hold her breath and stifle her gag reflex.

The elaborately-decorated, so-called dictator smelled like a burnt cigar soaked in the anal gland discharge of a dead skunk. She wasn't even sure which part of his body the offensive odor was coming from.

Maybe it was best she didn't know.

Thankfully, the introductions lasted just long enough for a handshake, a distracted smile in her direction, and a brief conversation with Tiago in Spanish. Then his brigade of uptight assistants ushered him off to the next partygoer.

Tiago hooked an arm around her back and touched

his mouth to her ear. "The air is safe to breathe again."

"Jesus," she whispered on an exhale. "What was that?"

"The aroma of corruption and power." He steered her toward the bar.

"You don't smell like that." She smirked.

He smirked back before calling out his drink order to the bartender.

On the way to this majestic beachfront mansion, he'd explained they were going to a private island owned by one of the President's diplomats. The last jog of the journey had involved a car ferry from the mainland. She hadn't been able to see the ocean in the dark, but for the first time in her life, she'd detected the scent of salt and brine and heard the roll of waves.

They'd only been on the island for thirty minutes, entering the main hall at the end of dinner. The hundreds of tuxedos and gowns in attendance had been too busy stuffing their faces to pay any attention to the late arrivals.

But she felt their eyes now.

Pinched-faced, scowling men and women filled the ballroom, all of them glaring at the man at her side. Apparently, they didn't like the King of Caracas in their presence.

"Some of these people are staring so hard," she said under her breath, leaning back against the bar, "when you leave tonight, your ears are going to be on fire."

"They want my city." With his body facing the bar, his assertive hand glided across her stomach and closed around her hip. "And the gorgeous woman on my arm."

"Pretty sure they just want you dead." She spotted

Arturo at the entrance of the ballroom, his gaze ever-watchful.

"That, too. But we're safe tonight. No one will try to kill each other with the President's armed forces on the premises."

If there were armed guards in the room, their weapons were concealed beneath tuxedos. Arturo was the only face she recognized, and he didn't have a gun. Every visitor in this house had to go through a metal detector.

She'd asked Tiago a thousand questions during the drive, and he'd only answered a few. While he was hunted by American government agencies and Mexican cartel, he'd assured her the President of Venezuela had more enemies than he did.

That did nothing to calm her nerves.

The bartender handed him the finished drinks. Tiago kept the tumbler of clear fluid and offered her the wine glass.

"What is this?" She took a small sip and widened her eyes.

"*Vino Pasita.* Wine made from bananas."

"Wow." She swallowed another greedy gulp and licked her lips, savoring the burst of sweet, fruity flavors. "This is heaven."

"You only get one. The hangover is a slow death of agonizing pain." He clasped her hand and guided her through the crowds of formal wear, his whisper a caress at her ear. "I need to rub some elbows and finalize a few deals. Enjoy your *vino* and don't leave my side."

For the next hour, she remained on his arm like a silent gold ornament, mesmerized by his sensual Spanish parlance as he hobnobbed with politicians, Venezuelan celebrities, and random powerful bad guys.

During each introduction, he announced her as Kate. Some of the faces she recognized. Others she knew by name. If she had a phone, she would've been burning up the Internet in an attempt to learn about these people.

After another hour of standing around in six-inch heels, her feet throbbed. Her delicious wine was long gone, and maybe she was just overstimulated by all the conversations, but something niggled. She felt edgy. Almost paranoid.

Her scalp tingled, and the constant itch between her shoulder blades had her searching the crowds at her back every few seconds.

Arturo hadn't moved from his position near the door. Nothing seemed amiss.

She needed another drink.

With no servers in the vicinity, she lifted Tiago's tumbler from his hand. He glanced at her while continuing his conversation with the Minister of Foreign Affairs.

She gave them a soft smile and sipped from the glass.

Well, crap. He was drinking water? Useless.

A younger man stood beside the old politician. She couldn't remember his name, but she didn't like his eyes. Especially when they fell to her chest. It was quick. A dip down and back up. But it happened, and Tiago didn't miss it.

His neck rolled, and his biceps hardened, crushing her fingers in the bend of his arm.

Desperate to diffuse his temper, she glanced around the room, and an idea struck.

"Sorry to interrupt your conversation." She set his

glass aside and rubbed a soothing hand over his clenched
fist. "Will you dance with me?"

"Yes." He said his goodbyes through gritted teeth
and escorted her across the room to the dance floor.
"Trying to distract me?"

"Absolutely."

"Do you know how to dance to this?"

Dozens of couples spun to the fast, creole-like
music. Hands clasped, they faced each other, making
small, stomping steps. They all moved in the same speed
and style, using waltz turns and sweeping foot
movements. She'd never seen anything like it. Maybe it
was the fandango. Definitely not the tango.

"I have no clue." She didn't know how to dance at
all.

"It's the joropo, the national dance of Venezuela."
He led her to the side of the dance floor where the band
congregated.

At least twenty musicians played guitars, maracas,
harps, mandolins, and multiple other instruments she
couldn't name.

He whispered something to the maestro, and a
moment later, the music segued into a slow Spanish
number.

"Better?" He stared at her mouth and brushed a
thumb across her lower lip.

She nodded. "I think so?"

He guided her to the center of the dance floor and
held her tight against the front of his body. Then he
swayed into an easy rhythm, keeping his steps simple
and slow, as if he knew she didn't know how to dance.

If the room was watching, she didn't notice. She
was only aware of the strength of his arms around her

back and the heat of his breath on her neck.

She ran her hands up the strong column of his neck and spoke against his mouth in an almost-kiss. "I like you like this."

"That so?"

"Yeah." She pressed her smile against his cheek, delighting in the scratch of stubble that had grown in within a few hours.

"Then I'll dance with you every night."

He carried her through another song, gently rocking, pacing the rise and fall of her breaths. But something started to shift under his skin. A tension that wasn't there before.

Or maybe it was just her earlier unease seeping in?

She ignored it for a few moments, until his muscles grew tighter beneath her fingers, and his movements stiffened with each note of the song. He was bracing for something.

"What's wrong?" She looked around and didn't register anything out of place.

"Let's take a walk." His fingers intertwined with hers, and he strolled off the dance floor with a nod to the maestro.

Panic seized her as he wove through the room, keeping his gait slow to accommodate her clicking high-heels. His expression was too calm, too blank. What was he hiding beneath that emotionless mask?

He didn't make eye contact or stop to talk to anyone. His gaze flitted between Arturo and the side door, where he was leading her.

She pinned her lips tight, knowing not to ask questions or draw attention with so many people around.

"This way." He directed her into a quiet corridor

and around a few clusters of mingling partygoers.

Stalking down the hallway, around the corner, and past a vacant dining room, he seemed to know his way around. She glanced back and found Arturo trailing at a distance.

"Are we in danger?" she whispered.

"Just one more meeting. Then we'll leave."

"That's not an answer. Where are we going?"

"Not sure." He flicked a finger at the wood flooring. "Following the beer."

"What?" She squinted in confusion. "The beer?"

He stopped and lowered to a crouch. With a swipe of his thumb, he collected a tiny drop of wetness from the floor and held it to his nose. "A trail of beer."

"Why? Who left it?"

He rose and touched his lips to the sensitive skin beneath her ear, shushing her. "Through here."

With a hand at the small of her back, he turned her into a dark, empty service kitchen.

"Where is everyone?" She craned her neck, searching the shadows amid commercial appliances. Her pulse skittered out of control.

"The main kitchen is on the other side of the house." He ushered her toward an industrial steel door.

An entrance to a walk-in freezer?

A beer bottle sat on the floor in front of it. He moved it out of the way and shrugged off his tuxedo coat.

In the doorway to the hall, Arturo stood with his back to the kitchen, keeping watch.

"Tiago, you're scaring me." She rubbed her arms. "Tell me what's going on."

"It's going to be cold." He draped the jacket over

her shoulders and pulled the lapels together at her chest.

With a hard, tense kiss against her lips, he turned and opened the steel door.

A blast of frigid air punched through her, but that wasn't what froze the breath in her lungs.

Standing at the rear of the walk-in freezer was a man she never expected to see.

Dressed to the nines in a black tuxedo, he looked like an apparition in a swirling cloud of wintry air.

She gasped. "Cole?"

THIRTY

Kate blinked rapidly, struggling to believe her eyes. Her pulse thundered, and her palms slicked with sweat, despite the frosty air.

"Kate." Cole Hartman folded his hands behind him, shoulders back, as if he were *expecting* her. "Are you okay?"

"I'm kind of freaking out." Her gaze snapped to Tiago as he shut the freezer door behind him.

Not a hint of surprise or anger on his stern face. What the almighty fuck?

Her mind reeled to make a connection between the two men. They seemed to look at each other with familiarity, and that kind of made sense. Cole had appeared on the video with Lucia when she found Tate in the shack.

But Tiago had never mentioned Cole's name to her. Did he know Tate had hired Cole to locate Lucia?

In all likelihood, Cole was here for *her*. To rescue her.

What if he'd sneaked in a gun? Would he shoot Tiago?

Were her friends here, too?

Elation and terror jolted through her, trembling her limbs and making every breath a workout. "Are you alone?"

"Yes." Cole narrowed his eyes at Tiago.

"Don't kill each other." She gripped Tiago's hand and squeezed. "We can figure out whatever this is without spilling blood."

Cole stared at their entwined fingers, and lines formed in his brow.

She would have to explain her relationship to him, even if she wasn't sure how to explain it to herself.

First, she needed answers.

"You purposefully left a trail of beer to this freezer," she said to Cole. "For Tiago?"

"Yes."

She stared up at Tiago's unreadable expression. "How did you know he did that?"

"I spotted him while we were dancing, and he tipped his beer bottle at me. A helpful clue." He scanned the ceilings and shelves of frozen foods. "Is this—?"

"I did a sweep." Cole's words rode on a flume of white steam. "The area is clean."

"Clean of what?" She glanced between them, taken back by the way their eyes connected so...comfortably. "I'm sorry. Do you two know each other?"

"*Clean* means no bugs. We're not being recorded or spied on." Tiago banded an arm around her back, pulling her against the heat of his body. "And yes, we know each other."

"Took you long enough to mark me." Cole cocked

his head. "I've been here all night."

"I was distracted." Tiago stroked a thumb along her arm.

"You shouldn't have come out of hiding," Cole said.

"We both know I didn't have a choice." His jaw hardened. "How's Trace?"

Cole crossed his arms over his chest, nostrils flaring.

"Who's Trace?" She adjusted Tiago's tuxedo coat tighter around her, shivering.

"He was our handler." Tiago turned, putting his dark eyes inches from her face. "Cole and I have known each other for a long time."

"What?" Shock strangled her voice. "How?"

"We worked for the U.S. government."

Her mouth fell open, closed, and opened again. "But you're Venezuelan."

"My mother was American. I was born in the U.S. and raised here, in my father's country."

"Were you military?" She recalled what little she knew of Cole and the fog of secrecy surrounding the man's credentials. "Or some kind of spy or assassin?"

His gaze slid to Cole, and they exchanged an indecipherable look.

"He can't discuss the job." Cole's lips slanted in a harsh line.

"But you both knew this Trace guy?" She trembled uncontrollably, fighting to keep warm in the subzero temperatures. "You worked together? On the same side?"

Her whirling thoughts jumped to FBI, CIA, top-secret espionage stuff. Except weren't those the very organizations that were hunting Tiago?

The night he told her about his wife, she'd asked him why he became like the man who had his family killed. His response hadn't made sense at the time.

I didn't. He was my colleague. When he betrayed me, I became the opposite of him. I became his enemy.

"Many years ago, Cole and I had the same employer, on the right side of the law." Tiago tugged her against his chest and enclosed his arms around her, running a hand up and down her back to create warmth. "We didn't work closely together, but we both reported to Trace. He was the handler who gave us our orders."

Just...mind-blowing.

"Trace is also Cole's best friend. Or *was*." He shot Cole a cruel smirk. "Is he still banging your fiancée?"

Cole bared his teeth. "He married her, you fucking asshole."

"Then he's definitely banging her."

"You know, you weren't always such an insensitive dick." Cole lowered his arms to his sides, and the hard lines of his face smoothed away. "I'm sorry about Semira and your family. Had I known what was happening, I swear, Tiago, I would've warned you. I would've done something to stop it."

Her throat tightened, and she grabbed Tiago's hand. God, they really did know each other. No wonder Cole had located Lucia so easily. Tate would shit himself if he knew about this crazy connection.

"The job came with risks." Tiago said softly. "They told us no attachments. No spouses. No weaknesses. We knew that going in, and we walked away losing everything that mattered to us."

"You were both betrayed?" Her mind churned to fit the pieces together. "It sounds like you were the good guys, fighting on the right side, and that side fucked you over. Is that what happened? You lost a fiancée, a wife, and a family because people you trusted turned on you?"

"Something like that." Cole stared at Tiago.

"Explain it to me," she said.

"There was a defection in our ranks." Tiago flexed his hand around hers. "Two of our colleagues—a man and a woman—defected from the agency and leaked our personal information to known enemies who were willing to pay a small fortune for it. The female traitor threatened Cole's fiancée, but his best friend protected her."

Did the best friend fuck her before or after he protected her? Maybe there was more to the story, but holy crap... Poor Cole.

"The other defector was responsible for the deaths of my family." Tiago's voice scratched, and he cleared it. "He sold classified information about me to an enemy, fully aware it would turn my home into a bloodbath. It wasn't personal. He just wanted the money."

"That's why you both switched sides."

Cole straightened. "I didn't—"

"I know for a fact you did a job for Van Quiso." She glared. "Which side do you think he's on?"

"Given your friendship with the capo of the Restrepo cartel," Tiago said, "it's safe to assume you're no longer working for the American people."

"Right." Cole blew out a breath. "Sometimes I work for criminals and walk a blurry line. But I don't murder or kidnap innocent people for money. And when I was betrayed, I didn't go on a ruthless killing spree. I faked my own death, went into hiding, and lost my goddamn soul mate."

"Good for you." Tiago laughed hollowly. "I guess that makes you a better man than me."

"No." Her hackles flared, and she grabbed Tiago's arm, turning him toward her. "I've never condoned the things you've done, but you know what? Cole didn't lose his parents and only brother. He didn't watch someone heartlessly gut his wife. There is *no* comparison. I don't know him that well, but if someone murdered his fiancée in front of him..." She jabbed a finger at Cole. "I think there would be a very different man standing there."

"You're defending him?" Cole asked with more hostility than she appreciated. "Do you know what he did to Tate and Lucia?"

"Yes." She jutted her chin.

"Are you free?"

"What?"

"Are you free to walk away from him? Right now?"

A numb, paralyzing thud echoed in her ears, and her neck ached to shake her head. Now was the time to tell him, to let him know she couldn't escape.

Tiago would never release her. He would never let her see her friends, or pursue a career, or carry a loaded gun, or go for a walk alone. Cole needed to know this. He could help her. But her muscles wouldn't work, and her voice deserted her.

"She's not free." Tiago's fingers shackled her wrist as he shoved open the freezer door. "If she wants to go with you, I won't allow it. If you try to take her—"

"You'll kill me. I figured as much." Cole flicked his gaze to her. "This isn't over, Kate. I'll get you out."

"The fuck you will." Tiago ushered her out of the freezer, into the warm kitchen, and toward the hallway, where Arturo waited.

"Hang on." She dug in her heels, trying to slow his long strides so she could explain the situation to Cole. "I just need to—"

An enormous explosion erupted somewhere in the house. The percussion was so forceful it reverberated in her ribcage and rang in her ears. She lost her balance in the heels, and in the next breath, strong arms came around her and her feet left the floor.

Tiago hoisted her against his chest and swung back toward Cole. "Tell me that isn't an assassination attempt on the President."

"With that bomb? It must be." Cole raced past them and poked his head in the corridor. "It probably dropped from overhead."

"Drones." Tiago's entire body turned to stone. "Goddammit, there will be more. We need to get the fuck out of here."

She choked down the sound of undiluted fear as it tried to escape.

A cloud of dust shook from the ceiling. Alarms, shrill and deafening, blared to life, and in the distance, the blast of gunfire rent the air.

"Opposition activists." Cole shoved a hand through his brown hair. "I heard a rumor the Colombian president was rallying an attack."

"And we're caught in the middle of it?" Her heart lurched.

"Gonna need you to run, Kate." Tiago lowered her feet to the floor. "Kick off your shoes."

He supported her balance as she toed off each heel. Then he guided her arms into the sleeves of the jacket still draped over her shoulders.

At her questioning look, he said, "In case there's any flying debris, the jacket is better than nothing."

"The rear exit is blocked by the gunfight." Arturo appeared in the doorway. "We'll have to leave out the front with everyone else."

"Mass fucking exodus." Tiago pulled her into the hall and laced their fingers together. "No matter what, don't let go."

The flashing, screeching alarms in the ceiling fucked with her bearings. By the time she scrounged up a nod, he was already dragging her at full speed toward the ballroom.

Cole and Arturo stayed on their heels. Until the second bomb hit.

It detonated so close it threw her against the wall. The acrid scent of smoke burned her nose, and she tasted the grit of dust as she coughed.

Given the noise of glass, the ear-splitting howls of people, and the rush of nearby footsteps, the explosion must've blown through the ballroom. If her sense of direction could be trusted, that was just around the next bend.

"Keep moving." Tiago hadn't let go of her hand and pulled on it roughly, urgently, propelling her forward again.

Her pulse thrashed past her ears as she sprinted to keep pace with his strides. Around the corner and through a doorway, they burst into what was left of the ballroom.

Dirt and smoke scattered into the atmosphere, creating a nebulous, eye-burning fog. Windows shattered. Shards of glass and twisted steel continued to drop in a groaning, deadly rainfall from the huge bite that had been taken out of the far side of the room.

Furniture tipped upside down, legs in the air. Debris and breakage covered the dance floor, the musicians gone. And the partygoers...

Some lay on the floor in fetal positions, trying to protect their ears and organs. Most ran toward the exit. Others stood off to the side, shell-shocked and unmoving. The rest had been tossed amid the blast, at least a dozen dead.

Tiago spun toward her and gripped her shoulders, shouting with his eyes. His mouth barked commands, but she couldn't hear him over the deafening noise.

He surveyed the glass-covered floor, glanced at her feet, and scooped her up into his arms. It was a considerable distance to carry her over the wreckage from one end of the demolished ballroom to the other, but gratitude overrode her stubbornness.

Wrapping her arms around his shoulders, she pressed her face into his neck and held on.

She assumed Arturo and Cole followed behind, but she was afraid to look. A barrage of closely spaced gunshots broke out around them, firing close enough to damage her eardrums.

The President's opposition might've been here to assassinate him, but if they were willing to bomb a house full of people, they didn't care who they hit in the crossfire.

Tiago tucked her close to his body, bowing over her with his head ducked as he ran like hell.

She wished she had a gun, so she could shoot back. She wished they'd stayed in bed and skipped the fucking party. But wishes wouldn't help them. They needed a fucking miracle.

The din of the surrounding chaos redlined her heart rate. The blaring alarms, panicked screams, and approaching gunfire pounded from every direction. She lifted her head.

Twenty feet from the exit. Almost there.

As every nerve ending in her body stretched toward that door, a great thunderous clap blew apart the world.

One second, she was in Tiago's arms beneath a vaulted ceiling. The next, she was airborne under the open nighttime sky.

Then everything went black.

THIRTY-ONE

Kate floated in a painless state of silence and disorientation. Every few seconds, a series of flashes burst through, like the intermittent vibrations of a dying heartbeat.

She couldn't hear anything. Not her cries or her breath. Was her head detached from her body? Or her limbs? That didn't make sense. But why couldn't she move?

"Tiago." His name chanted from her mind, but she wasn't sure her voice touched the air.

The floor shook violently beneath her. More explosions, farther away. Alarms strobed, but the wailing didn't penetrate her ears. People stumbled and ran, but she couldn't hear their screams.

As she attempted to recover her senses, a blanket of hellish heat saturated the front of her body. Blinking through semi-blindness, she stared up at a pillar of fiery smoke and dust. It rushed out through sections of the roof that had been destroyed by the blast.

Blackened orange flames billowed from the rubble near the exit, baking the startled air. A pressurized wind swept through the room, pulling on her, as if trying to draw her into the fire.

"Tiago!" She struggled to turn her neck and found herself lying by a wall some distance from where he'd been carrying her.

Panic tortured her heart, and her muscles refused to respond. It was so dark, so confusing. Why couldn't she see him? Or feel his hands on her? He would never leave her behind.

The blackness shuddered with jarring flickers of light. Bullets ricocheted, kicking up dirt across the floor. She tried to sit, until she felt the reverberation of approaching feet.

She held still, her stomach clenching as a dozen black-clad men with guns ran past her, their boots stepping close enough to bounce the broken pieces of wood beneath her.

Her hearing detected fragmented sound within her body, like the whooshing of blood and crackling static. Was she hurt? She couldn't sense pain or time, and her brain didn't seem to be working right.

Consciousness shriveled to a pinprick of light, and she strained for it, desperate to stay alert.

After a while, something touched her. Frantic hands, shaking her shoulders and rousing her awake.

Oh God, she'd passed out? For how long?

She opened her eyes, her mouth, struggling to identify the face hovering over her.

Brown hair, blue bow tie, American features — none of the details she ached to see.

Cole Hartman jostled her limp body, his lips

moving without sound.

"Where's Tiago?" She braced a hand against the splintered debris beneath her and pushed up. "Where is he?"

Her head pounded something fierce, and sporadic noises filtered in, making the pain unbearably worse.

She must not have been unconscious for very long, because the same chaotic level of disorder raged around her — the fire, the gunfight, the exodus of terrified people.

Tiago was nowhere in sight.

They were on an island. Did that mean there wouldn't be fire crews or ambulances? Where the hell was the mob of people running to? Where would they go?

Away from the fire and spraying bullets.

As Cole tried to speak to her, she focused on reading his lips.

Can you stand?

Are you hurt?

We need to go.

She wasn't going anywhere without Tiago.

Shoving off the floor with trembling muscles, she staggered to her feet and scanned the darkness. "Have you seen him?"

A rush of adrenaline accelerated her pulse, shaking away the crippling shock that had pinned her to the floor during those long, wasted minutes.

Cole's arms wrapped around her, lifting her off the floor and forcing her with him. She pushed against his chest, trying to get down, to stand on her own.

He tightened his hold and took her away from the rubble where Tiago must've been buried.

"Nooooo!" She screamed in horror, frantically

searching the destruction for his body. "I'm not leaving without him!"

Cole didn't slow as he veered around crumbled piles of masonry, wood, and steel. With each step, her hearing returned. As did her determination.

"Go back!" She thrashed in his unbending arms. "Take me back!"

A shooter sprinted past, sweating the room with bullets. Cole took cover, dodging the gunfire while fighting down her flailing hands. Then he burst into a sprint, carrying her through a demolished doorway and into a thick haze of smoke.

"Tiago!" She choked through the suffocating smog and realized the blackness overhead was the sky.

He'd taken her outside and wasn't stopping. His legs ate up the ground, hauling her farther and farther away from the burning mansion.

No, no no!

A sob opened her throat, and a flood of wailing screams fell out.

"Can't leave him! Put me down. I have to go back!" She couldn't stop crying. Couldn't see through her blinding panic and tears.

She howled and writhed until his hand clapped over her mouth and his furious eyes came into view.

"You're going to get us killed," he whispered harshly. "Shut the fuck up."

She shoved his hand away. "But Tiago—"

"He's dead or missing." He ran down an embankment and jumped onto a small deserted dock. "If you run back there, you'll be dead, too."

He dumped her in a waiting speedboat. Before she had a chance to scramble out, he slipped the tether free, fired up the engine, and shot into the black expanse of the ocean.

The sudden momentum knocked her into one of the vinyl seats. She twisted toward the rear, gripping the headrest as the island drifted away.

Rags of fire whipped along the skyline and wafted plumes of smoke above it, making the darkness even darker. The boat crashed against the waves, and as the distance stretched, reality clawed its way in.

Tiago was in that inferno, and she'd left him there.

Grief consumed her, wracking her body with violent, shuddering sobs. She'd abandoned him, something he would've never, ever done to her. He would've launched himself onto an exploding bomb before he let someone drag him away without her.

Because he loved her.

Not once had she said those words back to him, and the thought only made her more miserable. Guilt lashed in her stomach. Defeat bunched her shoulders around her ears. Despondency pounded in her head, and emptiness carved out her chest. She was utterly wretched and inconsolable.

Cole must've thought she'd completely lost her mind. She didn't know how to explain her feelings, but she had about thirty minutes to figure it out before he stopped the boat.

He killed the motor, and waves lapped around them. The ocean bled into darkness. Nothing to see or hear for miles.

After checking something on his phone, he turned his angry gaze to her.

"I don't extract unwilling people." He rose from the driver's seat and approached her in the rear of the boat. "Tell me I didn't make a mistake."

"You made a mistake." She was numb. Depleted. Heartsick. "Turn the boat around. Take me back."

"You want to go back to the man who poisoned Lucia for eleven years, mutilated Tate's back, shackled him in a shack for three months, and held you against your will?" He crouched beside her and softened his tone. "Did he rape you?"

An ugly mass of emotion swelled in her throat, and she looked away.

"You care about him." A sigh billowed past his lips. "It's okay, Kate. You have Stockholm syndrome. I see it all time in these situations and—"

"What if it's not that? What if my feelings are real? And I just..." Another sob rose up. "I just left him there to die."

"He received the same military training I did. If he's alive, he'll get out." His brows knitted together, and he glanced down at her thigh, where her scars peeked through the slit in the gown.

He spent the next few seconds examining her for injuries. Cuts and bruises marred her body. Her ankle was sprained, and he claimed she had a concussion.

She felt none of it. Nothing but emptiness.

"You've been through a lot. You need safety and friends and time to heal." He checked his phone and returned it to his pocket. "Your ride will be here any minute."

"What ride? Who's coming?"

"People who care about you." He removed a small device from another pocket. "I need to do a sweep for transmitters. Did Tiago put anything on your body? Like a small chip under your skin or maybe a piece of jewelry?"

"You mean a GPS chip?"

"Yes. You can't go to the Restrepo estate until we're certain you're not being tracked. The location is a highly guarded secret."

Her heart slammed as a fresh wave of sorrow washed over her. Tiago would've absolutely chipped her, and she knew exactly how. She didn't even care if he meant to track her. In fact, she loved that about him.

She loved his possessiveness.

She loved his bossy mouth, his sexy Spanish accent, his cruel eyes, and his addictive masculine taste when he kissed her. She loved everything about him, and so what if that made her a head case?

"He hasn't put anything on me." She rolled her shoulders forward so the material would hang more loosely across her breasts. "We have to go back for him, Cole."

He narrowed his eyes and waved that device right over her breasts until it sounded a low beep.

Her molars crashed together.

"You have piercings." He removed a tiny flashlight from his pocket. "I need to see them."

"I'm not removing them." She hardened her voice. "Take me back to the island."

"Not going back, Kate." He pinched the bridge of his nose and exhaled. "You can take out the piercings or leave them in. I don't give a fuck. I just need to see if there's a tracker on them."

"The thing beeped, so you already know."

"It detected metal. You'll get the same response when you go through an X-ray machine at the airport."

"Oh." She released a breath.

If he needed to see them, he would have to do it while they stayed in.

Without removing Tiago's tuxedo coat, she wriggled the straps of the dress down her arms. When her breasts hit the warm air, he powered on the flashlight and angled the beam on the glimmering red stones.

"The fuck?" He leaned in, eyes bulging as he stared at the jewelry. "It can't be."

"What?"

"Did he tell you what these stones are?"

"Uh... Pawneets... Or no, it was pennet..."

"Painites."

"Yes. Painites. Why?"

He barked out a strangled laugh and sat back on his heels. "That son of a bitch."

"What's wrong?"

He shook his head and gripped the back of his neck, his eyes fixed on the piercings, as if he couldn't believe they were real.

"Did you find a tracker?" She straightened, startled by his strange reaction.

"No. The barbells are too small. It's not that. It's just..." He scrubbed a hand down his face. "You can fix your dress."

Tiago hadn't put a tracker on her?

Her breath stuttered as she put the gown back in order. "Is it the stones?"

"Yeah, Kate. Those fucking stones..." He shifted to the seat across from her and rested his elbows on his knees. "Painites are one of the rarest gemstones on the planet. Extremely valuable. But that's not important. It's..."

Something thundered in the distance, a clap-clap-

clap whir of noise that grew louder, closer. In the next breath, she recognized the sound. A helicopter was coming.

"That's your ride. Listen…" Cole ran the device along the rest of her body as he spoke. "There's a rumor going around in the criminal underground that Tiago Badell sold his entire syndicate to some unknown investor in exchange for…" A swallow jogged in his throat. "Four rare painite stones."

"What?" Her face chilled, and she pressed a hand over one of the piercings.

"That sort of hearsay runs rampant in his world, usually conceived as a means of subterfuge and rarely accurate. I didn't even bother fact checking it. But the evidence…" He glanced at her chest and cleared his throat. "Jesus, Kate. If those gemstones are real…"

"He wouldn't give me fake gems and call them real. Not his style."

Cole nodded, his voice stunned. "You're wearing the last twelve years of his life. His entire goddamn livelihood."

"What does that mean?" Tears welled in her eyes as the whomping sound of the helicopter sped closer. "Did he give up his organization?"

"It appears so."

"But he gave the stones to me a month ago, and he's been going to the compound every day, conducting meetings with all his men."

"Meetings about what?"

"I don't know. They're always in Spanish."

"He was probably transitioning everything. Or dissolving operations."

"Oh my God." She jumped from the seat, rocking

unsteadily as waves slapped at the boat. "Take me back. I need to go back!"

The helicopter swept in above her, swallowing her voice and enveloping her in a mist of ocean water. She covered her ears against the god-awful noise, unable to make out its silhouette against the night sky.

No way would she agree to board that thing. How would it even work?

She turned back to Cole and shouted over the wind, "Take me back!"

He gripped her face, catching the hair whipping around her. "I'll go back. I'll find him."

His words didn't reach her ears, but she read them on his lips and saw the promise in his dark eyes.

"I'll go with you."

He shook his head and pointed behind her. "Go."

Steel arms encircled her from behind, and she turned, falling into the warm, familiar eyes of one of her roommates. "Martin!"

A tether ran from his harness to the helicopter. Evidently, he'd been lowered on some kind of pulley system.

Her chest squeezed as she absorbed the worried expression on his handsome face. Damn, she'd missed him, and the roar of the wind made it impossible to tell him as much.

A gust smacked her sideways, and she braced her legs to remain upright. Cole held her in place as Martin quickly attached a belt around her hips, between her legs, and secured the contraption to his. Then he shined a flashlight into the darkness overhead.

The harness pulled tight and his arms even tighter as they were lifted into the air. The blades beat the wind against them like a hurricane.

With her heart in her stomach, she stared down at Cole and demanded with her eyes. *Find him.*

He stared back with a silent vow tensing his face.

Digging her hands into Martin's shoulders, she held her breath and closed her eyes. She had to trust Cole to go back to the island, but it left her feeling completely useless and terrified as that boat sank farther away from her feet.

When they reached the helicopter, hands grabbed, and arms pulled, until she was lying on her back and safely inside the aircraft.

Familiar faces filled her view. Smiles. Cheering roars. Even a few wet eyes.

"Kate!" Camila tackled her as soon as she was disconnected from Martin. "Fucking shit, girl! You've given me a dozen heart attacks."

Matias nodded at her from the cockpit. She caught a glimpse of Luke's red hair, before Ricky hauled her into the seat beside him and strapped her in. Martin plopped down on her other side, and the helicopter's nose dipped as it raced into the night.

The blaring noise from the blades made conversation difficult, but she felt their relief and happiness pouring off them. Four of her old roommates had shown up for her rescue—Martin, Camila, Ricky, and Luke—and she suspected Tomas and others were waiting at Matias' Colombian estate.

After being gone for four months, it was surreal to be sitting here with them. A consuming, head-spinning kind of surreal that crashed in with a flood of pain.

Her eyes burned with that achy feeling that always came right before she cried. She tried to hold back the tears, but they were persistent and full of so many conflicting emotions — gratitude, fear, joy, desolation, and hope.

She was finally free, and it hurt to the depths of her soul.

The one thing that mattered most in her freedom was missing.

She needed Tiago.

Whether he joined her in her freedom or took it away, she just needed them to experience whatever came next together.

THIRTY-TWO

Eight people have been arrested after Saturday's apparent assassination attempt on the President of Venezuela. The President survived the ambush after several drones dropped explosives on his dinner party at a private residence, an attack he blamed on opposition activists and Colombia's president. Thirty-seven people are confirmed dead. Twelve others are still missing.

Kate powered off the TV and stared at the blank screen, her voice brittle with pain. "Tiago's alive."

A throat cleared. Feet shuffled. Someone sighed.

Sitting in one of the many living rooms at Matias' Colombian estate, she was surrounded by her friends. All of them. Liv and Josh, Van and Amber, Camila and Matias, Tate and Lucia, her roommates — everyone was here, seeking refuge within the cartel's stronghold while awaiting the verdict on Tiago Badell.

No one trusted him, and maybe that was smart. As long as she was separated from him, they weren't safe.

Cole Hartman had returned to the island as promised, but after a night of searching for Tiago and

Arturo, he came up empty.

The next day, he went to Tiago's penthouse and slipped past the building's supposed impenetrable security. Everything was still there, but the entire staff had vanished, including Boones.

That was four days ago.

He hadn't been able to confirm the list of casualties on the island. The President had buried that information. No surprise. Most of the names at the party belonged to the sort of unsavory people no president should be associated with.

Cole assured her he would learn who died and who was missing, but it would take time.

Didn't matter. She already decided Tiago was alive. She just needed to figure out how to find him. That was the tricky part.

Tiago had enemies, and now they knew who she was and what she meant to him. The moment she stepped outside of Matias' fortress, they would find her.

It didn't dissuade her. She had powerful friends, and they were extremely protective of her.

Except that was the problem. Her friends were *too* protective.

When she'd asked Matias for a security team to accompany her to Venezuela, he refused. Then he threatened to lock her in a cell if she tried to leave. Her roommates supported that threat.

When she'd asked Cole to somehow get a message to Tiago in the criminal underground, that request was refused, as well. Cole said it would end up in the wrong hands and only put her in more danger.

But Cole kept a diligent watch on Caracas, and he'd been able to confirm one thing.

Tiago was no longer associated with his organization.

Smuggling routes had been dismantled. Rival gangs had moved in. There was even a new leader running what was left of his compound.

He'd given it all up. Forfeited his livelihood. Surrendered his protection.

For the four gemstones he'd attached to her nipples.

The man had a filthy dark sense of chivalry.

"We need to consider the possibility he'll never resurface." Tate paced to the window and stared out at the moonlit landscape of the rain forest. "We can't hide here forever."

"He won't harm you," Kate murmured.

Tate pivoted and tilted his head to the side, regarding her. "Have you seen my back, Kate?"

"Yes." She glided a hand over her thigh, seeking comfort in the scars that lay beneath her borrowed jeans. "He and I made a deal. He promised me he would never hurt you again."

"His promises mean nothing to me."

Her chest was empty, drained of tears and breath. It felt as though she'd left her insides in that fire. Everything under her skin was simply gone. Except the hum of determination. That was still there, rising up from the chasm where her soul once lived, where he used to be.

"He's alive, and I'll find him." She met Tate's eyes. "Unless he finds me first."

He pressed his lips together, biting back a retort.

Every hour that passed reinforced her belief that Tiago was alive. That meant she wasn't the only one hurting. He had vulnerabilities that could only be comforted and healed by her. He needed her, missed her, feared for her as much as she did for him. They were two halves of a whole.

Since arriving here, she'd heard the term *Stockholm syndrome* from every mouth in every conversation. It didn't upset her or make her defensive. Because honestly, how many times had she thrown those very words at Tiago?

How sad that she had to lose him in order to see what had been right in front of her all along.

She knew what she felt was love — not coercion, not lust, not Stockholm syndrome — because it had become an artery that ran through the deepest part of her heart. She felt it beating and knew if she severed it, she would bleed out. She wouldn't survive.

The night she reunited with Tate, she sat down with him and explained this. Since he was so utterly wrapped up in Lucia, he understood the madness that came with love. He couldn't fully comprehend her position with regard to Tiago, but he listened. He was trying.

Then she had a heart-to-heart with everyone else, individually, paired off with couples, and together as a group. It'd been four days of discussing, soul-searching, and analyzing until her emotional shields were eradicated and there was nowhere to hide from their hard questions.

It felt like a form of group therapy. She endured it because she appreciated their life experiences, valued their opinions, and trusted their intentions.

Josh and Amber related to her the most. They'd both fallen in love with their captors, so they understood her on the darkest, most vulnerable level. Their journeys hadn't been pretty, and look at them now. They fucking glowed with happiness.

There was comfort in that. Validation. Hope.

So here they all were, the whole gang sitting together in Matias' estate, talking, monitoring the news, and waiting. Because the man she loved was missing, and that made him a threat to everyone.

On the bright side, she had her friends back. Thanks to Van Quiso, they shared a remarkable bond, one born in shackles and strengthened in survival.

For the rest of the night, they lounged around in the living room, pouring drinks, sharing stories, enjoying one another's company, and musing about the future.

She didn't know what the future held for her, but she never saw herself as a vigilante warrior. Not like them.

She told them she wanted to heal people, and maybe someday, she would become the Freedom Fighters' resident doctor.

A doctor like Boones.

If she located the old man, she would find Tiago.

Maybe Boones had returned to his brothers in his home village? She didn't know where that was, but through her observations, she'd collected four months of clues, including the unique sounds of his native language.

A plan started to form, thrumming through her blood and bouncing her leg.

"I'm going to head to bed." She rose, said her good-nights, and strolled through the maze of corridors in the sprawling, contemporary estate.

Verandas and scenic breezeways led her to her

suite. The fortress reminded her of an all-inclusive resort, equipped with every amenity. Commercial kitchens, dining rooms filled with dozens of tables, Olympic-sized pool, and full-service staff... With all the surrounding luxury, she could almost overlook the scary, heavily-armed cartel members who roamed the halls.

When she stepped inside her room, the tread of approaching footsteps sounded behind her.

"Hey, Kate." Martin caught the door before it closed. "Can I come in?"

"Like you have to ask." She strode past the bed, lowered into the armchair, and pulled Tiago's tuxedo coat over her lap, instantly finding solace in the crisp feel of the fabric. "Want a drink?"

Every suite had a fully-stocked wet bar, laptop, sitting area, and private bathroom.

"Nah. Just wanted to check on you." He sprawled on the loveseat beside her.

She grew up with three older brothers, and none of them had been even a fraction as protective as her five alpha roommates.

As he stared at her, a glint of aggression hardened his green eyes before melting away into the shadows of his handsome face.

His model-like features, perfectly-combed blond hair, and muscular build fit the requisite mold of beauty and seduction. They all had that in common.

Over a span of seven years, Van and Liv had captured six beautiful men and two women. Plucked out of the ghettos along the Mexican border, Kate and the others didn't have families who would miss them.

Joshua Carter was the exception, the one who shattered Liv's façade and brought down the entire sex trafficking operation.

Martin had been slave number five. He was also the pack leader among her male roommates.

"You sleep with that thing?" He nodded at the tuxedo coat.

"Maybe." She pulled it up to her nose and inhaled the scent of fire and masculinity from the collar.

"You're a fucking mess."

"You should talk. How's Ricky?"

His jaw set. "I'm not touching that conversation."

She loved to pester him about the sexual tension that vibrated between him and his best friend. Ricky was openly bisexual, flirtatious as hell, and had a very obvious, soul-deep crush on Martin.

Martin, on the other hand, grunted and growled like a homophobic every time she mentioned the attraction. He claimed to be straight and banged a different woman every night. But there was so much more going on beneath the surface. He carried a freight load of baggage, most of which had compounded during his captivity with Van.

Everyone knew he wanted to fuck Ricky's brains out. He just hadn't come to terms with it.

"How are you doing with Van?" she asked. "Is it still hard for you to be around him?"

"If I ever get him alone, I'm going to take him for a ride in the country."

"What does that mean?"

"It's what my dad used to say. Whenever one of our old dogs needed to be put down, he'd load up the dog in the truck, drive to an isolated field, and shoot it." A dark smirk twisted his lips. "It's time for a ride in the country."

"Please, don't." Her stomach caved in.

"You're telling me you've forgiven him?"

"No." She nodded. "Maybe. I don't know. Being around him isn't as hard as it used to be. He doesn't scare me."

There was a bigger, meaner, much more terrifying man in the world, and goddammit, she missed his brutal mouth.

"That's good, Kate. It's great." He pushed up from his sprawl and leaned forward to grip her hand. "You're a fucking fighter, you know that?"

"Can't shoot a gun or throw a fist to save my life." She laughed.

"You fight with this crazy, fathomless inner strength. I've never worried about losing you to depression or insanity or…" He squeezed her hand. "A broken heart. It seems you've figured out how to survive the emotional shit better than the rest of us. I envy that."

"Thank you." Her throat tightened.

"You're not going back to Texas, are you?"

She hadn't thought about it, but her answer was certain. "No."

"None of us are returning."

"You're all staying here?"

"I don't know what Tate and Lucia will do, but the guys and I need to be here, with Camila."

It made sense. Camila was their leader in a dangerous fight against human sex trafficking. Most of their missions sent them to South America. There was no reason for them to continue to live in Texas.

"We should sell the house." She gave him a sad smile.

"Agreed." He cocked his head. "This isn't a break-up, Kate."

"No." Her smile turned upward, stretching her cheeks. "It's a merger. The Freedom Fighters and the Restrepo cartel. An unstoppable force to be reckoned with."

"Ricky and I are leaving next week. I don't know when we'll return."

"What's the mission?"

"Camila's planting us in a Mexican prison to gather information on the leader of the inmates. He happens to be the capo of La Rocha cartel. A nasty piece of work. His incarceration hasn't stopped him from running one of the biggest slave trade operations south of the border." His gaze lost focus beneath a cloud of barely restrained fury. "He's trafficking kids, Kate. We have to end that motherfucker."

"You're going into a Mexican prison? Undercover? As inmates?" Her pulse sprinted. "What the fuck, Martin? You can't—"

"Ricky and I have been training for this for months. We know what we're doing."

She closed her eyes, released a breath, and met his gaze. "Please, be careful."

"Same to you, when you capture your captor." He winked.

They talked for a little while longer before she walked him out. Then she took a shower, put on pajamas she'd borrowed from Camila, and slipped her arms into the sleeves of Tiago's dinner jacket.

Maybe sleeping in it every night had taken her desperation too far, but she missed him terribly. It had only been four days, and the pain had become more than she could bear.

To think, he'd been such a dick to her. He'd hurt her, brought her to tears, made her vulnerable, and took away all her defenses.

He'd also kept every promise, showed genuine regret, protected her, and loved her unconditionally. Through his cruelty and his tenderness, she realized she could trust him at the deepest level. And those defenses and freedoms he'd taken from her? She didn't need any of it. Not with him.

She just needed his love.

As she crawled into bed, his absence hit her in a torrent of tears. She pulled the tuxedo coat around her, breathed him in, and silently wept.

"Where are you, Tiago?"

A knock sounded on the door.

After living with five roommates, she'd grown used to late-night visitors in her room. Someone always needed something, even if it was just conversation.

Since Martin had just left, she suspected Ricky would be waiting on the other side. But when she opened the door, Lucia's brown gaze collided with hers.

"Hi." Kate wiped her cheeks, certain all the crying had made her eyes red and swollen.

"Hey, um... I know we don't know each other, but I thought since we have a mutual...acquaintance..."

"You mean Tiago?"

"Yeah."

"He's more than an acquaintance to me."

"Poor choice of words. Look, I just..." Lucia rested her hands on her hips and stared at the floor. "I can't sleep. Tate hogs all your time, and I just really wanted to talk to you alone."

"You want me to tell you about Tiago."

"Yes." Her expression softened, her gaze pleading. "I spent eleven years with him, and I... Shit, I know it's late, so if you want to talk another time—"

"I can't sleep, either." She opened the door wider and motioned for Lucia to enter.

"Is that his?" Lucia nodded at the dinner jacket that engulfed her shoulders.

"Yeah." She ran a hand along the black sleeve.

"I never saw him wear a tux, but I can picture it." Lucia perched on the loveseat. "He's very easy on the eyes."

"He looked devastating that night, especially when he danced with me." Her chin trembled.

"Tiago *danced* with you?"

"Yeah." She took a seat in the armchair. "What do you want to know?"

"Everything."

She started at the beginning and walked through every interaction, every fight, every tender moment, the good and ugly, the brutality and rape, the kindness and beautiful acts of devotion.

By the time she finished, she hadn't left out a single detail from the past four months. Tears streaked her cheeks. A smile rested on her mouth, and she felt wonderfully copacetic.

"Damn." Lucia slumped into the loveseat with her jaw hanging open. "I can't even comprehend him being like that. He wasn't like that with me. I mean, the cruelty? Of course. The threats and the control? He ruled my damn life. But I never saw that devoted side of him. No one did. And what the hell? He was married?"

"Yeah, that took me by surprise, too."

"I'm really fucking in awe of you. That man scares

the shit out of me. I spent eleven years in fear of my life. But you? You walk in, and within four months, he's kneeling at your feet. You changed him."

"He hasn't changed, and he certainly doesn't fucking kneel. Believe me, he's just as vicious as ever. Don't forget about the scars on my body, the golden showers, the handcuffs in the jungle. If it hadn't been for those bombs, I would still be his captive."

"True. But he gave up Caracas and the protection it gave him."

"I don't know why. I didn't do anything to make him—"

"He loves you. That's huge, Kate. It's everything."

"Somewhere along the way, I fell in love with him, too. I guess that's why this hurts so badly. Not knowing where he is or if he's okay... I can't even let myself consider the possibility he was injured in that explosion. Or worse..."

"What are you going to do?"

She had over six-hundred-thousand dollars sitting in her bank account. The money Van had distributed among his ex-slaves.

It would take her some time to put all the clues together and pinpoint the location of Boones' village. She would need travel documents, a passport, and maybe a hired security guard. But once she had all that in place...

"I'm going to buy a plane ticket to Africa."

THIRTY-THREE

"Reconsider this trip, Kate." Liv Reed stood at the center of Kate's room, arms at her sides and shoulders back. A pillar of grace and dominance.

"No." Wrapped in Tiago's worn tuxedo coat, Kate sat in the corner of the loveseat, buzzing with nervous energy. "You would do the same thing if you lost Josh."

It had been one month since she left Tiago on that burning island.

One long fucking month.

Cole Hartman had finally acquired the names of the casualties from that night.

Both Tiago and Arturo were on the list.

They'd been counted among the dead.

Deceased.

Gone.

When Cole gave her the devastating news, she could've let it destroy her. But she wasn't ready to curl up and die. She couldn't give up.

So she decided that Tiago had taken a page from

Cole's book and faked his own death. There was no evidence to support her claim. Nothing to go on but hope.

Hope was all she had.

She spent the past month hunting for Boones' village.

His scarification, the jewelry and clothing from the photo of his daughter, the sounds of his native tongue, and a thousand other tiny little details led her to Northeast Africa.

She contacted a linguistic specialist at a university in Texas. Weeks of correspondence with the professor helped her narrow down Boones' vernacular to Tigre, an Afroasiatic language spoken in Sudan, Ethiopia, and Eritrea.

The three countries sat together along the Red Sea. She was getting closer, but not close enough.

The language had a lot of dialects, and those unique nuances helped her determine that Boones used the patois of the Tigre people in Eritrea.

That was the break she needed.

He was Eritrean, and they referred to their language as Tigrayit.

She had the country of Boones' home, but nothing more specific. After another week of digging, she hadn't been able to pinpoint a town or village.

Impatience dug in its claws.

Throughout her search, she tried so hard to control the emotions that swarmed inside her. It had been one month. At this point, she didn't think she could survive another day without him.

But she would. She would survive as long as it took.

TAKE

Her flight departed in four days. Luggage lined the far wall of her room, packed with the essentials for her trip to Eritrea.

She'd worked with Matias' staff to purchase everything she needed — clothes, travel documents, fake passport, and ID. She funded every cost and set every demand, all while keeping her destination as secret as possible.

Those involved knew she was going to Africa. Nothing more. Tiago hadn't shared the location for a reason, and she wouldn't, either.

Liv crossed the room and stood near the window, watching her teenage daughter through the glass.

Livana sat on the veranda of Kate's suite, with her nose in a book. She'd grown into a beautiful girl and seemed to be thriving in Colombia. Matias provided her with private tutors and an education far superior than what she received in the States.

"Have you decided to stay here for good?" Kate asked.

"We're working out the details. Van and Amber want to stay and join Camila's fight. Josh and I are willing to do the same, but the shared custody with Livana's adoptive mother complicates a permanent move."

"You could always fight for full custody."

"Yes, but that would be selfish. Livana was raised by her and — "

An urgent, rapid knock pounded on the door.

"Kate." Van barged in without waiting, and his silver eyes cut through the room until they landed on her. "He's here."

"Who?" She leapt from the loveseat, staggering to

right herself as her heart pounded out of her chest. "Who's here?"

But she knew.

She knew before Van said his name.

"Tiago Badell."

A gust of dizziness hit her sideways.

He was here. What did it mean? Was he hurting? Angry? Completely insane?

Her blood pressure skyrocketed as she sucked in breath after breath. She was going to hyperventilate. Or pass out.

She needed to go, run, get to him right now.

"Where?" She sprinted to the door, her voice rising to an explosive shrill. "Which way?"

"The west wing." He followed her into the hall and nodded to the right.

The hairs rose on her nape as she bolted in the direction he pointed her.

She hadn't visited the west wing but knew enough about the horrors Matias imprisoned there. Slave traders, traitors, and rival cartel members — the captives were the worst of the worst and deserved every punishment they received within those walls. She heard that Frizz, one of the men in Matias' inner circle, often sewed up their mouths to match his own.

If Tiago was there, did that mean he'd been captured? Were they torturing him?

Her stomach threatened to empty as she picked up her pace, racing through the halls with no idea which way to go.

The sound of sneakers gave chase, and a moment later, Van caught up with her.

"Turn left at the next bend." He directed her

through the halls, sprinting easily alongside her.

"How did Tiago get here?" She panted, her legs burning through the strides.

"The crazy motherfucker broke in."

"What?" She faltered, recovered, and sped up her gait. "How did he find this place?"

"Fuck if I know. Another left here." He raced her down a long corridor, his breathing so much calmer than hers. "He came in with guns blazing, ready to take down the whole goddamn cartel."

Her chest tightened painfully, and her lungs wheezed for air. "Did he get hurt? Is anyone dead?"

"Don't know."

Her limbs trembled with terror and anticipation as she skidded to a stop at the entrance to the wing.

The guards let them pass, and she followed the sounds of shouting through two more corridors.

Up ahead, Lucia leaned her back against the wall with a hand clutching her throat. When she spotted Kate, her eyes widened. "Kate! Wait!"

"Where is he?" She ran to the steel door across from Lucia and peered through the small window.

In the concrete room, Tiago lay on his side on the floor, eyes closed, dressed in only a pair of briefs. He bared his teeth and jerked his arms, going nowhere with his hands shackled behind him.

Her heart splintered, and she grabbed the door handle, shaking it. Locked.

Tate paced through the cell, shouting furiously as he demanded answers about Lucia and everything that had happened over the past eleven years.

Blood trickled from cuts on Tiago's face and chest, but there were no visible bullet or stab wounds.

Why was he bleeding and lying on the floor?

A rabid sound wrenched from her throat. She needed to get to him and hold him and let him know she was here.

"Open the door!" She shook the handle harder, more frantically, losing control when it wouldn't budge.

His eyes opened and unerringly found hers through the glass.

"Tiago!" She pressed her hand against the window, and a sharp burn stabbed through her chest.

He'd lost weight, his muscles radically leaner, his jaw more angular and covered in a full beard. What happened to him?

Tate's hands clenched at his sides, his face and neck bright red as he prowled a circle around Tiago's body. He looked as if he were seconds from murder.

"Let me in right now!" She pounded on the tiny window. "Swear to God, if you hurt him—"

Matias appeared on the other side of the glass and narrowed his eyes.

"Open the door," she screamed, banging her fists against the steel.

He slammed a metal cover over the window, blocking her view. Shutting her out.

She lost it.

In an explosion of rage, she threw her body against the door, yelling at the top of her lungs, kicking, and pounding until Van's arms locked around her and yanked her away.

"They're going to torture him." Tears blurred her eyes, and great sobs shook her shoulders. "They'll kill him."

"Kate, listen to me." Lucia gripped her face,

capturing her attention. "Only reason Tiago's alive is because of you. Matias and Tate know you love him. They're not going to hurt him."

"He's bleeding." She yanked on her arms, where Van held them at her back. "Let go of me."

He released her and stepped to the side, studying her with those bladed eyes of his. "He's bleeding because he broke into the secret headquarters of a Colombian cartel and attacked the guards."

"Did anyone die?" she asked Lucia.

"No. But they had to subdue him by physical force."

She wiped away her tears and pulled in a steeling breath. A little calmer now, she stepped back to the door and pressed her ear against it.

"Why won't they let me in?" She couldn't detect sound through the thick steel. "What are they doing to him?"

"Just talking." Lucia stared at the door, her expression tight. "Tate needs a resolution."

Tiago had tortured him, forced him to have sex with Van, and separated him from Lucia for three months. Kate wasn't sure there was a resolution for that.

"Why aren't you in there with him?" She flexed her hands, unable to quell the shaking.

"I've made peace with what he did to me." Lucia leaned her back against the wall and gazed at the door. "Hearing about your relationship with him helped. It gave me a sense of understanding, like maybe everything happened for a reason. I mean, I got Tate out of it."

"What about you?" She turned to Van. "I know what he did to you."

"Hm." He removed a toothpick from his pocket

and rested the end between his lips. "I'm the last person to throw stones. I don't like the guy, but I'll get over it. Forgive, forget, move on — any of that is better than holding on to hatred."

He gave her a knowing look, and for the first time since she'd met him, she stared directly into his razor eyes and didn't wince.

She didn't know whether she forgave Van or had simply moved on, but she no longer felt fear or hatred for the man.

"Tate's not in there for himself." Van rolled the toothpick to the corner of his mouth. "He's in there for his girl. He needs to flex his strength, make some threats, and prove to Tiago he's willing to do anything to protect her."

"Men," Lucia mumbled.

Kate shifted back to the door, aching to be on the other side. "Is there a first-aid kit around here?"

"I think so. Hang on." Lucia strode down the hall and returned a few minutes later with a bag of supplies, water bottles, and clean towels.

"Thank you." Kate gathered it in her arms and waited.

Another five minutes passed before the door swung open.

Tate stepped out, and his bloodshot eyes darted to Lucia. As Kate tried to squeeze past him, he caught her around the waist and enveloped her in a hug.

"Get him out of here before I start hating him again." He kissed the top of her head and let her go.

That sounded promising. Kind of.

Matias exited next, his expression brooding as he pressed a keyring into her hand. "He doesn't leave this cell."

Her heart burst into a gallop, and she darted into the room, swallowing down a month's worth of stress and tears.

Don't cry. Don't fall apart.

Matias closed the door behind her and sounded the dead bolt.

Her attention turned to Tiago, and her entire world filled with his harsh, imposing presence.

"Kate."

That deep, rich, dark timbre resonated in her soul. She felt his voice, *really* felt it, and in that moment, she experienced the truest form of freedom.

She had choices, endless choices and paths, and she picked him, willingly, freely.

Sitting on the floor with his hands shackled between his back and the wall, he watched her with an intensity that sucked the air from the room. The weight of his abrasive gaze ground against her, rubbing and heating her everywhere, his silence thick and penetrating, sinking inside her and pulling her toward him.

"What if I told you I tried to let you go?" He licked his lips. "Would you believe me?"

She shook her head, more in confusion than in answer. "Did you try to let me go?"

"Fuck no." He laughed, a cruel, humorless sound. "Never, Kate. Not even in death."

The tears she tried to keep in check rose, blurring her vision as she lowered to her knees beside him.

"I have so many questions. Things to tell you." She dumped the supplies on the floor and fumbled with the key. "I don't know where to start."

"Start with getting me out of these fucking

restraints." He shifted, giving her access to his arms. "I need you. Christ, I just need to feel you."

She twisted the key into the metal cuffs, and the instant they fell off, he dragged her onto his lap and captured her mouth with his.

The contact burned flames of hunger and energy around them, powering through her in billows of panting breaths.

Their tongues swept together, connecting, releasing, and chasing in frenzied lashes. Hands sailed everywhere, exploring and reacquainting with every muscle, scar, and curve of bone.

How strange and wonderful to feel his beard scratching her face. To feel his hands on her body. To taste his dark, minty essence on her tongue.

He was actually here.

Alive.

Growling.

Biting.

Mine.

When they came up for air, their gazes clung, neither of them blinking or speaking. There was so much to say, but she wanted to bask in the moment, let it settle through her, and commit every glorious detail to memory.

She sketched a thumb along the puckered, lifted scars that curved from his eye to the side of his skull. Her touch lowered to his beard, scraping through the thick, wiry black hairs.

Questions bubbled up, spooling and unraveling in her throat, but what came out first were the most important words she'd ever spoken.

"I love you."

"What?" He stopped breathing, his expression stark and unbelieving.

"I love you."

His eyes closed, and his head tipped back, as if the impact of her confession was too much.

"I love you, Tiago Badell."

He pulled in a broken breath. Relief melted across his face, and his shoulders and back lost strength and tension.

No lover had ever given him those words. It was perhaps the one thing he'd always wanted and never thought he could have.

When his eyes found hers again, he opened his demanding mouth, but no sound came out. It seemed she'd stolen his voice.

Straddling his lap, she gathered the water, towels, and antiseptic. Then she cleaned his wounds, starting with the cuts on his face.

She glided the towel across his wide shoulders, down the lines of his strong neck, and around the deep cut of muscles that sculpted his chest.

His weight loss was most evident in the flat terrain of his abdomen. Fewer ridges lined his lower stomach, and his hipbones protruded from his narrow waist, sharper than normal beneath the waistband of his briefs.

But the strength of him wasn't defined by bone and muscle. His power circulated behind his eyes and charged through his voice. She'd never come in contact with a more overbearing, viciously beautiful man.

Running a clean towel over every inch of his torso, she mourned the raised bumps of new scars. Some etched into the skin on his chest. Others lanced down his side and leg. Most would've required stitches. All of them hurt her heart.

As she examined him, he did the same with her, his hands caressing and probing, his breaths growing deeper, faster.

"You were injured in the explosion." She traced the slash on his ribs.

"Just cuts. You made it out unharmed?"

"A few bumps and bruises and a sprained ankle. No scars."

"I'm so fucking sorry, Kate. I failed — "

"What happened?" She searched his warm brown eyes. "One second, you were carrying me. Then you were gone. I didn't want to leave you, Tiago, but you were *no where*. It killed me."

"You got out. That's all that matters. And no thanks to me. I was knocked unconscious, unable to protect you." His jaw clenched. "I came to, buried under concrete." He gestured at the scar along his side. "When I couldn't find you and Cole, I knew he had you. You were safe. It made it easier to focus on saving my own ass."

"What about Arturo?"

His eyes shuddered. "He didn't make it."

"Fuck. I'm so sorry."

"Me, too." He tucked a lock of hair behind her ear.

"Cole said your names were on the deceased list."

"How the fuck did he get that list?" His dark eyebrows formed an angry *V*.

"I don't know."

"Jesus, Kate. I didn't want you to think I was dead."

"I didn't. I decided you were alive, because I couldn't... I couldn't accept anything else."

He tangled a hand in her hair and brought her

forehead to his lips. "I called in a favor to the President of Venezuela, had him put my name on that list before he released it to the authorities. It's not public information, but my enemies will get their hands on it, if they haven't already. As far as the U.S. government is concerned, I'm officially dead."

"They won't hunt you anymore?"

"No active searching, but I still have to lay low. Change my identity. That's if Restrepo ever allows me to leave this cell."

She flinched. "He's not going to keep you locked up!"

A rueful smile pulled at his mouth. "I know the location of his headquarters. No one walks away with that information."

She would see about that. "How did you find me?"

"There was no question *who* Cole placed you with. Problem was I didn't know where the fuck this place was. Took me a couple of weeks to narrow the location down to this section of the Amazon rain forest. I spent the next two weeks living in the surrounding jungle, tracking activity and listening for traffic."

"That's why you lost weight." She gripped his jaw through the beard, soaking in his dark features and beautiful brown eyes. "You look like a Latino Viking."

A feral growl vibrated in his chest. "I need you."

"I love you." She trailed a path of kisses across his cheek.

"Say it again." His hips lifted, rocking his rigid length between her legs.

"I love you."

"I want you." He wrapped his arms around her and ground her body against his lap.

"Take me."

"I'll never stop."

In the next breath, she was on her back, trapped beneath the hard concrete floor and his even harder body.

An addictive, burning desire inflamed her senses, and she writhed beneath him, desperate for his touch, his kiss, his heavy cock.

He didn't waste time, his fingers fumbling with the fly on her shorts. He stripped her from waist to feet, came down on top of her, and shoved up her shirt and bra, baring her breasts.

His gaze made a greedy sweep across her chest, and a devious grin tugged at the corner of his mouth.

"You kept the piercings." His eyes returned to hers.

"You told me not to remove them." She gripped one between her finger and thumb. "Is it true? Did you give up your entire syndicate for these stones?"

"No, Kate. I gave up everything for *you*."

Guilt pinched her stomach. "I was such a bitch when you gave me the piercings. I didn't know what it meant."

His lips crashed down on hers, hard and demanding. She arched against him, yearning for more contact, needing him closer.

Jolts of electricity shot through her as his assertive tongue swept in and out, doing wicked things in her mouth. Every nerve in her body electrified, and she moaned, grinding against the steel bar of his cock.

She ran her fingers down his strong, smooth back, pulling him closer, and her gaze landed on a black lens in the ceiling. "There's a camera."

"Let them watch." He reached between them, his hand brushing her pussy as he shoved down the front of his briefs. "Thank you for believing in us."

She could only nod. If he didn't fuck her soon, she might start crying again.

He met her eyes and pushed slowly, achingly inside her body.

Blissful sensations rippled through her, stealing her breath and scrambling her brain. Her skin heated. Her nipples hardened painfully, a throb that intensified as he drove faster, harder inside her.

They held each other as close as possible, touching everything at once. She swirled her tongue around his earlobe, inhaling his sinful, masculine scent. He turned his head and took her mouth, devouring, possessing, staking his claim.

"I'm yours." She met every thrust, surrendered every kiss.

"Say it again."

"I'm yours." She twitched, fighting the flood of stimulation, and started to come. "I love you."

He fell with her, groaning her name, jerking his hips, his heavy body shaking with the force of his climax.

As he caught his breath, he rolled to his back, taking her with him.

"That was too fast." His cock pulsed inside her. "Need to do it again."

"We will. But first, I need to get you out of here." With great reluctance, she pushed off him and dragged on her clothes. "Where's Boones?"

"I sent him home." He straightened his briefs and sat up. "Why?"

"Do you have a fake passport?"

"Several." He narrowed his eyes. "Start talking, Kate."

"Well…" She lifted a shoulder. "I have a plane ticket to go see him. I'm going to buy a second seat and have Matias arrange us transportation out of here."

She strode to the door and knocked.

"You don't know where Boones is." He was on his feet with an arm locked across her waist before she could blink.

"I narrowed it down to a small country." She angled her neck back and whispered in his ear, "Eritrea."

"How?" His eyes widened.

"It was the only way I knew how to find you." She twisted in his hold and lifted on toes to kiss his beard. "Desperation makes a woman dangerous."

The door opened.

He flicked his gaze over her shoulder and returned to her face. "Hurry back to me."

"Always."

THIRTY-FOUR

One month later, Tiago leaned against a pillar at the entrance of a fish market in a small Eritrean village. His gaze hungrily tracked the beautiful blonde as she picked her way through stalls of fruits, vegetables, spices, chickens, and bric-a-brac.

The sunlight caught the white-gold strands of her hair as she gripped Boones' arm and spoke animatedly about something she'd found on the vendor's table.

Tiago's pulse hammered, and he scanned the crowd, probing faces and clothing, searching for threats.

She wanted freedom and demanded to take these outings without him.

He was trying to give her that, even if it went against every instinct.

They'd settled in a small fishing village on the Red Sea, several hundred miles from where his family was murdered. Didn't mean his enemies couldn't find him. He could live anywhere, and danger would follow.

But he let her have her shopping trips, her walks

alone, and her quality time with Boones and his brothers. Kind of. He always followed at a distance. Always watching. He couldn't stop.

Some people simply couldn't change.

He would always tie her up, fuck her, cut her, and control her every move. And she would always fight him, challenge him, and fill his lungs with air.

Thank fucking God, because he couldn't breathe without her.

Thirty feet away, she stopped talking and went still. He slipped into the shadows as she turned her neck and searched the crowds behind her.

After a few sweeps, her huge blue eyes homed in on his location. Shrouded in darkness, he was certain she couldn't see him.

She bit her lip, said something to Boones, and strode directly toward his hiding spot.

His entire body tightened in anticipation.

A brightly-colored flowery sundress clung to her flawless, slender physique, and her pale complexion glowed beneath the Eritrean sun.

Africa looked fucking stunning on her.

A few steps away, she shook her head and fisted her hands on her hips.

"You." She cocked her sexy head. "Need a hobby."

"I have one."

"Stalking isn't a hobby."

"I call it guarding."

"You're a control freak."

"Control enthusiast." He clutched her neck and dragged her to him. "I want to fuck your ass."

"Of course, you do." Her sassy mouth curved into a grin. "You enjoyed it too much last time."

"So did you." He laced his fingers through hers and steered her in the direction of their home.

"You're a terrible influence." She couldn't contain her smile.

Hand in hand, they strolled toward the beach and followed the coastline. Slipping off their sandals, they let the waves lick at their feet as they walked.

"I love it here." She lifted her face to the cloudless sky and sighed.

"I love you."

She was his whole, his entire being, more himself than he was. If she ceased to exist, he would be a stranger, no longer part of this world.

She was his constant, his evermore, not just in the physical sense. She was the inexplicable *something* that made up his soul.

The two-mile stroll along the Red Sea brought them to an isolated beach house tucked away in a thick copse of foliage.

Boones and his brothers lived in the center of the village, with all the conveniences of the local shopping and transportation.

Tiago had installed heavy security in both places, relying on technology instead of the presence of armed men. Maybe none of it was needed, but he would never risk their lives. Never let his guard down. Never again.

He no longer had the protection of his syndicate or its allies in Caracas. Nor did he have the income from that business. But he'd saved a great deal of money over the years, enough to never need to work again.

She wanted to learn how to heal people and talked about pursuing a degree in medicine. Boones was beside himself when she asked for his guidance.

When they left Colombia, she told her friends it wasn't a goodbye. She fully intended to return as a doctor, and Tiago would be with her.

He would take her wherever she wanted to go, as long as she never left his sight. If she could deal with his possessive, overprotective inclinations, he would handle everything else.

"What do you want for dinner?" He opened the door to their two-bedroom bungalow and followed her inside.

"Whatever you're making."

A few hours later, he made an Eritrean traditional stew served with flatbread and a paste made from lentil and faba beans.

After dinner, they lay side by side on a blanket on the beach behind their house. The moon was bright in the sky, the tequila smooth as water, and the woman beside him more beautiful than the majestic landscape that stretched out around him.

"You're always in my mind, Tiago." She stretched out on her back and smiled up at the stars. "Perhaps not always a happy thought. Sometimes I'm plotting your demise. But you're always there, always a part of me." She turned her neck and looked at him. "Is that weird?"

"No." He rolled toward her and slid the hem of the dress up her thighs. "I want to live in your mind, your heart, and—"

"Don't say it."

"—your cunt."

"You said it." She laughed.

"I meant it."

"I know." She drew in a breath and ran a hand across his shaved jaw. "Nothing's ever felt more real than this. It scares me sometimes."

"Surrender to it." He gathered the dress above her waist, and the sight of her bare pussy made him painfully hard. "Open your legs."

She let her knees fall open and looked at him with all the trust in the world. He deserved none of it, but he would spend the rest of his life making sure she never regretted her gift.

Removing the finger blade from his pocket, he fit it onto his finger.

She swallowed. Her eyes glistened. Then she lifted her chin and smiled.

Sweet surrender.

He made small shallow cuts that wouldn't scar, and between each nick, he kissed her cunt until she came.

As the tide rolled in and warm water gathered beneath them, they fused together in a slow dance of seduction and heavy breaths. She stroked his cock. He made love to her mouth. She sucked him off, and he cut her again.

Perspiration slicked their skin, easing the glide of their bodies, the slip of hands, and the drive of his thrusts as they licked and fucked and bled together.

Some might consider their love dark and disturbing, but he thought of it as spiritual, unearthly, and wickedly filthy.

Despite all their fights and trials and mistakes, they never lost their sense of selves.

In the end, she saw something in him no one else had been able to see.

She saw a heart worthy enough to take.

The DELIVER series continues with:

MANIPULATE (#6)
Martin and Ricky's story

UNSHACKLE (#7)
Luke's story

DOMINATE (#8)
Tomas' story

COMPLICATE (#9) - *the final book*
Cole's story

OTHER BOOKS

LOVE TRIANGLE ROMANCE
TANGLED LIES TRILOGY
One is a Promise
Two is a Lie
Three is a War

DARK COWBOY ROMANCE
TRAILS OF SIN
Knotted #1
Buckled #2
Booted #3

DARK PARANORMAL ROMANCE
TRILOGY OF EVE
Heart of Eve
Dead of Eve #1
Blood of Eve #2
Dawn of Eve #3

STUDENT-TEACHER / PRIEST
Lessons In Sin

STUDENT-TEACHER ROMANCE
Dark Notes

ROCK-STAR DARK ROMANCE
Beneath the Burn

ROMANTIC SUSPENSE
Dirty Ties

EROTIC ROMANCE
Incentive

DARK HISTORICAL PIRATE ROMANCE
King of Libertines
Sea of Ruin

ABOUT

New York Times and USA Today Bestselling author, Pam Godwin, lives in the Midwest with her husband, their two children, and a foulmouthed parrot. When she ran away, she traveled fourteen countries across five continents, attended three universities, and married the vocalist of her favorite rock band.

Java, tobacco, and dark romance novels are her favorite indulgences, and might be considered more unhealthy than her aversion to sleeping, eating meat, and dolls with blinking eyes.

EMAIL: pamgodwinauthor@gmail.com